ROMOLA.

BY

GEORGE ELIOT,
AUTHOR OF "ADAM BEDE," "SILAS MARNER," ETC.

COPYRIGHT EDITION.

IN TWO VOLUMES.
VOL. I.

LEIPZIG
BERNHARD TAUCHNITZ
1863.

CONTENTS

OF VOLUME I.

		Page
PROEM		7

BOOK I.

CHAPTER	I.	The Shipwrecked Stranger	17
—	II.	A Breakfast for Love	35
—	III.	The Barber's Shop	41
—	IV.	First Impressions	56
—	V.	The blind Scholar and his Daughter	61
—	VI.	Dawning Hopes	80
—	VII.	A learned Squabble	101
—	VIII.	A Face in the Crowd	109
—	IX.	A Man's Ransom	126
—	X.	Under the Plane-Tree	136
—	XI.	Tito's Dilemma	152
—	XII.	The Prize is nearly grasped	157
—	XIII.	The Shadow of Nemesis	174
—	XIV.	The Peasants' Fair	183
—	XV.	The dying Message	203

Page
Chapter XVI. A Florentine Joke 215
— XVII. Under the Loggia 233
— XVIII. The Portrait 241
— XIX. The old Man's Hope 250
— XX. The Day of the Betrothal 255
BOOK II.
Chapter I. Florence expects a Guest 268
— II. The Prisoners 278
— III. After-Thoughts 288
— IV. Inside the Duomo 293
— V. Outside the Duomo 301
— VI. The Garment of Fear 308
— VII. The young Wife 315
— VIII. The painted Record 329
— IX. A Moment of Triumph 335
— X. The Avenger's Secret 345
— XI. Fniit is Seed 358
— XII. A Revelation 366
— XIII. Baldassarre makes an Acquaintance . . . 380

ROMOLA.

PROEM,

More than three centuries and a half ago, in the mid-spring-time of 1492, we are sure that the angel of the dawn, as he travelled with broad slow wing from the Levant to the Pillars of Hercules, and from the summits of the Caucasus across all the snowy Alpine ridges to the dark nakedness of the Western isles, saw nearly the same outline of firm land and unstable sea saw the same great mountain shadows on the same valleys as he has seen to-day saw olive mounts, and pine forests, and the broad plains, green with young corn or rain-freshened grass saw the domes and spires of cities rising by the river sides or mingled with the sedge-like masts on the many-curved sea coast, in the same spots where they rise to-day. And as the faint light of his course pierced into the dwellings of men, it fell, as now, on the rosy warmth of nestling children; on the haggard waking of sorrow and sickness; on the hasty uprising of the hard-handed labourer; and on the late sleep of the night-student, who had been questioning the stars or the sages, or his own soul, for that hidden knowledge which would break through the barrier of man's brief life, and show its dark path, that seemed to bend no whither, to be an arc in an immeasurable circle of light and glory. The great river courses which have shaped

the lives of men have hardly changed; and those other streams, the life-currents that ebb and flow in human hearts, pulsate to the same great needs, the same great loves and terrors. As our thought follows close in the slow wake of the dawn, we are impressed with the broad sameness of the human lot, which never alters in the main headings of its history hunger and labour, seed-time and harvest, love and death.

PROEM.

Even if, instead of following the dim daybreak, our imagination pauses on a certain historical spot, and awaits the fuller morning, we may see a world-famous city, which has hardly changed its outline since the days of Columbus, seeming to stand as an almost unviolated symbol, amidst the flux of human things, to remind us that we still resemble the men of the past more than we differ from them, as the great mechanical principles on which those domes and towers were raised must make a likeness in human building that will be broader and deeper than all possible change. And doubtless, if the spirit of a Florentine citizen, whose eyes were closed for the last time while Columbus was still waiting and arguing for the three poor vessels with which he was to set sail from the port of Palos, could return from the shades, and pause where our thought is pausing, he would believe that there must still be fellowship and understanding for him among the inheritors of his birthplace.

Let us suppose that such a Shade has been permitted to revisit the glimpses of the golden morning, and is standing once more on the famous hill of San Miniato, which overlooks Florence from the south.

The Spirit is clothed in his habit as he lived: the folds of his well-lined black silk garment or lucco hang in grave unbroken lines from neck to ankle; his plain cloth Cap, with its becchetto, or long hanging strip of drapery.

PROEM.

to serve as a scarf in case of need, surmounts a penetrating face, not, perhaps, very handsome, but with a firm, well-cut mouth, kept distinctly human by a close-shaven lip and chin. It is a face charged with memories of a keen and various life passed below there on the banks of the gleaming river; and as he looks at the scene before him, the sense of familiarity is so much stronger than the perception of change, that he thinks it might be possible to descend once more amongst the streets, and take up that busy life where he left it. For it is not only the mountains and the westward-bending river that he recognises; not only the dark sides of Mount Morello opposite to him, and the long valley of the Arno that seems to stretch its grey low-tufted luxuriance to the far-off ridges of Carrara; and the steep height of Fiesole, with its crown of monastic walls and cypresses; and all the green and grey slopes sprinkled with villas which he can name as he looks at them. He sees other familiar objects much closer to his daily walks. For though he misses the seventy or more towers that once surmounted the walls, and encircled the city as with a regal diadem, his eyes will not dwell on that blank; they are drawn irresistibly to the unique tower springing, like a tall flower-stem drawn towards the sun, from the square turreted mass of the Old Palace in the very heart of the city—the tower that looks none the worse for the four centuries that have passed since he used to walk under it. The great dome, too, greatest in the world, which, in his early boyhood, had been only a daring thought in the mind of a small, quick-eyed man there it raises its large curves still, eclipsing the hills. And the well-known bell-towers Giotto's, with its distant hint of rich colour, and the graceful spired Badia, and the rest-he looked at them all from the shoulder of his nurse.

ROMOLA.

"Surely," he thinks, "Florence can still ring her bells with the solemn hammer-sound that used to beat on the hearts of her citizens and strike out the fire there. And here, on the right, stands the long dark mass of Santa Croce, where we buried our famous dead, laying the laurel on their cold brows and fanning them with the breath of praise and of banners. But Santa Croce had no spire then: we Florentines were too full of great building projects to carry them all out in stone and marble; we had our frescoes and our shrines to pay for, not to speak of rapacious condottieri, bribed royalty, and purchased territories, and our fagades and spires must needs wait. But what architect can the Frati Minori* have employed to build that spire for them? If it had been built in my day, Filippo Brunelleschi or Michelozzo would have devised something of another fashion than that—something worthy to crown the church of Arnolfo."

At this the Spirit, with a sigh, lets his eyes travel on to the city walls, and now he dwells on the change there with wonder at these modern times. Why have five out of the eleven convenient gates been closed? And why, above all, should the towers have been levelled that were once a glory and defence? Is the world become so peaceful, then, and do Florentines dwell in such harmony, that there are no longer conspiracies to bring ambitious exiles home again with armed bands at their back? These are difficult questions: it is easier and pleasanter to recognise the old than to account for the new. And there flows Arno, with its bridges just where they used to be the Ponte Vecchio, least like other bridges in the world, laden with the same quaint shops, where our Spirit remembers lingering a little, on his way perhaps to look at the pro-

Franciscans,

gress of that great palace which Messer Luca Pitti had set a-building with huge stones got from the Hill of Bogoli* close behind, or perhaps to transact a little business with the cloth-dressers in Oltrarno. The exorbitant line of the Pitti roof is hidden from San Miniato; but the yearning of the old Florentine is not to see Messer Luca's too ambitious palace which he built unto himself; it is to be down among those narrow streets and busy humming Piazze where he inherited the eager life of his fathers. Is not the anxious voting with black and white beans still going on down there? Who are the Priori in these months, eating soberly-regulated official dinners in the Palazzo Vecchio, with removes of tripe and boiled partridges, seasoned by practical jokes against the ill-fated butt among those potent signors? Are not the significant banners still hung from the windows still distributed with decent pomp under Orcagna's Loggia every two months?

Life had its zest for the old Florentine when he, too, trod the marble steps and shared in those dignities. His politics had an area as wide as his trade, which stretched from Syria to Britain, but they had also the passionate intensity, and the detailed practical interest, which could belong only to a narrow scene of corporate action; only to the members of a community shut in close by the hills and by walls of six miles' circuit, where men knew each other as they passed in the street, set their eyes every day on the memorials of their commonwealth, and were conscious of having not only the right to vote, but the chance of being voted for. He loved his honours and his gains, the business of his counting-house, of his guild, of the public council-chamber; he loved his enmities too, and fingered the white bean which was to keep a hated name

Now Boboli.

out of the horsa with more complacency than if it had been a golden florin. He loved to strengthen his family by a good alliance, and went home with a triumphant light in his eyes after conclud ng a satisfactory marriage for his son or daughter, under his favourite loggia in the evening cool; he loved his game at chess under that same loggia, and his biting jest, and even his coarse joke, as not beneath the dignity of a man eligible for the highest magistracy. He had gained an insight into all sorts of affairs at home and abroad: he had been of the "Ten" who managed the war department, of the "Eight" who attended to home discipline, of the Priori or Signori who were the heads of the executive government; he had even risen to the supreme office of Gonfaloniere; he had made one in embassies to the Pope and to the Venetians; and he had been commissary to the hired army of the Republic, directing the inglorious bloodless battles in which no man died of brave breast wounds virtuosi colpi but only of casual falls and tramplings. And in this way he had learned to distrust men without bitterness; looking on life mainly as a game of skill, but not dead to traditions of heroism and clean-handed honour. For the human soul is hospitable, and will entertain conflicting sentiments and contradictory opinions with much impartiality. It was his pride, besides, that he was duly tinctured with the learning of his age and judged not altogether with the vulgar, but in harmony with the ancients: he, too, in his prime, had been eager for the most correct manuscripts, and had paid many florins for antique vases and for disinterred busts of the ancient immortals some, perhaps, inincis naribiis, wanting as to the nose, but not the less authentic; and in his old age he had made haste to look at the first sheets of that fine Homer which was among

the early glories of the Florentine press. But he had not, for all that, neglected to hang up a waxen image or double of himself under the protection of the Madonna Annunziata, or to do penance for his sins in large gifts to the shrines of saints whose lives had not been modelled on the study of the classics; he had not even neglected making liberal bequests towards buildings for the Frati, against whom he had levelled many a jest.

For the Unseen Powers were mighty. Who knew Vv-ho was sure that there was afiy name given to them behind which there was no angry force to be appeased, no intercessory pity to be won? Were not gems medicinal, though they only pressed the finger? Were not all things charged with occult virtues? Lucretius might be right— he was an ancient and a great poet; Luigi Pulci, too, who was suspected of not believing anything from the roof upward (dal tetto in sii), had very much the air of being right over the supper-table, when the wine and riboboli were circulating fast, though he was only a poet in the vulgar tongue. There were even learned personages who maintained that Aristotle, wisest of men (unless, indeed, Plato were wiser?), was a thoroughly irreligious philosopher; and a liberal scholar must entertain all speculations. But the negatives might, after all, prove false; nay, seemed manifestly false, as the circling hours swept past him, and turned round with graver faces. For had not the world become Christian? Had he not been baptised in San Giovanni, where the dome is awful with the s\'7dtii-bols of coming judgment, and where the altar bears a crucified Image disturbing to perfect complacency in oneself and the world? Our resuscitated Spirit was not a pagan philosopher, nor a philosophising pagan poet, but a man of the fifteenth centur\'7d^, inheriting its strange web of

belief and unbelief; of Epicurean levity and fetichistic dread; of pedantic impossible ethics uttered by rote, and crude passions acted out with childish impulsiveness: of inclination towards a self-indulgent paganism, and inevitable subjection to that human conscience which, in the unrest of a new growth, was filling the air with strange prophecies and presentiments.

He had smiled, perhaps, and shaken his head dubiously, as he heard simple folk talk of a Pope Angelico, who was to come by-and-by and bring in a new order of things, to purify the Church from simony, and the lives of the clergy from scandal a state of affairs too different from what existed under Innocent the Eighth for a shrewd merchant and politician to regard the prospect as worthy of entering into his calculations. But he felt the evils of the time, nevertheless; for he was a man of public spirit, and public spirit can never be wholly immoral, since its essence is care for a common good. That very Quaresima, or Lent, of 1492, in which he died, still in his erect old age, he had listened in San Lorenzo, not without a mixture of satisfaction, to the preaching of a Dominican Friar, named Girolamo Savonarola, who denounced with a rare boldness the worldliness and vicious habits of the clergy, and insisted on the duty of Christian men not to live for their own ease when wrong was triumphing in high places, and not to spend their wealth in outward pomp even in the churches, when their fellow-citizens were suffering from want and sickness. The Frate carried his doctrine rather too far for elderly ears; yet it was a memorable thing to see a preacher move his audience to such a pitch that the women even took off their ornaments, and delivered them up to be sold for the benefit of the needy.

"He was a noteworthy man, that Prior of San Marco,"

thinks our Spirit; "somewhat arrogant and extreme, perhaps, especially in his denunciations of speedy vengeance. Ah, Iddio no7i paga il Sabato the wages of men's sins often linger in their payment, and I myself saw much established wickedness of long-standing prosperity. But a Frate Predicatore who wanted to move the people— how could he be moderate? He might have been a little less defiant and curt, though, to Lorenzo de' Medici, whose family had been the very makers of San Marco: was that quarrel ever made up? And our Lorenzo himself, with the dim outward eyes and the subtle inward vision, did he get over that illness at Careggi? It was but a sad, uneasy-looking face that he would carry out of the world which had given him so much, and there were strong suspicions that his handsome son would play the part of Rehoboam. How has it all turned out? Which party is likely to be banished and have its houses sacked just now? Is there any successor of the incomparable Lorenzo, to whom the great Turk is so gracious as to send over presents of rare animals, rare relics, rare manuscripts, or fugitive enemies, suited to the tastes of a Christian Magni-fico who is at once lettered and devout and also slightly vindictive? And what famous scholar is dictating the Latin letters of the Republic what fiery philosopher is lecturing on Dante in the Duomo, and going home to write bitter invectives against the father and mother of the bad critic who may have found fault with his classical spelling? Are our wiser heads leaning towards alliance with the Pope and the Regno, or are they rather inclining their ears to the orators of France and of Milan?

"God does not pay on a Saturday."

The name given to Naples by way of distinction among the Italian States.

"There is knowledge of these things to be had in the streets below, on the beloved ?narnii in front of the churches, and under the sheltering Loggie, where surely our citizens have still their gossip and debates, their bitter and merry jests as of old. For are not the well-remembered buildings all there? The changes have not been so great in those uncounted years. I will go down and hear—I will tread the familiar pavement, and hear once again the speech of Florentines."

Go not down, good Spirit! for the changes are great, and the speech of Florentines would sound as a riddle in your ears. Or, if you go, mingle with no politicians on the marmi, or elsewhere; ask no questions about trade in the Calimara; confuse yourself with no inquiries into scholarship, official or monastic. Only look at the sunlight and shadows on the grand walls that were built solidly, and have endured in their grandeur; look at the faces of the little children, making another sunlight amid the shadows of age; look, if ybu will, into the churches, and hear the same chants, see the same images as of old—the images of willing anguish for a great end, of beneficent love and ascending glory; see upturned living faces, and lips moving to the old prayers for help. These things have not changed. The sunlight and shadows bring their old beauty and waken the old heart-strains at morning, noon, and eventide; the little children are still the symbol of the eternal marriage between love and duty; and men still yearn for the reign of peace and righteousness—still, own that life to be the highest, which is a conscious voluntary sacrifice. For the Pope Angelico is not come yet.

CHAPTER I.
THE SHIPWRECKED STRANGER.

The Loggia de' Cherchi stood in the heart of old Florence, within a labyrinth of narrow streets behind the Badia, now rarely threaded by the stranger, unless in a dubious search for a certain severely simple door-place, bearing this inscription:

QUI NACQUE IL DIVING PGETA.

To the ear of Dante, the same streets rang with the shout and clash of fierce battle between rival families; but in the fifteenth century, they were only noisy with the un-historical quarrels and broad jests of wool-carders in the cloth-producing quarters of San Martino and

Garbo.

Under this loggia, in the early morning of the gth of April 1492, two men had their eyes fixed on each other: one was stooping slightly, and looking downward with the scrutiny of cariosity; the other, lying on the pavement, was looking upward with the startled gaze of a suddenly-awakened dreamer.

Romola.

The standing figure was the first to speak. He was a grey-haired, broad-shouldered man, of the type which, in Tuscan phrase, is moulded with the fist and polished with the pickaxe; but the self-important gravity which had written itself out in the deep lines about his brow and mouth seemed intended to correct any contemptuous inferences from the hasty workmanship which Nature had bestowed on his exterior. He had deposited a large well-filled bag, made of skins, on the pavement, and before him hung a pedlar's basket, garnished partly with small woman's-ware, such as thread and pins, and partly with fragments of glass, which had probably been taken in exchange for those commodities.

"Young man," he said, pointing to a ring on the finger of the reclining figure, "when your chin has got a stiffer crop on it, you'll know better than to take your nap in street corners with a ring like that on your forefinger. By the holy 'vangels! if it had been anybody but me standing over you two minutes ago but Bratti Ferravecchi is not the man to steal. The cat couldn't eat her mouse if she didn't catch it alive, and Bratti couldn't relish gain if it had no taste of a bargain. Why, young man, one San Giovanni, three years ago, the Saint sent a dead body in my way a blind beggar, with his cap well-lined with pieces but, if you'll beheve me, my stomach turned against the testoni I'd never bargained for, till it came into my head that San Giovanni owed me the pieces for what I spend yearly at the Festa: besides, I buried the body and paid for a mass—and so I saw it was a fair bargain. But how comes a young man like you, with the face of Messer San Michele, to be sleeping on a stone bed with the wind for a curtain?"

The deep guttural sounds of the speaker were scarcely

intelligible to the newly-waked, bewildered listener, but he understood the action of pointing to his ring: he looked down at it, and, with a half-automatic obedience to the warning, took it off and thrust it within his doublet, rising at the same time and stretching himself.

"Your tunic and hose match ill with that jewel, young man," said Bratti, deliberately. "Anybody might say the saints had sent you a dead body; but if you took the jewels, I hope you buried him—and you can afford a mass or two for him into the bargain."

Something like a painful thrill appeared to dart through the frame of the listener, and arrest the careless stretching of his arms and chest. For an instant he turned on Bratti with a sharp frown; but he immediately recovered an air of indifference, took off the red Levantine cap which hung like a great purse over his left ear, pushed back his long dark-brown curls, and glancing at his dress, said, smilingly,

"You speak truth, friend: my garments are as weather-stained as an old sail, and they are not old either, only, like an old sail, they have had a sprinkling of the sea as well as the rain. The fact is, I'm a stranger in Florence, and when I came in foot-sore last night I preferred flinging myself in a corner of this hospitable porch to hunting any longer for a chance hostelry, which might turn out to be a nest of blood-suckers of more sorts than one."

"A stranger in good sooth," said Bratti, "for the words come all melting out of your throat, so that a Christian and a Florentine can't tell a hook from a hanger. But you're not from Genoa? More likely from Venice, by the cut of your clothes?"

"At this present moment," said the stranger, smiling, "it is of less imporance where I come from than where can go to for a mouthful of breakfast. This city of yours turns a grim look on me just here: can you show me the way to a more lively quarter, where I can get a meal and a lodging?"

"That I can," said Bratti, "and it is your good fortune, young man, that I have happened to be walking in from Rovezzano this morning, and turned out of my way to Mercato Vecchio to say an Ave at the Badia. That, I say, is your good fortune. But it remains to be seen what is my profit in the matter. Nothing for nothing, young man. If I show you the way to Mercato Vecchio, you'll swear by your patron saint to let me have the bidding for that stained suit of yours, when you set up a better—as doubtless you will."

"Agreed, by San Niccolo," said the other, laughing. "But now let us set off to this said Mercato, for I feel the want of a better lining to this doublet of mine which you are coveting."

"Coveting? Nay," said Bratti, heaving his bag on his back and setting out. But he broke off in his reply, and burst out in loud, harsh tones, not unlike the creaking and grating of a cart-wheel: "Chi abbaratta — baratta — b'ratta — chi abbarata cenci e vetri b'ratta ferri veccln?"*

"It's worth but little," he said presently, relapsing into his conversational tone. "Hose and altogether, your clothes are worth but little. Still, if you've a mind to set yourself up with a lute worth more than any new one, or with a sword that's been worn by a Ridolfi, or with a paternoster of the best mode, I could let you have a great bargain, by making an allowance for the clothes; for, simple as I stand here, I've got the best-furnished shop in the Ferravecchi, and it's close by the Mercato. The Virgin * "Who wants to exchange rags, broken glass, or old iron?"

be praised! it's not a pumpkin I cany on my shoulders. But I don't stay caged in my shop all day: I've got a wife and a raven to stay at home and mind the stock. Clii ahbaraila — haratta — b'ratta? .... And now, young man, where do you come from, and what's your business in Florence?"

"I thought you liked nothing that came to you without a bargain," said the stranger. "You've offered me nothing yet in exchange for that information."

"Well, well; a Florentine doesn't mind bidding a fair price for news: it stays the stomach a little, though he may win no hose by it. If I take you to the prettiest damsel in the Mercato to get a cup of milk—that will be a fair bargain."

"Nay; I can find her myself, if she be really in the Mercato; for pretty heads are apt to look forth of doors and windows. No, no. Besides, a sharp trader, like you, ought to know that he who bids for nuts and news, may chance to find them hollow."

"Ah! young man," said Bratti, with a sideway glance of some admiration, "you were not born of a Sunday— the salt shops were open when you came into the world. You're not a Hebrew, eh?come from Spain or Naples, eh? Let me tell you the Frati Minori are trying to make Florence as hot as Spain for those dogs of hell that want to get all the profits of usury to themselves and leave none for Christians; and when you walk the Calimara with a piece of yellow cloth in your cap, it will spoil your beauty more than a sword-cut across that smooth olive cheek of yours. Abbaratta, baraita chi abbaratta? I tell you, young man, gray cloth is against yellow cloth; and there's as much gray cloth in Florence as would make a gown and cowl for the Duomo, and there's not

SO much yellow cloth as would make hose for Saint Christopher—blessed be his name, and send me a sight of him this day! Abharatta, haratta, b'ratta chi ab-baratta?"

"All that is very amusing information you are parting with for nothing," said the stranger, rather scornfully; "but it happens not to concern me. I am no Hebrew."

"See, now!" said Bratti, triumphantly; "I've made a good bargain with mere words. I've made you tell me something, young man, though you're as hard to hold as a lamprey. San Giovanni be praised! a blind Florentine is a match for two one-eyed men. But here we are in the

Mercato."

They had now emerged from the narrow streets into a broad piazza, known to the elder Florentine writers as the Mercato Vecchio, or the Old Market. This piazza, though it had been the scene of a provision market from time immemorial, and may perhaps, says fond imagination, be the very spot to which the Fesulean ancestors of the Florentines descended from their high fastness to traffic with the rustic population of the valley, had not been shunned as a place of residence by Florentine wealth. In the early decades of the fifteenth century, which was now near its end, the Medici and other powerful families of the popolani grassi, or commercial nobility, had their houses there, not perhaps finding their ears much offended by the loud roar of mingled dialects, or their eyes much shocked by the butchers' stalls, which the old poet Antonio Pucci accounts a chief glory, or dignita, of a market that, in his esteem, eclipsed the markets of all the earth beside. But the glory, of mutton and veal (well attested to be the flesh of the right animals; for were not the skins, with the heads attached, duly displayed, according

to the decree of the Signoria?) was just now wanting to the Mercato, the time of Lent not being yet over. The proud corporation, or "Art," of butchers was in abeyance, and it was the great harvest-time of the market-gardeners, the cheesemongers, the vendors of macaroni, corn, eggs, milk, and dried fruits: a change which was apt to make the women's voices predominant in the chorus. But in all seasons there was the experimental ringing of pots and pans, the chinking of the money-changers, the tempting offers of cheapness at the-old-clothes' stalls, the challenges of the dicers, the vaunting of new linens and woollens, of excellent wooden-ware, kettles, and frying-pans; there was the choking of the narrow inlets with mules and carts, together with much uncomplimentary remonstrance in terms remarkably identical with the insults in use by the gentler sex of the present day, under the same imbrowning and heating circumstances. Ladies and gentlemen, who came to market, looked on at a larger amount of amateur fighting than could easily be seen in these later times, and beheld more revolting rags, beggary, and rascaldom, than modern householders could well picture to themselves. As the day wore on, the hideous drama of the gaminghouse might be seen here by any chance open-air spectator the quivering eagerness, the blank despair, the sobs, the blasphemy, and the blows.

"E vedesi clii perde con gran soffi, E bestemmiar colla mano alia mascella, E ricever e dar dimolti ingofli."

But still there was the relief of prettier sights: there were brood-rabbits, not less innocent and astonished than those of our own period; there were doves and singing-birds to be bought as presents for the children; there were even kittens for sale, and here and there a handsome gattuccio.

or "Tom," with the highest character for mousing; and, better than all, there were young, softly rounded cheeks and bright eyes, freshened by the start from the far-off castello* at daybreak, not to speak of older faces with the unfading charm of honest good-will in them, such as are never quite wanting in scenes of human industry. And high on a pillar in the centre of the place—a venerable pillar, fetched from the church of San Giovanni —stood Donatello's stone statue of Plenty, with a fountain near it, where, says old Pucci, the good wives of the market freshened their utensils, and their throats also— not because they were unable to buy wine, but because they wished to save the money for their husbands.

But on this particular morning a sudden change seemed to have come over the face of the market. The deschi, or stalls, were indeed partly dressed with their various commodities, and already there were purchasers assembled, on the alert to secure the finest, freshest vegetables and the most unexceptionable butter. But when Bratti and his companion entered the piazza, it appeared that some common preoccupation had for the moment distracted the attention both of buyers and sellers from their proper business. Most of the traders had turned their backs on their goods, and had joined the knots of talkers who were concentrating themselves at different points in the piazza. A vendor of old clothes, in the act of hanging out a pair of long hose, had distractedly hung them round his neck in his eagerness to join the nearest group; an oratorical cheesemonger, with a piece of cheese in one hand and a knife in the other, was incautiously making notes of his emphatic pauses on that excellent specimen of marzolino; and elderly market-

    Walled village.

women, with their egg-baskets in a dangerously obHque position, contributed a wailing fugue of invocation.In this general distraction, the Florentine boys, who were never wanting in any street scene, and were of an especially mischievous sort—as who should say, very sour crabs indeed saw a great opportunity. Some made a rush at the nuts and dried figs, others preferred the farinaceous delicacies at the cooked provision stalls— delicacies to which certain four-footed dogs also, who had learned to take kindly to Lenten fare, applied a discriminating nostril, and then disappeared with much rapidity under the nearest shelter; while the mules, not without some kicking and plunging among impeding baskets, were stretching their muzzles towards the aromatic green-meat.

"Diavolo!" said Bratti, as he and his companion came, quite unnoticed, upon the noisy scene; "the Mercato is gone as mad as if the most Holy Father had excommunicated us again. I must know what this is. But never fear; it seems a thousand years to you till you see the pretty Tessa, and get your cup of milk; but keep hold of me, and I'll hold to my bargain. Remember, I'm to have the first bid for your suit, specially for the hose, which, with all their stains, are the best parnio di garbo — as good as ruined, though, with mud and weather stains."

"Ola, Monna Trecca," Bratti proceeded, turning towards an old woman on the outside of the nearest group, who for the moment had suspended her wail to listen, and shouting close in her ears: "Here are the mules upsetting all your bunches of parsley: is the world coming to an end, then?"

"Monna Trecca" (equivalent to "Dame Greengrocer") turned round at this unexpected trumpeting in her right ear, with a half-fierce, half-bewildered look, first at the speaker, then at her disarranged commodities, and then at the speaker again.

"A bad Easter and a bad year to you, and may you die by the sword!" she burst out, rushing towards her stall, but directing this first volley of her wrath against Bratti, who, without heeding the malediction, quietly slipped into her place, within hearing of the narrative which had been absorbing her attention; making a sign at the same time to the young stranger to keep near him.

"I tell you I saw it myself," said a fat man, with a bunch of newly-purchased leeks in his hand. "I was in Santa Maria Novella, and saw it myself The woman started up and threw out her arms, and cried out and said she saw a big bull with fiery horns coming down on the church to crush it. I saw it myself."

"Saw what, Goro?" said a man of slim figure, whose eye twinkled rather roguishly. He wore a close jerkin, a skull-cap lodged carelessly over his left ear as if it had fallen there by chance, a delicate linen apron tucked up on one side, and a razor stuck in his belt. "Saw the bull, or only the woman?"

"Why, the woman, to be sure; but it's all one, mi pare: it doesn't alter the meaning val" answered the fat man, with some contempt.

"Meaning? no, no; that's clear enough," said several voices at once, and then followed a confusion of tongues, in which "Lights shooting over San Lorenzo for three nights together

Thunder in the clear starlight Lantern of the Duomo struck with the sword of St. Michael Palle All smashed Lions tearing each other to pieces Ah! and they might well Arms of the Medici.

"Boio caduto in Santissiina Nunziala! Died like the best of Christians "God will have pardoned him" —were often-repeated phrases, which shot across each other like storm-driven hailstones, each speaker feeling rather the necessity of utterance than of finding a listener. Perhaps the only silent members of the group were Bratti, who, as a xitw comer, was busy in mentally piecing together the flying fragments of information; the man of the razor; and a thin-lipped, eager-looking personage in spectacles, wearing a pen-and-ink case at his belt.

"Ebbene, Nello," said Bratti, skirting the group till he was within hearing of the barber. "It appears the Magnifico is dead rest his soul and the price of wax will rise?"

"Even as you say," answered Nello; and then added, with an air of extra gravity, but with marvellous rapidity, "and his waxen image in the Nunziata fell at the same moment, they say; or at some other time, whenever it pleases the Frati Serviti, who know best. And several cows and women have had still-born calves this Quare-sima; and for the bad eggs that have been broken since the Carnival, nobody has counted them. Ah! a great man a great politician a greater poet than Dante. And yet the cupola didn't fall, only the lantern. Che viiracolo ! "

A sharp and lengthened "Pst!" was suddenly heard darting across the pelting storm of gutturals. It came from the pale man in spectacles, and had the effect he intended; for the noise ceased, and all eyes in the group were fixed on him with a look of expectation.

A votive image of Lorenzo, in wax, hung up in the Church of the Annunziata, supposed to have fallen at the time of his death. Boto is popular Tuscan for Voto.

"'Tis well said you Florentines are blind," he began, in an incisive high voice. "It appears to me, you need nothing but a diet of hay to make cattle of you. What! do you think the death of Lorenzo is the scourge God has prepared for Florence? Go! you are sparrows chattering praise over the dead hawk. What! a man who was trying to slip a noose over every neck in the Republic that he might tighten it at his pleasure! You like that; you like to have the election of your magistrates turned into closet-work, and no man to use the rights of a citizen unless he is a Medicean. That is what is meant by qualification now: neito di specchio* no longer means that a man pays his dues to the Republic: it means that he'll wink at robbery of people's money at robbery of their daughters' dowries; that he'll play the chamberer and the philosopher by turns listen to bawdy songs at the Carnival and cry 'Bellissimi!' and listen to sacred lauds and cry again 'Bel-lissimi!' But this is what you love: you grumble and raise a riot over yoiw qtiattritii bianchi" (white farthings); "but you take no notice when the public treasury has got a hole in the bottom for the gold to run into Lorenzo's drains. You like to pay for staffieri to walk before and behind one of your citizens, that he may be affable and condescending to you. 'See, what a tall Pisan we keep,' say you, 'to march before him with the drawn sword flashing in our eyes; and yet Lorenzo smiles at us. What goodness!' And you think the death of a man, who would soon have saddled and bridled you as the Sforza has saddled and bridled Milan—you think his death is the scourge God is warning you of by portents. I tell you there is another sort of scourge in the air."

* The phrase used to express the absence of disqualification, ?'. e. the not being entered as a debtor in the pubhc book \'7bspecchio).

"Nay, nay, Ser Cioni, keep astride your politics, and never mount your prophecy; politics is the better horse," said Nello. "But if you tallc of portents, what portent can be greater than a pious notary? Balaam's ass was nothing to it."

"Ay, but a notary out of work, with his ink-bottle dry," said another bystander, very much out at elbows. "Better don a cowl at once, Ser Cioni; everybody will believe in your fasting."

The notary turned and left the group with a look of indignant contempt, disclosing, as he did so, the sallow but mild face of a short man who had been standing behind him, and whose bent shoulders told of some sedentary occupation.

"By San Giovanni, though," said the fat purchaser of leeks, with the air of a person rather shaken in his theories, "I'm not sure there isn't some truth in what Ser Cioni says. For I know I've good reason to find fault with the quattrini bianchi myself. Grumble, did he say? Suffocation! I should think we do grumble; and, let anybody say the word, I'll turn out into the piazza with the readiest, sooner than have our money altered in our hands as if the magistracy were so many necromancers. And it's true Lorenzo might have hindered such work if he would and for the bull with the flaming horns, why, as Ser Cioni says, there may be many meanings to it, for the matter of that; it may have more to do with the taxes than we think. For when God above sends a sign, it's not to be supposed he'd have only one meaning."

"Spoken like an oracle, Goro!" said the barber. "Why, when we poor mortals can pack two or three meanings into one sentence, it were mere blasphemy not

to believe that your miraculous bull means everything that any man in Florence likes it to mean."

"Thou art pleased to scoff, Nello," said the sallow, round-shouldered man, no longer eclipsed by the notary, "but it is not the less true that every revelation, whether by visions, dreams, portents, or the written word, has many meanings, which it is given to the illuminated only to unfold."

"Assuredly," answered Nello. "Haven't I been to hear the Frate in San Lorenzo? But then, I've been to hear Fra Menico da Ponzo in the Duomo too; and according to him, your Fra Girolamo, with his visions and interpretations, is running after the wind of Mongibello, and those who follow him are like to have the fate of certain swine that ran headlong into the sea or some hotter place. With San Domenico roaring e vero in one ear, and San Francisco screaming e also in the other, what is a poor barber to do unless he were illuminated? But it's plain our Goro here is beginning to be illuminated, for he already sees that the bull with the flaming horns means first himself, and secondly all the other aggrieved taxpayers of Florence, who are determined to gore the magistracy on the first opportunity."

"Goro is a fool!" said a bass voice, with a note that dropped like the sound of a great bell in the midst of much tinkling. "Let him carry home his leeks and shake his flanks over his wool-beating. He'll mend matters more that way than by showing his tun-shaped body in the piazza, as if everybody might measure his grievances by the size of his paunch. The burdens that harm him most are his heavy carcass and his idleness."

The speaker had joined the group only in time to hear the conclusion of Nello's speech, but he was one of those figures for whom all the world instinctively makes way, as it would for a battering-ram. He was not much above the middle height, but the impression of enormous force which was conveyed by his capacious chest and brawny arms bared to the shoulder, was deepened by the keen sense and quiet resolution expressed in his glance and in every furrow of his cheek and brow. He had often been an unconscious model to Domenico Ghirlandajo, when that great painter was making the walls of the churches reflect the life of Florence, and translating pale aerial traditions into the deep colour and strong lines of the faces he knew. The naturally dark tint of his skin was additionally bronzed by the same powdery deposit that gave a polished black surface to his leathern apron: a deposit which habit had probably made a necessary condition of perfect ease, for it was not washed off with punctilious regularity.

Goro turned his fat cheek and glassy eye on the frank speaker with a look of deprecation rather than of resentment.

"Why, Niccolo," he said, in an injured tone, "I've heard you sing to another tune than that, often enough, when you've been laying down the law at San Gallo on a festa. I've heard you say yourself, that a man wasn't a mill-wheel, to be on the grind, grind, as long as he was driven, and then stick in his place without stirring when the water was low. And you're as fond of your vote as any man in Florence—ay, and I've heard you say, if Lorenzo "

"Yes, yes," said Niccolo. "Don't you be bringing up my speeches again after you've swallowed them, and handing them about as if they were none the worse. I vote and I speak when there's any use in it: if there's hot metal on the anvil, I lose no time before I strike; but I don't spend good hours in tinkling on cold iron, or in standing on the pavement as thou dost, Goro, with snout upward, like a pig under an oak-tree. And as for Lorenzo—who's dead and gone before his time he was a man who had an eye for curious iron-work; and if anybody says he wanted to make himself a tyrant, I say, ' Sia; I'll not deny which way the wind blows when every man can see the weathercock.' But that only means that Lorenzo was a crested hawk, and there are plenty of hawks without crests whose claws and beaks are as good for tearing. Though if there was any chance of a real reform, so that Marzocco might shake his mane and roar again, instead of dipping his head to lick the feet of anybody that will mount and ride him, I'd strike a good blow for it."

"And that reform is not far off, Niccolo," said the sallow, mild-faced man, seizing his opportunity like a missionary among the too light-minded heathens; "for a time of tribulation is coming, and the scourge is at hand. And when the Church is purged of cardinals and prelates who traffic in her inheritance that their hands may be full to pay the price of blood and to satisfy their own lusts, the State will be purged too—and Florence will be purged of men who love to see avarice and lechery under the red hat and the mitre because it gives them the screen of a more hellish vice than their own."

"Ay, as Goro's broad body would be a screen for my narrow person in case of missiles," said Nello; "but if that excellent screen happened to fall, I were stifled under it, surely enough. That is no bad image of thine, Nanni or, rather of the Prate's; for I fancy there is no room in * The stone Lion, emblem of the Republic. the small cup of thy understanding for any other liquor than what he pours into it."

"And it were well for thee, Nello," replied Nanni, "if thou could'st empty thyself of thy scoffs and thy jests, and take in that liquor too. The warning is ringing in the ears of all men: and it's no new story; for the Abbot Joachim prophesied of the coming time three hundred years ago, and now Fra Girolamo has got the message afresh. He has seen it in a vision, even as the prophets of old: he has seen the sword hanging from the sky."

"Ay, and thou wilt see it thyself, Nanni, if thou wilt stare upward long enough," said Niccolo; "for that pitiable tailor's work of thine makes thy noddle so overhang thy legs, that thy eyeballs can see nought above the stitching-board but the roof of thy own skull."

The honest tailor bore the jest without bitterness, bent on convincing his hearers of his doctrine rather than of his dignity. But Niccolo gave him no opportunity for replying; for he turned away to the pursuit of his market business, probably considering further dialogue as a tinkling on cold iron.

"Ebbene," said the man with the hose round his neck, who had lately migrated from another knot of talkers, "they are safest who cross themselves and jest at nobody. Do you know that the Magnifico sent for the Frate at the last, and couldn't die without his blessing?"

"Was it so—in truth?" said several voices. "Yes, yes —God will have pardoned him." "He died like the best of Christians." "Never took his eyes from the holy crucifix." "And the Frate will have given him his blessing?"

"Well, I know no more," said he of the hosen; "only Guccio there met a staffiere going back to Careggi, and he told him the Frate had been sent for yesternight, after the Magnifico had confessed and had the holy sacraments."

"It's hkely enough the Frate will tell the people something about it in his sermon this morning; is it not true, Nanni?" said Goro. "What do you think?"

But Nanni had already turned his back on Goro, and the group was rapidly thinning; some being stirred by the impulse to go and hear "new things" from the Frate ("new things" were the nectar of Florentines); others by the sense that it was time to attend to their private business. In this general movement, Bratti got close to the barber, and said,—

"Nello, you've a ready tongue of your own, and are used to worming secrets out of people when you've once got them well-lathered. I picked up a stranger this morning as I was coming in from Rovezzano, and I can spell him out no better than I can the letters on that scarf I bought from the French cavalier. It isn't my wits are at fault, I want no man to help me tell peas from paternosters, but when you come to foreign fashions, a fool may happen to know more than a wise man."

"Ay, thou hast the wisdom of Midas, who could turn rags and rusty nails into gold, even as thou dost," said Nello, "and he had also something of the ass about him. But where is thy bird of strange plumage?"

Bratti was looking round, with an air of disappointment.

"Diavolo!" he said, with some vexation. "The bird's flown. It's true he was hungry, and I forgot him. But we shall find him in the Mercato, within scent of bread and savours, I'll answer for him."

"Let us make the round of the Mercato, then," said Nello.

"It isn't his feathers that puzzle me," continued Bratti, as they pushed their way together. "There isn't much in the way of cut and cloth on this side the Holy Sepulchre that can puzzle a Florentine."

"Or frighten him, either," said Nello, "after he has seen an Inglese or a Tedesco."

"No, no," said Bratti, cordially; "one may never lose sight of the Cupola and yet know the world, I hope. Besides, this stranger's clothes are good Italian merchandise, and the hose he wears were dyed in Ognissanti before ever they were dyed with salt water, as he says. But the riddle about him is—"

Here Bratti's explanation was interrupted by some jostling as they reached one of the entrances of the piazza, and before he could resume it they had caught sight of the enigmatical object they were in search of.

CHAPTER II. A BREAKFAST FOR LOVE.

After Bratti had joined the knot of talkers, the young stranger, hopeless of learning what was the cause of the general agitation, and not much caring to know what was probably of little interest to any but born Florentines, soon became tired of waiting for Bratti's escort; and chose to stroll round the piazza, looking out for some vendor of estables who might happen to have less than the average curiosity about public news. But as if at the suggestion of a sudden thought, he thrust his hand into a purse or wallet that hung at his waist, and explored it again and again with a look of frustration.

"Not an obolus, by Jupiter!" he murmured, in a language which was not Tuscan or even Italian. "I thought I had one poor piece left. I must get my breakfast for love, then!"

He had not gone many steps farther before it seemed likely that he had found a quarter of the market where that medium of exchange might not be rejected.

In a corner, away from any group of talkers, two mules were standing, well adorned with red tassels and collars. One of them carried wooden milk-vessels, the other a pair of panniers filled with herbs and salads. Resting her elbow on the neck of the mule that carried the milk, there leaned a young girl, apparently not more than sixteen, with a red hood surrounding her face, which was all the more baby-like in its prettiness from the entire concealment of her hair. The poor child, perhaps, was weary after her labour in the morning twilight in preparation for her walk to market from some castello three or four miles off, for she seemed to have gone to sleep in that half-standing, half-leaning posture. Nevertheless, our stranger had no com]3unction in awaking her, but the means he chose were so gentle that it seemed to the damsel in her dream as if a little sprig of thyme had touched her lips while she was stooping to gather the herbs. The dream was broken, however, for she opened her blue baby-eyes, and started up with astonishment and confusion to see the young stranger standing close before her. She heard him speaking to her in a voice which seemed so strange and soft, that even if she had been more collected she would have taken it for granted that he said something hopelessly unintelligible to her, and her first movement was to turn her head a little away, and lift up a corner of her green serge mantle as a screen. He repeated his words

A BREAKFAST FOR LOVE.

"Forgive me, pretty one, for awaking you. I'm dying witla hunger, and the scent of milk makes breakfast seem more desirable than ever."

He had chosen the words "miioio di fame," because he knew they would be familiar to her ears; and he had uttered them playfully, with the intonation of a mendicant. This time he was understood; the corner of the mantle was dropped, and in a few moments a large cup of fragrant milk was held out to him. He paid no further compliments before raising it to his lips, and while he was drinking, the little maiden found courage to look up at the long brown curls of this singular-voiced stranger, who had asked for food in the tones of a beggar, but who, though his clothes were much damaged, was unlike any beggar she had ever seen.

While this process of survey was going on, there was another current of feeling that carried her hand into a bag which hung by the side of the mule, and when the stranger set down his cup, he saw a large piece of bread held out towards him, and caught a glance of the blue eyes that seemed intended as an encouragement to him to take this additional gift.

"But perhaps that is your own breakfast," he said. "No, I have had enough without payment. A thousand thanks, my gentle one."

There was no rejoinder in words; but the piece of bread was pushed a little nearer to him, as if in impatience at his refusal; and as the long dark eyes of the stranger rested on the baby face, it seemed to be gathering more and more courage to look up and meet them.

"Ah, then, if I must take the bread," he said, laying his hand on it, "I shall get bolder still, and beg for another kiss to make the bread sweeter."

His speech was getting wonderfully intelligible in spite of the strange voice, which had at first almost seemed a thing to make her cross herself. She blushed deeply, and lifted up a corner of her mantle to her mouth again. But just as the too presumptuous stranger was leaning forward, and had his fingers on the arm that held up the screening mantle, he was startled by a harsh voice close upon his ear.

"Who are yon —with a murrain to you? No honest buyer, I'll warrant, but a hanger-on of the dicers—or something worse. Go! dance off, and find fitter company, or I'll give you a tune to a little quicker time than you'll like."

The young stranger drew back and looked at the speaker with a glance provokingly free from alarm and deprecation, and his slight expression of saucy amusement broke into a broad beaming smile as he surveyed the figure of his threatener. She was a stout but brawny woman, with a man's jerkin slipped over her green serge gamurra or gown, and the peaked hood of some departed mantle fastened round her sunburnt face, which, under all its coarseness and premature wrinkles showed a half-sad, half ludicrous maternal resemblance to the tender baby-face of the little maiden—the sort of resemblance which often seems a more croaking, shudder-creating prophecy than that of the death's head.

There was something irresistibly propitiating in that bright young smile, but Monna Ghita was not a woman to betray any weakness, and she went on speaking, apparently with heightened exasperation.

"Yes, yes, you can grin as well as other monkeys in cap and jerkin. You're a minstrel or a mountebank, I'll be sworn; you look for all the world as silly as a tumbler when he's been upside down and has got on his heels again. And what fool's tricks hast thou been after, Tessa?" she added, turning to her daughter, whose frightened face was more inviting to abuse. "Giving away the milk and victuals, it seems; ay, ay, thou'dst carry water in thy ears for any idle vagabond that didn't like to stoop for it, thou silly staring rabbit! Turn thy back, and lift the herbs out of the panniers, else I'll make thee say a few Aves without counting."

"Nay, Madonna," said the stranger, with a pleading smile, "don't be angry with your pretty Tessa for taking pity on a hungry traveller, who found himself unexpectedly without a quattrino. Your handsome face looks so well when it frowns, that I long to see it illuminated by a smile."

" Va via! I know what paste you are made of You may tickle me with that straw a good long while before I shall laugh, I can tell you. Get along, with a bad Easter! else I'll make a beauty spot or two on that face of yours that shall spoil your kissing on this side Advent."

As Monna Ghita lifted her formidable talons by way of complying with the first and last requisite of eloquence, Bratti, who had come up a minute or two before, had been saying to his companion, "What think you of this pappagallo, Nello? Doesn't his tongue smack of Venice?"

"Nay, Bratti," said the barber in an undertone, "thy wisdom has much of the ass in it, as I told thee just now; especially about the ears. This stranger is a Greek, else I'm not the barber who has had the sole and exclusive shaving of the excellent Demetrio, and drawn more than one sorry tooth from his learned jaw. And this youth might be taken to have come straight from Olympus—at least when he has had a touch of my razor."

" Orsii! Monna Ghita!" continued Nello, not sorry to see some sport; "what has happened to cause such a thunderstorm? Has this young stranger been misbehaving himself?"

"By San Giovanni!" said the cautious Bratti, who had not shaken off his original suspicions concerning the shabbily-clad possessor of jewels, "he did right to run away from me, if he meant to get into mischief. I can swear that I found him under the Loggia de' Cerchi, with a ring on his finger such as I've seen worn by Bernardo Rucellai himself. Not another rusty nail's worth do I know about him."

"The fact is," said Nello, eyeing the stranger good-humouredly, "this hello giovane has been a little too presumptuous in admiring the charms of Monna Ghita, and has attempted to kiss her while her daughter's back is turned; for I observe that the pretty Tessa is too busy to look this way at present. Was is not so, Messer?" Nello concluded, in a tone of courtesy.

"You have divined the offence like a soothsayer," said the stranger, laughingly. "Only that I had not the good fortune to find Monna Ghita here at first. I begged a cup of milk from her daughter, and had accepted this gift of bread, for which I was making a humble offering of gratitude, before I had the higher pleasure of being face to face with these riper charms which I was perhaps too bold in admiring."

"Va, va! be off, every one of you, and stay in purgatory till I pay to get you out, will you?" said Monna Ghita, fiercely, elbowing Nello, and leading forward her mule so as to compel the stranger to jump aside. "Tessa, thou simpleton, bring forward thy mule a bit: the cart will be upon us."

As Tessa turned to take the mule's bridle, she cast one timid glance at the stranger, who was now moving with Nello out of the way of an approaching market-cart; and the glance was just long enough to seize the beckoning movement of his hand, which indicated that he had been watching for this opportunity of an adieu.

"Ebbene," said Bratti, raising his voice to speak across the cart; "I leave you with Nello, young man, for there's no pushing my bag and basket any farther, and I have business at home. But you'll remember our bargain, because if you found Tessa without me, it was not my fault.. Nello will show you my shop in the Ferravecchi, and I'll not turn my back on you."

"A thousand thanks, friend!" said the stranger, laughing, and then turned away with Nello up the narrow street which led most directly to the Piazza del Duomo.

CHAPTER III.

THE barber's shop.

"To tell you the truth," said the young stranger to Nello, as they got a little clearer of the entangled vehicles and mules, "I am not sorry to be handed over by that patron of mine to one who has a less barbarous accent, and a less enigmatical business. Is it a common thing among you Florentines for an itinerant trafficker in broken glass and rags to talk of a shop where he sells lutes and swords?"

"Common? No: our Bratti is not a common man. He has a theory, and lives up to it, which is more than I can say for any philosopher I have the honour of shaving," answered Nello, whose loquacity, like an over-full bottle, could never pour forth a small dose. "Bratti means to extract the utmost possible amount of pleasure, that is to say, of hard bargaining, out of this lifej winding it up with a bargain for the easiest possible passage through purgatory, by giving Holy Church his winnings when the game is over. He has had his will made to that effect on the cheapest terms a notary could be got for. But I have often said to him, 'Bratti, thy bargain is a limping one, and thou art on the lame side of it. Does it not make thee a little sad to look at the pictures of the Para-diso? Thou wilt never be able there to chaffer for rags and rusty nails: the saints and angels want neither pins nor tinder; and except with San Bartolomeo, who carries his skin about in an inconvenient manner, I see no chance of thy making a bargain for second-hand clothing.' But God pardon me," added Nello, changing his tone, and crossing himself, "this light talk ill beseems a morning when Lorenzo lies dead, and the Muses are tearing their hair—always a painful thought to a barber; and you yourself, Messere, are probably under a cloud, for when a man of your speech and presence takes up with so sorry a night's lodging, it argues some misfortune to have befallen him."

"What Lorenzo is that whose death you speak of?" said the stranger, appearing to have dwelt with too anxious an interest on this point to have noticed the indirect inquiry that followed it.

"What Lorenzo? There is but one Lorenzo, I imagine, whose death could throw the Mercato into an uproar, set the lantern of the Duomo leaping in desperation, and cause the lions of the Republic to feel under an immediate necessity to devour one another. I mean Lorenzo de' Medici, the Pericles of our Athens—if I may make such a comparison in the ear of a Greek."

"Why not?" said the other, laughingly; "for I doubt whether Athens, even in the days of Pericles, could have produced so learned a barber."

"Yes, yes; I thought I could not be mistaken," said the rapid Nello, "else I have shaved the venerable Demetrio Calcondila to little purpose; but pardon me, I am lost in wonder: your Italian is better than his, though he has been in Italy forty years—better even than that of the accomplished Marullo, who may be said to have married the Italic Muse in more senses than one, since he has married our learned and lovely Alessandra Scala."

"It will lighten your wonder to know that I come of a Greek stock, planted in Italian soil much longer than the mulberry-trees which have taken so kindly to it. I was born at Bari, and' my I mean, I was brought up by an Italian—and, in fact, may rather be called a Grseculus than a Greek. The Greek dye was subdued in me, I suppose, till I had been dipped over again by long abode and much travel in the land of gods and heroes. And, to confess something of my private affairs to you, this same Greek dye, with a few ancient gems I have about me, is the only fortune shipwreck has left me. But when the towers fall, you know, it is an ill business for the small nest-builders—the death of your Pericles makes me wish I had rather turned my steps towards Rome, as I should have done, but for a fallacious Minerva in the shape of an Augustinian monk. 'At Rome,' he said, 'you will be lost in a crowd of hungry scholars; but at Florence, every corner is penetrated by the sunshine of Lorenzo's patronage: Florence is the best market in Italy for such commodities as yours.'"

" Gnaffe, and so it will remain, I hope," said Nello. "Lorenzo vas not the only patron and judge of learning

in our city heaven forbid! Because he was a large melon, every other Florentine is not a pumpkin, mi pare. Have vie not Bernardo Rucellai, and Alamanno Rinuccini, and plenty more? And if you want to be informed on such matters, I, Nello, am your man. It seems to me a thousand years till I can be of service to a hel enidito like yourself. And, first of all, in the matter of your hair. That beard, my fine young man, must be parted with, were it as dear to you as the nymph of your dreams. Here at Florence, we love not to see a man with his nose projecting over a cascade of hair. But, remember, you will have passed the Rubicon, when once you have been shaven: if you repent, and let your beard grow after it has acquired stoutness by a struggle with the razor, your mouth will by-and-by show no longer what Messer Angelo calls the divine prerogative of lips, but will appear like a dark cavern fringed with horrent brambles."

"That is a terrible prophecy," said the Greek, "especially if your Florentine maidens are many of them as pretty as the little Tessa I stole a kiss from this morning."

"Tessa? she is a rough-handed contadina: you will rise into the favour of dames who bring no scent of the mule-stables with them. But to that end, you must not have the air of a sgherro, or a man of evil repute: you must look like a courtier, and a scholar of the more polished sort, such as our Pietro Crinito—like one who sins among well-bred, well-fed people, and not one who sucks down vile vijio di soito in a chance tavern."

"With all my heart," said the stranger. "If the Florentine Graces demand it, I am willing to give up this small matter of my beard, but—"

"Yes, yes," interrupted Nello. "I know what you

would say. It is the hella zazzera the hyacinthine locks, you do not choose to part with; and there is no need. Just a little pruning ecco! and you will look not unlike the illustrious prince Pico di Mirandola in his prime. And here we are in good time in the Piazza San Giovanni, and at the door of my shop. But you are pausing, I see: naturally, you want to look at our wonder of the world, our Duomo, our Santa Maria del Fiore. Well, well, a mere glance; but I beseech you to leave a closer survey till you have been shaved: I am quivering with the inspiration of my art even to the very edge of my razor. Ah, then, come round this way."

The mercurial barber seized the arm of the stranger, and led him to a point, on the south side of the piazza, from which he could see at once the huge dark shell of the cupola, the slender soaring grace of Giotto's campanile, and the quaint octagon of San Giovanni in front of them, showing its unique gates of storied bronze, which still bore the somewhat dimmed glory of their original gilding. The inlaid marbles were then fresher in their pink, and white, and purple, than they are now, when the winters of four centuries have turned their white to the rich ochre of well-mellowed meerschaum; façade of the cathedral did not stand ignominious in faded stucco, but had upon it the magnificent promise of the half-completed marble inlaying and statued niches, which Giotto had devised a hundred and fifty years before; and as the campanile in all its harmonious variety of colour and form led the eyes upward, high into the clear air of this April morning, it seemed a prophetic symbol, telling that human life must somehow and some time shape itself into accord with that pure aspiring beauty.

But this was not the impression it appeared to pro-duce on the Greek. His eyes were irresistibly led upward, but as he stood with his arms folded and his curls falling backward, there was a slight touch of scorn on his lip, and when his eyes fell again they glanced round with a scanning coolness which was rather piquing to Nello's Florentine spirit.

"Well, my fine young man," he said, with some impatience, "you seem to make as little of our Cathedral as if you were the Angel Gabriel come straight from Paradise. I should like to know if you have ever seen finer work than our Giotto's tower, or any cupola that would not look a mere mushroom by the side of Brunelleschi's there, or any marbles finer or more cunningly wrought than these that our Signoria got from far-off quarries, at a price that would buy a dukedom. Come, now, have you ever seen anything to equal them?"

"If you asked me that question with a scimitar at my throat, after the Turkish fashion, or even your own razor," said the young Greek, smiling gaily, and moving on towards the gates of the Baptistery, "I daresay you might get a confession of the true faith from me. But with my throat free from peril, I venture to tell you that your buildings smack too much of Christian barbarism for my taste. I have a shuddering sense of what there is inside —hideous smoked Madonnas; fleshless saints in mosaic, staring down idiotic astonishment and rebuke from the apse; skin-clad skeletons hanging on crosses, or stuck all over with arrows, or stretched on gridirons; women and monks with heads aside in perpetual lamentation. I have seen enough of those wry-necked favourites of heaven at Constantinople. But what is this bronze door rough with imagery? These women's figures seem moulded in a different spirit from those starved and staring saints I spoke

of: these heads in high reUef speak of a human mind within them, instead of looking hke an index to perpetual spasms and colic."

"Yes, yes," said Nello, with some triumph. "I think we shall show you by-and-by that our Florentine art is not in a state of barbarism. These gates, my fine young man, were moulded half a century ago, by our Lorenzo Ghiberti, when he counted hardly so many years as you do."

"Ah, I remember," said the stranger, turning away, like one whose appetite for contemplation was soon satisfied. "I have heard that your Tuscan sculptors and painters have been studying the antique a little. But with monks for models, and the legends of mad hermits and martyrs for subjects, the vision of Olympus itself would be of small use to them."

"I understand," said Nello, with a significant shrug, as they walked along. "You are of the same mind as Michele Marullo, ay, and as Angelo Poliziano himself, in spite of his canonicate, when he relaxes himself a little in my shop after his lectures, and talks of the gods awaking from their long sleep and making the woods and streams vital once more. But he rails against the Roman scholars who want to make us all talk Latin again: 'My ears,' he says, 'are sufficiently flayed by the barbarisms of the learned, and if the vulgar are to talk Latin I would as soon have been in Florence the day they took to beating all the kettles in the city because the bells were not enough to stay the wrath of the saints.' Ah, Messer Greco, if you want to know the flavour of our scholarship, you must frequent my shop: it is the focus of Florentine intellect, and in that sense the navel of the earth—as my great predecessor, Burchiello, said of his shop, on the more frivolous pre-tension that his street of the CaUmara was the centre of our city. And here we are at the sign of 'Apollo and the Razor.' Apollo, you see, is bestowing the razor on the Triptolemus of our craft, the first reaper of beards, the sublime Anonimo, whose mysterious identity is indicated by a shadowy hand."

"I see thou hast had custom already, Sandro," continued Nello, addressing a solemn-looking dark-eyed youth, who made way for them on the threshold. "And now make all clear for this signor to sit down. And prepare the finest scented lather, for he has a learned and a handsome chin."

" You have a pleasant little adytum there, I see," said the stranger, looking through a latticed screen which divided the shop from a room of about equal size, opening into a still smaller walled enclosure, where a few bays and laurels surrounded a stone Hermes. "I suppose your conclave of eruditi meets there?"

"There, and not less in my shop," said Nello, leading the way into the inner room, in which were some benches, a table, with one book in manuscript and one printed in capitals lying open upon it, a lute, a few oil-sketches, and a model or two of hands and ancient masks. "For my shop is a no less fitting haunt of the Muses, as you will acknowledge when you feel the sudden illumination of understanding and the serene vigour of inspiration that will come to you with a clear chin. Ah! you can make that lute discourse, I perceive. I, too, have some skill that way, though the serenata is useless when daylight discloses a visage like mine, looking no fresher than an apple that has stood the winter. But look at that sketch: it is a fancy of Piero di Cosimo's, a strange freakish painter, who says he saw it by long looking at a mouldy wall."

The sketch Nello pointed to represented three masks —one a drunken laughing Satyr, another a sorrowing Magdalen, and the third, which lay between them, the rigid, cold face of a Stoic: the masks rested obliquely on the lap of a little child, whose cherub features rose above them with something of the supernal promise in the gaze which painters had by that time learned to give to the Divine Infant.

"A symbolical picture, I see," said the young Greek, touching the lute while he spoke, so as to bring out a slight musical murmur. "The child, perhaps, is the Golden Age, wanting neither worship nor philosophy. And the Golden Age can always come back as long as men are born in the form of babies, and don't come into the world in cassock or furred mantle. Or, the child may mean the wise philosophy of Epicurus, removed alike from the gross, the sad, and the severe."

"Ah! everybody has his own interpretation for that picture," said Nello; "and if you ask Piero himself what he meant by it, he says his pictures are an appendix which Messer Domeneddio has been pleased to make to the universe, and if any man is in doubt what they mean, he had better inquire of Holy Church. He has been asked to paint a picture after the sketch, but he puts his fingers to his ears and shakes his head at that: the fancy is passed, he says—a strange animal, our Piero. But now all is ready for your initiation into the mysteries of the razor."

"Mysteries they may well be called," continued the barber, with rising spirits at the prospect of a long monologue, as he imprisoned the young Greek in the shroudlike shaving-cloth; "mysteries of Minerva and the Graces. I get the flower of men's thoughts, because I seize them in the first moment after shaving. (Ah! you wince a little at the lather; it tickles the outlying limits of the nose, I admit.) And that is what makes the peculiar fitness of a barber's shop to become a resort of wit and learning. For, look now at a druggist's shop: there is a dull conclave at the sign of Mow, that pretends to rival mine; but what sort of inspiration, I beseech you, can be got from the scent of nauseous vegetable decoctions? to say nothing of the fact that you no sooner pass the threshold than you see a doctor of physic, like a gigantic spider disguised in fur and scarlet, waiting for his prey; or even see him blocking up the doorway seated on a bony hack, inspecting saliva. (Your chin a little elevated, if it please you: contemplate that angel who is blowing the trumpet at you from the ceiling. I had it painted expressly for the regulation of my clients' chins.) Besides, your druggist, who herborises and decocts, is a man of prejudices: he has poisoned people according to a system, and is obliged to stand up for his system to justify the consequences. Now a barber can be dispassionate; the only thing he necessarily stands by is the razor, always providing he is not an author. That was the flaw in my great predecessor Burchiello: he was a poet, and had consequently a prejudice about his own poetry. I have escaped that; I saw very early that authorship is a narrowing business, in conflict with the liberal art of the razor, which demands an impartial affection for all men's chins. Ecco, Messer! the outline of your chin and lip is as clear as a maiden's; and now fix your mind on a knotty question—ask yourself whether you are bound to spell Virgil with an i or an e, and say if you do not feel an unwonted clearness on the point. Only, if you decide for the i, keep it to yourself till your fortune is made, for the

e hath the stronger following in Florence. Ah! I thuik I see a gleam of still quicker wit in your eye. I have it on the authority of our young Niccolo Macchiavelli, himself keen enough to discern il pelo neW novo, as we say, and a great lover of delicate shaving, though his beard is hardly of two years' date, that no sooner do the hairs begin to push themselves, than he perceives a certain grossness of apprehension creeping over him."

"Suppose you let me look at myself," said the stranger, laughing. "The happy effect on my intellect is perhaps obstructed by a little doubt as to the effect on my appearance."

"Behold yourself in this mirror, then; it is a Venetian mirror from Murano, the true ?iosce tcipsum, as I have named it, compared with which the finest mirror of steel or silver is mere darkness. See now, how by diligent shaving, the nether region of your face may preserve its human outline, instead of presenting no distinction from the physiognomy of a bearded owl or a Barbary ape. I have seen men whose beards have so invaded their cheeks, that one might have pitied them as the victims of a sad, brutalising chastisement befitting our Dante's Inferno, if they had not seemed to strut with a strange triumph in their extravagant hairiness."

"It seems to me," said the Greek, still looking into the mirror, "that you have taken away some of my capital with your razor—I mean a year or two of age, which might have won me more ready credit for my learning. Under the inspection of a patron whose vision has grown somewhat dim, I shall have a perilous resemblance to a maiden of eighteen in the disguise of hose and jerkin."

"Not at all," said Nello, proceeding to cHp the too extravagant curls; "your proportions are not those of a

maiden. And for your age, I myself remember seeing Angelo Poliziano begin his lectures on the Latin language when he had a younger beard than yours; and between ourselves, his juvenile ugliness was not less signal than his precocious scholarship. Whereas you—no, no, your age is not against you; but between ourselves, let me hint to you that your being a Greek, though it be only an Apulian Greek, is not in your favour. Certain of our scholars hold that your Greek learning is but a wayside degenerate plant until it has been transplanted into Italian brains, and that now there is such a plentiful crop of the superior quality, your native teachers are mere propagators of degeneracy. Ecco! your curls are now of the right proportion to neck and shoulders; rise, Messer, and I will free you from the encumbrance of this cloth! Gnaffe! I almost advise you to retain the faded jerkin and hose a little longer; they give you the air of a fallen prince."

"But the question is," said the young Greek, leaning against the high back of a chair, and returning Nello's contemplative admiration with a look of inquiring anxiety; "the question is, in what quarter I am to carry my princely air, so as to rise from the said fallen condition. If your Florentine patrons of learning share this scholarly hostility to the Greeks, I see not how your city can be a hospitable refuge for me, as you seemed to say just now."

"Plan Piatio —not so fast," said Nello, sticking his thumbs into his belt and nodding to Sandro to restore order. "I will not conceal from you that there is a prejudice against Greeks among us; and though, as a barber unsnared by authorship, I share no prejudices, I must admit that the Greeks are not always such pretty youngsters as yourself: their erudition is often of an uncombed, un-

mannerly aspect, and encrusted with a barbarous utterance of Italian, that makes their converse hardly more euphonious than that of a Tedesco in a state of vinous loquacity. And then, again, excuse me—we Florentines have liberal ideas about speech, and consider that an instrument which can flatter and promise so cleverly as the tongue, must have been partly made for those purposes; and that truth is a riddle for eyes and wit to discover, which it were a mere spoiling of sport for the tongue to betray. Still we have our limits beyond which we call dissimulation treachery. But it is said of the Greeks that their honesty begins at what is the hanging-point with us, and that since the old Furies went to sleep, your Christian Greek is of so easy a conscience that he would make a stepping-stone of his father's corpse."

The flush on the stranger's face indicated what seemed so natural a movement of resentment, that the good-natured Nello hastened to atone for his want of reticence.

"Be not offended, bel giova?ie; I am but repeating what I hear in my shop; as you may perceive, my eloquence is simply the cream which I skim off my clients' talk. Heaven forbid I should fetter my impartiality by entertaining an opinion. And for that same scholarly objection to the 'Greeks," added Nello, in a more mocking tone, and with a significant grimace, "the fact is, you are heretics, Messer; jealousy has nothing to do with it: if you would just change your opinion about Heaven, and alter your Doxology a little, our Italian scholars would think it a thousand years till they could give up their chairs to you. Yes, yes; it is chiefly religious scruple, and partly also the authority of a great classic,—Juvenal, is it not? He, I gather, had his bile as much stirred by the swarm of Greeks as our Messer Angelo, who is fond of

quoting some passage about their incorrigible impudence — audacia pcrdita."

"Pooh! the passage is a compliment," said the Greek, who had recovered himself, and seemed wise enough to take the matter gaily—

" 'Ingenium velox, audacia perdita, sermo Promptus, et Isseo torrentior,'

A rapid intellect and ready eloquence may carry off a little impudence."

"Assuredly," said Nello. "And since, as I see, you know Latin literature as well as Greek, you will not fall into the mistake of Giovanni Argiropulo, who ran full tilt against Cicero, and pronounced him all but a pumpkin-head. For, let me give you one bit of advice, young man trust a barber who has shaved the best chins, and kept his eyes and ears open for twenty years oil your tongue well when you talk of the ancient Latin writers, and give it an extra dip when you talk of the modern. A wise Greek may win favour among us; witness our excellent Demetrio, who is loved by many, and not hated immoderately even by the most renowned scholars."

"I discern the wisdom of your advice so clearly," said the Greek, with the bright smile which was continually lighting up the fine form and colour of his young face, "that I will ask you for a little more. Who now, for example, would be the most likely patron for me? Is there a son of Lorenzo who inherits his tastes? Or is there any other wealthy Florentine specially addicted to purchasing antique gems? I have a fine Cleopatra cut in sardonyx, and one or two other intaglios and cameos, both curious and beautiful, worthy of being added to the cabinet of a prince. Happily, I had taken the precaution of fastening them within the lining of my doublet before

I set out on my voyage. Moreover, I should like to raise a small sum for my present need on this ring of mine" (here he took out the ring and replaced it on his finger), "if you could recommend me to any honest trafficker."

"Let us see, let us see," said Nello, perusing the floor, and walking up and down the length of his shop. "This is no time to apply to Piero de' Medici, though he has the will to make such purchases if he could always spare the money; but I think it is another sort of Cleopatra that

he covets most Yes, yes, I have it. What you

want is a man of wealth, and influence, and scholarly tastes not one of your learned porcupines, bristling all over with critical tests, but one whose Greek and Latin are of a comfortable laxity. And that man is Bartolom-meo Scala, the secretary of our Republic. He came to Florence as a poor adventurer himself a miller's son a 'branny monster,' as he has been nicknamed by our honey-lipped Poliziano, who agrees with him as well as my teeth agree with lemon-juice. And, by-the-bye, that may be a reason why the secretary may be the more ready to do a good turn to a strange scholar. For, between you and me, bel giovane trust a barber who has shaved the best scholars friendliness is much such a steed as Ser Benghi's: it will hardly show much alacrity unless it has got the thistle of hatred under its tail. However, the secretary is a man who'll keep his word to you, even to the halving of a fennel seed; and he is not unlikely to buy some of your gems."

"But how am I to get at this great man?" said the Greek, rather impatiently.

"I was coming to that," said Nello. "Just now everybody of any public importance will be full of Lorenzo's death, and a stranger may find it difficult to get any

notice. But in the meantime, I could take you to a man who, if he has a mind, can help you to a chance of a favourable interview with Scala sooner than anybody else in Florence— worth seeing for his own sake too, to say nothing of his collections, or of his daughter Romola, who is as fair as the Florentine lily before it got quarrelsome, and turned red."

"But if this father of the beautiful Romola makes collections, why should he not like to buy some of my gems himself?"

Nello shrugged his shoulders. "For two good reasons —want of sight to look at the gems, and want of money to pay for them. Our old Bardo de' Bardi is so blind that he can see no more of his daughter than, as he says, a glimmering of something bright when she comes very near him: doubtless her golden hair, which, as Messer Luigi Pulci says of his Meridiana's, ' raggia come stella per sereno.' Ah, here come some clients of mine, and I shouldn't wonder if one of them could serve your turn about that ring."

CHAPTER IV.

FIRST IMPRESSIONS.

"Good-day, Messer Domenico," said Nello to the foremost of the two visitors who entered the shop, while he nodded silently to the other. "You come as opportunely as cheese on macaroni. Ah! you are in haste—wish to be shaved without delay—ecco! And this is a morning when everyone has grave matter on his mind. Florence orphaned—the very pivot of Italy snatched away—heaven itself at a loss what to do next. Oime! Well, well; the

sun is nevertheless travelling on towards dinner-time again; and, as I was saying, you come like cheese ready grated. For this young stranger was wishing for an honourable trader who would advance him a sum on a certain ring of value, and if I had counted every goldsmith and moneylender in Florence on my fingers, I couldn't have found a better name than Menico Cennini. Besides, he hath other ware in which you deal Greek learning, and young eyes a double implement which you printers are always in need of"

The grave elderly man, son of that Bernardo Cennini, who, twenty years before, having heard of the new process of printing carried on by Germans, had cast his own types in Florence, remained necessarily in lathered silence and passivity while Nello showered this talk in his ears, but turned a slow sideway gaze on the stranger.

"This fine young man has unlimited Greek, Latin, or Italian at your service," continued Nello, fond of interpreting by very ample paraphrase. "He is as great a wonder of juvenile learning as Francesco Filelfo or our own incomparable Poliziano. A second Guarino, too, for he has had the misfortune to be shipwrecked, and has doubtless lost a store of precious manuscripts that might have contributed some correctness even to your correct editions, Domenico. Fortunately, he has rescued a few gems of rare value. His name is—you said your name, Messer, was ?"

"Tito Melema," said the stranger, slipping the ring from his finger, and presenting it to Cennini, whom Nello, not less rapid with his razor than with his tongue, had now released from the shaving-cloth.

Meanwhile the man who had entered the shop in company with the goldsmith a tall figure, about fifty, with a short trimmed beard, wearing an old felt hat and a threadbare mantle had kept his eye fixed on the Greek, and now said abruptly,

"Young man, I am painting a picture of Sinon deceiving old Priam, and I should be glad of your face for my Sinon, if you'd give me a sitting."

Tito Melema started and looked round with a pale astonishment in his face as if at a sudden accusation; but Nello left him no time to feel at a loss for an answer: "Piero," said the barber, "thou art the most extraordinary compound of humours and fancies ever packed into a human skin. What trick wilt thou play with the fine visage of this young scholar to make it suit thy traitor? Ask him rather to turn his eyes upward, and thou may'st make a Saint Sebastian of him that will draw troops of devout women, or, if thou art in a classical vein, put myrtle about his curls and make him a young Bacchus, or say rather a Phœbus Apollo, for his face is as warm and bright as a summer morning; it made me his friend in the space of a 'credo.'"

"Aye, Nello," said the painter, speaking with abrupt pauses; "and if thy tongue can leave off its everlasting chirping long enough for thy understanding to consider the matter, thou may'st see that thou hast just shown the reason why the face of Messere will suit my traitor. A perfect traitor should have a face which vice can write no marks on lips that will lie with a dimpled smile eyes of such agate-like brightness and depth that no infamy can dull them cheeks that will rise from a murder and not look haggard. I say not this young man is a traitor: I mean, he has a face that would make him the more perfect traitor if he had the heart of one, which is saying neither more nor less than that he has a beautiful face,

informed with rich young blood, that will be nourished enough by food, and keep its colour without much help of virtue. He may have the heart of a hero along with it; I aver nothing to the contrary. Ask Domenico there if the lapidaries can always tell a gem by the sight alone. And now I'm going to put the tow in my ears, for thy chatter and the bells together are more than I can endure: so say no more to me, but trim my beard."

With these last words Piero (called "di Cosimo," from his master, Cosimo Rosselli) drew out two bits of tow, stuffed them in his ears, and placed himself in the chair before Nello, who shrugged his shoulders and cast a grimacing look of intelligence at the Greek, as much as to say,

"A whimsical fellow, you perceive! Everybody holds his speeches as mere jokes."

Tito, who had stood transfixed, with his long dark eyes resting on the unknown man who had addressed him so equivocally, seemed recalled to his self-command by Piero's change of position, and, apparently satisfied with his explanation, was again giving his attention to Cennini, who presently said,—

"This is a curious and a valuable ring, young man. This intaglio of the fish with the crested serpent above it, in the black stratum of the onyx, or rather nicolo, is well shown by the surrounding blue of the upper stratum. The ring has, doubtless, a history?" added Cennini, lookmg up keenly at the young stranger.

"Yes, indeed," said Tito, meeting the scrutiny very frankly. "The ring was found in Sicily, and I have understood from those who busy themselves with gems and sigils, that both the stone and intaglio are of virtue to make the wearer fortunate, especially at sea, and also to restore to him whatever he may have lost. But," he con- tinued smiling, "though I have worn it constantly since I quitted Greece, it has not made me altogether fortunate I at sea, you perceive, unless I am to count escape from drowning as a sufficient proof of its virtue. It remains to be seen whether my lost chests will come to light; but to lose no chance of such a result, Messer, I will pray you j only to hold the ring for a short space as pledge for a small sum far beneath its value, and I will redeem it as soon as I can dispose of certain other gems which are secured within my doublet, or indeed as soon as I can earn something by any scholarly employment, if I may be so fortunate as to meet with such."

"That may be seen, young man, if you will come with me," said Cennini. "My brother Pietro, who is a better judge of scholarship than I, will perhaps be able to supply you with a task that may test your capabilities. Meanwhile, take back your ring until I can hand you the necessary florins, and, if it please you, come along with me."

"Yes, yes," said Nello, "go with Messer Domenico, you cannot go in better company; he was born under the constellation that gives a man skill, riches, and integrity, whatever that constellation may be, which is of the less consequence because babies can't choose their own horoscopes, and, indeed, if they could, there might be an inconvenient rush of babies at particular epochs. Besides, our Phoenix, the incomparable Pico, has shown that your horoscopes are all a nonsensical dream—which is the less troublesome opinion. Addio, bel giovane! don't forget to come back to me."

"No fear of that," said Tito, beckoning a farewell, as he turned round his bright face at the door. "You are to do me a great service: — that is the most positive security for your seeing me again."

"Say what thou wilt, Piero," said Nello, as the young stranger disappeared, "I shall never look at such an outside as that without taking it as a sign of a loveable nature. Why, thou wilt say next that Lionardo, whom thou art always raving about, ought to have made his Judas as beautiful as St. John! But thou art as deaf as the top of Mount Morello with that accursed tow in thy ears. Well, well: I'll get a little more of this young man's history from him before I take him to Bardo Bardi."

CHAPTER V. THE BLIND SCHOLAR AND HIS DAUGHTER.

The Via de' Bardi, a street noted in the history of Florence, lies in Oltrarno, or that portion of the city which clothes the southern bank of the river. It extends from the Ponte Vecchio to the Piazza de' Mozzi at the head of the Ponte alle Grazie; its right-hand line of houses and walls being backed by the rather steep ascent which in the fifteenth century was known as the Hill of Bogoli, the famous stone-quarry whence the city got its pavement—of dangerously unstable consistence when penetrated by rains; its left-hand buildings flanking the river and making on their northern side a length of quaint, irregUlarly-pierced facade, of which the waters give a softened loving reflection as the sun begins to decline towards the western heights. But quaint as these buildings are, some of them seem to the historical memory a too modern substitute for the famous houses of the Bardi family, destroyed by popular rage in the middle of the fourteenth century.

They were a proud and energetic stock, these Bardi:
conspicuous among those who ckitched the sword in the eariiest world-famous quarrels of Florentines with Florentines, when the narrow streets were darkened with the high towers of the nobles, and when the old tutelar god Mars, as he saw the gutters reddened with neighbours' blood, might well have smiled at the centuries of lip-service paid to his rival, the Baptist. But the Bardi hands were of the sort that not only clutch the sword-hilt with vigour, but love the more delicate pleasure of fingering minted metal: they were matched, too, with true Florentine eyes, capable of discerning that power was to be won by other means than by rending and riving, and by the middle of the fourteenth century we find them risen from their original condition oi popolani to be possessors, by purchase, of lands and strongholds, and the feudal dignity of Counts of Vernio, disturbing to the jealousy of their republican fellow-citizens. These lordly purchases are explained by our seeing the Bardi disastrously signalised only a few years later as standing in the very front of European commerce—the Christian Rothschilds of that time—undertaking to furnish specie for the wars of our Edward the Third, and having revenues "in kind" made over to them; especially in wool, most precious of freights for Florentine galleys. Their august debtor left them with an august deficit, and alarmed Sicilian creditors made a too sudden demand for the payment of deposits, causing a ruinous shock to the credit of the Bardi and of associated houses, which was felt as a commercial calamity along all the coasts of the Mediterranean. But, like more modern bankrupts, they did not, for all that, hide their heads in humiliation; on the contrary, they seem to have held them higher than ever, and to have been among the most arrogant of those grandi, who under certain noteworthy circumstances, open to all who will read the honest pages of Giovanni Villani, drew upon themselves the exasperation of the armed people in 1343. The Bardi, who had made themselves fast in their street between the two bridges, kept these narrow inlets, like panthers at bay, against the oncoming gonfalons of the people, and were only made to give way by an assault from the hill behind them. Their houses by the river, to the number of twenty-two [palagi e case grandi), were sacked and burnt, and many among the chief of those who bore the Bardi name were driven from the city. But an old Florentine family was many-rooted, and we find the Bardi maintaining importance and rising again and again to the surface of Florentine affairs in a more or less creditable manner, implying an untold family history that would have included even more vicissitudes and contrasts of dignity and disgrace, of wealth and poverty, than are usually seen on the background of wide kinship.* But the Bardi never resumed their proprietorship in the old street on the banks of the river, which in 1492 had long been associated with other names of mark, and especially with the Neri, who possessed a considerable range of houses on the side towards the hill.

In one of these Neri houses there lived, however, A sign that such contrasts were peculiarly frequent in Florence is the fact that Saint Antonine, Prior of San Marco, and afterwards archbishop, in the first half of this fifteenth century, founded the society of Buonuomini di San Martino (Good Men of St. Martin) with the main object of succouring the povert vergognosi in other words, paupers of good family. In the records of the famous Panciatichi family we find a certain Girolamo in this century who was reduced to such a state of poverty that he was obliged to seek charity for the mere means of sustaining life, though other members of his family were enormously wealthy.

descendant of the Bardi, and of that very branch which a century and a half before had become Counts of Vernio: a descendant who had inherited the old family pride and energy, the old love of pre-eminence, the old desire to leave a lasting track of his footsteps on the fast-whirling earth. But the family passions lived on in him under altered conditions: this descendant of the Bardi was not a man swift in street warfare, or one who loved to play the signor, fortifying strongholds and asserting the right to hang vassals, or a merchant and usurer of keen daring, who delighted in the generalship of wide commercial schemes: he was a man with a deep-veined hand cramped by much copying of manuscripts, who ate sparing dinners, and wore threadbare clothes, at first from choice and at last from necessity; who sat among his books and his marble fragments of the past, and saw them only by the light of those far-off younger days which still shone in his memory: he was a moneyless, blind old scholar— the Bar do de' Bardi to whom Nello, the barber, had promised to introduce the young Greek, Tito Melema,

The house in which Bardo lived was situated on the side of the street nearest the hill, and was one of those large sombre masses of stone building pierced by comparatively small windows, and surmounted by what may be called a roofed terrace or loggia, of which there are many examples still to be seen in the venerable city. Grim doors, with conspicuous scrolled hinges, having high up on each side of them a small window defended by iron bars, opened on a groined entrance court, empty of everything but a massive lamp-iron suspended from the centre of the groin. A smaller grim door on the left hand admitted to the stone staircase, and the rooms on the ground floor. These last were used as a warehouse

by the proprietor; so was the first floor; and both were filled with precious stores, destined to be carried, some perhaps to the banks of the Scheldt, some to the shores of Africa, some to the isles of the Egean, or to the banks of the Euxine. Maso, the old serving-man, who returned from the Mercato, with the stock of cheap vegetables, had to make his slow way up to the second story before he reached the door of his master, Bardo, through which we are about to enter only a few mornings after Nello's conversation with the Greek.

We follow Maso across the antechamber to the door on the left hand, through which we pass as he opens it. He merely looks in and nods, while a clear young voice says, "Ah, you are come back, Maso. It is well. We have wanted nothing."

The voice came from the farther end of a long, spacious room, surrounded with shelves, on which books and antiquities were arranged in scrupulous order. Here and there, on separate stands in front of the shelves, were placed a beautiful feminine torso; a headless statue, with an uplifted muscular arm wielding a bladeless sword; rounded, dimpled, infantine limbs severed from the trunk, inviting the lips to kiss the cold marble; some well-preserved Roman busts; and two or three vases of Magna Grecia. A large table in the centre was covered with antique bronze lamps and small vessels in dark pottery. The colour of these objects was chiefly pale or sombre: the vellum bindings, with their deep-ridged backs, gave little relief to the marble, livid with long burial; the once si^lendid patch of carpet at the farther end of the room had long been worn to dimness; the dark bronzes wanted sunlight upon them to bring out their tinge of green, and the sun was not yet high enough to send gleams of brightness through the narrow windows that looked on the Via de' Bardi.

The only spot of bright colour in the room was made by the hair of a tall maiden of seventeen or eighteen, who was standing before a carved leggio, or reading-desk, such as is often seen in the choirs of Italian churches. The hair was of a reddish gold colour enriched by an unbroken small ripple, such as may be seen in the sunset clouds on grandest autumnal evenings. It was confined by a black fillet above her small ears, from which it rippled forward again, and made a natural veil for her neck above her square-cut gown of black rascia, or serge. Her eyes were bent on a large volume placed before her: one long white hand rested on the reading-desk, and the other clasped the back of her father's chair.

The blind father sat with head uplifted and turned a little aside towards his daughter, as if he were looking at her. His delicate paleness, set off by the black velvet cap which surmounted his drooping white hair, made all the more perceptible the likeness between his aged features and those of the young maiden, whose cheeks were also without any tinge of the rose. There was the same refinement of brow and nostril in both, counterbalanced by a full though firm mouth and powerful chin, which gave an expression of proud tenacity and latent impetuousness: an expression carried out in the backward poise of the girl's head, and the grand line of her neck and shoulders. It was a type of face of which one could not venture to say whether it would inspire love or only that unwilling admiration which is mixed with dread: the question must be decided by the eyes, which often seem charged with a more direct message from the soul. But the eyes of the father had long been silent, and the eyes of the daughter

were bent on the Latin pages of Politian's Miscellanea, from which she was reading aloud at the eightieth chapter, to the following effect:—

"There was a certain nymph of Thebes named Chariclo, "especially dear to Pallas; and this nymph was the mother "of Teiresias. But once when in the heat of summer, 'Pallas, in company with Chariclo, was bathing her dis-" robed limbs in the Heliconian Hippocrene, it happened "that Teiresias coming as a hunter to quench his thirst "at the same fountain, inadvertently beheld Minerva un-"veiled, and immediately became blind. For it is de-"clared in the Saturnian laws, that he who beholds the "gods against their will, shall atone for it by a heavy "penalty. . . . When Teiresias had fallen into this calamity, "Pallas, moved by the tears of Chariclo, endowed him "with prophecy and length of days, and even caused his "prudence and wisdom to continue after he had entered "among the shades, so that an oracle spake from his "tomb: and she gave him a staff, wherewith, as by a "guide, he might walk without stumbling. . . . And hence, "Nonnus, m the fifth book of the Dionysiaca, introduces "Actseon exclaiming that he calls Teiresias happy, since, "without dying, and with the loss of his eyesight merely, "he had beheld IVIinerva unveiled, and thus, though blind, "could for evermore carry her image in his soul."

At this point in the reading, her daughter's hand slipped from the back of the chair and met her father's, which he had that moment upUfted; but she had not oked round, and was going on, though with a voice a ittle altered by some suppressed feeling, to read the Greek quotation from Nonnus, when the old man said—

"Stay, Romola; reach me my own copy of Nonnus.

It is a more correct copy than any in Poliziano's hands, for I made emendations in it which have not yet been communicated to any man. I finished it in 1477, when my sight was fast faiUng me."

Romola walked to the farther end of the room, with the queenly step which was the simple action of her tall, finely-wrought frame, without the slightest conscious adjustment of herself.

"Is it in the right place, Romola?" asked Bardo, who was perpetually seeking the assurance that the outward fact continued to correspond with the image which lived to the minutest detail in his mind.

"Yes, father; at the west end of the room, on the third shelf from the bottom, behind the bust of Hadrian, above Apollonius Rhodius and CaUimachus, and below Lucan and Silius Italicus."

As Romola said this, a fine ear would have detected in her clear voice and distinct utterance, a faint suggestion of weariness struggling with habitual patience. But as she approached her father and saw his arms stretched out a little with nervous excitement to seize the volume, her hazel eyes filled with pity; she hastened to lay the book on his lap, and kneeled down by him, looking up at him as if she believed that the love in her face must surely make its way through the dark obstruction that shut out everything else. At that moment the doubtful attractiveness of Romola's face, in which pride and passion seemed to be quivering in the balance with native refinement and intelligence, was transfigured to the most loveable womanliness by mingled pity and affection: it was evident that the deepest fount of feeling within her had not yet wrought its way to the less changeful features, and only found its outlet through her eyes.

But the father, unconscious of that soft radiance, looked flushed and agitated as his hand explored the edges and back of the large book.

"The vellum is yellowed in these thirteen years, Romola."

"Yes, father," said Romola, gently; "but your letters at the back are dark and plain still—fine Roman letters; and the Greek character," she continued, laying the book open on her father's knee, "is more beautiful than that of any of your bought manuscripts."

"Assuredly, child," said Bardo, passing his finger across the page, as if he hoped to discriminate line and margin. "What hired amanuensis can be equal to the scribe who loves the words that grow under his hand, and to whom an error or indistinctness in the text is more painful than a sudden darkness or obstacle across his path? And even these mechanical printers who threaten to make learning a base and vulgar thing—even they must depend on the manuscript over which we scholars have bent with that insight into the poet's meaning which is closely akin to the viens divinior of the poet himself; unless they would flood the world with grammatical falsities and inexplicable anomalies that would turn the very fountains of Parnassus into a deluge of poisonous mud. But find the passage in the fifth book, to which Poliziano refers—I know it very well."

Seating herself on a low stool, close to her father's knee, Romola took the book on her lap and read the four verses containing the exclamation of Actaeon.

"It is true, Romola," said Bardo, when she had finished; "it is a true conception of the poet; for what is that grosser, narrower light by which men behold merely the petty scene around them, compared with that far-stretching, lasting light which spreads over centuries of thought, and over the life of nations, and makes clear to us the minds of the immortals who have reaped the great harvest and left us to glean in their furrows? For me, Romola, even when I could see, it was with the great dead that I lived; while the living often seemed to me mere spectres—shadows dispossessed of true feeling and intelligence; and unlike those Lamise, to whom Poliziano, with that superficial ingenuity which I do not deny to him, compares our inquisitive Florentines, because they put on their eyes when they went abroad, and took them off when they got home again, I have returned from the converse of the streets as from a forgotten dream, and have sat down among my books, saying with Petrarca, the modern who is least unworthy to be named after the ancients, 'Libri medullitus delectant, colloquuntur, consulunt, et viva quadam nobis atque arguta familiaritate junguntur.' "

"And in one thing you are happier than your favourite Petrarca, father," said Romola, affectionately humouring the old man's disposition to dilate in this way; "for he used to look at his copy of Homer and think sadly that the Greek was a dead letter to him: so far, he had the inward blindness that you feel is worse than your outward blindness."

"True, child; for I carry within me the fruits of that fervid study which I gave to the Greek tongue under the teaching of the younger Crisolora, and Filelfo, and Argiro-pulo; though that

great work in which I had desired to gather, as into a firm web, all the threads that my research had laboriously disentangled, and which would have been the vintage of my life, was cut off by the failure of my sight and my want of a fitting coadjutor. For the sustained zeal and unconquerable patience demanded from those who would tread the unbeaten paths of knowledge
       are still less reconcilable with the wandering, vagrant propensity of the feminine mind than with the feeble powers of the feminine body."

"Father," said Romola, with a sudden flush and in an injured tone, "I read anything you wish me to read; and I will look out any passages for you, and make whatever notes you want."

Bar do shook his head, and smiled with a bitter sort of pity. "As well try to be a pentathlos and perform all the five feats of the palfestra with the limbs of a nymph. Have I forgotten thy fainting in the mere search for the references I needed to explain a single passage of Callimachus?"

"But, father, it was the weight of the books, and Maso can help me; it was not want of attention and patience."

Bardo shook his head again. "It is not mere bodily organs that I want: it is the sharp edge of a young mind to pierce the way for my somewhat blunted faculties. For blindness acts like a dam, sending the streams of thought backward along the already travelled channels and hindering the course onward. If my son had not forsaken me, deluded by debasing fanatical dreams, worthy only of an energumen whose dwelling is among tombs, I might have gone on and seen my path broadening to the end of my life; for he was a youth of great promise. . . . But it has closed in now," the old man continued, after a short pause; "it has closed in now;—all but the narrow track he has left me to tread—alone, in my blindness."

Romola started from her seat, and carried away the large volume to its place again, stung too acutely by her father's last words to remain motionless as well as silent; and when she turned away from the shelf again, she remained standing at some distance from him, stretching

ROMOLA.

her arms downward and clasping her fingers tightly as she looked with a sad dreariness in her young face at the lifeless objects around her—the parchment backs, the unchanging mutilated marble, the bits of obsolete bronze and clay.

Bardo, though usually susceptible to Romola's movements and eager to trace them, was now too entirely preoccupied by the pain of rankling memories to notice her departure from his side.

"Yes," he went on, "with my son to aid me, I might have had my due share in the triumphs of this century: the names of the Bardi, father and son, might have been held reverently on the lips of scholars in the ages to come; not on account of frivolous verses or philosophic treatises, which are superfluous and presumptuous attempts to imitate the inimitable, such as allure vain men like Pan-hormita, and from which even the admirable Poggio did not keep himself sufficiently free; but because we should have given a lamp whereby men might have studied the supreme productions of the past. For why is a young man like Poliziano, who was not yet born when I was already held worthy to maintain a discussion with Thomas of Sarzana, to have a glorious memory as a commentator on the Pandects—why is Ficino, whose Latin is an offence to me, and who wanders purblind among the superstitious fancies that marked the decline at once of art, literature, and philosophy, to descend to posterity as the very high priest of Platonism, while I, who am more than their equal, have not effected anything but scattered work, which will be appropriated by other men? Why? but because my son, whom I had brought up to replenish my ripe learning with young enterprise, left me and all liberal pursuits that he might lash himself and howl at midnight with besotted friars—that he might go wandering on pilgrimages befitting men who know of no past older than the missal and the crucifix?—left me when the night was already beginning to fall on me."

In these last words the old man's voice, which had risen high in indignant protest, fell into a tone of reproach so tremulous and plaintive that Romola, turning her eyes again towards the blind aged face, felt her heart swell with forgiving pity. She seated herself by her father again, and placed her hand on his knee—too proud to obtrude consolation in words that might seem like a vindication of her own value, yet wishing to comfort him by some sign of her presence.

"Yes, Romola," said Bardo, automatically letting his left hand, with its massive prophylactic rings, fall a little too heavily on the delicate blue-veined back of the girl's right, so that she bit her lip to prevent herself from starting. "If even Florence only is to remember me, it can but be on the same ground that it will remember Niccolo Niccoli—because I forsook the vulgar pursuit of wealth in commerce that I might devote myself to collecting the precious remains of ancient art and wisdom, and leave them, after the example of the munificent Romans, for an everlasting possession to my fellow-citizens. But why do I say Florence only? If Florence remembers me, will not the world remember me? . . . Yet," added Bardo, after a short pause, his voice falling again into a saddened key, "Lorenzo's untimely death has raised a new difficulty. I had his promise—I should have had his bond—that my collection should always bear my name and should never be sold, though the harpies might clutch everything else; but there is enough for them—there is more than enough and for thee, too, Romola, there will be enough. Besides,

thou wilt marry; Bernardo reproaches me that I do not seek a fitting parentado for thee, and we will delay no longer, we will think about it."

"No, no, father; what could you do? besides, it is useless: wait till someone seeks me," said Romola, hastily.

"Nay, my child, that is not the paternal duty. It was not so held by the ancients, and in this respect Florentines have not degenerated from their ancestral customs."

"But I will study diligently," said Romola, her eyes dilating with anxiety. "I will become as learned as Cassandra Fedele: I will try and be as useful to you as if I had been a boy, and then perhaps some great scholar will want to marry me, and will not mind about a dowry; and he will like to come and live with you, and he will be to you in place of my brother . . . and you will not be sorry that I was a daughter."

There was a rising sob in Romola's voice as she said the last words, which touched the fatherly fibre in Bardo. He stretched his hand upward a little in search of her golden hair, and as she placed her head under his hand, he gently stroked it, leaning towards her as if his eyes discerned some glimmer there.

"Nay, Romola mia, I said not so; if I have pronounced an anathema on a degenerate and ungrateful son, I said not that I could wish thee other than the sweet daughter thou hast been to me. For what son could have tended me so gently in the frequent sickness I have had of late? And even in learning thou art not, according to thy measure, contemptible. Something perhaps were to be wished in thy capacity of attention and memory, not incompatible even with the feminine mind. But as Cal-condila bore testimony, when he aided me to teach thee,

thou hast a ready apprehension, and even a wide-glancing intelligence. And thou hast a man's nobility of soul: thou hast never fretted me with thy petty desires as thy mother did. It is true, I have been careful to keep thee aloof from the debasing influence of thy own sex, with their sparrow-like frivolity and their enslaving superstition, except, indeed, from that of our cousin Brigida, who may well serve as a scarecrow and a warning. And though— since I agree with the divine Petrarca, when he declares, quoting the Aulularia of Plautus, who again was indebted for the truth to the supreme Greek intellect, 'Optimam foeminam nullam esse, alia licet alia pejor sit'—I cannot boast that thou art entirely lifted out of that lower category to which Nature assigned thee, nor even that in erudition thou art on a par with the more learned women of this age; thou art, nevertheless—yes, Romola mia," said the old man, his pedantry again melting into tenderness, "thou art my sweet daughter, and thy voice is as the lower notes of the flute, 'dulcis, durabilis, clara, pura, secans aera et auribus sedens,' according to the choice words of Quintilian; and Bernardo tells me thou art fair, and thy hair is like the brightness of the morning, and indeed it seems to me that I discern some radiance from thee. Ah! I know how all else looks in this room, but thy form I only guess at. Thou art no longer the little woman six years old, that faded for me into darkness; thou art tall, and thy arm is but little below mine. Let us walk together."

The old man rose, and Romola, soothed by these beams of tenderness, looked happy again as she drew his arm within hers, and placed in his right hand the stick which rested at the side of his chair. While Bardo had been sitting, he had seemed hardly more than sixty: his face, though pale, had that refined texture in which wrinkles and lines are never deep; but now that he began to walk he looked as old as he really was—rather more than seventy; for his tall spare frame had the student's stoop of the shoulders, and he stepped with the undecided gait of the blind.

"No, Romola," he said, pausing against the bust of Hadrian, and passing his stick from the right to the left that he might explore the familiar outline with a "seeing hand." "There will be nothing else to preserve my memory and carry down my name as a member of the great republic of letters—nothing but my library and my collection of antiquities. And they are choice," continued Bardo, pressing the bust and speaking in a tone of insistance. "The collections of Niccolo I know were larger: but take any collection which is the work of a single man—that of the great Boccaccio even—mine will surpass it. That of Poggio was contemptible compared with mine. It will be a great gift to unborn scholars. And there is nothing else. For even if I were to yield to the wish of Aldo Manuzio when he sets up his press at Venice, and give him the aid of my annotated manuscripts, I know well what would be the result: some other scholar's name would stand on the title-page of the edition—some scholar who would have fed on my honey and then declared in his preface that he had gathered it all himself fresh from Hymettus. Else, why have I refused the loan of many an annotated codex? why have I refused to make public any of my translations? why? but because scholarship is a system of licensed robbery, and your man in scarlet and furred robe who sits in judgment on thieves, is himself a thief of the thoughts and the fame that belong to his fellows. But against that robbery Bardo de' Bardi shall struggle— though blind and forsaken, he shall struggle. I too have a right to be remembered—as great a right as Pontanus or Merula, whose names will be foremost on the lips of posterity, because they sought patronage and found it; because they had tongues that could flatter, and blood that was used to be nourished from the client's basket. I have a right to be remembered."

The old man's voice had become at once loud and tremulous, and a pink flush overspread his proud, delicately-cut features, while the habitually raised attitude of his head gave the idea that behind the curtain of his blindness he saw some imaginary high tribunal to which he was appealing against the injustice of Fame.

Romola was moved with sympathetic indignation, for in her nature too there lay the same large claims, and the same spirit of struggle against their denial. She tried to calm her father by a still prouder word than his.

"Nevertheless, father, it is a great gift of the gods to be born with a hatred and contempt of all injustice and meanness. Yours is a higher lot, never to have lied and truckled, than to have shared honours won by dishonour. There is strength in scorn, as there was in the martial fury by which men became insensible to wounds."

"It is well said, Romola. It is a Promethean word thou hast uttered," answered Bardo, after a little inteival in which he had begun to lean on his stick again, and to walk on. "And I indeed am not to be pierced by the shafts of Fortune. My armour is the œs triplex of a clear conscience, and a mind nourished by the precepts of philosophy. 'For men,' says Epictetus, 'are disturbed not by things themselves, but by their opinions or thoughts concerning those things.' And again, 'whosoever will be free, let him not desire or dread that which it is in the power of others either to deny or inflict: otherwise, he is

a slave/ And of all such gifts as are dependent on the caprice of fortune or of men, I have long ago learned to say, with Horace—who, however, is too wavering in his philosophy, vacillating between the precepts of Zeno and the less worthy maxims of Epicurus, and attempting, as we say, 'duabus sellis sedere'—concerning such accidents, I say, with the pregnant brevity of the poet—

'Sunt qui non habeant, est qui non curat habere.'

He is referring to gems, and purple, and other insignia of wealth; but I may apply his words not less justly to the tributes men pay us with their lips and their pens, which are also matters of purchase, and often with base coin. Yes, 'inanis'—hollow, empty—is the epithet justly bestowed on Fame."

They made the tour of the room in silence after this; but Bardo's lip-born maxims were as powerless over the passion which had been moving him, as if they had been written on parchment and hung round his neck in a sealed bag; and he presently broke forth again in a new tone of insistance.

"Inanis? yes, if it is a lying fame; but not if it is the just meed of labour and a great purpose. I claim my right: it is not fair that the work of my brain and my hands should not be a monument to me—it is not just that my labour should bear the name of another man. It is but little to ask," the old man went on, bitterly, "that my name should be over the door—that men should own themselves debtors to the Bardi Library in Florence. They will speak coldly of me, perhaps: 'a diligent collector and transcriber,' they will say, 'and also of some critical ingenuity, but one who could hardly be conspicuous in an age so fruitful in illustrious scholars. Yet he merits our

pity, for in the latter years of his hfe he was bUnd, and his only son, to whose education he had devoted his best years—' Nevertheless, my name will be remembered, and men will honour me: not with the breath of flattery, purchased by mean bribes, but because I have laboured, and because my labour will remain. Debts! I know there are debts; and there is thy dowry, Romola, to be paid. But there must be enough—or, at least, there can lack but a small sum, such as the Signoria might well provide. And if Lorenzo had not died, all would have been secured and settled. But now . . . ."

At this moment Maso opened the door, and advancing to his master, announced that Nello, the barber, had desired him to say, that he was come with the Greek scholar whom he had asked leave to introduce.

"It is well," said the old man. "Bring them in." Bardo, conscious that he looked more dependent when he was walking, liked always to be seated in the presence of strangers, and Romola, without needing to be told, conducted him to his chair. She was standing by him at her full height, in quiet majestic self-possession, when the visitors entered; and the most penetrating observer would hardly have divined that this proud pale face, at the slightest touch on the fibres of affection or pity, could become passionate with tenderness, or that this woman, who imposed a certain awe on those who approached her, was in a state of girlish simplicity and ignorance concerning the world outside her father's books.

CHAPTER VI.
DAWNING HOPES.

When Maso opened the door again, and ushered in the two visitors, Nello, first making a deep reverence to Romola, gently pushed Tito before him, and advanced with him towards her father.

"Messer Bar do," he said, in a more measured and respectful tone than was usual with him, "I have the honour of presenting to you the Greek scholar, who has been eager to have speech of you, not less from the report I made to him of your learning and your priceless collections, than because of the furtherance your patronage may give him under the transient need to which he has been reduced by shipwreck. His name is Tito Melema, at your service."

Romola's astonishment could hardly have been greater if the stranger had worn a panther-skin and carried a thyrsus; for the cunning barber had said nothing of the Greek's age or appearance; and among her father's scholarly visitors, she had hardly ever seen any but middle-aged or grey-headed men. There was only one masculine face, at once youthful and beautiful, the image of which remained deeply impressed on her mind: it was that of her brother, who long years ago had taken her on his knee, kissed her, and never come back again: a fair face, with sunny hair, like her own. But the habitual attitude of her mind towards strangers—a proud self-dependence and determination to ask for nothing even by a smile— confirmed in her by her father's complaints against the world's injustice, was like a snowy embankment hemming in the rush of admiring surprise. Tito's bright face showed

its rich-tinted beauty without any rivahy of colour above his black sajo or tunic reaching to the knees. It seemed like a wreath of spring, dropped suddenly in Romola's young but wintry life, which had inherited nothing but memories—memories of a dead mother, of a lost brother, of a blind father's happier time—memories of far-off light, love, and beauty, that lay embedded in dark mines of books, and could hardly give out their brightness again until they were kindled for her by the torch of some known joy. Nevertheless, she returned Tito's bow, made to her on entering, with the same pale proud face as ever; but, as he approached, the snow melted, and when he ventured to look towards her again, while Nello was speaking, a pink flush overspread her face, to vanish again almost immediately, as if her imperious will had recalled it. Tito's glance, on the contrary, had that gentle, beseeching admiration in it which is the most propitiating of appeals to a proud, shy woman, and is perhaps the only atonement a man can make for being too handsome. The finished fascination of his air came chiefly from the absence of demand and assumption. It was that of a fleet, soft-coated, dark-eyed animal that delights you by not bounding away in indifference from you, and unexpectedly pillows its chin on your palm, and looks up at you desiring to be stroked—as if it loved you.

"Messere, I give you welcome," said Bardo, with some condescension; "misfortune wedded to learning, and especially to Greek learning, is a letter of credit that should win the ear of every instructed Florentine; for, as you are doubtless aware, since the period when your countryman, Manuello Crisolora, diffused the light of his teaching in the chief cities of Italy, now nearly a century ago, no man is held worthy of the name of scholar who has acquired merely the transplanted and derivative literature of the) Latins; rather, such inert students are stigmatised as opici or barbarians, according to the phrase of the Romans themselves, who frankly replenished their urns at the fountain head. I am, as you perceive, and as Nello has doubtless forewarned you, totally blind: a calamity to which we Florentines are held especially liable, whether owing to the cold winds which rush upon us in spring from the passes of the Apennines, or to that sudden transition from the cool gloom of our houses to the dazzling brightness of our summer sun, by which the lippi are said to have been made so numerous among the ancient Romans; or, in fine, to some occult cause which eludes our superficial surmises. But I pray you be seated: Nello, my friend, be seated."

Bardo paused until his fine ear had assured him that the visitors were seating themselves, and that Romola was taking her usual chair at his right hand. Then he said:

"From what part of Greece do you come, Messere? I had thought that your unhappy country had been almost exhausted of those sons who could cherish in their minds any image of her original glory, though indeed the barbarous Sultans have of late shown themselves not indisposed to engraft on their wild stock the precious vine which their own fierce bands have hewn down and trampled under foot. From what part of Greece do you come?"

"I sailed last from Naupha," said Tito; "but I hav resided both at Constantinople and Thessalonica and hav travelled in various parts little visited by Western Christians since the triumph of the Turkish arms. I should tell you, however, Messere, that I was not born in Greece, but at Bari. I spent the first sixteen years of my life in Southern Italy and Sicily."

While Tito was speaking, some emotion passed, like a breath on the waters, across Bardo's delicate features; he leaned forward, put out his right hand towards Romola, and turned his head as if about to speak to her; but then, correcting himself, turned away again, and said, in a subdued voice,—

"Excuse me; is it not true—you are young?"

"I am three and twenty," said Tito.

"Ah," said Bardo, still in a tone of subdued excitement, "and you had, doubtless, a father who cared for your early instruction—who, perhaps, was himself a scholar?"

There was a slight pause before Tito's answer came to the ear of Bardo; but for Romola and Nello it commenced with a slight shock that seemed to pass through [lim, and cause a momentary quivering of the lip; doubtless at the revival of a supremely painful remembrance.

"Yes," he replied; "at least a father by adoption. He was a Neapolitan, and of accomplished scholarship, both Latin and Greek. But," added Tito, after another slight pause, "he is lost to me—was lost on a voyage he too rashly undertook to Delos."

Bardo sank backward again, too delicate to ask another question that might probe a sorrow which he divined to be recent. Romola, who knew well what were the fibres that Tito's voice had stirred in her father, felt that this new acquaintance had with wonderful suddenness got within the barrier that lay between them and the alien v.orld. Nello, thinking that the evident check given to the conversation offered a graceful opportunity for relieving himself from silence, said

"In truth, it is as clear as Venetian glass that this fine young man has had the best training; for the two Cennini have set him to work at their Greek sheets already, and it seems to me they are not men to begin cutting before they have felt the edge of their tools; they tested him well beforehand, we may be sure, and if there are two things not to be hidden love and a cough I say there is a third, and that is ignorance, when once a man is obliged to do something besides wagging his head. The tonsor inequalis is inevitably betrayed when he takes the shears in his hand; is it not true, Messer Bardo? I speak after the fashion of a barber, but, as Luigi Puici says

'Perdonimi s'io fallo: clii m'ascolta Intenda il mio volgar col suo latino.'"

"Nay, my good Nello," said Bardo, with an air of friendly severity, "you are not altogether illiterate, and might doubtless have made a more respectable progress in learning if you had abstained somewhat from the cica-lata and gossip of the street-corner, to which our Florentines are excessively addicted; but still more if you had not clogged your memory with those frivolous productions of which Luigi Pulci has furnished the most peccant exemplar a compendium of extravagancies and incongruities the farthest removed from the models of a pure age, and resembling rather the grylli or conceits of a period when mystic meaning was held a warrant for monstrosity of form; with this difference, that while the monstrosity is retained, the mystic meaning is absent; in contemptible contrast with the great poem of Virgil, who, as I long held with Filelfo, before Landino had taken upon him to expound the same opinion, embodied the deepest lessons of philosophy in a graceful and well-knit fable. And I cannot but regard the multiplication of these babbling, lawless productions, albeit countenanced by the patronage, and in some degree the example of Lorenzo himself, other-

wise a friend to true learning, as a sign that the glorious hopes of this century are to be quenched in gloom; nay, that they have been the delusive prologue to an age worse than that of iron—the age of tinsel and gossamer, in which no thought has substance enough to be moulded into consistent and lasting form."

"Once more, pardon," said Nello, opening his palms outwards, and shrugging his shoulders, "I find myself knowing so many things in good Tuscan before I have time to think of the Latin for them; and Messer Luigi's rhymes are always slipping off the lips of my customers: —that is what corrupts me. And, indeed, talking of customers, I have left my shop and my reputation too long in the custody of my slow Sandro, who does not deserve even to be called a tonsor inequalis, but rather to be pronounced simply a bungler in the vulgar tongue. So with your permission, Messer Bardo, I will take my leave —well understood that I am at your service whenever Maso calls upon me. It seems a thousand years till I dress and perfume the damigella's hair, which deserves to shine in the heavens as a constellation, though indeed it were a pity for it ever to go so far out of reach."

Three voices made a fugue of friendly farewells to Nello, as he retreated with a bow to Romola and a beck to Tito. The acute barber saw that the pretty youngster, who had crept into his liking by some strong magic, was well launched in Bardo's favourable regard; and satisfied that his introduction had not miscarried so far, he felt the propriety of retiring.

The little burst of wrath, called forth by Nello's unlucky quotation, had diverted Bardo's mind from the feelings which had just before been hemming in further speech,

and he now addressed Tito again with his ordinary cahn-ness.

"Ah! young man, you are happy in having been able to unite the advantages of travel with those of study, and you will be welcome among us as a bringer of fresh tidings from a land which has become sadly strange to us, except through the agents of a now restricted commerce and the reports of hasty pilgrims. For those days are in the far distance which I myself witnessed, when men like Aurispa and Guarino went out to Greece as to a storehouse, and came back laden with manuscripts which every scholar was eager to borrow—and, be it owned with shame, not always willing to restore; nay, even the days when erudite Greeks flocked to our shores for a refuge, seem far off now — farther off than the oncoming of my blindness. But, doubtless, young man, research after the treasures of antiquity was not alien to the purpose of your travels?"

"Assuredly not," said Tito. "On the contrary, my companion—my father—was willing to risk his life in his zeal for the discovery of inscriptions and other traces of ancient civilisation."

"And I trust there is a record of his researches and their results," said Bardo, eagerly, "since they must be even more precious than those of Ciriaco, which I have diligently availed myself of, though they are not always illuminated by adequate learning."

"There was such a record," said Tito, "but it was lost, like everything else, in the shipwreck I suffered below Ancona. The only record left is such as remains in our —in my memory."

"You must lose no time in committing it to paper, young man," said Bardo, with growing interest. "Doubtless you remember much, if you aided in transcription;

DAWNING HOPES.

for when I was your age, words wrought themselves into my mind as if they had been fixed by the tool of the graver; wherefore I constantly marvel at the capriciousness of my daughter's memory, which grasps certain objects with tenacity, and lets fall all those minutia3 whereon depends accuracy, the very soul of scholarship. But I apprehend no such danger with you, young man, if your will has seconded the advantages of your training."

When Bardo made this reference to his daughter, Tito ventured to turn his eyes towards her, and at the accusation against her memory his face broke into its brightest smile, which was reflected as inevitably as sudden sunbeams in Romola's. Conceive the soothing delight of that smile to her! Romola had never dreamed that there was a scholar in the world who would smile at her for a deficiency for which she was constantly made to feel herself a culprit. It was like the dawn of a new sense to her—the sense of comradeship. They did not look away from each other immediately, as if the smile had been a stolen one; they looked and smiled with frank enjoyment.

"She is not really so cold and proud," thought Tito.

"Does he forget too, I wonder?" thought Romola. "But I hope not, else he will vex my father."

But Tito was obliged to turn away, and answer Bardo's question.

"I have had much practice in transcription," he said, "but in the case of inscriptions copied in memorable scenes, rendered doubly impressive by the sense of risk and adventure, it may have happened that my retention of written characters has been weakened. On the plain of the Eurotas, or among the gigantic stones of Mycence and Tyrins especially when the fear of the Turk hovers -Over one like a vulture—the mind wanders, even though the hand writes faithfully what the eye dictates. But something doubtless I have retained," added Tito, with a modesty which was not false, though he was conscious that it was politic, "something that might be of service if illustrated and corrected by a wider learning than my own."

"That is well-spoken, young man," said Bardo, delighted. "And I will not withhold from you such aid as I can give, if you like to communicate with me concerning your recollections. I foresee a work which will be a useful supplement to the Isolario of Cristoforo Buondelmonte, and which may take rank with the Itineraria of Ciriaco and the admirable Ambrogio Traversari. But we must prepare ourselves for calumny, young man," Bardo went on with energy, as if the work were already growing so fast that the time of trial was near; "if your book contains novelties you will be charged with forgery; if my elucidations should clash with any principles of interpretation adopted by another scholar, our personal characters will be attacked, we shall be impeached with foul actions; you must prepare yourself to be told that your mother was a fish-woman, and that your father was a renegade priest or a hanged malefactor. I myself, for having shown error in a single preposition, had an invective written against me wherein I was taxed with treachery, fraud, indecency, and even hideous crimes. Such, my young friend —such are the flowers with which the glorious path of scholarship is strewed! But tell me, then: I have learned much concerning Byzantium and Thessalonica long ago from Demetrio Calcondila, who has but lately departed from Florence; but you, it seems, have visited less familiar scenes?"

"Yes; we made what I may call a pilgrimage full of danger, for the sake of visiting places which have almost died out of the memory of the West, for they lie away from the track of pilgrims; and my father used to say that scholars themselves hardly imagine them to have any existence out of books. He was of opinion that a new and more glorious era would open for learning when men should begin to look for their commentaries on the ancient writers in the remains of cities and temples, nay, in the paths of the rivers, and on the face of the valleys and the mountains."

"Ah!" said Bardo, fervidly, "your father, then, was not a common man. Was he fortunate, may I ask? Had he many friends?" These last words were uttered in a tone charged with meaning.

"No; he made enemies—chiefly, I believe, by a certain impetuous candour; and they hindered his advancement, so that he lived in obscurity. And he would never stoop to conciliate: he could never forget an injury."

"Ah!" said Bardo again, with a long, deep intonation. "Among our hazardous expeditions," continued Tito, willing to prevent further questions on a point so personal, "I remember with particular vividness a hastily snatched visit to Athens. Our hurry, and the double danger of being seized as prisoners by the Turks, and of our galley raising anchor before we could return, made it seem like a fevered vision of the night—the wide plain, the girdling mountains, the ruined porticos and columns, either standing far aloof, as if receding from our hurried footsteps, or else jammed in confusedly among the dwellings of Christians degraded into servitude, or among the forts and turrets of their Moslem conquerors, who have their stronghold on the Acropolis."

"You fill me with surprise," said Bardo. "Athens,

ROMOLA.

then, is not utterly destroyed and swept away, as I had imagined?"

"No wonder you should be under that mistake, for few even of the Greeks themselves, who live beyond the mountain boundary of Attica, know anything about the present condition of Athens, or Setine, as the sailors call it. I remember, as we were rounding the promontory of Sunium, the Greek pilot we had on board our Venetian galley pointed to the mighty columns that stand on the summit of the rock—the remains, as you know well, of the great temple erected to the goddess Athena, who looked down from that high shrine with triumph at her conquered rival Poseidon;—well, our Greek pilot, pointing to those columns, said, 'That was the school of the great pMosopher Aristotle.' And at Athens itself, the monk who acted as our guide in the hasty view we snatched, insisted most on showing us the spot where St. Philip baptised the Ethiopian eunuch, or some such legend."

"Talk not of monks and their legends, young man!" said Bardo, interrupting Tito impetuously. "It is enough to overlay human hope and enterprise with an eternal frost to think that the ground which was trodden by philosophers and poets is crawled over by those insect-swarms of besotted fanatics or howling hypocrites."

"Perdio, I have no affection for them," said Tito, with a shrug; "servitude agrees well with a religion like theirs, which lies in the renunciation of all that makes life precious to other men. And they carry the yoke that befits them: their matin chant is drowned by the voice of the muezzin, who, from the gallery of the high tower on the Acropolis, calls every Mussulman to his prayers. That tower springs from the Parthenon itself; and every time we paused and directed our eyes toward it, our guide set up a wail, that a temple which had once been won from the diaboHcal uses of the Pagans to become the temple of another virgin than Pallas—the Virgin-Mother of God— was now again perverted to the accursed ends of the Moslem. It was the sight of those walls of the Acropolis, which disclosed themselves in the distance as we leaned over the side of our galley when it was forced by contrary winds to anchor in the Pirteus, that fired my father's mind with the determination to see Athens at all risks, and in spite of the sailors' warnings that if we lingered till a change of wind they would depart without us: but after all, it was impossible for us to venture near the Acropolis, for the sight of men eager in examining 'old stones' raised the suspicion that we were Venetian spies, and we had to hurry back to the harbour."

"We will talk more of these things," said Bardo, eagerly. "You must recal everything, to the minutest traces left in your memory. You will win the gratitude of after-times by leaving a record of the aspect Greece bore while yet the barbarians had not swept away every trace of the structures that Pausanias and Pliny described: you will take those great writers as your models; and such contribution of criticism and suggestion as my riper mind can supply shall not be wanting to you. There will be much to tell; for you have travelled, you said, in the Peloponnesus?"

"Yes; and in Boeotia also: I have rested in the groves of Helicon, and tasted of the fountain Hippocrene. But on every memorable spot in Greece conquest after conquest has set its seal, till there is a confusion of ownership even in ruins, that only close study and comparison could unravel. High over every fastness, from the plains of Lace-doemon to the Straits of Thermopylae, there towers some

ROMOLA.

huge Frankish fortress, once inhabited by a French or ItaUan marquis, now either abandoned or held by Turkish bands."

"Stay!" cried Bardo, whose mind was now too thoroughly pre-occupied by the idea of the future book to attend to Tito's further narration. "Do you think of writing in Latin or Greek? Doubtless Greek is the more ready clothing for your thoughts, and it is the nobler language. But, on the other hand, Latin is the tongue in which we shall measure ourselves with the larger and more famous number of modern rivals. And if you are less at ease in it, I will aid you—yes, I will spend on you that long-accumulated study which was to have been thrown into the channel of another work—a work in which I myself was to have had a helpmate."

Bardo paused a moment, and then added,—

"But who knows whether that work may not be executed yet? For you, too, young man, have been brought up by a father who poured into your mind all the long-gathered stream of his knowledge and experience. Our aid might be mutual."

Romola, who had watched her father's growing excitement, and divined well the invisible currents of feehng that determined every question and remark, felt herself in a glow of strange anxiety: she turned her eyes on Tito continually, to watch the impression her father's words made on him, afraid lest he should be inclined to dispel these visions of co-operation which were lighting up her father's face with a new hope. But no! He looked so bright and gentle: he must feel, as she did, that in this eagerness of blind age there was piteousness enough to call forth inexhaustible patience. How much more strongly he would feel this if he knew about her brother! A girl of eighteen

imagines the feelings behind the face that has moved her with its sympathetic youth, as easily as primitive people imagined the humours of the gods in fair weather: what is she to believe in, if not in this vision woven from within?

And Tito was really very far from feeling impatient. He delighted in sitting there with the sense that Romola's attention was fixed on him, and that he could occasionally look at her. He was pleased that Bardo should take an interest in him; and he did not dwell with enough seriousness on the prospect of the work in which he was to be aided, to feel moved by it to anything else than that easy, good-humoured acquiescence which was natural to him.

"I shall be proud and happy," he said, in answer to Bardo's last words, "if my services can be held a meet offering to the matured scholarship of Messere. But doubtless"—here he looked towards Romola—"the lovely damigella, your daughter, makes all other aid superfluous; for I have learned from Nello that she has been nourished on the highest studies from her earliest years."

"You are mistaken," said Romola; "I am by no means sufficient to my father: I have not the gifts that are necessary for scholarship."

Romola did not make this self-depreciatory statement in a tone of anxious humility, but with a proud gravity.

"Nay, my Romola," said her father, not willing that the stranger should have too low a conception of his daughter's powers; "thou art not destitute of gifts; rather, thou art endowed beyond the measure of women; but thou hast withal the woman's delicate frame, which ever craves repose and variety, and so begets a wandering imagination. My daughter"—turning to Tito—"has been very precious to me, filling up to the best of her power the place of a son. For I had once a son . . ."

Bardo checked himself; he did not wish to assume an attitude of complaint in the presence of a stranger, and he remembered that this young man, in whom he had unexpectedly become so much interested, was still a stranger, towards whom it became him rather to keep the position of a patron. His pride was roused to double activity by the fear that he had forgotten his dignity.

"But," he resumed, in his original tone of condescension, "we are departing from what I believe is to you the most important business. Nello informed me that you had certain gems which you would fain dispose of, and that you desired a passport to some man of wealth and taste who would be likely to become a purchaser."

"It is true; for, though I have obtained employment as a corrector with the Cennini, my payment leaves little margin beyond the provision of necessaries, and would leave less but that my good friend Nello insists on my hiring a lodging from him, and saying nothing about the rent till better days."

"Nello is a good-hearted prodigal," said Bardo; "and though, with that ready ear and ready tongue of his, he is too much like the ill-famed Margites—knowing many things and knowing them all badly, as I hinted to him but now—he is nevertheless 'abnormis sapiens,' after the manner of our born Florentines. But have you the gems with you? I would willingly know what they are—yet it is useless: no, it might only deepen regret. I cannot add to my store."

"I have one or two intaglios of much beauty," said Tito, proceeding to draw from his wallet a small case.

But Romola no sooner saw the movement than she looked at him with significant gravity, and placed her finger on her lips,

"Con viso che tacendo dicea, Taci." If Bardo were made aware that the gems were withha reach, she knew well he would want a minute description of them, and it would become pain to him that they should go away from him, even if he did not insist on some device for purchasing them in spite of poverty. But she had no sooner made this sign than she felt rather guilty and ashamed at having virtually confessed a weakness of her father's to a stranger. It seemed that she was destined to a sudden confidence and familiarity with this young Greek, strangely at variance with her deeply-seated pride and reserve; and this consciousness again brought the unwonted colour to her cheeks,

Tito understood her look and sign, and immediately withdrew his hand from the case, saying, in a careless tone, so as to make it appear that he was merely following up his last words,

"But they are usually in the keeping of Messer Domenico Cennini, who has strong and safe places for these things. He estimates them as worth at least five hundred ducats."

"Ah, then, they are fine intagli," said Bardo. "Five hundred ducats! Ah, more than a man's ransom!"

Tito gave a slight, almost imperceptible start, and opened his long dark eyes with questioning surprise at Bardo's blind face, as if his words—a mere phrase of common parlance, at a time when men were often being ransomed from slavery or imprisonment—had had some special meaning for him. But the next moment he looked towards Romola, as if her eyes must be her father's interpreters. She, intensely pre-occupied with what related to her father, imagined that Tito was looking to her agairil for some guidance, and immediately spoke.

"Alessandra Scala delights in gems, you know, father; she calls them her winter flowers; and the Segretario would be almost sure to buy any gems that she wished for. Besides, he himself sets great store by rings and sigils, which he wears as a defence against pains in the joints."

"It is true," said Bardo. "Bartolommeo has overmuch confidence in the efficacy of gems—a confidence wider than is sanctioned by Pliny, who clearly shows that he regards many beliefs of that sort as idle superstitions; though not to the utter denial of medicinal virtues in gems. Wherefore, I myself, as you observe, young man, wear certain rings, which the discreet Camillo Leonardi prescribed to me by letter when two years ago I had a certain infirmity of sudden numbness. But thou hast spoken well, Romola. I will dictate a letter to Bartolommeo, which Maso shall carry. But it were well that Messere should notify to thee what the gems are, together with the intagli they bear, as a warrant to Bartolommeo that they will be worthy of his attention."

"Nay, father," said Romola, whose dread lest a paroxysm of the collector's mania should seize her father, gave her the courage to resist his proposal. "Your word will be sufficient that Messere is a scholar and has travelled much. The Segretario will need no further inducement to receive him."

"True, child," said Bardo, touched on a chord that was sure to respond. "I have no need to add proofs and arguments in confirmation of my word to Bartolommeo. And I doubt not that this young man's presence is in accord with the tones of his voice, so that, the door being once opened, he will be his own best advocate."

Bardo paused a few moments, but his silence was evidently charged with some idea that he was hesitating

DAWNING HOPES.

to express, for he once leaned forward a little as if he were going to speak, then turned his head aside towards Romola and sank backward again. At last, as if he had made up his mind, he said in a tone which might have become a prince giving the courteous signal of dismissal,—

"I am somewhat fatigued this morning, and shall prefer seeing you again to-morrow, when I shall be able to give you the secretary's answer, authorising you to present yourself to him at some given time. But before you go—" here the old man, in spite of himself, fell into a more faltering tone—"you will perhaps permit me to touch your hand? It is long since I touched the hand of a young man."

Bardo had stretched out his aged white hand and Tito immediately placed his dark but delicate and supple fingers within it. Bardo's cramped fingers closed over them, and he held them for a few minutes in silence. Then he said,—

"Romola, has this young man the same complexion as thy brother—fair and pale?"

"No, father," Romola answered, with determined composure, though her heart began to beat violently with mingled emotions. "The hair of Messere is dark—his complexion is dark." Inwardly she said, "Will he mind it? will it be disagreeable? No, he looks so gentle and good-natured." Then aloud again,

"Would Messere permit my father to touch his hair and face?"

Her eyes inevitably made a timid entreating appeal while she asked this, and Tito's met them with soft brightness as he said, "Assuredly," and, leaning forward, raised Bardo's hand to his curls, with a readiness of assent which was the greater relief to her because it was unaccompanied by any sign of embarrassment.

Bardo passed his hand again and again over the long curls and grasped them a little, as if their spiral resistance made his inward vision clearer; then he passed his hand over the brow and cheek, tracing the profile with the edge of his palm and fourth finger, and letting the breadth of his hand repose on the rich oval of the cheek.

"Ah!" he said, as his hand glided from the face and rested on the young man's shoulder. "He must be very unlike thy brother, Romola: and it is better. You see no visions, I trust, my young friend?"

At this moment the door opened, and there entered, unannounced, a tall elderly man in a handsome black silk lucco, who, unwinding his becchetto from his neck and taking off his cap, disclosed a head as white as Bardo's. He cast a keen glance of surprise at the group before him — the young stranger leaning in that filial attitude, while Bardo's hand rested on his shoulder, and Romola sitting near with eyes dilated by anxiety and agitation. But there was an instantaneous change: Bardo let fall his hand, Tito raised himself from his stooping posture, and Romola rose to meet the visitor with an alacrity which implied all the greater intimacy, because it was unaccompanied by any smile.

"Well, figlioccina," said the stately man, as he touched Romola's shoulder; "Maso said you had a visitor, but I came in nevertheless."

"It is thou, Bernardo," said Bardo. "Thou art come at a fortunate moment. This, young man," he continued, while Tito rose and bowed, "is one of the chief citizens of Florence, Messer Bernardo del Nero, my oldest, I had almost said my only friend—whose good opinion, if you

DAWNING HOPES.

tan win it, may carry you far. He is but three-and-twenty, Bernardo, yet he can doubtless tell thee much which thou wilt care to hear; for though a scholar, he has already travelled far, and looked on other things besides the manuscripts for which thou hast too light an esteem."

"Ah, a Greek, as I augur," said Bernardo, returning Tito's reverence but slightly, and surveying him with that sort of glance which seems almost to cut like fine steel. "Newly arrived in Florence, it appears. The name of Messere—or part of it, for it is doubtless a long one?"

"On the contrary," said Tito, with perfect good humour, "it is most modestly free from polysyllabic pomp. My name is Tito Melema."

"Truly?" said Bernardo, rather scornfully, as he took a seat; "I had expected it to be at least as long as the names of a city, a river, a province and an empire all put together. We Florentines mostly use names as we do prawns, and strip them of all flourishes before we trust them to our throats."

"Well, Bardo," he continued, as if the stranger were not worth further notice, and changing his tone of sarcastic suspicion for one of sadness, "we have buried him!"

"Ah!" replied Bardo, with corresponding sadness, "and a new epoch has come for Florence—a dark one, I fear. Lorenzo has left behind him an inheritance that is but like the alchemist's laboratory when the wisdom of the alchemist is gone."

"Not altogether so," said Bernardo. "Piero de' Medici has abundant intelligence; his faults are only the faults of hot blood. I love the lad—lad he will always be to me, as I have always been padricciuolo (little father) to him."

"Yet all who want a new order of things are likely to conceive new hopes," said Bardo. "We shall have the old strife of parties, I fear."

"If we could have a new order of things that was something else than knocking down one coat of arms to put up another," said Bernardo, "I should be ready to say, 'I belong to no party: I am a Florentine.' But as long as parties are in question, I am a Medicean, and will be a Medicean till I die. I am of the same mind as Farinata degli Uberti: if any man asks me what is meant by siding with a party, I say, as he did, 'To wish ill or well, for the sake of past wrongs or kindnesses.'"

During this short dialogue, Tito had been standing, and now took his leave.

"But come again at the same hour to-morrow," said Bardo, graciously, before Tito left the room, "that I may give you Bartolommeo's answer."

"From what quarter of the sky has this pretty Greek youngster alighted so close to thy chair, Bardo?" said Bernardo del Nero, as the door closed. He spoke with dry emphasis, evidently intended to convey something more to Bardo than was implied by the mere words.

"He is a scholar who has been shipwrecked and has saved a few gems, for which he wants to find a purchaser. I am going to send him to Bartolommeo Scala, for thou knowest it were more prudent in me to abstain from further purchases."

Bernardo shrugged his shoulders and said, "Romola, wilt thou see if my servant is without? I ordered him to wait for me here." Then, when Romola was at a sufficient distance, he leaned forward and said to Bardo in a low, emphatic tone:—

"Remember, Bardo, thou hast a rare gem of thy own; take care no man gets it who is not likely to pay a worthy price. That pretty Greek has a Hthe sleekness about him, that seems marvellously fitted for slipping easily into any nest he fixes his mind on."

Bardo was startled: the association of Tito with the image of his lost son had excluded instead of suggesting the thought of Romola. But almost immediately there seemed to be a reaction which made him grasp the warning as if it had been a hope.

"But why not, Bernardo? If the young man approved himself worthy—he is a scholar—and—and there would be no difficulty about the dowry, which always makes thee gloomy,"

CHAPTER VII.

A LEARNED SQUABBLE.

Bartolommeo Scala, secretary of the Florentine Republic, on whom Tito Melema had been thus led to anchor his hopes, lived in a handsome palace close to the Porta a Pinti, now known as the Casa Gherardesca. His arms —an azure ladder transverse on a golden field, with the motto Gradatim placed over the entrance—told all comers that the miller's son held his ascent to honours by his own efforts a fact to be proclaimed without wincing. The secretary was a vain and pompous man, but he was also an honest one: he was sincerely convinced of his own merit, and could see no reason for feigning. The topmost round of his azure ladder had been reached by this time: he had held his secretaryship these twenty years— had long since made his orations on the rmghtera, or platform, of the Old Palace, as the custom was, in the presence of princely visitors, while Marzocco, the republican lion, wore his gold crown on the occasion, and all tlie people cried, "Viva Messer Bartolommeo!"—had been on an embassy to Rome, and had there been made titular Senator, Apostolical Secretary, Knight of the Golden Spur; and had, eight years ago, been Gonfalconiere—last gaol of the Florentine citizen's ambition. Meantime he had got richer and richer, and more and more gouty, after the manner of successful mortality; and the Knight of the Golden Spur had often to sit with helpless cushioned heel under the handsome loggia he had built for himself, overlooking the spacious gardens and lawn at the back of his palace.

He was in this position on the day when he hacl granted the desired interview to Tito Melema. The May afternoon sun was on the flowers and the grass beyond the pleasant shade of the loggia; the too stately silk lucco was cast aside, and a light loose mantle was thrown over his tunic; his beautiful daughter Alessandra and her husband, the Greek soldier-poet Marullo, were seated on one side of him: on the other, two friends, not oppressively illustrious, and, therefore, the better listeners. Yet, to say nothing of the gout, Messer Bartolommeo's felicity was far from perfect: it was embittered by the contents of certain papers that lay before him, consisting chiefly of a correspondence between himself and Politian. It was a human foible at that period (incredible as it may seem) to recite quarrels, and favour scholarly visitors with the communication of an entire and lengthy correspondence; and this was neither the first nor the second time that Scala had asked the candid opinion of his friends as to the balance of right and wrong in some half-score Latin letters between himself and Politian, all springing out of certain epigrams written in the most playful tone in the worl4.

It was the story of a very typical and pretty quarrel, in which we are interested, because it supphed precisely that thistle of hatred necessary, according to Nello, as a stimulus to the sluggish paces of the cautious steed, Friendship.

Politian, having been a rejected pretender to the love and the hand of Scala's daughter, kept a very sharp and learned tooth in readiness against the too prosperous and presumptuous secretary, who had declined the greatest scholar of the age for a son-in-law. Scala was a meritorious public servant, and, moreover, a lucky man— naturally exasperating to an offended scholar; but then— O beautiful balance of things!—he had an itch for authorship, and was a bad writer—one of those excellent people who, sitting in gouty slippers, "penned poetical trifles" entirely for their own amusement, without any view to an audience, and, consequently, sent them to their friends in letters, which were the literary periodicals of the fifteenth century. Now Scala had abundance of friends who were ready to praise his writings: friends like Ficino and Landino—amiable browsers in the Medicean park along with himself—who found his Latin prose style elegant and masculine; and the terrible Joseph Scaliger, who was to pronounce him totally ignorant of Latinity, was at a comfortable distance in the next century. But when was the fatal coquetry inherent in superfluous authorship ever quite contented with the ready praise of friends? That critical, supercilious Politian—a fellow-browser, who was far from amiable—must be made aware that the solid secretary showed, in his leisure hours, a pleasant fertility in verses, that indicated pretty clearly how much he might do in that way if he were not a man of affairs.

Ineffable moment! when the man you secretly hate

sends you a Latin epigram with a false gender—hen-decasyllables with a questionable elision, at least a toe too much—attempts at poetic figures which are manifest solecisms. That moment had come to Politian: the secretary had put forth his soft head from the official shell, and the terrible lurking crab was down upon him. Politian had used the freedom of a friend, and pleasantly, in the form of a Latin epigram, corrected the mistake of Scala in making the adcx (an insect too well known on the banks of the Arno) of the inferior or feminine gender. Scala replied by a bad joke, in suitable Latin verses, referring to Politian's unsuccessful suit. Better and better. Politian found the verses very pretty and highly facetious: the more was the pity that they were seriously incorrect, and inasmuch as Scala had alleged that he had written them in imitation of a Greek epigram, Politian, being on such friendly terms, would enclose a Greek epigram of his own, on the same interesting insect—not, we may presume, out of any wish to humble Scala, but rather to iti-struct him; said epigram containing a lively conceit about Venus, Cupid, and the culex, of a kind much tasted at that period, founded partly on the zoological fact that the gnat, like Venus, was born from the waters. Scala, in reply, begged to say that his verses were never intended for a scholar with such delicate olfactories as Politian, nearest of all living men to the perfection of the ancients, and of a taste so fastidious that sturgeon itself must seem insipid to him; defended his own verses, nevertheless, though indeed they were written hastily, without correction, and intended as an agreeable distraction during the summer heat to himself and such friends as were satisfied with mediocrity, he, Scala, not being like some other people, who courted publicity through the booksellers.

For the rest, he had barely enough Greek to make out the sense of the epigram so graciously sent him, to say nothing of tasting its elegancies; but—the epigram was Politian's: what more need be said? Still, by way of postscript, he feared that his incomparable friend's comparison of the gnat to Venus on account of its origin from the waters, was in many ways ticklish. On the one hand, Venus might be offended; and on the other, unless the poet intended an allusion to the doctrine of Thales, that cold and damp origin seemed doubtful to Scala in the case of a creature so fond of warmth: a fish were perhaps the better comparison, or, when the power of flying was in question, an eagle, or, indeed, when the darkness was taken into consideration, a bat or an owl were a less obscure and more apposite parallel, &c. &c. Here was a great opportunity for Politian. He was not aware, he wrote, that when he had Scala's verses placed before him, there was any question of sturgeon, but rather of frogs and gudgeons: made short work with Scala's defence of his own Latin, and mangled him terribly on the score of the stupid criticisms he had ventured on the Greek epigram kindly forwarded to him as a model. Wretched cavils, indeed! for as to the damp origin of the gnat, tliere was the authority of Virgil himself, who had called it the "altimmis of the waters;" and as to what his dear dull friend had to say about the fish, the eagle, and the rest, it was "nihil ad rem;" for because the eagle could fly higher, it by no means followed that the gnat could not fly at all, &c. &c. He was ashamed, however, to dwell on such trivialities, and thus to swell a gnat into an elephant; but, for his own part, would only add that he had nothing deceitful or double about him, neither was he to be caught when present by the false blandishments of

those who slandered him in his absence, agreeing rather with a Homeric sentiment on that head—which furnished a Greek quotation to serve as powder to his bullet.

The quarrel could not end there. The logic could hardly get worse, but the secretary got more pompously self-asserting, and the scholarly poet's temper more and more venomous. Politian had been generously willing to hold up a mirror, by which the too-inflated secretary, beholding his own likeness, might be induced to cease setting up his ignorant defences of bad Latin against ancient authorities whom the consent of centuries had placed beyond question,—unless, indeed, he had designed to sink in literature in proportion as he rose in honours, that by a sort of compensation men of letters might feel themselves his equals. In return, Politian was begged to examine Scala's writings; nowhere would he find a more devout admiration of antiquity. The secretary was ashamed of the age in which he lived, and blushed for it. Some, indeed, there were who wanted to have their own works praised and exalted to a level with the divine monuments of antiquity; but he, Scala, could not oblige them. And as to the honours which were offensive to the envious, they had been well earned: witness his whole life since he came in penury to Florence. The elegant scholar, in reply, was not surprised that Scala found the Age distasteful to him, since he himself was so distasteful to the Age; nay, it was with perfect accuracy that he, the elegant scholar, had called Scala a branny monster, inasmuch as he was formed from the offscourings of monsters, born amidst the refuse of a mill, and eminently worthy the long-eared office of turning the paternal millstones \'7bin pistrini sordihus natus et quideni pistrino dignissimiis)\

It was not without reference to Tito's appointed visit
that the papers containing this correspondence were brought out to-day. Here was a new Greek scholar Avliose accomphshments were to be tested and on nothing did Scala more desire a dispassionate opinion from persons of superior knowledge than that Greek epigram of Politian's. After sufficient introductory talk concerning Tito's travels, after a survey and discussion of the gems, and an easy passage from the mention of the lamented Lorenzo's eagerness in collecting such specimens of ancient art to the subject of classical tastes and studies in general and their present condition in Florence, it was inevitable to mention Politian, a man of eminent ability indeed, but a little too arrogant—assuming to be a Hercules, whose office it was to destroy all the literary monstrosities of the age, and writing letters to his elders without signing them, as if they were miraculous revelations that could only have one source. And after all, were not his own criticisms often questionable and his tastes perverse? He was fond of saying pungent things about the men who thought tliey wrote like Cicero because they ended every sentence with "esse videtur:" but while he was boasting of his freedom from servile imitation, did he not fall into the other extreme, running after strange words and affected l)lirases? Even in his much belauded Miscellanea was every point tenable? And Tito, who had just been looking in the Miscellanea, found so much to say that wis agreeable to the secretary—he would have done so from the mere disposition to please, without further motive— that he showed himself quite worthy to be made a judge in the notable correspondence concerning the culex. Here was the Greek epigram which Politian had doubtless thought the finest in the world, though he had pretended -to believe that the "transmarini," the Greeks themselves,

ROMOLA.

would make light of it: had he not been unintentionally speaking the truth in his false modesty?

Tito was ready, and scarified the epigram to Scala's content. O wise young judge! He could doubtless appreciate satire even in the vulgar tongue, and Scala—who, excellent man, not seeking publicity through the booksellers, was never unprovided with "hasty uncorrected trifles," as a sort of sherbet for a visitor on a hot day, or, if the weather were cold, why then as a cordial— had a few little matters in the shape of Sonnets, turning on well-known foibles of Politian's, which he would not like to go any farther, but which would, perhaps, amuse the company.

Enough: Tito took his leave under an urgent invitation to come again. His gems were interesting; especially the agate, with the liisus naturce in it—a most wonderful semblance of Cupid riding on the lion; and the "Jew's stone," with the lion-headed serpent enchased in it; both of which the secretary agreed to buy—the latter as a reinforcement of his preventives against the gout, which gave him such severe twinges that it was plain enough how intolerable it would be if he were not well supplied with rings of rare virtue, and with an amulet worn close under the right breast. But Tito was assured that he himself was more interesting than his gems. He had won his way to the Scala Palace by the recommendation of Bardo de' Bardi, who, to be sure, was Scala's old acquaintance and a worthy scholar, in spite of his overvaluing himself a little (a frequent foible in the secretary's friends); but he must come again on the ground of his own manifest accomplishments.

The interview could hardly have ended more auspiciously for Tito, and as he walked out at the Porta a Pinti

A FACE IN THE CROVD.

that he might laugh a Httle at his ease over the affair of the culex, he felt that Fortune could hardly mean to turn her back oa him again at present, since she had taken him by the hand in this decided way.

CHAPTER Vm. A FACE IN THE CROWD.

It is easy to northern people to rise early on Midsummer morning, to see the dew on the grassy edge of the dusty pathway, to notice the fresh shoots among the darker green of the oak and fir in the coppice, and to look over the gate at the shorn meadow, without recollecting that it is the Nativity of Saint John the Baptist.

Not so to the Florentine—still less to the Florentine of the fifteenth century; to him on that particular morn-ino: the brightness of the eastern sun on the Arno had something special in it; the ringing of the bells was articulate, and declared it to be the great summer festival ot Florence, the day of San Giovanni.

San Giovanni had been the patron saint of Florence for at least eight hundred years—ever since the time when the Lombard Queen Theodolinda had commanded her subjects to do him peculiar honour; nay, says old Villain, to the best of his knowledge, ever since the days of Constantine the Great and Pope Sylvester, when the Florentines deposed their idol Mars, whom they were nevertheless careful not to treat with contumely; for while they consecrated their beautiful and noble temple to the honour of God and of the "Beato Messere Santo Giovanni," they placed old Mars respectfully on a high tower near the River Arno, finding in certain ancient memorials that he

had been elected as their tutelar deity under such astral influences that if he were broken, or otherwise treated with indignity, the city would suffer great damage and mutation. But in the fifteenth century that discreet regard to the feelings of the Man-destroyer had long vanished: the god of the spear and shield had ceased to frown by the side of the Arno, and the defences of the Republic were held to lie in its craft and its coffers. For spear and shield could be hired by gold florins, and on the gold florins there had always been the image of San Giovanni.

Much good had come to Florence since the dim time of struggle between the old patron and the new: some quarrelling and bloodshed, doubtless, between Guelf and Ghibelline, between Black and White, between orthodox sons of the Church and heretic Paterini; some floods, famine, and pestilence; but still much wealth and glory. Florence had achieved conquests over walled cities once mightier than itself, and especially over hated Pisa, whose marble buildings were too high and beautiful, whose masts were too much honoured on Greek and Italian coasts. The name of Florence had been growing prouder and prouder in all the courts of Europe, nay, in Africa itself, on the strength of purest gold coinage, finest dyes and textures, pre-eminent scholarship and poetic genius, and wits of the most serviceable sort for statesmanship and banking: it was a name so omnipresent that a Pope with a turn for epigram had called Florentines "the fifth element." And for this high destiny, though it might partly depend on the stars and Madonna dell' Impruneta, and certainly depended on other higher Powers less often named, the praise was greatly due to San Giovanni, whose image was on the fair gold florins.

Therefore it was fitting that the day of San Giovanni that ancient Church festival ah-eady venerable in the days of St. Augustine—should be a day of peculiar rejoicing to Florence, and should be ushered in by a vigil duly kept in strict old Florentine fashion, with much dancing, with much street jesting, and perhaps with not a little stone-throwing and window-breaking, but emphatically with certain street sights such as could only be provided by a city which held in its service a clever Cecca, engineer and architect, valuable alike in sieges and shows. By the help of Cecca, the very Saints, surrounded with their almond-shaped glory, and floating on clouds with their joyous companionship of winged cherubs, even as they may be seen to this day in the pictures of Perugino, seemed, on the eve of San Giovanni, to have brought their piece of the heavens down into the narrow streets, and to pass slowly through them; and, more wonderful still, saints of gigantic size, with attendant angels, might be seen, not seated, but moving in a slow, mysterious manner along the streets, like a procession of colossal figures come down from the high domes and tribunes of the churches. The clouds were made of good woven stuff, the saints and cherubs were unglorified mortals supported by firm bars, and those mysterious giants were really men of very steady brain, balancing themselves on stilts, and enlarged, like Greek tragedians, by huge masks and stuffed shoulders; but he was a miserably unimaginative Florentine who thought only of that—nay, somewhat impious, for in the images of sacred things was there not some of the virtue of sacred things themselves? And if, after that, there came a company of merry black demons well-armed with claws and thongs, and other implements of sport, ready to per-form impromptu farces of bastinadoing and clothes-tearing, why, that was the demons' way of keeping a vigil, and they, too, might have descended from the domes and the tribunes. The Tuscan mind slipped from the devout to the burlesque, as readily as water round an angle; and the saints had already had their turn, had gone their way, and made their due pause before the gates of San Giovanni, to do him honour on the eve of his festa. And on the morrow, the great day thus ushered in, it was fitting that the tributary symbols paid to Florence by all its dependent cities, districts, and villages, whether conquered, protected, or of immemorial possession, should be offered at the shrine of San Giovanni in the old octagonal church, once the cathedral, and now the baptistery, where every Florentine had had the sign of the Cross made with the anointing chrism on his brov; that all the city, from the white-haired man to the stripling, and from the matron to the lisping child, should be clothed in its best to do honour to the great day, and see the great sight; and that again, when the sun was sloping and the streets were cool, there should be the glorious race or Corso, when the unsaddled horses, clothed in rich trappings, should run right across the city, from the Porta al Prato on the northwest, through the Mercato Vecchio, to the Porta Santa Croce on the south-east, where the richest of Palii, or velvet and brocade banners with silk linings and fringe of gold, such as became a city that half-clothed the well-dressed world, were mounted on a triumphal car awaiting the winner or winner's owner.

And thereafter followed more dancing; nay, through the whole day, says an old chronicler at the beginning of that century, there were weddings and the grandest gather-
ings, with so much piping, music and song, with balls and feasts and gladness and ornament, that this earth might have been mistaken for Paradise!

In this year of 1492, it was, perhaps, a little less easy to make that mistake. Lorenzo the magnificent and subtle was dead, and an arrogant, incautious Piero was come in his room, an evil change for Florence, unless, indeed, the wise horse prefers the bad rider, as more easily thrown from the saddle; and already the regrets for Lorenzo were getting less predominant over the murmured desire for government on a broader basis, in which corruption might be arrested, and there might be that free play for everybody's jealousy and ambition, which made the ideal liberty of the good old quarrelsome, struggling times, when Florence raised her great buildings, reared her own soldiers, drove out would-be tyrants at the sword's point, and was proud to keep faith at her own loss. Lorenzo was dead, Pope Innocent was dying, and a troublesome Neapolitan succession, with an intriguing, ambitious Milan, might set Italy by the ears before long: the times were likely to be difficult. Still, there was all the more reason that the Republic should keep its religious festivals.

And Midsummer morning, in this year 1492, was not less bright than usual. It was betimes in the morning that the symbolic offerings to be carried in grand procession were all assembled at their starting point in the Piazza della Signoria—that famous piazza, where stood then, and stand now, the massive turreted Palace of the People, called the Palazzo Vecchio, and the spacious Loggia, built by Orcagna—the scene of all grand State ceremonial. The sky made the fairest blue tent, and under it the bells swung so vigorously that every evil spirit with sense enough to be formidable, must long since

ROMOLA.

have taken his flight; windows and terraced roofs were aUve with human faces; sombre stone houses were bright with hanging draperies; the boldly soaring palace tower, the yet older square tower of the Bargello, and the spire of the neighbouring Badia, seemed to keep watch above; and below, on the broad polygonal flags of the piazza, was the glorious show of banners and horses, with rich trappings and gigantic ceri, or tapers, that were fitly called towers—strangely aggrandised descendants of those torches by whose faint light the Church worshipped in the Catacombs. Betimes in the morning all processions had need to move under the Midsummer sky of Florence, where the shelter of the narrow streets must every now and then be exchanged for the glare of wide spaces; and the sun would be high up in the heavens before the long pomp had ended its pilgrimage in the Piazza di San Giovanni.

But here, where the procession was to pause, the magnificent city, with its ingenious Cecca, had provided another tent than the sky; for the whole of the Piazza del Duomo, from the octagonal baptistery in the centre to the facade of the cathedral and the walls of the houses on the other sides of the quadrangle, was covered, at the height of forty feet or more, with blue drapery, adorned with well-stitched yellow lilies and the familiar coats of arms, while sheaves of many-coloured banners drooped at fit angles under this superincumbent clue—a gorgeous rainbow-lit shelter to the waiting spectators who leaned from the windows, and made a narrow border on the pavement, and wished for the coming of the show.

One of these spectators was Tito Milema. Bright, in the midst of brightness, he sat at the window of the room above Nello's shop, his right elbow resting on the red drapery hanging from the window-sill, and his head sup-

ported in a backward position by the right hand, which pressed the curls against his ear. His face wore that bland hvehness, as far removed from excitability as from heaviness or gloom, which marks the companion popular alike amongst men and women—the companion who is never obtrusive or noisy from uneasy vanity or excessive animal spirits, and whose brow is never contracted by resentment or indignation. He showed no other change from the two months and more that had passed since his first appearance in the weather-stained tunic and hose, than that added radiance of good fortune, which is like the just perceptible perfecting of a flower after it has drunk in a morning's sunbeams. Close behind him, ensconced in the narrow angle between his chair and the window-frame, stood the slim figure of Nello in holiday suit, and at his left the younger Cennini—Pietro, the erudite corrector of proof-sheets, not Domenico the practical. Tito was looking alternately down on the scene below, and upward at the varied knot of gazers and talkers immediately around him, some of whom had come in after witnessing!: the commencement of the procession in the Piazza della Signoria. Piero di Cosimo was raising a laugh among them by his grimaces and anathemas at the noise of the bells, against which no kind of ear-stuffing was a sufficient barricade, since the more he stuffed his ears the more he felt the vibration of his skull; and declaring that he would bury himself in the most solitary spot of the Valdamo on a festa, if he were not condemned, as a painter, to lie in wait for the secrets of colour that were sometimes to be caught from the floating of banners and the chance grouping of the multitude.

    Tito had just turned his laughing face away from the whimsical painter to look down at the small drama going on among the chequered border of spectators, when at the angle of the marble steps in front of the Duomo, nearly opposite Nello's shop, he saw a man's face upturned towards him, and fixing on him a gaze that seemed to have more meaning in it than the ordinary passing observation of a stranger. It was a face with tonsured head, that rose above the black mantle and white tunic of a Dominican friar—a very common sight in Florence; but the glance had something peculiar in it for Tito, There was a faint suggestion in it, certainly not of an unpleasant kind. Yet what pleasant association had he ever had with monks? None. The glance and the suggestion hardly took longer than a flash of lightning.

"Nello!" said Tito, hastily, but immediately added in a tone of disappointment, "Ah, he has turned round. It was that tall, thin friar who is going up the steps. I wanted you to tell me if you knew aught of him?"

"One of the Frati Predicatori," said Nello, carelessly; "you don't expect me to know the private history of the crows."

"I seem to remember something about his face," said Tito. "It is an uncommon face."

"What? you thought it might be our Fra Girolamo? Too tall; and he never shows himself in that chance way."

"Besides, that loud-barking 'hound of the Lord'* is not in Florence just now," said Francesco Cei, the popular poet; "he has taken Piero de' Medici's hint, to carry his railing prophecies on a journey for awhile."

"The Frate neither rails nor prophesies against any man," said a middle-aged personage seated at the otheri

* A play on the name of the Dominicans \'7bDomini Canes) which [, was accepted by themselves, and which is pictorially represented in a fresco painted for them by Simone Memmi.

corner of the window; "he only prophesies against vice. If you think that an attack on your poems, Francesco, it is not the Frate's fault."

"Ah, he's gone into the Duomo now," said Tito, who had watched the figure eagerly. "No, I was not under that mistake, Nello. Your Fra Girolamo has a high nose and a large under-lip. I saw him once—he is not handsome; but this man . . . ."

"Truce to your descriptions!" said Cennini. "Hark! see! Here come the horsemen and the banners. That standard," he continued, laying his hand familiarly on Tito's shoulder,—"that carried on the horse with white trappings that with the red eagle holding the green dragon between his talons, and the red lily over the eagle is the gonfalon of the Guelf party, and those cavaliers close round it are the chief officers of the Guelf party. That is one of our proudest banners, grumble as we may; it means the triumph of the Guelfs, which means the triumph of Florentine will, which means triumph of the popolani."

"Nay, go on, Cennini," said the middle-aged man, seated at the window, "which means triumph of the fat popolani over the lean, which again means triumph of the fattest popolano over those who are less fat."

"Cronaca, you are becoming sententious," said the printer; "Fra Girolamo's preaching will spoil you, and make you take life by the wrong handle. Trust me, your cornices will lose half their beauty if you begin to mingle bitterness with them; that is the maniera Tedesca which you used to declaim against when you came from Rome. The next palace you build we shall see you trying to put the Frate's doctrine into stone."

"That is a goodly show of cavaliers," said Tito, who had learned by this time the best way to please Florentines; "but are there not strangers among them? I see foreign costumes."

"Assuredly," said Cennini; "you see there the Orators! from France, Milan, and Venice, and behind them are English and German nobles; for it is customary that all foreign visitors of distinction pay their tribute to San Giovanni in the train of that gonfalon. For my part, I think our Florentine cavaliers sit their horses as well as, any of those cut-and-thrust northerns, whose wits lie in their heels and saddles; and for yon Venetian, I fancy he would feel himself more at ease on the back of a dolphin. We ought to know something of horsemanship, for we excel all Italy in the sports of the Giostra, and the money we spend on them. But you will see a finer show of our chief men by-and-by, Melema; my brother himself will be among the officers of the Zecca."

"The banners are the better sight," said Piero di Cosimo, forgetting the noise in his delight at the winding stream of colour as the tributary standards advanced round the piazza. "The Florentine men are so-so; they make but a sorry show at this distance with their patch of sallow flesh-tint above the black garments; but those banners with their velvet, and satin, and minever, and brocade, and their endless play of delicate light and shadow!— Vaf your human talk and doings are a tame jest; the only passionate life is in form and colour."

"Ay, Piero, if Santanasso could paint, thou wouldst sell thy soul to learn his secrets," said Nello. "But there is little likelihood of it, seeing the blessed angels themselves are such poor hands at chiaroscuro, if one may judge from their capo-d'opera, the Madonna Nunziata."

"There go the banners of Pisa and Arezzo," said Cennini. "Ay, Messer Pisano, it is no use for you to look sullen; you may as well carry your banner to our San Giovanni with a good grace. 'Pisans false, Florentines blind' — the second half of that proverb will hold no longer. There come the ensigns of our subject towns and signories, Melema; they will all be suspended in San Giovanni until this day next year, when they will give place to new ones."

"They are a fair sight," said Tito; "and San Giovanni will surely be as well satisfied with that produce of Italian looms as Minerva with her peplos, especially as he contents himself with so little drapery. But my eyes are less delighted with those whirling towers, which would soon make me fall from the window in sympathetic vertigo."

The "towers" of which Tito spoke were a part of the procession esteemed very glorious by the Florentine populace; and having their origin, perhaps, in a confused combination of the tower-shaped triumphal car which the Romans borrowed from the Etruscans, with a kind of hyperbole for the all-efficacious wax taper, were also called cen. But inasmuch as all hyperbole is impracticable in a real and literal fashion, these gigantic cefi, some of them so large as to be of necessity carried on wheels, were not solid but hollow, and had their surface made not solely of wax, but of wood and pasteboard, gilded, carved, and painted, as real sacred tapers often are, with successive circles of fingers—warriors on horseback, foot soldiers with lance and shield, dancing maidens, animals, trees and fruits, and in fine, says the old chronicler, "all things that could delight the eye and the heart;" the hoUowness having the further advantage that men could stand inside these hyperbolic tapers and whirl them continually, so as to produce a phantasmagoric effect, which,

considering the towers were numerous, must have been calculated to produce dizziness on a truly magnificent scale.

"Pesiilenza!" said Piero di Cosimo, moving from the window, "those whirling circles one above the other are worse than the jangling of all the bells. Let me know when the last taper has passed."

"Nay, you will surely like to be called when the con-tadini come carrying their torches," said Nello; "you would not miss the men of the Mugello and the Casentino, of whom your favourite Lionardo would make a hundred grotesque sketches."

"No," said Piero, resolutely; "I will see nothing till the car of the Zecca comes. I have seen clowns enough holding tapers aslant, both with and without cowls, to last me for my life."

"Here it comes, then, Piero—the car of the Zecca," called out Nello, after an interval during which towers and tapers in a descending scale of size had been making their slow transit.

"Fediddio!" exclaimed Francesco Cei, "that is a well-tanned San Giovanni! some sturdy Romagnole beggar-man, I'll warrant. Our Signoria plays the host to all the Jewish and Christian scum that every other city shuts its gates against, and lets them fatten on us like Saint Anthony's swine."

To make clear this exclamation of Cei's, it must be understood that the car of the Zecca, or Mint, was originally an immense wooden tower or cero adorned after the same fashion as the other tributary ceri, mounted on a splendid car, and drawn by two mouse-coloured oxen, whose mild heads looked out from rich trappings bearing the arms of the Zecca. But the latter half of the century was getting rather ashamed of the towers with their circular or spiral paintings, which had delighted the eyes and the hearts of the other half, so that they had become a contemptuous proverb, and any ill-painted figure looking, as will sometimes happen to figures in the best ages of art, as if it had been boned for a pie, was called 2. fantoccio da cero, a tower-puppet; consequently improved taste, with Cecca to help it, had devised for the magnificent Zecca a triumphal car like a pyramidal catafalque, with ingenious wheels warranted to turn all corners easily. Round the base were living figures of saints and angels arrayed in sculpturesque fashion; and on the summit, at the height of thirty feet, well bound to an iron rod and holding an iron cross also firmly infixed, stood a living representative of St. John the Baptist, with arms and legs bare, a garment of tigerskins about his body, and a golden nimbus fastened on his head—as the Precursor was wont to appear in the cloisters and churches, not having yet revealed himself to painters as the brown and sturdy boy who made one of the Holy Family. For where could the image of the patron saint be more fitly placed than on the symbol of the Zecca? Was not the royal prerogative of coining money the surest token that a city had won its independence? and by the blessing of San Giovanni this "beautiful sheepfold" of his had shown that token earliest among the Italian cities. Nevertheless, the annual function of representing the patron saint was not among the high prizes of public life; it was paid for with ten lire, a cake weighing fourteen pounds, two bottles of wine, and a handsome supply of light eatables; the money being furnished by the magnificent Zecca, and the payment in kind being by peculiar "privilege" presented in a basket suspended on a pole from an upper window of a private house, whereupon the eidolon of the austere saint at once invigorated himself with a reasonable share of the sweets and wine, threw the remnants to the crowd, and embraced the mighty cake securely with his right arm through the remainder of his passage. This was the attitude in which the mimic San Giovanni presented himself as the, tall car jerked and vibrated on its slow way round the piazza to the northern gate of the Baptistery.

"There go the Masters of the Zecca, and there is my brother—you see him, Melema?" cried Cennini, with an agreeable stirring of pride at showing a stranger what was too familiar to be remarkable to fellow-citizens. "Behind come the members of the Corporation of Calimara,* the dealers in foreign cloth, to which we have given our Florentine finish, men of ripe years, you see, who were matriculated before you were born; and then comes the famous Art of Money-changers."

"Many of them matriculated also to the noble art of usury before you were born," interrupted Francesco Cei, "as you may discern by a certain fitful glare of the eye and sharp curve of the nose which manifest their descent from the ancient Harpies, whose portraits you saw supporting the arms of the Zecca. Shaking off old prejudices now, such a procession as that of some four hundred passably ugly men carrying their tapers in open daylight, Diogenes-fashion, as if they were looking for a lost quattrino, would make a merry spectacle for the Feast of Fools."

"Blaspheme not against the usages of our city," said Pietro Cennini, much offended.

"There are new wits who think they see things more truly because they stand on

* "Arte di Calimara," "arte" being, in this use of it, equivalent to corporation.

their heads to look at them, Hke tumblers and mountebanks, instead of keeping the attitude of rational men. Doubtless it makes little difference to Maestro Vaiano's monkeys whether they see our Donatello's statue of Judith with their heads or their tails uppermost."

"Your solemnity will allow some quarter to playful fancy, I hope," said Cei, with a shrug, "else what becomes of the ancients, whose example you scholars are bound to revere, Messer Pietro? Life was never anything but a perpetual seesaw between gravity and jest."

"Keep your jest then till your end of the pole is uppermost," said Cennini, still angry, "and that is not when the great bond of our republic is expressing itself in ancient symbols without which the vulgar—the popolo minnto —would be conscious of nothing beyond their own petty wants of back and stomach, and never rise to the sense of community in religion and law. There has been no great people without processions, and the man who thinks himself too wise to be moved by them to anything but contempt is like the puddle that was proud of standing alone while the river rushed by."

No one said anything after this indignant burst of Cennini's till he himself spoke again.

"Hark! the trumpets of the Signoria: now comes the last stage of the show, Melema. That is our Gonfaloniere in the middle, in the starred mantle, with the sword carried before him. Twenty years ago we used to see our foreign Podesta, who was our judge in civil causes, walking on his right hand; but our republic has been over-doctored by clever Medici. That is the Proposto* of the Priori on the left; then come the other seven Priori;

* Spokesman or Moderator.

then all the other magistracies and officials of our Republic, You see your patron the Segretario?"

"There is Messer Bernardo del Nero also," said Tito; "his visage is a fine and venerable one, though it has worn rather a petrifying look towards me."

"Ah," said Nello, "he is the dragon that guards the remnant of old Bardo's gold, which, I fancy, is chiefly that virgin gold that falls about the fair Romola's head and shoulders; eh, my ApoUino?" he added, patting Tito's head.

Tito had the youthful grace of blushing, but he had also the adroit and ready speech that prevents a blush from looking like embarrassment. He replied at once:—

"And a very Pactolus it is—a stream with golden ripples. If I were an alchemist—"

He was saved from the need for further speech by ,j the sudden fortissimo of drums and trumpets and fifes, bursting into the breadth of the piazza in a grand storm of sound—a roar, a blast, and a whistling, well befitting a city famous for its musical instmments, and reducing the members of the closest group to a state of deaf isolation, j

During this interval Nello observed Tito's fingers mov- ' ing in recognition of someone in the crowd below, but not seeing the direction of his glance he failed to detect the object of this greeting—the sweet round blue-eyed face under a white hood—immediately lost in the narrow border of heads, where there was a continual eclipse of round contadina cheeks by the harsh-lined features or bent shoulders of an old spadesman, and where profiles turned as sharply from north to south as weathercocks under a shifting wind.

But when it was felt that the show was ended—when the twelve prisoners released in honour of the day, and

the very barheri or race-horses, with the arms of their owners embroidered on their cloths, had followed up the Signoria, and been duly consecrated to San Giovanni, and everyone was moving from the window—Nello, whose Florentine curiosity was of that lively canine sort which thinks no trifle too despicable for investigation, put his hand on Tito's shoulder and said,—

"What acquaintance was that you were making signals to, eh, giovane mio?"

"Some little contadina who probably mistook me for an acquaintance, for she had honoured me with a greeting."

"Or who wished to begin an acquaintance," said Nello. "But you are bound for the Via de' Bardi and the feast of the Muses: there is no counting on you for a frolic, else we might have gone in search of adventures together in the crowd, and had some pleasant fooling in honour of San Giovanni. But your high fortune has come on you too soon: I don't mean the professor's mantle — that is roomy enough to hide a few stolen chickens, but—Messer Endymion minded his manners after that singular good fortune of his; and what says our Luigi Pulci?

*Da quel giorno in qua cli'amor m'accese Per lei son fatto e gentile e cortese.'"

"Nello, amico mio, thou hast an intolerable trick of making life stale by forestalling it with thy talk," said Tito, shrugging his shoulders, with a look of patient resignation, which was his nearest approach to anger: "not to mention that such ill-founded babbling would be held a great offence by that same goddess whose humble worshipper you are always professing yourself."

"I will be mute," said Nello, laying his finger on his

lips, with a responding shrug. "But it is only under our four eyes that I talk any folly about her."

"Pardon! you were on the verge of it just now in the hearing of others. If you want to ruin me in the minds of Bardo and his daughter—"

"Enough, enough!" said Nello. "I am an absurd old barber. It all comes from that abstinence of mine, in not making bad verses in my youth: for want of letting my folly run out that way when I was eighteen, it runs out at my tongue's end now I am at the unseemly age of fifty. But Nello has not got his head muffled for all that; he can see a buffalo in the snow. Addio, giovane mio."

CHAPTER IX.

A man's ransom.

Trro was soon down among the crowd, and, notwithstanding his indifferent reply to Nello's question about his chance acquaintance, he was not without a passing wish, as he made his way round the piazza to the Corso degli Adimari, that he might encounter the pair of blue eyes which had looked up towards him from under the square bit of white linen drapery that formed the ordinary hood of the contadina at festa time. He was perfectly well aware that that face was Tessa's; but he had not chosen to say so. What had Nello to do with the matter? Tito had an innate love of reticence—let us say a talent for it—which acted as other impulses do, without any conscious motive, and, like all people to whom concealment is easy, he would now and then conceal something which

had as little the nature of a secret as the fact that he had seen a flight of crows.

But the passing wish about pretty Tessa was almost immediately eclipsed by the recurrent recollection of that friar whose face had some irrecoverable association for him. Why should a sickly fanatic, worn with fasting, have looked at him in particular, and where in all his travels could he remember encountering that face before? Folly! such vague memories hang about the mind like cobwebs, with tickling importunity—best to sweep them away at a dash: and Tito had pleasanter occupation for his thoughts. By the time he was turning out of the Corso degli Adimari into a side-street he was caring only that the sun was high, and that the procession had kept him longer than he had intended from his visit to that room in the Via de' Bardi, where his coming, he knew, was anxiously awaited. He felt the scene of his entrance beforehand: the joy beaming diffusedly in the blind face like the light in a semi-transparent lamp: the transient pink flush on Romola's face and neck, which subtracted nothing from her majesty, but only, gave it the exquisite charm of womanly sensitiveness, heightened still more by what seemed the paradoxical boy-like frankness of her look and smile. They were the best comrades in the world during the hours they passed together round the blind man's chair: she was constantly appealing to Tito, and he was informing her, yet he felt himself strangely in subjection to Romola with that majestic simplicity of hers: he felt for the first time, without defining it to himself, that loving awe in the presence of noble womanhood, which is perhaps something like the worship paid of old to a great nature-goddess, who was not all-knowing, but whose life and power were something deeper and more

primordial than knowledge. They had never been alone together, and he could frame to himself no probable image of love scenes between them: he could only fancy and wish wildly—what he knew was impossible—that Romola would some day tell him that she loved him. One day in Greece, as he was leaning over a wall in the sunshine, a little black-eyed peasant girl, who had rested her water-pot on the wall, crept gradually nearer and nearer to him, and at last shyly asked him to kiss her, putting up her round olive cheek very innocently. Tito was used to love that came in this unsought fashion. But Romola's love would never come in that way: would it ever come at all?—and yet it was that topmost apple on which he had set his mind. He was in his fresh youth—not passionate, but impressible: it was as inevitable that he should feel lovingly towards Romola as that the white irises should be reflected in the clear sunlit stream; but he had no coxcombry, and he had an intimate sense that Romola was something very much above him. Many men have felt the same before a large-eyed, simple child. Nevertheless, Tito had had the rapid success which would have made some men presuming, or would have warranted him in thinking that there would be no great presumption in entertaining an agreeable confidence that he might one day be the husband of Romola—nay, that her father himself was not without a vision of such a future for him. His first auspicious interview with Bar-tolommeo Scala had proved the commencement of a growing favour on the secretary's part, and had led to an issue which would have been enough to make Tito decide on Florence as the place in which to establish himself, even if it had held no other magnet. Politian was professor of Greek as well as Latin at Florence, professorial

chairs being maintained there, although the university had been removed to Pisa; but for a long time Demetrio Cal-condila, one of the most eminent and respectable among the emigrant Greeks, had also held a Greek chair, simultaneously with the too predominant Italian. Calcondila was now gone to Milan, and there was no counterpoise or rival to Politian such as was desired for him by the friends who wished him to be taught a little propriety and humility. Scala was far from being the only friend of this class, and he found several who, if they were not among those thirsty admirers of mediocrity that were glad to be refreshed with his verses in hot weather, were yet quite willing to join him in doing that moral service to Politian. It was finally agreed that Tito should be supported in a Greek chair, as Demetrio Calcondila had been by Lorenzo himself, who, being at the same time the affectionate patron of Politian, had shown by precedent that there was nothing invidious in such a measure, but only a zeal for true learning and for the instruction of the Florentine youth.

Tito was thus sailing under the fairest breeze, and besides convincing fair judges that his talents squared with his good fortune, he wore that fortune so easily and unpretentiously that no one had yet been offended by it. He was not unlikely to get into the best Florentine society: society where there was much more plate than the circle of enamelled sUver in the centre of the brass dishes, and where it was not forbidden by the Signory to wear the richest brocade. For where could a handsome young scholar not be welcome when he could touch the lute and troll a gay song? That bright face, that easy smile, that liquid voice, seemed to give life a holiday aspect; just as a strain of gay music and the hoisting of colours make the work-worn and the sad rather ashamed of showing themselves. Here was a professor hkely to render the Greek classics amiable to the sons of great houses.

And that was not the whole of Tito's good fortune; for he had sold all his jewels, except the ring he did not choose to part with, and he was master of full five hundred gold florins.

Yet the moment when he first had this sum in his possession was the crisis of the first serious struggle his facile, good-humoured nature had known. An importunate thought, of which he had till now refused to see more than the shadow as it dogged his footsteps, at last rushed upon him and grasped him: he was obliged to pause and decide whether he would surrender and obey, or whether he would give the refusal that must carry irrevocable consequences. It was in the room above Nello's shop, which Tito had now hired as a lodging, that the elder Cennini handed him the last quota of the suni on behalf of Bernardo Rucellai, the purchaser of the two most valuable gems.

"Ecco, giovane mio!" said the respectable printer and goldsmith, "you have now a pretty little fortune; and if you will take my advice, you will let me place your florins in a safe quarter, where they may increase and multiply, instead of slipping through your fingers for banquets and other follies which are rife among our Florentine youth. And it has been too much the fashion of scholars, especially when, like our Pietro Crinito, they think their scholarship needs to be scented and broidered, to squander with one hand till they have been fain to beg with the other. I have brought you the money, and you are free to make a wise choice or an unwise: I shall see on which side the balance dips. We Florentines hold no man a member of an Art till he has shown his skill and been matriculated; and no man is matriculated to the art of life till he has been well tempted. If you make up your mind to put your florins out to usury, you can let me know to-morrow. A scholar may marry, and should , have something in readiness for the morgen-cap. * Addio."

As Cennini closed the door behind him, Tito turned round with the smile dying out of his face, and fixed his eyes on the table where the florins lay. He made no other movement, but stood with his thumbs in his belt, looking down, in that transfixed state which accompanies the concentration of consciousness on some inward image.

"A man's ransom!—who was it that had said five hundred florins was more than a man's ransom? If now under this mid-day sun, on some hot coast far away, a man somewhat stricken in years—a man not without high thoughts and with the most passionate heart—a man who long years ago had rescued a little boy from a life of beggary, filth, and cruel wrong, had reared him tenderly, and been to him as a father—if that man were now under this summer sun toiling as a slave, hewing wood and drawing water, perhaps being smitten and buffeted because he was not deft and active? If he were saying to himself, 'Tito will find me: he had but to carry our manuscripts and gems to Venice; he will have raised money, and will never rest till he finds me out?' If that were certain, could he, Tito, see the price of the gems lying before him, and say, 'I will stay at Florence, where I am fanned by soft airs of promised love and prosperity: I will not risk myself for his sake?'" No, surely not, if it ivere certain. But nothing could be

* A srnn given by the bridegroom to the bride the day after the marriage \'7bMorgevgahe).farther from certainty. The galley had been taken by a Turkish vessel on its way

to Delos: that was known by the report of the companion galley, which had escaped. But there had been resistance, and probable bloodshed; a man had been seen falling overboard: who were the survivors, and what had befallen them amongst all the multitude of possibilities? Had not he, Tito, suffered shipwreck, and narrowly escaped drowning? He had good cause for feeling the omnipresence of casualties that threatened all projects with futility. The rumour that there were pirates who had a settlement in Delos was not to be depended on, or might be nothing to the purpose. What, probably enough, would be the result if he were to quit Florence and go to Venice; get authoritative letters—yes, he knew that might be done—and set out for the Archipelago? Why, that he should be himself seized, and spend all his florins on preliminaries, and be again a destitute wanderer—with no more gems to sell.

Tito had a clearer vision of that result than of the possible moment when he might find his father again, and carry him deliverance. It would surely be an unfairness that he, in his full ripe youth, to whom life had hitherto had some of the stint and subjection of a school, should turn his back on promised love and distinction, and perhaps never be visited by that promise again. "And yet," he said to himself, "if I were certain—yes, if I were certain that Baldassarre Calvo was alive, and that I could free him, by whatever exertions or perils, I would go now —now I have the money: it was useless to debate the matter before. I would go now to Bardo and Bartolom-meo Scala, and tell them the whole truth." Tito did not say to himself so distinctly that if those two men had

known the whole truth he was aware there would have been no alternative for him but to go in search of his benefactor, who, if alive, was the rightful owner of the gems, and whom he had always equivocally spoken of as "lost;" he did not say to himself, what he was not ignorant of, that Greeks of distinction had made sacrifices, taken voyages again and again, and sought help from crowned and mitred heads for the sake of freeing relatives from slavery to the Turks. Public opinion did not regard that as exceptional virtue.

This was his first real colloquy with himself: he had gone on following the impulses of the moment, and one of those impulses had been to conceal half the fact: he had never considered this part of his conduct long enough to face the consciousness of his motives for the concealment. What was the use of telling the whole? It was true, the thought had crossed his mind several times since he had quitted Nauplia that, after all, it was a great relief to be quit of Baldassarre, and he would have liked to know tvho it was that had fallen overboard. But such thoughts spring inevitably out of a relation that is irksome. Baldassarre was exacting, and had got stranger as he got older: he was constantly scrutinising Tito's mind to see whether it answered to his own exaggerated expectations; and age—the age of a thick-set, heavy-browed, bald man beyond sixty, whose intensity and eagerness in the grasp of ideas have long taken the character of monotony and repetition, may be looked at from many points of view without being found attractive. Such a man, stranded among new acquaintances, unless he had the philosopher's stone, would hardly find rank, youth, and beauty at his feet. The feelings that gather fervour from novelty will be of little help towards making the world a home for

dimmed and faded human beings; and if there is any love of which they are not widowed, it must be the love that is rooted in memories and distils perpetually the sweet balms of fidelity and forbearing tenderness.

But surely such memories were not absent from Tito's mind. Far in the backward vista of his remembered life, when he was only seven years old, Baldassarre had rescued him from blows, had taken him to a home that seemed like opened paradise, where there was sweet food and soothing caresses, all had on Baldassarre's knee; and from that time till the hour they had parted, Tito had been the one centre of Baldassarre's fatherly cares.

And he had been docile, pliable, quick of apprehension, ready to acquire: a very bright lovely boy, a youth of even splendid grace, who seemed quite without vices, as if that beautiful form represented a vitality so exquisitely poised and balanced that it could know no uneasy desires, no unrest—a radiant presence for a lonely man to have won for himself. If he were silent when his father expected some response, still he did not look moody; if he declined some labour—why, he flung himself down with such a charming, half-smiling, half-pleading air, that the pleasure of looking at him made amends to one who had watched his growth with a sense of claim and possession: the curves of Tito's mouth had ineffable good humour in them. And then, the quick talent to which everything came readily, from philosophic systems to the rhymes of a street ballad caught up at a hearing! Would anyone have said that Tito had not made a rich return to his benefactor, or that his gratitude and affection would fail on any great demand?

He did not admit that his gratitude had failed; but rvas not certain that Baldassarre was in slavery, not certain that he was Hving.

"Do I not owe something to myself?" said Tito, inwardly, with a slight movement of his shoulders, the first he had made since he had turned to look down at the florins. "Before I quit everything, and incur again all the risks of which I am even now weary, I must at least have a reasonable hope. Am I to spend my life in a wandering search? believe he is dead. Cennini was right about my florins: I will place them in his hands to-morrow."

When, the next morning, Tito put this determination into act he had chosen his colour in the game, and had given an inevitable bent to his wishes. He had made it impossible that he should not from henceforth desire it to be the truth that his father was dead; impossible that he should not be tempted to baseness rather than that tlie precise facts of his conduct should not remain for ever concealed.

Under every guilty secret there is hidden a brood of guilty wishes, whose unwholesome infecting life is cherished by the darkness. The contaminating effect of deeds often lies less in the commission than in the consequent adjustment of our desires—the enlistment of our self-interest on the side of falsity; as, on the other hand, the purifying influence of public confession springs from the fact, that by it the hope in lies is for ever swept away, and the soul recovers the noble attitude of simplicity.

Besides, in this first distinct colloquy with himself the ideas which had previously been scattered and interrupted had now concentrated themselves: the little rills of selfishness had united and made a channel, so that they could never again meet with the same resistance. Hitherto Tito had left in vague indecision the question whether,

with the means in his power, he would not return, and ascertain his father's fate; he had now made a definite excuse to himself for not taking that course; he had avowed to himself a choice which he would have been ashamed to avow to others, and which would have made him ashamed in the resurgent presence of his father. But the inward shame, the reflex of that outward law which the great heart of mankind makes for every individual man, a reflex which will exist even in the absence of the sympathetic impulses that need no law, but rush to the deed of fidelity and pity as inevitably as the brute mother shields her young from the attack of the hereditary enemy—that inward shame was showing its blushes in Tito's determined assertion to himself that his father was dead, or that at least search was hopeless.

CHAPTER X.

UNDER THE PLANE-TREE.

On the day of San Giovanni it was already three weeks ago that Tito had handed his florins to Cennini, and we have seen that as he set out towards the Via de' Bardi he showed all the outward signs of a mind at ease. How should it be otherwise? He never jarred with what was immediately around him, and his nature was too joyous, too unapprehensive, for the hidden and the distant to grasp him in the shape of a dread. As he turned out of the hot sunshine into the shelter of a narrow street, took off the black cloth berretta, or simple cap with upturned lappet, which just crowned his brown curls, pushing his hair and tossing his head backward to court the cooler air, there was no brand of duplicity on his brow; neither

was there any stamp of candour: it was simply a finely formed, square, smooth young brow. And the slow absent glance he cast around at the upper windows of the houses had neither more dissimulation in it, nor more ingenuousness, than belongs to a youthful well-opened eyelid with its unwearied breadth of gaze; to perfectly pellucid lenses; to the undimmed dark of a rich brown iris; and to a pure cerulean-tinted angle of whiteness streaked with the delicate shadows of long eyelashes. Was it that Tito's face attracted or repelled according to the mental attitude of the observer? Was it a cypher with more than one key? The strong, unmistakable expression in his whole air and person was a negative one, and it was perfectly veracious; it declared the absence of any uneasy claim, any restless vanity, and it made the admiration that followed him as he passed among the troop of holiday-makers a thoroughly willing tribute.

For by this time the stir of the Festa was felt even in the narrowest side streets; the throng which had at one time been concentrated in the lines through which the procession had to pass, was now streaming out in all directions in pursuit of a new object. Such intervals of a Festa are precisely the moments when the vaguely active animal spirits of a crowd are likely to be the most petulant and most ready to sacrifice a stray individual to the greater happiness of the greater number. As Tito entered the neighbourhood of San Martino, he found the throng rather denser; and near the hostelry of the Bertucce, or Baboons, there was evidently some object which was arresting the passengers and forming them into a knot. It needed nothing of great interest to draw aside passengers unfreighted with a purpose, and Tito was preparing to turn aside into an adjoining street, when, amidst the loud

laughter, his ear discerned a distressed childish voice cry- | ing. "Loose me! Holy Virgin, help me!" which at once 1 determined him to push his way into the knot of gazers. He had just had time to perceive that the distressed voice came from a young contadina, whose white hood had fallen off in the struggle to get her hands free from the grasp of a man in the parti-coloured dress of a cerreiano, j or conjuror, who was making laughing attempts to soothe ' and cajole her, evidently carrying with him the amused , sympathy of the spectators, who by a persuasive variety j of words, signifying simpleton, for which the Florentine dialect is rich in equivalents, seemed to be arguing with the contadina against her obstinacy. At the first moment the girl's face was turned away, and he saw only her light brown hair plaited and fastened with a long silver pin; but in the next, the struggle brought her face opposite to Tito's, and he saw the baby features of Tessa, her blue eyes filled with tears, and her under-lip quivering. Tessa, too, saw him, and through the mist of her swelling tears there beamed a sudden hope, like that in the face of a little child, when, held by a stranger against its will, it sees a familiar hand stretched out.

In an instant Tito had pushed his way through the barrier of bystanders, whose curiosity made them ready to turn aside at the sudden interference of this handsome young signor, had grasped Tessa's waist, and had said, "Loose this child! What right have you to hold her against her will?"

The conjuror—a man with one of those faces in which the angles of the eyes and eyebrows, of the nostrils, mouth, and sharply defined jaw, all tend upward—showed his small regular teeth in an impish but not ill-natured grin, as he let go Tessa's hands, and stretched out his own

backward, slirngging his shoulders, and bending them forward a little in a half apologetic, half protesting manner.

"I meant the ragazza no evil in the world, Messere: ask this respectable company. I was only going to show them a few samples of my skill, in which this little damsel might have helped me the better because of her kitten face, which would have assured them of open dealing; and I had promised her a lapful of confetti as a reward. But what then? Messer has doubtless better confetti at hand, and she knows it."

A general laugh among the bystanders accompanied these last words of the conjuror, raised, probably, by the look of relief and confidence with which Tessa clung to Tito's arm, as he drew it from her waist and placed her hand within it. She only cared about the laugh as she might have cared about the roar of wild beasts from which she was escaping, not attaching any meaning to it; but Tito, who had no sooner got her on his arm than he foresaw some embarrassment in the situation, hastened to get clear of observers, who, having been despoiled of an expected amusement, were sure to re-establish the balance by jests.

"See, see, little one! here is your hood," said the conjuror, throwing the bit of white drapery over Tessa's head. " Orsii, bear me no malice; come l3ack to me when Messere can spare you."

"Ah! Maestro Vaiano, she'll come back presently, as the toad said to the harrow," called out one of the spectators, seeing how Tessa started and shrank at the action of the conjuror.

Tito pushed his way vigorously towards the corner of a side street, a little vexed at this delay in his progress to the Via de' Bardi, and intending to get rid of the poor

little contadina as soon as possible. The next street, too, had its passengers inclined to make holiday remarks at so unusual a pair; but they had no sooner entered it than he said, in a kind but hurried manner, "Now, little one, where were you going? Are you come by yourself to the Festa?"

"Ah, no!" said Tessa, looking frightened and distressed again; "I have lost my mother in the crowd—her and my father-in-law. They will be angry—he will beat me. It was in the crowd in San Pulinari—somebody pushed me along and I couldn't stop myself, so I got away from them. Oh, I don't know where they're gone! Please, don't leave me!"

Her eyes had been swelling with tears again, and she' ended with a sob.

Tito hurried along again: the Church of the Badia was not far off. They could enter it by the cloister that opened at the back, and in the church he could talk to Tessa—perhaps leave her. No! it was an hour at which the church was not open; but they paused under the shelter of the cloister, and he said, "Have you no cousin or friend in Florence, my little Tessa, whose house you could find; or are you afraid of walking by yourself since you have been frightened by the conjuror? I am in a hurry to get to Oltrarno, but if I could take you anywhere near "

"Oh, I am frightened: he was the devil—I know he was. And I don't know where to go—I have nobody: and my mother meant to have her dinner somewhere, and I don't know where. Holy Madonna! I shall be beaten."

The corners of the pouting mouth went down piteously, and the poor little bosom with the beads on it above the

green serge gown heaved so, that there was no longer any help for it: a loud sob would come, and the big tears fell as if they were making up for lost time. Here was a situation! It would have been brutal to leave her, and Tito's nature was all gentleness. He wished at that moment that he had not been expected in the Via de' Bardi. As he saw her lifting up her holiday apron to catch the hurrying tears, he laid his hand, too, on the apron, and rubbed one of the cheeks and kissed the babylike roundness.

"My poor little Tessa! leave off crying. Let us see what can be done. Where is your home—where do you live?"

There was no answer, but the sobs began to subside a little and the drops to fall less quickly.

"Come! I'll take you a little way, if you'll tell me where you want to go."

The apron fell, and Tessa's face began to look as contented as a cherub's budding from a cloud. The diabolical conjuror, the anger and the beating seemed a long way off.

"I think I'll go home, if you'll take me," she said, in a half whisper, looking up at Tito with wide blue eyes, and with something sweeter than a smile—with a childlike calm.

"Come, then, little one," said Tito, in a caressing tone, putting her arm within his again. "Which way is it?"

"Beyond Peretola—where the large pear-tree is."

"Peretola? Out at which gate, pazzarella? I am a stranger, you must remember."

"Out at the For del Prato," said Tessa, moving along with a very fast hold on Tito's arm.

He did not know all the turnings well enough to venture on an attempt at choosing the quietest streets; and besides, it occurred to him that where the passengers were most numerous there was, perhaps, the most chance of meeting with Monna Ghita and finding an end to his knight-errantship. So he made straight for Porta Rossa, and on to Ognissanti, showing his usual bright propitiatory-face to the mixed observers who threw their jests at him and his little heavy-shod maiden with much liberality. Mingled with the more decent holiday-makers there were frolicsome apprentices, rather envious of his good fortune; bold-eyed women with the badge of the yellow veil; beggars who thrust forward their caps for alms, in derision at Tito's evident haste; dicers, sharpers, and loungers of the worst sort; boys whose tongues were used to wag in concert at the most brutal street games: for the streets of Florence were not always a moral spectacle in those times, and Tessa's terror at being lost in the crowd was not wholly unreasonable.

When they reached the Piazza d'Ognissanti, Tito slackened his pace: they were both heated with their hurried walk, and here was a wider space where they could take breath. They sat down on one of the stone benches which were frequent against the walls of old Florentine houses.

"Holy Virgin!" said Tessa; "I am glad we have got away from those women and boys; but I was not frightened, because you could take care of me."

"Pretty little Tessa!" said Tito, smiling at her. "What makes you feel so safe with me?"

"Because you are so beautiful—like the people going into Paradise—they are all good."

"It is a long while since you had your breakfast, Tessa," said Tito, seeing some stalls near, with fruit and sweetmeats upon them, "Are you hungry?"

"Yes, I think I am—if you will have some too."

Tito bought some apricots, and cakes, and comfits, and put them into her apron.

"Come," he said, "let us walk on to the Prato, and then perhaps you will not be afraid to go the rest of the way alone."

"But you will have some of the apricots and things," said Tessa, rising obediently and gathering up her apron as a bag for her store,

"We will see," said Tito aloud; and to himself he said, "Here is a little contadina who might inspire a better idyl than Lorenzo de' Medici's Nencia da Barherino, that Nello's friends rave about; if I were only a Theocritus, or had time to cultivate the necessary experience by unseasonable walks of this sort! However, the mischief is done now: I am so late already that another half hour will make no difference. Pretty little pigeon!"

"We have a garden and plenty of pears," said Tessa, "and two cows, besides the mules; and I'm very fond of them. But the pairigno is a cross man: I wish my mother had not married him. I think he is wicked; he is very ugly."

"And does your mother let him beat you, poverina? You said you were afraid of being beaten."

"Ah, my mother herself scolds me: she loves my young sister better, and thinks I don't do work enough. Nobody speaks kindly to me, only the Pievano (parish priest) when I go to confession. And the men in the Mercato laugh at me and make fun of me. Nobody ever kissed me and spoke to me as you do; just as I talk to my little black-faced kid, because I'm very fond of it."

It seemed not to have entered Tessa's mind that there was any change in Tito's appearance since the morning he begged the milk from her, and that he looked now hke a personage for whom she must summon her little stock of reverent words and signs. He had impressed her too differently from any human being who had ever come near her before, for her to make any comparison of details; she took no note of his dress; he was simply a voice and a face to her, something come from Paradise into a world where most things seemed hard and angry; and she prattled with as little restraint as if he had been an imaginary companion born of her own lovingness and the sunshine.

They had now reached the Prato, which at that time was a large open' space within the walls, where the Florentine youth played at their favourite Calcio —a peculiar kind of football— and otherwise exercised themselves. At this midday time it was forsaken and quiet to the very gates, where a tent had been erected in preparation for the race. On the border of this wide meadow Tito paused and said,

"Now, Tessa, you will not be frightened if I leave you to walk the rest of the way by yourself Addio! Shall I come and buy a cup of milk from you in the Mercato to-morrow morning, to see that you are quite safe?"

He added this question in a soothing tone, as he saw her eyes widening sorrowfully; and the corners of her mouth falling. She said nothing at first; she only opened her apron and looked down at her apricots and sweetmeats. Then she looked up at him again, and said complainingly,—

"I thought you would have some, and we could sit

down under a tree outside the gate, and eat them together."

"Tessa, Tessa, you httle siren, you would ruin me," said Tito, laughing, and kissing both her cheeks. "I ought to have been in the Via de' Bardi long ago. No! I must go back now; you are in no danger. There—I'll take an apricot. Addio!"

He had already stepped two yards from her when he said the last word. Tessa could not have spoken; she was pale, and a great sob was rising; but she turned round as if she felt there was no hope for her, and stepped on, holding her apron so forgetfully that the apricots began to roll out on the grass.

Tito could not help looking after her, and seeing her shoulders rise to the bursting sob, and the apricots fall— could not help going after her and picking them up. It was very hard upon him: he was a long way off the Via de' Bardi, and very near to Tessa.

"See, my silly one," he said, picking up the apricots. "Come, leave off crying, I will go with you, and we'll sit down under the tree. Come, I don't like to see you cry; but you know I must go back some time."

So it came to pass that they found a great plane-tree] not far outside the gates, and they sat down under it, and all the feast was spread out on Tessa's lap, she leaning with her back against the trunk of the tree, and he stretched opposite to her, resting his elbows on the rough green growth cherished by the shade, while the sunlight stole through the boughs and played about them like a winged thing. Tessa's face was all contentment again, and the taste of the apricots and sweetmeats seemed very good.

"You pretty bird!" said Tito, looking at her as she sat eyeing the remains of the feast with an evident mental debate about saving them, since he had said he would not have any more. "To think of anyone scolding you! What sins do you tell of at confession, Tessa?"

"Oh, a great many. I am often naughty. I don't like work, and I can't help being idle, though I know I shall be beaten and scolded; and I give the mules the best fodder when nobody sees me, and then when the Madre is angry I say I didn't do it, and that makes me frightened at the devil. I think the conjuror was the devil. I am not so frightened after I've been to confession. And see, I've got a Breve here that a good father who came to Prato preaching this Easter blessed and gave us all." Here Tessa drew from her bosom a tiny bag carefully fiistened up. "And I think the Holy Madonna will take care of me; she looks as if she would; and perhaps if I wasn't idle, she wouldn't let me be beaten."

"If they are so cruel to you, Tessa, shouldn't you like to leave them, and go and live with a beautiful lady who would be kind to you, if she would have you to wait upon her?"

Tessa seemed to hold her breath for a moment or two. Then she said doubtfully, "I don't know."

"Then should you like to be my little servant, and live with me?" said Tito, smiling. He meant no more than to see what sort of pretty look and answer she would give.

There was a flush of joy immediately. "Will you take me with you now? Ah! I shouldn't go home and be beaten then." She paused a little while, and then added more doubtfully, "But I should like to fetch my black-faced kid."

"Yes, you must go back to your kid, my Tessa," said Tito, rising, "and I must go the other way."

"By Jupiter!" he added, as he went from under the shade of the tree, "it is not a pleasant time of day to walk from here to the Via de' Bardi; I am more inclined to lie down and sleep in this shade."

It ended so. Tito had an unconquerable aversion to anything unpleasant, even when an object very much loved and desired was on the other side of it. He had risen early; had waited; had seen sights, and had been already walking in the sun: he was inclined for a siesta, and inclined all the more because little Tessa was there, and seemed to make the air softer. He lay down on the grass again, putting his cap under his head on a green, tuft by the side of Tessa. That was not quite comfortable; so he moved again, and asked Tessa to let him rest his head against her lap; and in that way he soon fell asleep. Tessa sat quiet as a dove on its nest, just venturing, when he was fast asleep, to touch the wonderful dark curls that fell backward from his ear. She was too happy to go to sleep—too happy to think that Tito would wake up, and that then he would leave her, and she must go home. It takes very little water to make a perfect pool for a tiny fish, where it will find its world and paradise all in one, and never have a presentiment of the dry bank. The fretted summer shade, and stillness, and the gentle breathing of some loved life near—it would be paradise to us all, if eager thought, the strong angel with the implacable brow, had not long since closed the gates.

It really was a long while before the waking came— before the long dark eyes opened at Tessa, at first with a little surprise, and then with a smile, which was soon quenched by some preoccupying thought. Tito's deeper sleep had broken into a doze, in which he felt himself in' the Via de' Bardi, explaining his failure to appear at the appointed time. The clear images of that doze urged him to start up at once to a sitting posture, and as he stretched his arms and shook his cap he said,—

"Tessa, little one, you have let me sleep too long. My hunger and the shadows together tell me that the sun has done much travel since I fell asleep. I must lose no more time. Addio," he ended, patting her cheek with one hand, and settling his cap with the other.

She said nothing, but there were signs in her face which made him speak again in as serious and chiding a tone as he could command,—

"Now, Tessa, you must not cry. I shall be angry; I shall not love you if you cry. You must go home to your black-faced kid, or if you like you may go back to the gate and see the horses start. But I can stay with you no longer, and if you cry, I shall think you are troublesome to me."

The rising tears were checked by terror at this change in Tito's voice. Tessa turned very pale, and sat in trembling silence, with her blue eyes widened by arrested tears.

"Look now," Tito went on, soothingly, opening the wallet that hung at his belt, "here is a pretty charm that I have had a long while—ever since I was in Sicily, a country a long way off."

His wallet had many little matters in it mingled with small coins, and he had the usual difficulty in laying his finger on the right thing. He unhooked his wallet, and turned out the contents on Tessa's lap. Among them was his onyx ring.

"Ah, my ring!" he exclaimed, slipping it on the forefinger of his right hand. "I forgot to put it on again this morning. Strange, I never missed it! See, Tessa," he added, as he spread out the smaller articles, and selected the one he was in search of "See this pretty little pointed bit of red coral—like your goat's horn, is it not?—and here is a hole in it, so you can put on the cord round your neck along with your Breve, and then the evil spirits can't hurt you; if you ever see them coming in the shadow round the corner, point this little coral horn at them, and they will run away. It is a 'buon fortuna,' and will keep you from harm when I am not with you. Come, undo the cord."

Tessa obeyed with a tranquillising sense that life was going to be something quite new, and that Tito would be with her often. All who remember their childhood remember the strange vague sense, when some new experience came, that everything else was going to be changed, and that there would be no lapse into the old monotony. So the bit of coral was hung beside the tiny bag with the scrap of scrawled parchment in it, and Tessa felt braver.

"And now you will give me a kiss," said Tito, economising time by speaking while he swept in the contents of the wallet and hung it at his waist again, "and look happy, like a good girl, and then—"

But Tessa had obediently put forward her lips in a moment, and kissed his cheek as he hung down his head.

"Oh, you pretty pigeon!" cried Tito, laughing, pressing her round cheeks with his hands and crushing her features together so as to give them a general impartial kiss.

Then he started up and walked away, not looking

round till he was ten yards from her, when he just turned and gave a parting beck. Tessa was looking after him, but he could see that she was making no signs of distress. It was enough for Tito if she did not cry while he was present. The softness of his nature required that all sorrow should be hidden away from him.

"I wonder when Romola will kiss my cheek in that way?" thought Tito, as he walked along. It seemed a tiresome distance now, and he almost wished he had not been so soft-hearted, or so tempted to linger in the shade. No other excuse was needed to Bardo and Romola than saying simply that he had been unexpectedly hindered; he felt confident their proud delicacy would inquire no farther. He lost no time in getting to Ognissanti, and hastily taking some food there, he crossed the Arno by the Ponte alia Carraja, and made his way as directly as possible towards the Via de' Bardi.

But it was the hour when all the world who meant to be in particularly good time to see the Corso were returning from the Borghi, or villages just outside the gates, where they had dined and reposed themselves; and the thoroughfares leading to the bridges were of course the issues towards which the stream of sightseers tended. Just as Tito reached the Ponte Vecchio and the entrance of the Via de' Bardi, he was suddenly urged back towards the angle of the intersecting streets. A company on horseback, coming from the Via Guicciardini, and turning up the Via de' Bardi, had compelled the foot-passengers to recede hurriedly. Tito had been walking, as his manner was, with the thumb of his right hand resting in his belt; and as he was thus forced to pause, and was looking carelessly at the passing cavaliers, he felt a very thin cold hand laid on his. He started round,

and saw the Dominican friar whose upturned face had so struck him in the morning. Seen closer, the face looked more evidently worn by sickness and not by age; and again it brought some strong but indefinite reminiscences to Tito.

"Pardon me, but—from your face and your ring,"— said the friar, in a faint voice, "is not your name Tito Melema?"

"Yes," said Tito, also speaking faintly, doubtly jarred by the cold touch and the mystery. He was not apprehensive or timid through his imagination, but through his sensations and perceptions he could easily be made to shrink and turn pale like a maiden.

"Then I shall fulfil my commission."

The friar put his hand under his scapulary, and drawing out a small linen bag which hung round his neck, took from it a bit of parchment, doubled and stuck firmly together with some black adhesive substance, and placed it in Tito's hand. On the outside was written in Italian, in a small but distinct character—

"Tito Melema, aged twenty three, with a dark, beautiful face, long dark curls, the brightest smile, and a large onyx ring on his right forefinger."

Tito did not look at the friar, but tremblingly broke open the bit of parchment. Inside, the words were—

"I am sold for a slave: I think they are going to take me to Antioch. The gems alone will serve to ransom me."

Tito looked round at the friar, but could only ask a question with his eyes.

"I had it at Corinth," the friar said, speaking with difficulty, like one whose small strength had been overtaxed, "I had it from a man who was dying."

"He is dead, then?" said Tito, with a bounding of the heart.

"Not the writer. The man who gave it me was a pilgrim, Hke myself, to whom the writer had entrusted it, because he was journeying to Italy."

"You know the contents?"

"I do not know them, but I conjecture them. Your friend is in slavery—you will go and release him. But I am unable to talk now." The friar, whose voice had become feebler and feebler, sank down on the stone bench against the wall from which he had risen to touch Tito's hand, adding,

"I am at San Marco; my name is Fra Luca."

CHAPTER XI. TITO'S DILEMMA.

When Fra Luca had ceased to speak, Tito still stood by him in irresolution, and it was not till, the pressure of the passengers being removed, the friar rose and walked slowly into the church of Santa Felicita, that Tito also went on his way along the Via de' Bardi.

"If this monk is a Florentine," he said to himself— "if he is going to remain at Florence, everything must be disclosed." He felt that a new crisis had come, but he was not, for all that, too agitated to pay his visit to Bardo, and apologise for his previous non-appearance. Tito's talent for concealment was being fast developed into something less neutral. It was still possible—perhaps it might be inevitable—for him to accept frankly the altered conditions, and avow Baldassarre's existence; but hardly without casting an unpleasant light backward on his original

reticence as studied equivocation in order to avoid the fulfilment of a secretly recognised claim, to say nothing of his quiet settlement of himself and investment of his florins, when, it would be clear, his benefactor's fate had not been certified. It was at least provisionally wise to act as if nothing had happened, and, for the present, he would suspend decisive thought; there was all the night for meditation, and no one would know the precise moment at which he had received the letter.

So he entered the room on the second story, where Romola and her father sat among the parchment and the marble, aloof from the life of the streets on holiday as well as on common days, with a face only a little less bright than usual, from regret at appearing so late: a regret which wanted no testimony, since he had given up the sight of the Corso in order to express it; and then set himself to throw extra animation into the evening, though all the while his consciousness was at work like a machine with complex action, leaving deposits quite distinct from the line of talk; and by the time he descended the stone stairs and issued from the grim door in the starlight, his mind had really reached a new stage in its formation of a purpose.

And when, the next day, after he was free from his professional work, he turned up the Via del Cocomero, towards the convent of San Marco, his purpose was fully shaped. He was going to ascertain from Fra Luca precisely how much he conjectured of the truth, and on what grounds he conjectured it; and, further, how long he was to remain at San Marco. And on that fuller knowledge he hoped to mould a statement which would in any case save him from the necessity of quitting Florence, Tito had never had occasion to fabricate an ingenious lie be-

fore: the occasion was come now—the occasion which circumstance never fails to beget on tacit falsity; and his ingenuity was ready. For he had convinced himself that he was not bound to go in search of Baldassarre. He had once said that on a fair assurance of his father's existence and whereabouts, he would unhesitatingly go after him. But, after all, why was he bound to go! What, looked at closely, was the end of all life, but to extract the utmost sum of pleasure? And was not his own blooming life a promise of incomparably more pleasure, not for himself only, but for others, than the withered wintry life of a man who was past the time of keen enjoyment, and whose ideas had stiffened into barren rigidity? Those ideas had all been sown in the fresh soil of Tito's mind, and were lively germs there: that was the proper order of things—the order of nature, which treats all maturity as a mere nidus for youth. Baldassarre had done his work, had had his draught of life: Tito said it was his turn now.

And the prospect was so vague:—"I think they are going to take me to Antioch:" here was a vista! After a long voyage, to spend months, perhaps years, in a search for which even now there was no guarantee that it would not prove vain: and to leave behind at starting a life of distinction and love: and to find, if he found anything, the old exacting companionship which was known by rote beforehand. Certainly the gems and therefore the florins were, in a sense, Baldassarre's: in the narrow sense by which the right of possession is determined in ordinary affairs; but in that large and more radically natural view by which the world belongs to youth and strength, they were rather his who could extract the most pleasure out of them. That, he was conscious, was not the sentiment

which the conipHcated play of human feeUngs had engendered m society. The men around him would expect that he should immediately apply those florins to his benefactor's rescue. But what was the sentiment of society? —a mere tangle of anomalous traditions and opinions, that no wise man would take as a guide, except so far as his own comfort was concerned. Not that he cared for the florins save perhaps for Romola's sake: he would give up the florins readily enough. It was the joy that was due to him and was close to his lips, which he felt he was not bound to thrust away from him and travel on, thirsting. Any maxims that required a man to fling away the good that was needed to make existence sweet, were only the linins: of human selfishness turned outward: they were made by men who wanted others to sacrifice themselves for their sake. He would rather that Baldassarre should not suffer: he liked no one to suffer; but could any philosophy prove to him that he was bound to care for another's suffering more than for his own? To do so he must have loved Baldassarre devotedly, and he did not love him: was that his own fault? Gratitude! seen closely, it made no valid claim: his father's life would have been dreary without him: are we convicted of a debt to men for the pleasures they give themselves?

Having once begun to explain away Baldassarre's claim, Tito's thought showed itself as active as a virulent acid, eating its rapid way through all the tissues of sentiment. His mind was destitute of that dread which has been erroneously decried as if it were nothing higher than a man's animal care for his own skin: that awe of the Divine Nemesis which was felt by religious pagans, and, though it took a more positive form under Christianity, is still felt by the mass of mankind simply as a vague fear at any-

thing which is called wrong-doing. Such terror of the unseen is so far above mere sensual cowardice that it will annihilate that cowardice: it is the initial recognition of a moral law restraining desire, and checks the hard bold scrutiny of imperfect thought into obligations which can. never be proved to have any sanctity in the absence of feeling. "It is good," sing the old Eumenides, in ^schy-lus, "that fear should sit as the guardian of the soul, forcing it into wisdom—good that men should carry a threatening shadow in their hearts under the fiill sunshine; else, how shall they learn to revere the right?" That guardianship may become needless; but only when all outward law has become needless—only when duty and love have united in one stream and made a common force.

As Tito entered the outer cloister of San Marco, and inquired for Fra Luca, there was no shadowy presentiment in his mind: he felt himself too cultured and sceptical for that: he had been nurtured in contempt for the tales of priests whose impudent lives were a proverb, and in erudite familiarity with disputes concerning the Chief Good, which had after all, he considered, left it a matter of taste. Yet fear was a strong element in Tito's nature—the fear of what he believed or saw was likely to rob him of pleasure: and he had a definite fear that Fra Luca might be the means of driving him from Florence.

"Fra Luca? ah, he is gone toFiesole—to the Dominican monastery there. He was taken on a litter in the cool of the morning. The poor Brother is very ill. Could you leave a message for him?" J

This answer was given by a/m converse, or lay brother, whose accent told plainly that he was a raw contadino, and whose dull glance implied no curiosity.

"Thanks; my business can wait."

Tito turned away with a sense of rehef. "This friar is not likely to live," he said to himself. "I saw he was worn to a shadow. And at Fiesole there will be nothing to recall me to his mind. Besides, if he should come back, my explanation will serve as well then as now. But I wish I knew what it was that his face recalled to me."

CHAPTER Xir.
THE PRIZE IS NEARLY GRASPED.

Tito walked along with a light step, for the immediate fear had vanished; the usual joyousness of his disposition reassumed its predominance, and he was going to see Romola. Yet Romola's life seemed an image of that loving, pitying devotedness, that patient endurance of irksome tasks, from which he had shrunk and excused himself. But he was not out of love with goodness, or prepared to plunge into vice: he was in his fresh youth, with soft pulses for all charm and loveliness; he had still a healthy appetite for ordinary human joys, and the poison could only work by degrees. He had sold himself to evil, but at present life seemed so nearly the same to him that he was not conscious of the bond. He meant all things to go on as they had done before, both within and without him: he meant to win golden opinions by meritorious exertion, by ingenious learning, by amiable compliance: he was not going to do anything that would throw him out of harmony with the beings he cared for. And he cared supremely for Romola; he wished to have her for his majestic, beautiful, and loving wife. There might be a wealthier alliance within the ultimate reach of success-

ful accomplishments like his, but there was no woman in all Florence like Romola. When she was near him, and looked at him with her sincere hazel eyes, he was subdued by a delicious influence as strong and inevitable as those musical vibrations which take possession of us with a rhythmic empire that no sooner ceases than we desire. it to begin again.

As he trod the stone stairs, when he was still outside the door, with no one but Maso near him, the influence seemed to have begun its work by the mere nearness of anticipation.

"Welcome, Tito mio," said the old man's voice, before Tito had spoken. There was a new vigour in the voice, a new cheerfulness in the blind face, since that first interview more than two months ago. "You have brought fresh manuscript, doubtless; but since we were talking last night I have had new ideas: we must take a wider scope—we must go back upon our footsteps."

Tito, paying his homage to Romola as he advanced, went, as his custom was, straight to Bardo's chair, and put his hand in the palm that was held to receive it, placing himself on the cross-legged leather seat with scrolled ends, close to Bardo's elbow.

"Yes," he said, in his gentle way; "I have brought the new manuscript, but that can wait your pleasure. I have young limbs, you know, and can walk back up the hill without any difficulty."

He did not look at Romola as he said this, but he knew quite well that her eyes were fixed on him with delight.

"That is well said, my son." Bardo had already addressed Tito in this way once or twice of late. "And I perceive with gladness that you do not shrink from labour.

without which, the poet has wisely said, Hfe has given nothing to mortals. It is too often the 'palma sine pulvere,' the prize of glory without the dust of the race, that young ambition covets. But what says the Greek? 'In the morning of life, work; in the midday, give counsel; in the evening, pray.' It is true, I might be thought to have reached that helpless evening; but not so, while I have counsel within me wdiich is yet unspoken. For my mind, as I have often said, was shut up as by a dam; the plenteous waters lay dark and motionless, but you, my Tito, have opened a duct for them, and they rush forward with a force that surprises myself And now, what I want is, that we should go over our preliminary ground again, with a wider scheme of comment and illustration: otherwise I may lose opportunities which I now see retrospectively, and which may never occur again. You mark what I am saying, Tito?"

He had just stooped to reach his manuscript, which had rolled dow^n, and Bardo's jealous ear was alive to the slight movement.

Tito might have been excused for shrugging his shoulders at the prospect before him, but he was not naturally impatient; moreover, he had been bred up in that laborious erudition, at once minute and copious, which was the chief intellectual task of the age; and with Romola near, he was floated along by waves of agreeable sensation that made everything seem easy.

"Assuredly," he said; "you wish to enlarge your comments on certain passages we have cited."

"Not only so; I wish to introduce an occasional ex-cursus, where we have noticed an author to whom I have given special study; for I may die too soon to achieve any separate work. And this is not a time for scholarly in-

tegrity and well-sifted learning to lie idle, when it is not only rash ignorance that we have to fear, but when there' are men like Calderino, who, as Poliziano has well shown, have recourse to impudent falsities of citation to serve the ends of their vanity and secure a triumph to their own mistakes. Wherefore, my Tito, I think it not well that we should let slip the occasion that lies under our hands. And now we will turn back to the point where we have cited the passage from Thucydides, and I wish you, by way of preliminary, to go with me through all my notes on the Latin translation made by Lorenzo Valla, for which the incomparable Pope Nicholas V.—with whose personal notice I was honoured while I was yet young, and when he was still Thomas of Sarzana—paid him (I say not unduly) the sum of five hundred gold scudi. But inasmuch as Valla, though otherwise of dubious fame, is held in high honour for his severe scholarship, so that the epigrammatist has jocosely said of him that since he went among the shades, Pluto himself has not dared to speak in the ancient languages, it is the more needful that his name should not be as a stamp warranting false wares; and therefore I would introduce an excursus on Thucydides, wherein my castigations of Valla's text may find a fitting place. My Romola, thou wilt reach the needful volumes—thou knowest them—on the fifth shelf of the cabinet."

Tito rose at the same moment with Romola, saying, "I will reach them, if you will point them out," and followed her hastily into the adjoining small room, where the walls were also covered with ranges of books in perfect order.

"There they are," said Romola, pointing upward;
"every book is just where it was when my father ceased to see them."

Tito stood by her without hastening to reach the books. They had never been in this room together before.

"I hope," she continued, turning her eyes full on Tito, with a look of grave confidence—"I hope he will not weary you; this work makes him so happy."

"And me too, Romola—if you will only let me say, I love you—if you will only think me worth loving a little."

His speech was the softest murmur, and the dark beautiful face, nearer to hers than it had ever been before, was looking at her with beseeching tenderness.

"I do love you," murmured Romola: she looked at him with the same simple majesty as ever, but her voice had never in her life before sunk to that murmur. It seemed to them both that they were looking at each other a long while before her lips moved again; yet it was but a moment till she said, "I know now what it is to be happy."

The faces just met, and the dark curls mingled for an instant with the rippling gold. Quick as lightning after that, Tito set his foot on a projecting ledge of the bookshelves and reached down the needful volumes. They were both contented to be silent and separate, for that : first blissful experience of mutual consciousness was all the more exquisite for being unperturbed by immediate sensation.

It had all been as rapid as the irreversible mingling of waters, for even the eager and jealous Bardo had not become impatient.

"You have the volumes, my Romola?" the old man said, as they came near him again.

"And now you will get your pen ready; for, as Tito marks off the scholia we determine on extracting, it will be well for you to copy them without delay—numbering them carefully, mind, to correspond with the numbers he will put in the text he will write."

Romola always had some task which gave her a share in this joint work. Tito took his stand at the leggio, where he both wrote and read, and she placed herself at a table just in front of him, where she was ready to give into her father's hands anything that he might happen to want, or relieve him of a volume that he had done with. They had always been in that position since the work began, yet on this day it seemed new: it was so different now for them to be opposite each other; so different for Tito to take a book from her, as she lifted it from her father's knee. Yet there was no finesse to secure an additional look or touch. Each woman creates in her own likeness the love-tokens that are offered to her; and Romola's deep calm happiness encompassed Tito like the rich but quiet evening light which dissipates all unrest.

They had been two hours at their work, and were just desisting because of the fading light, when the door opened and there entered a figure strangely incongruous with the current of their thoughts and with the suggestions of every object around them. It was the figure of a short stout black-eyed woman, about fifty, wearing a black velvet berretta, or close cap, embroidered with pearls, under which surprisingly massive black braids surmounted the little bulging forehead, and fell in rich plaited curves over the ears, while an equally surprising carmine tint on the upper region of the fat cheeks contrasted with the surrounding sallowness. Three rows of pearls and a lower necklace of gold reposed on the horizontal cushion of her neck; the embroidered border of her trailing black-velvet gown and her embroidered long-drooping sleeves of rose-coloured damask, were slightly faded, but they conveyed to the initiated eye the satisfactory assurance that they were the splendid result of six months' labour by a skilled workman; and the rose-coloured petticoat, with its dimmed white fringe and seed-pearl arabesques, was duly exhibited in order to suggest a similar pleasing reflection. A handsome coral rosary hung from one side of an inferential belt, which emerged into certainty with a large clasp of silver wrought in niello; and, on the other side, where the belt again became inferential, hung a scarsella, or large purse, of crimson velvet, stitched with pearls. Her little fat right hand, which looked as if it had been made of paste, and had risen out of shape under partial baking, held a small book of devotions, also splendid with velvet, pearls, and silver.

The figure was already too familiar to Tito to be startling, for Monna Brigida was a frequent visitor at Bardo's, being excepted from the sentence of banishment passed on feminine triviality, on the ground of her cousin-ship to his dead wife and her early care for Romola, who now looked round at her with an affectionate smile, and rose to draw the leather seat to a due distance from her father's chair, that the coming gush of talk might not be too near his ear.

"La cugina?" said Bardo, interrogatively, detecting the short steps and the sweeping drapery.

"Yes, it is your cousin," said Monna Brigida, in an alert voice, raising her fingers smiling at Tito, and then lifting up her face to be kissed by Romola. "Always the troublesome cousin breaking in on your wisdom," she went on, seating herself and beginning to fan herself with the white veil hanging over her arm. "Well, well; if I didn't bring you some news of the world now and then, I do believe you'd forget there was anything in life but these mouldy ancients, who want sprinkling with holy water if all I hear about them is true. Not but what the world is bad enough nowadays, for the scandals that turn up under one's nose at every corner—/ don't want to hear and see such things, but one can't go about with one's head in a bag; and it was only yesterday—well, well, you needn't burst out at me, Bardo, I'm not going to tell anything; if I'm not as wise as the three kings, I know how-many legs go into one boot. But, nevertheless, Florence is a wicked city—is it not true, Messer Tito? for you go into the world. Not but what one must sin a little— Messer Domeneddio expects that of us, else what are the blessed sacraments for? And what I say is, we've got to reverence the saints, and not to set ourselves up as if we could be like them, else life would be unbearable; as it will be if things go on after this new fashion. For what do you think? I've been at the wedding to-day— Dianora Acciajoli's with the young Albizzi that there has been so much talk of—and everybody wondered at its being to-day instead of yesterday: but del! such a wedding as it was might have' been put off till the next Quaresima for a penance. For there was the bride looking like a white nun—not so much as a pearl about her —and the bridegroom as solemn as San Giuseppe. It's true! And half the people invited were Piagnoni —they call them Piagnoni'*' now, these new saints of Fra Giro-| lamo's making. And to think of two families like the! Albizzi and the Acciajoli taking up such notions, whenfc they could afford to wear the best! Well, well, theyF invited me—but they could do no other, seeing my hus-j!; * Funereal mourners: properly, paid mourners.

band was Luca Antonio's uncle by the mother's side— and a pretty time I had of it while we waited under the canopy in front of the house, before they let us in. I couldn't stand in my clothes, it seemed, without giving offence; for there Monna Berta, who has had worse secrets in her time than any I could tell of myself, looking askance at me from under her hood like a pinzochera* and telling me to read the Frate's book about widows, from which she had found great guidance. Holy Madonna! it seems as if widows had nothing to do now but to buy their coffins, and think it a thousand years till they get into them, instead of enjoying themselves a little when they've got their hands free for the first time. And what do you think was the music we had, to make our dinner lively? A long discourse from Fra Domenico of San Marco, about the doctrines of their blessed Fra Girolamo—the three doctrines we are all to get by heart; and he kept marking them off on his fingers till he made my flesh creep: and the first is, Florence, or the Church—I don't know which, for first he said one and then the other—shall be scourged; but if he means the pestilence, the Signory ought to put a stop to such preaching, for it's enough to raise the swelling under one's arms with fright; but then, after that, he says Florence is to be regenerated; but what will be the good of that when we're all dead of the plague, or something else? And then, the third thing, and what he said oftenest, is, that it's all to be in our days: and he marked that off on his thumb, till he made me tremble like the very jelly before me. They had jellies, to be sure, with the anus of the Albizzi and the Acciajoli raised on them in all colours; they've not turned the world quite upside down yet. But all their talk is, that we are to go * A Sister of the Third Order of St. Francis j an uncloistered nun.

back to the old ways: for up starts Francesco Valorl," that I've danced with in the Via Larga when he was a bachelor and as fond of the Medici as anybody, and he makes a speech about the old times, before the Florentines had left off crying 'Popolo' and begun to cry 'Palle' —as if that had anything to do with a wedding!—and how we ought to keep to the rules the Signory laid down heaven knows when, that we were not to wear this and that, and not to eat this and that—and how our manners were corrupted and we read bad books; though he can't say that of f7ie —"

"Stop, cousin!" said Bardo, in his imperious tone, for, he had a remark to make, and only desperate measures; could arrest the rattling lengthiness of Monna Brigida's discourse. But now she gave a little start, pursed up her mouth and looked at him with round eyes.

"Francesco Valori is not altogether wrong," Bardo went on. "Bernardo, indeed, rates him not highly, and is rather of opinion that he christens private grudges by the name of public zeal; though I must admit that my good Bernardo is too slow of belief in that unalloyed patriotism which was found in all its lustre amongst the ancients. But it is true, Tito, that our manners have degenerated somewhat from that noble frugality which, as has been well seen in the public acts of our citizens, is the parent of true magnificence. For men, as I hear, will now spend on the transient show of a Giostra sums which would suffice to found a library, and confer a lasting possession on mankind. Still, I conceive, it remains true of us Florentines that we have more of that magnanimous sobriety which abhors a trivial lavishness that it may be grandly open-handed on grand occasions, that can be found in any other city of Italy; for I understand that the

Neapolitan and Milanese courtiers laugh at the scarcity of our plate, and think scorn of our great families for borrowing from each other that furniture of the table at their entertainments. But in the vain laughter of folly wisdom hears half its applause."

"Laughter, indeed!" burst forth Monna Brigida again, the moment Bardo paused. "If anybody wanted to hear laughter at the wedding to-day they were disappointed, for when young Niccolo Macchiavelli tried to make a joke, and told stories out of Franco Sacchetti's book, how it was no use for the Signoria to make rules for us women, because we were cleverer than all the painters, and architects, and doctors of logic in the world, for we could make black look white, and yellow look pink, and crooked look straight, and, if anything was forbidden, we could find a new name for it—Holy Virgin! the Piagnoni looked more dismal than before, and somebody said Sacchetti's book was wicked. Well, I don't read it—they can't accuse me of reading anything. Save me from going to a wedding again if that's to be the fashion; for all of us who were not Piagnoni were as comfortable as wet chickens. I was never caught in a worse trap but once before, and that was when I went to hear their precious Frate last Quaresima in San Lorenzo. Perhaps I never told you about it, Messer Tito?—it almost freezes my blood when I think of it. How he rated us poor women! and the men, too, to tell the truth, but I didn't mind that so much. He called us cows, and lumps of flesh, and wantons, and mischief-makers—and I could just bear that, for there were plenty others more fleshy and spiteful than I was, though every now and then his voice shook the very bench under me like a trumpet; but then he came to the false hair, and, O misericordia! he made a picture—I see

it now—of a young woman lying a pale corpse, and us light-minded widows—of course he meant me as well as the rest, for I had my plaits on, for if one is getting old, one doesn't want to look as ugly as the Befana*—us widows rushing up to the corpse, like bare-pated vultures as we were, and cutting off its young dead hair to deck our old heads with. Oh, the dreams I had after that! And then he cried, and wrung his hands at us, and I cried too. And to go home, and to take off my jewels, this very clasp, and everything, and to make them into a packet, fu tiitt'uno; and I was within a hair of sending them to the Good Men of St. Martin to give to the poor, but, by heaven's mercy, I bethought me of going first to my confessor, Fra Cristoforo, at Santa Croce, and he told me how it was all the work of the devil, this preaching and prophesying of their Fra Girolamo, and the Dominicans were trying to turn the world upside down, and I was never to go and hear him again, else I must do penance for it; for the great preachers Fra Mariano and Fra Menico, had shown how Fra Girolamo preached lies—and that was true, for I heard them both in the Duomo—and how the Pope's dream of San Francesco propping up the Church with his arms was being fulfilled still, and the Dominicans were beginning to pull it down. Well and good: I went away con Dio, and made myself easy. I am not going to be frightened by a Frate Predicatore again. And all I say is, I wish it hadn't been the Dominicans that poor Dino joined years ago, for then I should have been glad when I heard them say he was come back "

* The name given to the grotesque black-faced figures, supposed to represent the Magi, carried about or placed in the windows on Twelfth Night: a corruption of Epifania.

"Silenzio!" said Bardo, in a loud agitated voice, while Romola half started from her chair, clasped her hands, and looked round at Tito, as if now she might appeal to him. Monna Brigida gave a little scream, and bit her lip.

"Donna!" said Bardo, again, "hear once more my will. Bring no reports about that name to this house; and thou, Romola, I forbid thee to ask. My son is dead."

Bardo's whole frame seemed vibrating with passion, and no one dared to break silence again. Monna Brigida lifted her shoulders and her hands in mute dismay; then she rose as quietly as possible, gave many significant nods to Tito and Romola, motioning to them that they were not to move, and stole out of the room like a culpable fat spaniel who has barked unseasonably.

Meanwhile, Tito's quick mind had been combining ideas with lightning-like rapidity. Bardo's son was not really dead, then, as he had supposed: he was a monk; he was "come back:" and Fra Luca—yes! it was the likeness to Bardo and Romola that had made the face seem half-known to him. If he were only dead at Fiesole at that moment! This importunate selfish wish inevitably thrust itself before every other thought. It was true that Bardo's rigid will was a sufficient safeguard against any intercourse between Romola and her brother; but not against the betrayal of what he knew to others, especially when the subject was suggested by the coupling of Romola's name with that of the very Tito Melema whose description he had carried round his neck as an index. No! nothing but Fra Luca's death could remove all danger; but his death was highly probable, and after the momentary shock of the discovery, Tito let his mind fall back in repose on that confident hope.

They had sat in silence, and in a deepening twilight for many minutes, when Romola ventured to say—

"Shall I light the lamp, father, and shall we go on?"

"No, my Romola, we will work no more to-night. Tito, come and sit by me here."

Tito moved from the reading-desk and seated himself on the other side of Bardo, close to his left elbow.

"Come nearer to me, figliuola mia," said Bardo again, after a moment's pause. And Romola seated herself on a low stool and let her arm rest on her father's right knee, that he might lay his hand on her hair, as he was fond of doing.

"Tito, I never told you that I had once a son," said Bardo, forgetting what had fallen from him in the emotion raised by their first interview. The old man had been deeply shaken and was forced to pour out his feelings in spite of pride. "But he left me—he is dead to me—I have disowned him for ever. He was a ready scholar as you are, but more fervid and impatient, and yet sometimes rapt and self-absorbed, like a flame fed by some fitful source; showing a disposition from the very first to turn away his eyes from the clear fights of reason and philosophy, and to prostrate himself under the influences of a dim mysticism which eludes all rules of human duty as it eludes all argument. And so it ended. We will speak no more of him: he is dead to me. I wish his face could be blotted from that world of memory in which the distant seems to grow clearer and the near to fade."

Bardo paused, but neither Romola nor Tito dared to speak—his voice was too tremulous, the poise of his feelings too doubtful. But he presently raised his hand and found Tito's shoulder to rest it on, while he went on speaking, with an effort to be calmer.

"But you have come to me, Tito—not quite too late. I will lose no time in vain regret. When you are working by my side I seem to have found a son again."

The old man, preoccupied with the governing interest of his life, was only thinking of the much-meditated book which had quite thrust into the background the suggestion, raised by Bernardo del Nero's warning, of a possible marriage between Tito and Romola. But Tito could not allow the moment to pass unused.

"Will you let me be always and altogether your son? Will you let me take care of Romola—be her husband. I think she will not deny me. She has said she loves me. I know I am not equal to her in birth—in anything; but I am no longer a destitute stranger."

"Is it true, my Romola?" said Bardo, in a lower tone, an evident vibration passing through him and dissipating the saddened aspect of his features.

"Yes, father," said Romola, firmly. "I love Tito—I wish to marry him, that we may both be your children and never part."

Tito's hand met hers in a strong clasp for the first time, while she was speaking, but their eyes were fixed anxiously on her father.

"Why should it not be?" said Bardo, as if arguing against any opposition to his assent, rather than assenting. "It would be a happiness to me; and thou, too, Romola, wouldst be the happier for it."

He stroked her long hair gently and bent towards her.

"Ah, I have been apt to forget that thou needest some other love than mine. And thou wilt be a noble wife. Bernardo thinks I shall hardly find a husband fitting for thee. And he is perhaps right. For thou art not like the herd of thy sex! thou art such a woman as the immortal poets had a vision of, when they sang the lives of the heroes—tender but strong, like thy voice, which has been to me instead of the light in the years of my blindness. . . . And so thou lovest him?"

He sat upright again for a minute and then said, in the same tone as before, "Why should it not be? I will think of it; I will talk with Bernardo."

Tito felt a disagreeable chill at this answer, for Bernardo del Nero's eyes had retained their keen suspicion whenever they looked at him, and the uneasy remembrance of Fra Luca converted all uncertainty into fear.

"Speak for me, Romola," he said, pleadingly. "Messer Bernardo is sure to be against me."

"No, Tito," said Romola, "my godfather will not oppose what my father firmly wills. And it is your will that I should marry Tito—is it not true, father? Nothing has ever come to me before that I have wished for strongly: I did not think it possible that I could care so much for anything that could happen to myself."

It was a brief and simple plea; but it was the condensed story of Romola's self-repressing colourless young life, which had thrown all its passion into sympathy with aged sorrows, aged ambition, aged pride and indignation. It had never occurred to Romola that she should not speak as directly and emphatically of her love for Tito as of any other subject.

"Romola mia!" said her father fondly, pausing on the words, "it is true thou hast never urged on me any wishes of thy own. And I have no will to resist thine; rather, my heart met Tito's entreaty at its very first utterance. Nevertheless, I must talk with Bernardo about the measures needful to be observed. For we must not act in haste, or do anything unbeseeming my name. I am poor, and held of little account by the wealthy of our family—nay, I may consider myself a lonely man—but I must nevertheless remember that generous birth has its obligations. And I would not be reproached by my fellow-citizens for rash haste in bestowing my daughter. Bartolommeo Scala gave his Alessandra to the Greek Marullo, but Marullo's lineage was well known, and Scala himself is of no extraction, I know Bernardo will hold that we must take time: he will, perhaps, reproach me with want of due forethought. Be patient, my children: you are very young." No more could be said, and Romola's heart was perfectly satisfied. Not so Tito's. If the subtle mixture of good and evil prepares suffering for human truth and purity, there is also suffering prepared for the wrong-doer by the same mingled conditions. As Tito kissed Romola on their parting that evening, the very strength of the thrill that moved his whole being at the sense that this woman, whose beauty it was hardly possible to think of as anything but the necessary consequence of her noble nature, loved him with all the tenderness that spoke in her clear eyes, brought a strong reaction of regret that he had not kept himself free from that first deceit which had dragged him into the danger of being disgraced before her. There was a spring of bitterness mingling with that fountain of sweets. Would the death of Fra Luca arrest it? He hoped it would.

CHAPTER XIII.
THE SHADOW OF NEIVIESIS.

It was the lazy afternoon time on the seventh of September, more than two months after the day on which Romola and Tito had confessed their love to each other.

Tito, just descended into Nello's shop, had found the barber stretched on the bench with his cap over his eyes; one leg was drawn up, and the other had slipped towards the ground, having apparently carried with it a manuscript volume of verse, which lay with its leaves crushed. In a corner sat Sandro, playing a game at ?nora by himself, and watching the slow reply of his left fingers to the arithmetical demands of his right with solemn-eyed interest.

Treading with the gentlest step, Tito snatched up the lute, and bending over the barber, touched the strings lightly while he sang,—

Quant' e bella giovinezza, Che si fugge tuttavia!

Chi viiol esser Ueto sia, Di doman non c'e certezza."*

Nello was as easily awaked as a bird. The cap was off his eyes in an instant, and he started up.

"Ah, my Apollino! I am somewhat late with my siesta on this hot day, it seems. That comes of not going to sleep in the natural way, but taking a potion of potent poesy. Hear you, how I am beginning to match my words by the initial letter, like a Trovatore? That is one of my bad symptoms: I am sorely afraid that the good wine of my understanding is going to run off at the spigot

Whoso would be joyful—let him! There's no surety for the morrow."

* "Beauteous is life in blossom! And it fleeteth—fleeteth ever;

Carnival Song h^' Lorenzo de' Medici.

of authorship, and I shall be left an empty cask with an odour of dregs, like many another incomparable genius of my acquaintance. What is it, my Orpheus?" here Nello stretched out his arms to their full length, and then brought them round till his hands grasped Tito's curls, and drew them out playfully. "What is it you want of your well-tamed Nello? For I perceive a coaxing sound in that soft strain of yours. Let me see the very needle's eyes of your desire, as the sublime poet says, that I may thread it."

"That is but a tailor's image of your subHme poet's," said Tito, still letting his fingers fall in a light dropping way on the strings. "But you have divined the reason of my affectionate impatience to see your eyes open. I want you to give me an extra touch of your art—not on my chin, no; but on the zazzera, which is as tangled as your Florentine politics. You have an adroit way of inserting your comb, which flatters the skin, and stirs the animal spirits agreeably in that region; and a little of your most delicate orange scent would not be amiss, for I am bound to the Scala palace, and am to present myself in radiant company. The young Cardinal Giovanni de' Medici is to be there, and he brings with him a certain young Bernardo Dovizi of Bibbiena, whose wit is so rapid, that I see no way of outrivalling it save by the scent of orange-blossoms."

Nello had already seized and flourished his comb, and pushed Tito gently backward into the chair, wrapping the cloth round him.

"Never talk of rivalry, bel giovane mio: Bernardo Dovizi is a keen youngster, who will never carry a net out to catch the wind; but he has something of the same sharp-muzzled look as his brother Ser Piero, the weasel

that Piero de' Medici keeps at his beck to slip through small holes for him. No! you distance all rivals, and may soon touch the sky with your forefinger. They tell me you have even carried enough honey with you to sweeten the sour Messer Angelo; for he has pronounced you less of an ass than might have been expected, considering there is such a good understanding between you and the Secretary."

"And between ourselves, Nello mio, that Messer Angelo has more genius and erudition than I can find in all the other Florentine scholars put together. It may answer very well for them to cry me up now, when Poli-ziano is beaten down with grief, or illness, or something else; I can try a flight with such a sparrow-hawk as Pietro Crinito, but for Poliziano, he is a large-beaked eagle who would swallow me feathers and all, and not feel any difference."

"I will not contradict your modesty there, if you will have it so; but you don't expect us clever Florentines to keep saying the same things over again every day of our lives, as we must do if we always told the truth. We cry down Dante, and we cry up Francesco Cei, just for the sake of variety; and if we cry you up as a new Poliziano, heaven has taken care that it shall not be quite so great a lie as it might have been. And are you not a pattern of virtue in this wicked city? with your ears double-waxed against all siren invitations that would lure you from the Via de' Bardi, and the great work which is to astonish posterity?"

"Posterity in good truth, whom it will probably astonish as the universe does, by the impossibility of seeing what was the plan of it."

"Yes, something like that was being prophesied here

the other day. Cristoforo Landino said that the excellent Bardo was one of those scholars who lie overthrown in their learning, like cavaliers in heavy armour, and then get angry because they are over-ridden—which pithy remark, it seems to me, was not a herb out of his own garden; for of all men, for feeding one with an empty spoon and gagging one with vain expectation by long discourse, Messer Cristoforo is the pearl. Ecco! you are perfect now." Here Nello drew away the cloth. "Impossible to add a grace more! But love is not always to be fed on learning, eh? I shall have to dress the zazzera for the betrothal before long—is it not true?"

"Perhaps," said Tito, smiling, "unless Messer Bernardo should next recommend Bardo to require that I should yoke a lion and a wild boar to the car of the Zecca before I can win my Alcestis. But I confess he is right in holding me unworthy of Romola; she is a Pleiad that may grow dim by marrying any mortal."

"Gnaffe, your modesty is in the right place there. Yet Fate seems to have measured and chiselled you for the niche that was left empty by the old man's son, who, by the way, Cronaca was telling me, is now at San Marco. Did you know?"

A slight electric shock passed through Tito as he rose from the chair, but it was not outwardly perceptible, for he immediately stooped to pick up the fallen book, and busied his fingers with flattening the leaves, while he said,

"No; he was at Fiesole, I thought. Are you sure he is come back to San Marco?"

"Cronaca is my authority," said Nello, with a shrug. "I don't frequent that sanctuary, but he does. Ah," he added, taking the book from Tito's hands, "my poor

Nencia da Barberino! It jars your scholarly feelings to see the pages dog's-eared. I was lulled to sleep by the well-rhymed charms of that rustic maiden—'prettier than the turnip-flower,' 'with a cheek more savoury than cheese.' But to get such a well-scented notion of the contadina, one must lie on velvet cushions in the Via Larga—not go to look at the Fierucoloni stumping in to the Piazza della Nunziata this evening after sundown."

"And pray who are the Fierucoloni?" said Tito, indifferently, settling his cap.

"The contadine who come from the mountains of Pistoia, and the Casentino, and heaven knows where, to keep their vigil in the church of the Nunziata, and sell their yarn and dried mushrooms at the Fierucola (petty fair), as we call it. They make a queer show, with their paper lanterns, howling their hymns to the Virgin on this eve of her nativity—if you had the leisure to see them. No?—well, I have had enough of it myself, for there is wild work in the Piazza. One may happen to get a stone or two about one's ears or shins without asking for it, and I was never fond of that pressing attention. Addio."

Tito carried a little uneasiness with him on his visit, which ended earlier than he had expected, the boy-cardinal Giovanni de' Medici, youngest of red-hatted fathers, who has since presented his broad dark cheek very conspicuously to posterity as Pope Leo the Tenth, having been detained at his favourite pastime of the chase, and having failed to appear. It still wanted half an hour of sunset as he left the door of the Scala palace, with the intention of proceeding forthwith to the Via de' Bardi; but he had not gone far when, to his astonishment, he saw Romola advancing towards him along the Borgo Pinti.

She wore a thick veil and black mantle, but it was

impossible to mistake her figure and her walk and by her side was a short stout form, which he recognised as that of Monna Brigida, in spite of the unusual plainness of her attire. Romola had not been bred up to devotional observances, and the occasions on which she took the air elsewhere than under the loggia on the roof of the house, were so rare and so much dwelt on beforehand, because of Bardo's dislike to be left without her, that Tito felt sure there must have been some sudden and urgent ground for an absence of which he had heard nothing the day before. She saw him through her veil and hastened her steps.

"Romola, has anything happened?" said Tito, turning to walk by her side.

She did not answer at the first moment, and Monna Brigida broke in.

"Ah, Messer Tito, you do well to turn round, for we are in haste. And is it not a misfortune?—we are obliged to go round by the walls and turn up the Via del Maglio, because of the Fair; for the contadine coming in block up the way by the Nunziata, which would have taken us to San Marco in half the time."

Tito's heart gave a great bound, and began to beat violently.

"Romola," he said, in a lower tone, "are you going to San Marco?"

They were now out of the Borgo Pinti and were under the city walls, where they had wide gardens on their left hand, and all was quiet. Romola put aside her veil for the sake of breathing the air, and he could see the subdued agitation in her face.

"Yes, Tito mio," she said, looking directly at him with sad eyes. "For the first time I am doing something un-known to my father. It comforts me tliat I have met you, for at least I can tell you. But if you are going to him, it will be well for you not to say that you met me. He thinks I am only gone to the cugina, because she sent for me. I left my godfather with him: he knows where I am going, and why. You remember that evening when my brother's name was mentioned and my father spoke of him to you?"

"Yes," said Tito, in a low tone. There was a strange complication in his mental state. His heart sank at the probability that a great change was coming over his prospects, while at the same time his thoughts were darting over a hundred details of the course he would take when the change had come; and yet he returned Romola's gaze with a hungry sense that it might be the last time she would ever bend it on him with full unquestioning confidence.

"The cugina had heard that he was come back, and the evening before—the evening of San Giovanni—as I afterwards found, he had been seen by our good Maso near the door of our house; but when Maso went to inquire at San Marco, Dino, that is, my brother—he was christened Bernardino, after our godfather, but now he calls himself Fra Luca—had been taken to the monastery at Fiesole, because he was ill. But this morning a message came to Maso, saying that he was come back to San Marco, and Maso went to him there. He is very ill, and he has adjured me to go and see him. I cannot refuse it, though I hold him guilty: I still remember how I loved him when I was a little girl, before I knew that he would forsake my father. And perhaps he has some word of; penitence to send by me. It cost me a struggle to act in opposition to my father's feelings, which I have always

held to be just. I am almost sure you will think I have chosen rightly, Tito, because I have noticed that your nature is less rigid than mine, and nothing makes you angry: it would cost you less to be forgiving; though, if you had seen your father forsaken by one to whom he had given his chief love—by one in whom he had planted his labour and his hopes—forsaken when his need was becoming greatest—even you, Tito, would find it hard to forgive."

What could he say? He was not equal to the hypocrisy of telling Romola that such offences ought not to be pardoned; and he had not the courage to utter any words of dissuasion.

"You are right, my Romola; you are always right, except in thinking too well of me."

There was really some genuineness in those last words, and Tito looked very beautiful as he uttered them, with an unusual pallor in his face, and a slight quivering of his lip. Romola, interpreting all things largely, like a mind prepossessed with high beliefs, had a tearful brightness in her eyes as she looked at him, touched with keen joy that he felt so strongly whatever she felt. But without pausing in her walk, she sai

"And now, Tito, I wish you to leave me, for the cugina and I shall be less noticed if we enter the piazza alone."

"Yes, it were better you should leave us," said Monna Brigida; "for to say the truth, Messer Tito, all eyes follow you, and let Romola muffle herself as she will, everyone wants to see what there is under her veil, for she has that way of walking like a procession. Not that I find fault with her for it, only it doesn't suit my steps. And, indeed, I would rather not have us seen going to San

Marco, and that's why I am dressed as if I were one of the Piagnoni themselves, and as old as Sant' Anna; for if it had been anybody but poor Dino, who ought to be forgiven if he's dying, for what's the use of having a grudge against dead people?—make them feel while they live, say I "

No one made a scruple of interrupting Monna Brigida, and Tito, having just raised Romola's hand to his lips, and said, "I understand, I obey you," now turned away, lifting his cap—a sign of reverence rarely made at that time by native Florentines, and which excited Bernardo del Nero's contempt for Tito as a fawning Greek, while to Romola, who loved homage, it gave him an exceptional grace.

He was half glad of the dismissal, half disposed to cling to Romola to the last moment in which she would love him without suspicion. For it seemed to him certain that this brother would before all things want to know, and that Romola would before all things confide to him, what was her father's position and her own after the years which must have brought so much change. She would tell him that she was soon to be publicly betrothed to a young scholar, who was to fill up the place left vacant long ago by a wandering son. He foresaw the impulse that would prompt Romola to dwell on that prospect, and what would follow on the mention of the future husband's name. Fra Luca would tell all he knew and conjectured, and Tito saw no possible falsity by which he could now ward off: the worst consequences of his former dissimulation. It was all over with his prospects in Florence. There was Messer Bernardo del Nero, who would be delighted at seeing confirmed the wisdom of his advice about deferring the betrothal until Tito's character and position had been established by a longer residence; and the history of the

young Greek professor whose benefactor was in slavery, would be the talk under every loggia. For the first time in his life he felt too fevered and agitated to trust his power of self-command; he gave up his intended visit to Bardo, and walked up and down under the walls until the yellow light in the west had quite faded, when, without any distinct purpose, he took the first turning, which happened to be the Via San Sebastiano, leading him directly towards the Piazza dell' Annunziata.

He was at one of those lawless moments which come to us all if we have no guide but desire, and the pathway where desire leads us seems suddenly closed; he was ready to follow any beckoning that offered him an immediate purpose.

CHAPTER XIV.

THE PEASANTS' FAIR.

The moving crowd and the strange mixture of noises that burst on him at the entrance of the piazza, reminded Tito of what Nello had said to him about the Fierucoloni, and he pushed his way into the crowd with a sort of pleasure in the hooting and elbowing, that filled the empty moments, and dulled that calculation of the future which had so new a dreariness for him, as he foresaw himself wandering away solitary in pursuit of some unknown fortune, that his thought had even glanced towards going in search of Baldassarre after all.

At each of the opposite inlets he saw people struggling into the piazza, while above them paper lanterns, held aloft on sticks, were waving uncertainly to and fro. A rude monotonous chant made a distinctly traceable strand of

noise, across which screams, whistles, gibing chants in piping boyish voices, the beating of nacchere or drums, and the ringing of httle bells, met each other in confused din. Every now and then one of the dim floating lights disappeared with a smash from a stone launched more or less vaguely in pursuit of mischief, followed by a scream and renewed shouts. But on the outskirts of the whirling tumult there were groups who were keeping this vigil of the Nativity of the Virgin in a more methodical manner than by fitful stone-throwing and gibing. Certain ragged men, darting a hard sharp glance around them while their tongues rattled merrily, were inviting country people to game with them on fair and open-handed terms; two masquerading figures on stilts, who had snatched lanterns from the crowd, were swaying the lights to and fro in meteoric fashion, as they strode hither and thither; a sage trader was doing a profitable business at a small covered stall, in hot berlingozzi, a favourite farinaceous delicacy; one man standing on a barrel, with his back firmly planted against a pillar of the loggia in front of the Foundling Hospital (Spedale degl' Innocenti), was selling efficacious pills, invented by a doctor of Salerno, warranted to prevent toothache and death by drowning; and not far off, against another pillar, a tumbler was showing off his tricks on a small platform; while a handful of 'prentices, despising the slack entertainment of guerilla stone-throwing, were having a private concentrated match of that favourite Florentine sport at the narrow entrance of the Via de' Febbrai.

Tito, obliged to make his way through chance openings in the crowd, found himself at one moment close to the trotting procession of barefooted, hard-heeled conta-dine, and could see their sun-dried, bronzed faces, and

their strange, fragmentary garb, dim with hereditary dirt, and of obsolete stuffs and fashions, that made them look, in the eyes of the city people, a wayworn ancestry returning from a pilgrimage on which they had set out a century ago. Just then it was the hardy, scant-feeding peasant-women from the mountains of Pistoia, who were entering with a year's labour in a moderate bundle on their backs, and in their hearts that meagre hope of good and that wide dim fear of harm, which were somehow to be cared for by the Blessed Virgin, whose miraculous image, painted by the angels, was to have the curtain drawn away from it on this Eve of her Nativity, that its potency might stream forth without obstruction.

At another moment he was forced away towards the boundary of the piazza, where the more stationary candidates for attention and small coin had judiciously placed themselves, in order to be safe in their rear. Among these Tito recognised his acquaintance Bratti, who stood with his back against a pillar and his mouth pursed up in disdainful silence, eyeing everyone who approached him with a cold glance of superiority, and keeping his hand fast on a serge covering which concealed the contents of the basket slung before him. Rather surprised at a deportment so unusual in an anxious trader, Tito went nearer and saw two women go up to Bratti's basket with a look of curiosity, whereupon the pedlar drew the covering tighter, and looked another way. It was quite too provoking, and one of the women was fain to ask what there was in his basket?

"Before I answer that, Monna, I must know whether you mean to buy, I can't show such wares as mine in this fair for every fly to settle on and pay nothing. My goods are a little too choice for that. Besides, I've only two left, and I've no mind to sell them; for with the chances of the pestilence that wise men talk of, there is likelihood of their being worth their weight in gold. No, no; andate con Dio."

The two women looked at each other.

"And what may be the price?" said the second.

"Not within what you are likely to have in your purse, buona donna," said Bratti, in a compassionately supercilious tone. "I recommend you to trust in Messer Do-meneddio and the saints: poor people can do no better for themselves."

"Not so poor!" said the second woman, indignantly, drawing out her money-bag. "Come, now! what do you say to a gross?"

"I say you may get twenty-one quattrini for it," said Bratti, coolly; "but not of me, for I haven't got that small change."

"Come; two, then?" said the woman, getting exasperated, while her companion looked at her with some envy. "It will hardly be above two, I think."

After further bidding, and further mercantile coquetry, Bratti put on an air of concession.

"Since you've set your mind on it," he said, slowly raising the cover, "I should be loth to do you a mischief; for Maestro Gabbadeo used to say, when a woman sets her mind on a thing and doesn't get it, she's in worse danger of the pestilence than before. Ecco! I have but two left; and let me tell you, the fellow to them is on the finger of Maestro Gabbadeo, who is gone to Bologna—as wise a doctor as sits at any door."

The precious objects were two clumsy iron rings, beaten into the fashion of old Roman rings, such as were sometimes disinterred. The rust on them, and the entirely hidden character of their potency, were so satisfactory, that the grossi were paid without grumbhng, and the first woman, destitute of those handsome coins, succeeded after much show of rehictance on Bratti's part in driving a bargain with some of her yarn, and carried off the remaining ring in triumph. Bratti covered up his basket, which was now filled with miscellanies, probably obtained under the same sort of circumstances as the yarn, and, moving from his pillar, came suddenly upon Tito, who, if he had had time, would have chosen to avoid recognition.

"By the head of San Giovanni, now," said Bratti, drawing Tito back to the pillar; "this is a piece of luck. For I was talking of you this morning, Messer Greco; but, I said, he is mounted up among the signori now—and I'm glad of it, for I was at the bottom of his fortune—but I can rarely get speech of him, for he's not to be caught lying on the stones now—not he! But it's your luck, not mine, Messer Greco, save and except some small trifle to satisfy me for my trouble in the transaction."

"You speak in riddles, Bratti," said Tito. "Remember, I don't sharpen my wits, as you do, by driving hard bargains for iron rings: you must be plain."

"By the Holy 'Vangels! it was an easy bargain I gave them. If a Hebrew gets thirty-two per cent., I hope a Christian may get a little more. If I had not borne a conscience, I should have got twice the money and twice the yarn. But, talking of rings, it is your ring—that very ring you've got on your finger—that I could get you a purchaser for; ay, and a purchaser with a deep moneybag."

"Truly?" said Tito, looking at his ring and listening.

"A Genoese who is going straight away into Hungary, as I understand. He came and looked all over my shop to see if I had any old things I didn't know the price of; I warrant you, he thought I had a pumpkin on my shoulders. He had been rummaging all the shops in Florence. And he had a ring on—not like yours, but something of the same fashion; and as he was talking of rings, I said I knew a fine young man, who was a particular acquaintance of mine, who had a ring of that sort. And he said, 'Who is he, pray? Tell him I'll give him his price for it.' And I thought of going after you to Nello's to-morrow; for it's my opinion of you, Messer Greco, that you're not one who'd see the Arno run broth, and stand by without dipping your finger."

Tito had lost no word of what Bratti had said, yet his mind had been very busy all the while. Why should he keep the ring? It had been a mere sentiment, a mere fancy, that had prevented him from selling it with the other gems; if he had been wiser and had sold it, he might perhaps have escaped that identification by Fra Luca. It was true that it had been taken from Baldas-sarre's finger and put on his as soon as his young hand had grown to the needful size; but there was really no valid good to anybody in those superstitious scruples about inanimate objects. The ring had helped towards the recognition of him. Tito had begun to dislike recognition, which was a claim from the past. This foreigner's offer, if he would really give a good price, was an opportunity for getting rid of the ring without the trouble of seeking a purchaser.

"You speak with your usual wisdom, Bratti," said Tito. "I have no objection to hear what your Genoese will offer. But when and where shall I have speech of him?"

"To-morrow, at three hours after sunrise, he will be at my shop, and if your wits are of that sharpness I have always taken them to be, Messer Greco, you will ask him a heavy price; for he minds not money. It's my belief he's buying for somebody else, and not for himself—perhaps for some great signor."

"It is well," said Tito. "I will be at your shop, if nothing hinders."

"And you will doubtless deal nobly by me for old acquaintance' sake, Messer Greco, so I will not stay to fix the small sum you will give me in token of my service in tlie matter. It seems to me a thousand years now till I get out of the piazza, for a fair is a dull, not to say a \\icked thing, wlaen one has no more goods to sell."

Tito made a hasty sign of assent and adieu, and moving away from the pillar, again found himself pushed towards the middle of the piazza and back again, without the power of determining his own course. In this zigzag way he was carried along to the end of the piazza opposite tlie church, where, in a deep recess formed by an irregularity in the line of houses, an entertainment was going forward which seemed to be especially attractive to the crowd. Loud bursts of laughter interrupted a monologue which was sometimes slow and oratorical, at others rattling and buffoonish. Here a girl was being pushed forward into the inner circle with apparent reluctance, and there a loud laughing minx was finding a way with her own elbows. It was a strange light that was spread over the I piazza. There were the pale stars breaking out above, ' and the dim waving lanterns below, leaving all objects indistinct except when they were seen close under the fitfully moving lights; but in this recess there was a stronger light, against which the heads of the encircling spectators stood in dark relief as Tito was gradually pushed towards them, while above them rose the head of a man wearing a white mitre with yellow cabalistic figures upon it.

"Behold, my children!" Tito heard him saying, "behold your opportunity! neglect not the holy sacrament of matrimony when it can be had for the small sum of a white quattrino—the cheapest matrimony ever offered, and dissolved by special bull beforehand at every man's own will and pleasure. Behold the bull!" Here the speaker held up a piece of parchment with huge seals attached to it. "Behold the Indulgence granted by his Holiness Alexander the Sixth, who, being newly elected Pope for his peculiar piety, intends to reform and purify the Church, and wisely begins by abolishing that priestly abuse which keeps too large a share of this privileged matrimony to the clergy and stints the laity. Spit once, my sons, and pay a white quattrino! This is the whole and sole price of the Indulgence. The quattrino is the only difference the Holy Father allows to be put any longer between us and the clergy—who spit and pay nothing."

Tito thought he knew the voice, which had a peculiarly sharp ring, but the face was too much in shadow from the lights behind for him to be sure of the features. Stepping as near as he could, he saw within the circle behind the speaker an altar-like table raised on a small platform, and covered with a red drapery stitched all over with yellow cabalistical figures. Half-a-dozen thin tapers burned at the back of this table, which had a conjuring apparatus scattered over it, a large open book in the centre, and at one of the front angles a monkey fastened by a cord to a small ring and holding a small taper, which in his incessant fidgety movements fell more or less aslant, while an impish boy in a white surplice occupied

lumself chiefly in cuffing the monkey, and adjusting the j taper. The man in the mitre also wore a sur-phce, and over it a chasuble on which the signs of the zodiac were rudely marked in black upon a yellow ground. Tito was sure now that he recognised the sharp upward-tending angles of the face under the mitre: it was that of Maestro A'aiano, the cerreiano, from whom he had rescued Tessa. Pretty little Tessa! Perhaps she too had come in among ^ the troops of contadine ?

"Come, my maidens! This is the time for the pretty who can have many chances, and for the ill-favoured who have few. Matrimony to be had hot, eaten, and done with as easily as berlingozzi! And see!" here the conjuror held up a cluster of tiny bags. "To every bride I give a Breve with a secret in it—the secret alone worth the money you pay for the matrimony. The secret how to—no, no, I will not tell you what the secret is about, and that makes it a double secret. Hang it round your neck if you like, and never look at it; I don't say that will not be the best, for then you will see many things you don't expect: though if you open it you may break your leg, e vero, but you will know a secret! Something nobody knows but me! And mark—I give you the Breve, I don't sell it, as many another holy man would: the quattrino is for the matrimony, and the Breve you get for nothing. Orsii, giovanetti, come like dutiful sons of Ithe Church and buy the Indulgence of his Holiness I Alexander the Sixth."

This buffoonery just fitted the taste of the audience; the fierucola was but a small occasion, so the townsmen might be contented with jokes that were rather less indecent than those they were accustomed to hear at every carnival, put into easy rhyme by the Magnifico and his

poetic satellites; while the women, over and above any relish of the fun, really began to have an itch for the Brevi. Several couples had already gone through the ceremony, in which the conjuror's solemn gibberish and grimaces over the open book, the antics of the monkey, and even the preliminary spitting, had called forth peals of laughter; and now a well-looking, merry-eyed youth of seventeen, in a loose tunic and red cap, pushed forward, holding by the hand a plump brunette, whose scanty ragged dress displayed her round arms and legs very picturesquely,

"Fetter us without delay, Maestro!" said the youth, "for I have got to take my bride home and paint her under the light of a lantern."

"Ha! Mariotto, my son, I commend your pious observance. ..." The conjuror was going on, when a loud chattering behind warned him that an unpleasant crisis had arisen with his monkey.

The temper of that imperfect acolyte was a little tried by the over-active discipline of his colleague in the surplice, and a sudden cuff administered as his taper fell to a horizontal position, caused him to leap back with a violence that proved too much for the slackened knot by which his cord was fastened. His first leap was to the other end of the table, from which position his remonstrances were so threatening that the imp in the surplice took up a wand by way of an equivalent threat, whereupon the monkey leaped on to the head of a tall woman in the foreground, dropping his taper by the way, and chattering with increased emphasis from that eminence. Great was the screaming and confusion, not a few of the spectators having a vague dread of the Maestro's monkey, as capable of more hidden mischief than mere teeth and

claws could inflict; and the conjuror himself was in some alarm lest any harm should happen to his familiar. In the scuffle to seize the monkey's string, Tito got out of the circle, and, not caring to contend for his place again, he allowed himself to be gradually pushed towards the church of the Nunziata, and to enter amongst the worshippers.

The brilliant illumination within seemed to press upon his eyes with palpable force after the pale scattered lights and broad shadows of the piazza, and for the first minute or two he could see nothing distinctly. That yellow splendour was in itself something supernatural and heavenly to some of the peasant-women, for whom half the sky was hidden by mountains, and who went to bed in the twilight; and the uninterrupted chant from the choir was repose to the ear after the hellish hubbub of the crowd outside. Gradually the scene became clearer, though still there was a thin yellow haze from incense mingling with the breath of the multitude. In a chapel on the left hand of the nave, wreathed with silver lamps, was seen unveiled the miraculous fresco of the Annunciation, which, in Tito's oblique view of it from the right-hnnd side of the nave, seemed dark with the excess of light around it. The whole area of the great church was filled with peasant-women, some kneeling, some standing; the coarse bronzed skins, and the dingy clothing of the rougher dwellers on the mountains, contrasting with the softer-lined faces and white or red head-drapery of the well-to-do dwellers in the valley, who were scattered in irregular groups. And spreading high and far over the walls and ceiling there was another multitude, also pressing close against each other, that they might be nearer the potent Virgin. It was the crowd of votive waxen images,

ROMOLA.

the effigies of great personages, clothed in their habit as they hved; Florentines of high name in their black silk lucco, as when they sat in council; popes, emperors, kings, cardinals, and famous condottieri with plumed morion seated on their chargers; all notable strangers who passed through Florence or had aught to do with its affairs— Mahomedans, even, in well-tolerated companionship with Christian cavaliers; some of them with faces blackened and robes tattered by the corroding breath of centuries, others fresh and bright in new red mantle or steel corselet, the exact doubles of the living. And wedged in with all these were detached arms, legs, hands, and other members, with only here and there a gap where some image had been removed for public disgrace, or had fallen ominously, as Lorenzo's had done six months before. It was a perfect resurrection-swarm of remote mortals and fragments of mortals, reflecting, in their varying degrees of freshness, the sombre dinginess and sprinkled brightness of the crowd below.

Tito's glance wandered over the wide multitude in search of something. He had already thought of Tessa, and the white hoods suggested the possibility that he might detect her face under one of them. It was at least a thought to be courted, rather than the vision of Romola looking at him with changed eyes. But he searched in vain; and he was leaving the church, weary of a scene which had no variety, when, just against the doorway, he caught sight of Tessa, only two yards off him. She was kneeling with her back against the wall, behind a group of peasant-women, who were standing and looking for a spot nearer to the sacred image. Her head hung a little aside with a look of weariness, and her blue eyes were directed rather absently towards an altar-piece where the

Archangel Michael stood in his armour, with young face and floating hair, amongst bearded and tonsured saints. Her right hand, holding a bunch of cocoons, fell by her side listlessly, and her round cheek was paled, either by the light or by the weariness that was expressed in her attitude: her lips were pressed poutingly together, and every now and then her eyelids half fell: she was a large image of a sweet sleepy child. Tito felt an irresistible desire to go up to her and get her pretty trusting looks and prattle: this creature who was without moral judgments that could condemn him, whose little loving ignorant soul made a world apart, where he might feel in freedom from suspicions and exacting demands, had a new attraction for him now. She seemed a refuge from the threatened isolation that would come with disgrace. He glanced cautiously round, to assure himself that Monna Ghita was not near, and then, slipping quietly to her side, kneeled on one knee, and said, in the softest voice, "Tessa!"

She hardly started any more than she would have started at a soft breeze that fanned her gently when she was needing it. She turned her head and saw Tito's face close to her: it was very much more beautiful than the Archangel Michael, who was so mighty and so good that he lived with the Madonna and all the saints and was prayed to along with them. She smiled in happy silence, for that nearness of Tito quite filled her mind.

"My little Tessa! you look very tired. How long have you been kneeling here?"

She seemed to be collecting her thoughts for a minute or two, and at last she said—

"I'm very hungry."

"Come, then; come with me."

He lifted her from her knees, and led her out under

the cloisters surrounding the atrium, which were then open, and not yet adorned with the frescoes of Andrea del Sarto.

"How is it you are all by yourself, and so hungry, Tessa?"

"The Madre is ill; she has very bad pains in her legs, and sent me to bring these cocoons to the Santissima Nunziata, because they're so wonderful; see!"—she held up the bunch of cocoons, which were arranged with fortuitous regularity on a stem,—"and she had kept them to bring them herself, but she couldn't, and so she sent me because she thinks the Holy Madonna may take away her pains; and somebody took my bag with the bread and chestnuts in it, and the people pushed me back, and I was so frightened coming in the crowd, and I couldn't get anywhere near the Holy Madonna, to give the cocoons to the Padre, but I must—oh, I must."

"Yes, my little Tessa, you shall take them; but come first and let me give you some berlingozzi. There are some to be had not far off."

"Where did you come from?" said Tessa, a little bewildered. "I thought you would never come to me again, because you never came to the Mercato for milk any more. I set myself Aves to say, to see if they would bring you back, but I left off, because they didn't."

"You see I come when you want someone to take care of you, Tessa. Perhaps the Aves fetched me, only it took them a long while. But what shall you do if you are here all alone? Where shall you go?"

"Oh, I shall stay and sleep in the church—a great many of them do—in the church and all about here—1| did once when I came with my mother; and the patrigno is coming with the mules in the morning."

They were out in the piazza now, where the crowdl

"was rather less riotous than before, and the lights were fewer, the stream of pilgrims having ceased. Tessa clung fast to Tito's arm in satisfied silence, while he led her towards the stall where he remembered seeing the eatables. Their way was the easier because there was just now a great rush towards the middle of the piazza, where the masqued figures on stilts had found space to execute a dance. It was very pretty to see the guileless thing giving her cocoons into Tito's hand, and then eating her berlingozzi with the relish of a hungry child. Tito had really come to take care of her, as he did before, and that wonderful happiness of being with him had begun again for her. Her hunger was soon appeased, all the sooner for the new stimulus of happiness that had roused her from her languor, and, as they turned away from the stall, she said nothing about going into the church again, but looked round as if the sights in the piazza were not without attraction to her now she was safe under Tito's arm.

"How can they do that?" she exclaimed, looking up at the dancers on stilts. Then, after a minute's silence, "Do you think Saint Christopher helps them?"

"Perhaps. What do you think about it, Tessa?" said Tito, slipping his right arm round her, and looking down at her fondly.

"Because Saint Christopher is so very tall; and he is very good; if anybody looks at him he takes care of them all day. He is on the wall of the church—too tall to stand up there—but I saw him walking through the streets one San Giovanni, carrying the little Gesu."

"You pretty pigeon! Do you think anybody could help taking care oi you, if you looked at them?"

"Shall you always come and take care of me?" said

Tessa, turning her face up to him, as he crushed her cheek with his left hand. "And shall you always be a long while first?"

Tito was conscious that some bystanders were laughing at them, and though the licence of street fun among artists and young men of the wealthier sort, as well as among the populace, made few adventures exceptional, still less disreputable, he chose to move away towards the end of the piazza.

"Perhaps I shall come again to you very soon, Tessa," he answered, rather dreamily, when they had moved away. He was thinking that when all the rest had turned their backs upon him, it would be pleasant to have this little creature adoring him and nestling against him. The absence of presumptuous self-conceit in Tito made him feel all the more defenceless under prospective obloquy: he needed soft looks and caresses too much ever to be impudent.

"In the Mercato?" said Tessa. "Not to-morrow morning, because the patrigno will be there, and he is so cross. Oh! but you have money, and he will not be cross if you buy some salad. And there are some chestnuts. Do you like chestnuts?"

He said nothing, but continued to look down at her with a dreamy gentleness, and Tessa felt herself in a state of delicious wonder; everything seemed as new as if she were being carried on a chariot of clouds.

"Holy Virgin!" she exclaimed again presently. "There is a holy father like the Bishop I saw at Prato."

Tito looked up too, and saw that he had unconsciously advanced to within a few yards of the conjuror, Maestro Vaiano, who, for the moment, was forsaken by the crowd. His face was turned away from them, and he was occupied with the apparatus on his altar or table, preparing a new diversion by the time the interest in the dancing should be exhausted. The monkey was imprisoned under the red cloth, out of reach of mischief, and the youngster in the white surplice was holding a sort of dish or salver, from which his master was taking some ingredient. The altar-like table, with its gorgeous cloth, the row of tapers, the sham episcopal costume, the surpliced attendant, and even the movements of the mitred figure, as he alternately bent his head and then raised something before the lights, were a sufficiently near parody of sacred things to rouse poor little Tessa's veneration; and there was some additional awe produced by the mystery of their apparition in this spot, for when she had seen an altar in the street before, it had been on Corpus Christi Day, and there had been a procession to account for it. She crossed herself and looked up at Tito, but then, as if she had had time for reflection, said, "It is because of the Nativita."

Meanwhile Vaiano had turned round, raising his hands to his mitre with the intention of changing his dress, when his quick eye recognised Tito and Tessa who were both looking at him, their faces being shone upon by the light of his tapers, while his own was in shadow.

"Ha! my children!" he said, instantly, stretching out his hands in a benedictory attitude, "you are come to be married. I commend your penitence—the blessing of Holy Church can never come too late."

But whilst he was speaking, he had taken in the whole meaning of Tessa's attitude and expression, and he discerned an opportunity for a new kind of joke which required him to be cautious and solemn.

"Should you like to be married to me, Tessa?" said Tito, softly, half enjoying the comedy, as he saw the pretty

childish seriousness on her face, half prompted by hazy previsions which belonged to the intoxication of despair.

He felt her vibrating before she looked up at him and said, timidly, "Will you let me?"

He answered only by a smile, and by leading her forward in front of the cerretano, who, seeing an excellent jest in Tessa's evident delusion, assumed a surpassing sacerdotal solemnity, and went through the mimic ceremony with a liberal expenditure of lingua fnrbesca or thieves' Latin. But some symptoms of a new movement in the crowd urged him to bring it to a speedy conclusion and dismiss them with hands outstretched in a benedictory attitude over their kneeling figures. Tito, disposed always to cultivate goodwill, though it might be the least select, put a piece of four grossi into his hand as he moved away, and was thanked by a look which, the conjuror felt sure, conveyed a perfect understanding of the whole affair.

But Tito himself was very far from that understanding, and did not, in fact, know, whether the next moment, he should tell Tessa of the joke and laugh at her for a little goose, or whether he should let her delusion last, and see what would come of it—see what she would say and do next.

"Then you will not go away from me again," said Tessa, after they had walked a few steps, "and you will take me to where you live." She spoke meditatively, and not in a questioning tone. But presently she added, "I must go back once to the Madre, though, to tell her I brought the cocoons, and that I'm married, and shall not go back again."

Tito felt the necessity of speaking now; and, in the rapid thought prompted by that necessity, he saw that by undeceiving Tessa he should be robbing himself of some

at least of that pretty trustfulness which might, by-and-by, be his only haven from contempt. It would spoil Tessa to make her the least particle wiser or more suspicious.

"Yes, my little Tessa," he said, caressingly, "you must go back to the Madre; but you must not tell her you are married—you must keep that a secret from everybody; else some very great harm would happen to me, and you would never see me again.'"

She looked up at him with fear in her face.

"You must go back and feed your goats and mules, and do just as you have always done before, and say no word to anyone about me."

The corners of her mouth fell a little.

"And then, perhaps, I shall come and take care of you again when you want me, as I did before. But you must do just what I tell you, else you will not see me again."

"Yes, I will, I will," she said, in a loud whisper, frightened at that blank prospect.

They were silent a little while; and then Tessa, looking at her hand, said,—

"The Madre wears a betrothal ring. She went to church and had it put on, and then after that, another day, she was married. And so did the cousin Nannina. But then she married Gollo," added the poor little thing, entangled in the difficult comparison between her own case and others within her experience.

"But you must not wear a betrothal ring, my Tessa, because no one must know you are married," said Tito, feeling some insistance necessary. "And the buona fortuna that I gave you did just as well for betrothal. Some people are betrothed with rings and some are not."

"Yes, it is true, they would see the ring," said Tessa,

trying to convince herself that a thing she would like very much was really not good for her.

They were now near the entrance of the church again, ai:d she remembered her cocoons which were still in Tito's hand.

"Ah, you must give me the boto," she said; "and we must go in, and I must take it to the Padre, and I must tell the rest of my beads, because I was too tired before."

"Yes, you must go in, Tessa; but I will not go in. I must leave you now," said Tito, too fevered and weary to re-enter that stifling heat, and feeling that this was the least difficult way of parting with her.

"And not come back? Oh, where do you go?" Tessa's mind had never formed an image of his whereabouts or his doings when she did not see him: he had vanished, and her thought, instead of following him, had stayed in the same spot where he was with her.

"I shall come back some time, Tessa," said Tito, taking her under the cloisters to the door of the church. "You must not cry—you must go to sleep, when you have said your beads. And here is money to buy your breakfast. Now kiss me, and look happy, else I shall not come again."

She made a great effort over herself as she put up her lips to kiss him, and submitted to be gently turned round, with her face towards the door of the church. Tito saw her enter; and then with a shrug at his own resolution, leaned against a pillar, took off his cap, rubbed his hair backward, and wondered where Romola was now, and what she was thinking of him. Poor little Tessa had disappeared behind the curtain among the crowd of conta-dine; but the love which formed one web with all his worldly hopes, with the ambitions and pleasures that must

make the solid part of his days—the love that was identified with his larger self—was not to be banished from his consciousness. Even to the man who presents the most elastic resistance to whatever is unpleasant,' there will come moments when the pressure from without is too strong for him, and he must feel the smart and the bruise in spite of himself Such a moment had come to Tito. There was no possible attitude of mind, no scheme of action by which the uprooting of all his newly-planted hopes could be made otherwise than painful.

CHAPTER XV.

THE DYING MESSAGE.

When Romola arrived at the entrance of San Marco she found one of the Frati waiting there in expectation of her arrival. Monna Brigida retired into the adjoining church, and Romola was conducted to the door of the chapter-house in the outer cloister, whither the invalid had been conveyed; no woman being allowed admission beyond this precinct.

When the door opened, the subdued external light blending with that of two tapers placed behind a truckle-bed, showed the emaciated face of Fra Luca, with the tonsured crown of golden hair above it, and with deep-sunken hazel eyes fixed on a small crucifix which he held before him. He was propped up into nearly a sitting posture; and Romola was just conscious, as she threw aside her veil, that there was another monk standing by the bed, with the black cowl drawn over his head, and that he moved towards the door as she entered; just conscious that in the background there was a crucified form

rising high and pale on the frescoed wall, and pale faces of sorrow looking out from it below.

The next moment her eyes met Fra Luca's as they looked up at her from the crucifix, and she was absorbed in that pang of recognition which identified this monkish emaciated form with the image of her fair young brother.

"Dino!" she said, in a voice like a low cry of pain. But she did not bend towards him; she held herself erect, and paused at two yards' distance from him. There was an unconquerable repulsion for her in that monkish aspect; it seemed to her the brand of the dastardly undutifulness which had left her father desolate—of the grovelling superstition which could give such undutifulness the name of piety. Her father, whose proud sincerity and simplicity of life had made him one of the few frank pagans of his time, had brought her up with a silent ignoring of any claims the Church could have to regulate the belief and action of beings with a cultivated reason. The Church, in her mind, belonged to that actual life of the mixed multitude from which they had always lived apart, and she had no ideas that could render her brother's course an object of any other feeling than incurious, indignant contempt. Yet the lovingness of Romola's soul had clung to that image in the past, and while she stood rigidly aloof, there was a yearning search in her eyes for something too faintly discernible.

But there was no corresponding emotion in the face of the monk. He looked at the little sister returned to him in her full womanly beauty, with the far-off gaze of a revisiting spirit.

"My sister!" he said, with feeble and interrupted but yet distinct utterance, "it is well thou hast not longer de-

layed to come, for I have a message to deliver to thee, and my tune is short."

Romola took a step nearer: the message, she thought, would be one of affectionate penitence to her father, and her heart began to open. Nothing could wipe out the long years of desertion; but the culprit, looking back on those years with the sense of irremediable wrong committed, would call forth pity. Now, at the last, there would be understanding and forgiveness. Dino would poor out some natural filial feeling; he would ask questions about his father's blindness—how rapidly it had come on? how the long dark days had been filled? what the life was now in the home where he himself had been nourished?—and the last message from the dying lips would be one of tenderness and regret.

"Romola," Fra Luca began again, "I have had a vision concerning thee. Thrice I have had it in the last two months: each time it has been clearer. Tlierefore I came from Fiesole, deeming it a message from heaven that I was bound to deliver. And I gather a promise of mercy to thee in this, that my breath is preserved in order to—"

The difficult breathing which continually interrupted him would not let him finish the sentence.

Romola had felt her heart chilling again. It was a vision, then, this message—one of those visions she had so often heard her father allude to with bitterness. Her indignation rushed to her lips.

"Dino, I thought you had some words to send to my father. You forsook him when his sight was failing; you made his life very desolate. Have you never cared about that? never repented? What is this religion of yours, that places visions before natural duties?"

The deep-sunken hazel eyes turned slowly towards her, and rested upon her in silence for some moments, as if he were meditating whether he should answer her.

"No," he said at last; speaking, as before, in a low passionless tone, as if his voice were that of some spirit not human, speaking through dying human organs. "No; I have never repented fleeing from the stifling poison-breath of sin that was hot and thick around me, and threatened to steal over my senses like besotting wine. My father could not hear the voice that called me night and day; he knew nothing of the demon-tempters that tried to drag me back from following it. My father has lived amidst human sin and misery without believing in them: he has been like one busy picking shining stones in a mine, while there was a world dying of plague above him. I spoke, but he listened with scorn. I told him the studies he wished me to live for were either childish trifling—dead toys—or else they must be made warm and living by pulses that beat to worldly ambitions and fleshly lusts; for worldly ambitions and fleshly lusts made all the substance of the poetry and history he wanted me to bend my eyes on continually."

"Has not my father led a pure and noble life, then?" Romola burst forth, unable to hear in silence this implied accusation against her father. "He has sought no worldly honours; he has been truthful; he has denied himself all luxuries; he has lived like one of the ancient sages. He never wished you to live for worldly ambitions and fleshly lusts; he wished you to live as he himself has done, according to the purest maxims of philosophy, in which he brought you up."

Romola spoke partly by rote, as all ardent and sympathetic young creatures do; but she spoke with intense belief. The pink flush was in her face, and she quivered from head to foot. Her brother was again slow to answer, looking at her passionate face with strange passionless eyes.

"What were the maxims of philosophy to me? They told me to be strong, when I felt myself weak; when I was ready, like the blessed Saint Benedict, to roll myself among thorns, and court smarting wounds as a deliverance from temptation. For the Divine love had sought me, and penetrated me, and created a great need in me; like a seed that wants room to grow. I had been brought up in carelessness of the true faith; I had not studied the doctrines of our religion; but it seemed to take possession of me like a rising flood. I felt that there was a life of l)erfect love and purity for the soul; in which there would be no uneasy hunger after pleasure, no tormenting questions, no fear of suffering. Before I knew the history of the saints, I had a foreshadowing of their ecstasy. For the same truth had penetrated even into pagan philosophy; that it is a bliss within the reach of man to die to mortal needs, and live in the life of God as the Unseen Perfectness. But to attain that I must forsake the world: I must have no affection, no hope, that wedded me to that which passeth away; I must live with my fellow-beings only as human souls related to the eternal unseen life. That need was urging me continually: it came over me in visions when my mind fell away weary from the vain words which record the passions of dead men; it came over me after I had been tempted into sin and had turned away with loathing from the scent of the emptied cup. And in visions I saw the meaning of the Crucifix."

He paused, breathing hard for a minute or two: but Romola was not prompted to speak again. It was useless for her mind to attempt any contact with the mind of this unearthly brother: as useless as for her hand to try and grasp a shadow. He went on as soon as his heaving chest was quieter.

"I felt whom I must follow: but I saw that even among the servants of the Cross who professed to have renounced the world, my soul would be stifled with the fumes of hypocrisy, and lust, and pride. God had not chosen me, as he chose Saint Dominic and Saint Francis, to wrestle with evil in the Church and in the world. He called upon me to flee: I took the sacred vows and I'fled —fled to lands where danger and scorn and want bore me continually, like angels, to repose on the bosom of God. I have lived the life of a hermit, I have ministered to pilgrims; but my task has been short: the veil has worn very thin that divides me from my everlasting rest. I came back to Florence that—"

"Dino, you did want to know if my father was alive," interrupted Romola, the picture of that suffering life touching her again with the desire for union and forgiveness.

"—that before I died I might urge others of our brethren to study the Eastern tongues, as I had not done, and go out to greater ends than I did, and I find them already bent on the work. And since I came, Romola, I have felt that I was sent partly to thee—not to renew the bonds of earthly affection, but to deliver the heavenly warning conveyed in a vision. For I have had that vision thrice. And through all the years since first the Divine voice called me, while I was yet in the world, I have been taught and guided by visions. For in the painful linking together of our waking thoughts we can never be sure that we have not mingled our own error with the light we have prayed for; but in visions and dreams we

are passive, and our souls are as an instrument in the Divine hand. Therefore listen, and speak not again—for the time is short."

Romola's mind recoiled strongly from listening to this vision. Her indignation had subsided, but it was only because she had felt the distance between her brother and herself widening. But while Fra Luca was speaking, the figure of another monk had entered, and again stood on the other side of the bed, with the cowl drawn over his head.

"Kneel, my daughter, for the Angel of Death is present, and waits while the message of heaven is delivered: bend thy pride before it is bent for thee by a yoke of iron," said a strong rich voice, startlingly in contrast with Fra Luca's.

The tone was not that of imperious command, but of quiet self-possession and assurance of the right, blended with benignity. Romola, vibrating to the sound, looked round at the figure on the opposite side of the bed. His face was hardly discernible under the shadow of the cowl, and her eyes fell at once on his hands, which were folded across his breast and lay in relief on the edge of his black mantle. They had a marked physiognomy wliich enforced the influence of the voice: they were very beautiful and almost of transparent delicacy. Romola's disposition to rebel against command, doubly active in the presence of monks, whom she had been taught to despise, would have fixed itself on any repulsive detail as a point of support. But the face was hidden, and the hands seemed to have an appeal in them against all hardness. The next moment the right hand took the crucifix to relieve the fatigued grasp of Fra Luca, and the left touched Jiis lips with a wet sponge which lay near. In the act of

Romola. I. 14

bending, the cowl was pushed back, and the features of the monk had the full light of the tapers on them. They were very marked features, such as lend themselves to popular description. There was the high arched nose, the prominent under lip, the coronet of thick dark hair above the brow, all seeming to tell of energy and passion; there were the blue-grey eyes, shining mildly under auburn eyelashes, seeming, like the hands, to tell of acute sensitiveness. Romola felt certain they were the features of Fra Girolamo Savonarola, the prior of San Marco, whom she had chiefly thought of as more offensive than other monks, because he was more noisy. Her rebellion was rising against the first impression, which had almost forced her to bend her knees.

"Kneel, my daughter," the penetrating voice said again, "the pride of the body is a barrier against the gifts that purify the soul."

He was looking at her with mild fixedness while he spoke, and again she felt that subtle mysterious influence of a personality by which it has been given to some rare men to move their fellows.

Slowly Romola fell on her knees, and in the very act a tremor came over her; in the renunciation of her proud erectness, her mental attitude seemed changed, and she found herself in a new state of passiveness. Her brother began to speak again.

"Romola, in the deep night, as I lay awake, I saw my father's room—the library—with all the books and the marbles and the leggio, where I used to stand and read; and I saw you—you were revealed to me as I see you now, with fair long hair, sitting before my father's chair. And at the leggio stood a man whose face I could not see—I looked, and looked, and it was a blank to me, even as a painting effaced; and I saw him move and take thee, Romola, by the hand; and then I saw thee take my father by the hand; and you all three went down the stone steps into the streets, the man whose face was a blank to me leading the way. And you stood at the altar in Santa Croce, and the priest who married you had the face of death; and the graves opened, and the dead in their shrouds rose and followed you like a bridal train. And you passed on through the streets and the gates into the valley, and it seemed to me that he who led you hurried you more than you could bear, and the dead were weary of following you, and turned back to their graves. And at last you came to a stony place where there was no water, and no trees or herbage; but instead of water, I saw written parchment unrolling itself everywhere, and instead of trees and herbage I saw men of bronze and marble springing up and crowding round you. And my father was faint for want of water and fell to the ground; and the man whose face was a blank loosed thy hand and departed: and as he went I could see his face; and it was the face of the Great Tempter. And thou, Romola, didst wring thy hands and seek for water, and there was none. And the bronze and marble figures seemed to mock thee and hold out cups of water, and when thou didst grasp them and put them to my father's lips, they turned to parchment. And the bronze and marble figures seemed to turn into demons and snatch my father's body from thee, and the parchments shrivelled up, and blood ran everywhere instead of them, and fire upon the blood, till they all vanished, and the plain was bare and stony again, and thou wast alone in the midst of it. And then it seemed that the night fell and I saw no more. . . . Thrice I have had that vision, Romola. I believe it is a

revelation meant for thee—to warn thee against marriage as a temptation of the enemy—it calls upon thee to dedicate thyself "

His pauses had gradually become longer and more frequent, and he was now compelled to cease by a severe fit of gasping, in which his eyes were turned on the crucifix as on a light that was vanishing. Presently he found strength to speak again, but in a feebler, scarcely audible tone.

"To renounce the vain philosophy and corrupt thoughts of the heathens: for in the hour of sorrow and death their pride will turn to mockery, and the unclean gods will "

The words died away.

In spite of the thought that was at work in Romola, telling her that this vision was no more than a dream, fed by youthful memories and ideal convictions, a strange awe had come over her. Her mind was not apt to be assailed by sickly fancies; she had the vivid intellect and the healthy human passion, which are too keenly alive to the constant relations of things to have any morbid craving after the exceptional. Still the images of the vision she despised jarred and distressed her like painful and cruel cries. And it was the first time she had witnessed the struggle with approaching death: her young life had been sombre, but she had known nothing of the utmost human needs; no acute suffering—no heart-cutting sorrow; and this brother, come back to her in his hour of supreme agony, was like a sudden awful apparition from an invisible world. The pale faces of sorrow in the fresco on the opposite wall seemed to have come nearer, and to make one company with the pale face on the bed.

"Frate," said the dying voice.

Fra Girolamo leaned down. But no other word came for some moments.

"Romola," it said next.

She leaned forward too: but again there was silence. The words were struggling in vain.

"Fra Girolamo, give her "

"The crucifix," said the voice of Fra Girolamo.

No other sound came from the dying lips.

"Dino!" said Romola, with a low but piercing cry, as the certainty came upon her that the silence of misunderstanding could never be broken.

"Take the crucifix, my daughter," said Fra Girolamo, after a few minutes. "His eyes behold it no more."

Romola stretched out her hand to the crucifix, and this act appeared to relieve the tension of her mind. A great sob burst from her. She bowed her head by the side of her dead brother, and wept aloud. It seemed to her as if this first vision of death must alter the daylight for her for evermore.

Fra Girolamo moved towards the door, and called in a lay Brother who was waiting outside. Then he went up to Romola and said in a tone of gentle command, "Rise, my daughter, and be comforted. Our brother is with the blessed. He has left you the crucifix, in remembrance of the heavenly warning—that it may be a beacon to you in the darkness."

She rose from her knees, trembling, folded her veil over her head, and hid the crucifix under her mantle. Fra Girolamo then led the way out into the cloistered court, lit now only by the stars and by a lantern which was held by someone near the entrance. Several other figures in the dress of the dignified laity were grouped about the same spot. They were some of the numerous frequenters of San Marco, who had come to visit the Prior, and having heard that he was in attendance on the dying Brother in the chapter-house, had awaited him here.

Romola was dimly conscious of footsteps, and rustling forms moving aside: she heard the voice of Fra Girolamo, saying, in a low tone, "Our brother is departed;" she felt a hand laid on her arm. The next moment the door was opened, and she was out in the wide piazza of San Marco, with no one but Monna Brigida, and the servant carrying the lantern.

The fresh sense of space revived her, and helped her to recover her self-mastery. The scene which had just closed upon her was terribly distinct and vivid, but it began to narrow under the returning impressions of the life that lay outside it. She hastened her steps, with nervous anxiety to be again with her father—and with Tito—for were they not together in her absence? The images of that vision, while they clung about her like a hideous dream not yet to be shaken off, made her yearn all the more for the beloved faces and voices that would assure her of her waking life.

Tito, we know, was not with Bardo; his destiny was being shaped by a guUty consciousness, urging on him the despairing belief that by this time Romola possessed the knowledge which would lead to their final separation.

And the lips that could have conveyed that knowledge were for ever closed. The prevision that Fra Luca's words had imparted to Romola had been such as comes from the shadowy region where human souls seek wisdom apart from the human sympathies which are the very life and substance of our wisdom; the revelation that might have come from the simple questions of filial and brotherly affection had been carried into irrevocable silence.

CHAPTER XVI. A FLORENTINE JOKE.

Early the next morning Tito was returning from Bratti's shop in the narrow thoroughfare of the Ferra-vecchi. The Genoese stranger had carried away the onyx ring, and Tito was carrying away fifty florins. It did just cross his mind that if, after all, Fortune, by one of her able devices, saved him from the necessity of quitting Florence, it would be better for him not to have parted with his ring, since he had been understood to wear it for the sake of pecuHar memories and predilections; still, it was a slight matter, not worth dwelling on with any emphasis, and in those moments he had lost his confidence in fortune. The feverish excitement of the first alarm which had impelled his mind to travel into the future had given place to a dull, regretful lassitude. He cared so much for the pleasures that could only come to him through the good opinion of his fellow-men, that he wished now he had never risked ignominy by shrinking from what his fellow-men called obligations.

But our deeds are like children that are born to us; they live and act apart from our own will. Nay, children may be strangled, but deeds never: they have an indestructible life both in and out of our consciousness; and that dreadful vitality of deeds was pressing hard on Tito for the first time.

He was going back to his lodgings in the Piazza di San Giovanni, but he avoided passing through the Mercato Vecchio, which was his nearest way, lest he should see

Tessa. He was not in the humour to seek anything; he could only await the first sign of his altering lot.

The piazza with its sights of beauty was lit up by that warm morning sunlight under which the autumn dew still lingers and which invites to an idleness undulled by fatigue. It was a festival morning too, when the soft warmth seems to steal over one with a special invitation to lounge and gaze. Here too the signs of the fair were present; in the spaces round the octagonal baptistery, stalls were being! spread with fruit and flowers, and here and there laden|| mules were standing quietly absorbed in their nose-bags, while their drivers were perhaps gone through the hospitable sacred doors to kneel before the Blessed Virgin on this morning of her Nativity. On the broad marble steps 11 of the Duomo there were scattered groups of beggars and gossipping talkers: here an old crone with white hair and 'j hard sunburnt face encouraging a round-capped baby to try its tiny bare feet on the warmed marble, while a dog sitting near snuffed at the performance suspiciously; there i I a couple of shaggy-headed boys leaning to watch a small pale cripple who was cutting a face on a cherry-stone; and above them on the wide platform men were making changing knots in laughing desultory chat, or else were standing in close couples gesticulating eagerly.

But the largest and most important company of loungers was that towards which Tito had to direct his steps. It y was the busiest time of the day with Nello, and in this warm season and at an hour when clients were numerous, most men preferred being shaved under the pretty red and white awning in front of the shop rather than within narrow walls. It is not a sublime attitude for a man, to sit with lathered chin thrown backward, and have his nose made a handle of; but to be shaved was a fashion of

Florentine respectability, and it is astonishing how gravely men look at each other when they are all in the fashion. It was the hour of the day too when yesterday's crop of gossip was freshest, and the barber's tongue was always in its glory when his razor was busy; the deft activity of those two instruments seemed to be set going by a common spring. Tito foresaw that it would be impossible for him to escape being drawn into the circle; he must smile and retort, and look perfectly at his ease. Well! it was but the ordeal of swallowing bread and cheese pills after all. The man who let the mere anticipation of discovery choke him was simply a man of weak nerves.

But just at that time Tito felt a hand laid on his shoulder, and no amount of previous resolution could prevent the very unpleasant sensation with which that sudden touch jarred him. His face, as he turned it round, betrayed the inward shock; but the owner of the hand that seemed to have such evil magic in it broke into a light laugh. He was a young man about Tito's own age, with keen features, small close-clipped head, and close-shaven lip and chin, giving the idea of a mind as little encumbered as possible with material that was not nervous. The keen eyes were bright with hope and friendliness, as so many other young eyes have been that have afterwards closed on the world in bitterness and disappointment; for at that time there were none but pleasant predictions about Niccolo Macchiavelli, as a young man of promise, who was expected to mend the broken fortunes of his ancient family.

"Why, Melema, what evil dream did you have last night, that you took my light grasp for that of a shirro or something worse?"

"Ah, Messer Niccolo!" said Tito, recovering himself immediately; "it must have been an extra amount of dul-

ness in my veins this morning that shuddered at the approach of your wit. But the fact is, I have had a bad night."

"That is unlucky, because you will be expected to shine without any obstructing fog to-day in the Rucellai Gardens. I take it for granted you are to be there."

"Messer Bernardo did me the honour to invite me," said Tito; "but I shall be engaged elsewhere."

"Ah! I remember, you are in love," said Macchiavelli, with a shrug, "else you would never have such inconvenient engagements. Why, we are to eat a peacock and ortolans under the loggia among Bernardo Rucellai's rare trees; there are to be the choicest spirits in Florence and the choicest wines. Only, as Piero de' Medici is to be there, the choice spirits may happen to be swamped in the capping of impromptu verses. I hate that game; it is a device for the triumph of small wits, who are always inspired the most by the smallest occasions."

"What is that you are saying about Piero de' Medici and small wits, Messer Niccolo?" said Nello, whose light figure was at that moment predominating over the Herculean frame of Niccolo Caparra.

That famous worker in iron, whom we saw last with bared muscular arms and leathern apron in the Mercato Vecchio, was this morning dressed in holiday suit, and as he sat submissively while Nello skipped round him, lathered him, seized him by the nose, and scraped him with magical quickness, he looked much as a lion might if it had donned linen and tunic and was preparing to go into society.

"A private secretary will never rise in the world if he couples great and small in that way," continued Nello. "When great men are not allowed to marry their sons and daughters as they like, small men must not expect to

marry their words as they hke. Have you heard the news Domenico Cennini, here, has been telHng us?—that Pagol-antonio Soderini has given Ser Piero da Bibbiena a box on the ear for setting on Piero de' Medici to interfere with the marriage between young Tommaso Soderini and Fiam-metta Strozzi, and is to be sent ambassador to Venice as a punishment?"

"I don't know which I envy him most," said Macchia-velH, "the offence or the punishment. The offence will make him the most popular man in all Florence, and the punishment will take him among the only people in Italy who have known how to manage their own affairs."

"Yes, if Soderini stays long enough at Venice," said Cennini, "he may chance to learn the Venetian fashion, and brinar it home with him. The Soderini have been fast friends of the Medici, but what has happened is likely to open Pagolantonio's eyes to the good of our old Florentine trick of choosing a new harness when the old one galls us; if we have not quite lost the trick in these last fifty years."

"Not we," said Niccolo Caparra, who was rejoicing in the free use ot his lips again. "Eat eggs in Lent and the snow will melt. That's what I say to our people when they get noisy over their cups at San Gallo, and talk of raising a romor (insurrection): I say, never do you plan a rojjior; you may as well try to fill Arno with buckets. When there's water enough Arno will be full, and that will not be till the torrent is ready."

"Caparra, that oracular speech of yours is due to my excellent shaving," said Nello. "You could never have made it with that dark rust on your chin. Ecco, Messer Domenico, I am ready for you now. By the way, my bel erudito," continued Nello as he saw Tito moving towards the door, "here has been old Maso seeking for you, but your nest was empty. He will come again presently. The old man looked mournful, and seemed in haste. I hope there is nothing wrong in the Via de' Bardi."

"Doubtless Messer Tito knows that Bardo's son is dead," said Cronaca, who had just come up.

Tito's heart gave a leap—had the death happened before Romola saw him?

"No, I had not heard it," he said, with no more discomposure than the occasion seemed to warrant, turning and leaning against the doorpost, as if he had given up his intention of going away. "I knew that his sister had gone to see him. Did he die before she arrived?"

"No," said Cronaca; "I was in San Marco at the time, and saw her come out from the chapter-house with Fra Girolamo, who told us that the dying man's breath had been preserved as by a miracle, that he might make a disclosure to his sister."

Tito felt that his fate was decided. Again his mind rushed over all the circumstances of his departure from Florence, and he conceived a plan of getting back his money from Cennini before the disclosure had become public. If he once had liis money he need not stay long in endurance of scorching looks and biting words. He would wait now, and go away with Cennini and get the money from him at once. With that project in his mind he stood motionless—his hands in his belt, his eyes fixed absently on the ground. Nello, glancing at him, felt sure that he was absorbed in anxiety about Romola, and thought him such a pretty image of self-forgetful sadness, that he just perceptibly pointed his razor at him, and gave a challenging look at Piero di Cosimo, whom he had never forgiven for his refusal to see any prognostics of character in his favourite's handsome face. Piero, who was leaning against the other doorpost, close to Tito, shrugged his shoulders: the frequent recurrence of such challenges from Nello had changed the painter's first declaration of neutrality into a positive inclination to believe ill of the much-praised Greek.

"So you have got your Fra Girolamo back again, Cronaca? I suppose we shall have him preaching again this next Advent," said Nello.

"And not before there is need," said Cronaca, gravely. "We have had the best testimony to his words since the last Quaresima: for even to the wicked wickedness has become a plague; and the ripeness of vice is turning to rottenness in the nostrils even of the vicious. There has not been a change since the Quaresima, either in Rome or at Florence, but has put a new seal on the Frate's words—that the harvest of sin is ripe, and that God will reap it with a sword."

"I hope he has had a new vision, however," said Francesco Cei, sneeringly. "The old ones are somewhat stale. Can't your Frate get a poet to help out his imagination for him?"

: "He has no lack of poets about him," said Cronaca, with quiet contempt, "but they are great poets and not little ones; so they are contented to be taught by him, and no more think tlie truth stale which God has given him to utter, than they think the light of the moon is stale. But perhaps certain high prelates and princes who dislike the Frate's denunciations, might be pleased to hear that, though Giovanni Pico, and Poliziano, and Marsilio Ficino, and most other men of mark in Florence reverence Fra Girolamo, Messer Francesco Cei despises him."

"Poliziano?" said Cei, with a scornful laugh. "Yes, doubtless he believes in your new Jonah; witness the fine oration he wrote for the envoys of Sienna, to tell Alexander the Sixth that the world and the church were never so well off as since he became Pope."

"Nay, Francesco," said Macchiavelli, smiling, "a various scholar must have various opinions. And as for the Frate, whatever we may think of his saintliness, you judge his preaching too narrowly. The secret of oratory lies, not in saying new things, but in saying things with a certain power that moves the hearers—without which, as old Filelfo has said, your speaker deserves to be called, *non oratorem, sed oratorem.' And, according to that test, Fra Girolamo is a great orator."

"That is true, Niccolo," said Cennini, speaking from the shaving chair, "but part of the secret lies in the prophetic visions. Our people—no offence to you, Cronaca —will run after anything in the shape of a prophet, especially if he prophesies terrors and tribulations."

"Rather say, Cennini," answered Cronaca, "that the chief secret lies in the Frate's pure life and strong faith, which stamp him as a messenger of God."

"I admit it—I admit it," said Cennini, opening his palms, as he rose from the chair. "His life is spotless: no man has impeached it."

"He is satisfied with the pleasant lust of arrogance," Cei burst out, bitterly. "I can see it in that proud lip and satisfied eye of his. He hears the air filled with his own name—Fra Girolamo Savonarola, of Ferrara; the prophet, the saint, the mighty preacher, who frightens the very babies of Florence into laying down their wicked baubles."

" Come, come, Francesco, you are out of humour with waiting," said the conciliatory Nello. "Let me stop your

mouth with a little lather. I must not have my friend Cronaca made angry: I have a regard for his chin; and his chin is in no respect altered since he became a Piagnone. And for my own part, I confess, when the Frate was preaching in the Duomo last Advent, I got into such a trick of slipping in to listen to him, that I might have turned Piagnone too, if I had not been hindered by the liberal nature of my art—and also by the length of the sermons, which are sometimes a good while before they get to the moving point. But, as Messer Niccolo here says, the Frate lays hold of the people by some power over and above his prophetic visions. Monks and nuns who prophesy are not of that rareness. For what says Luigi Pulci? 'Dombruno's sharp-cutting scimitar had the fame of being enchanted; but,' says Luigi, 'I am rather of opinion that it cut sharp because it was of strongly-tempered steel.' Yes, yes; Paternosters may shave clean, but they must be said over a good razor."

"See, Nello!" said Macchiavelli, "what doctor is this advancing on his Bucephalus? I thought your piazza was free from those furred and scarlet-robed lacqueys of death. This man looks as if he had had some such night adventure as Boccaccio's Maestro Simone, and had his bonnet and mantle pickled a little in the gutter; though he himself is as sleek as a miller's rat."

"A-ah!" said Nello, with a low long-drawn intonation, as he looked up towards the advancing figure—a round-headed, round-bodied personage, seated on a raw young 'horse, which held its nose out with an air of threatening obstinacy, and by a constant effort to back and go off in an oblique line showed free views about authority very much in advance of the age.

"And I have a few more adventures in pickle for him,"

continued Nello, in an undertone, "which I hope will drive his inquiring nostrils to another quarter of the city. He's a doctor from Padua; they say he has been at Prato for three months, and now he's come to Florence to see what he can net. But his great trick is making rounds among the contadini. And do you note those great saddlebags he carries? They are to hold the fat capons and eggs and meal he levies on silly clowns with whom coin is scarce. He vends his own secret medicines, so he keeps away from the doors of the draggists; and for this last week he has taken to sitting in my piazza for two or three hours every day, and making it a resort for asthmas and squalling bambini. It stirs my gall to see the toad-faced quack fingering the greasy quattrini, or bagging a pigeon in exchange for his pills and powders. But I'll put a few thorns in his saddle, else I'm no Florentine. Laudamus! he is coming to be shaved; that's what I've waited for. Messer Domenico, go not away—wait; you shall see a rare bit of fooling, which I devised two days ago. Here, Sandro!"

Nello whispered in the ear of Sandro, who rolled his solemn eyes, nodded, and, following up these signs of understanding with a slow smile, took to his heels with surprising rapidity.

"How is it with you, Maestro Tacco?" said Nello, as the doctor, with difficulty, brought his horse's head round towards the barber's shop. "That is a fine young horse of yours, but something raw in the mouth, eh?"

"He is an accursed beast, the vermocane seize him!"* said Maestro Tacco, with a burst of irritation, descending from his saddle and fastening the old bridle, mended with string, to an iron staple in the wall. "Nevertheless," he added, recollecting himself, "a sound beast and a valuable, for one who wanted to purchase, and get a profit by training him. I had him cheap."

"Rather too hard riding for a man who carries your weight of learning: eh, Maestro?" said Nello. "You seem hot."

"Truly, I am likely to be hot," said the doctor, taking off his bonnet, and giving to full view a bald low head and that broad face, with high ears, wide lipless mouth, round eyes, and deep arched lines above the projecting eyebrows, which altogether made Nello's epithet "toad-faced" dubiously complimentary to the blameless batrachian. "Riding from Peretola, when the sun is high, is not the same thing as kicking your heels on a bench in the shade, like your Florence doctors. Moreover, I have had not a little pulling to get through the carts and mules into the Mercato, to find out the husband of a certain Monna Ghita, who had had a fatal seizure before I was called in! and if it had not been that I had to demand my fees—"

"Monna Ghita!" said Nello, as the perspiring doctor interrupted himself to rub his head and face. "Peace be with her angry soul! The Mercato will want a whip the more if her tongue is laid to rest."

Tito, who had roused himself from his abstraction, and was listening to the dialogue, felt a new rush of the vague half-formed ideas about Tessa, which had passed through his mind the evening before: if Monna Ghita were really taken out of the way, it would be easier for him to see Tessa again—whenever he wanted to see her.

"Gnaffe, Maestra," Nello went on, in a sympathising tone, "you are the slave of rude mortals, who, but for you, would die like brutes, without help of pill or powder. It is pitiful to see your learned lymph oozing from your pores as if it were mere vulgar moisture. You think my shaving will cool and disencumber you? One moment and I have done with Messer Francesco here. It seems to me a thousand years till I wait upon a man who carries all the science of Arabia in his head and saddle-bags. Ecco!"

Nello held up the shaving cloth with an air of invitation, and Maestro Tacco advanced and seated himself under a pre-occupation with his heat and his self-importance, which made him quite deaf to the irony conveyed in Nello's officiously friendly tones.

"It is but fitting that a great medicus like you," said Nello, adjusting the cloth, "should be shaved by the same razor that shaved the illustrious Antonio Benevieni, the greatest master of the chirurgic art."

"The chirurgic art!" interrupted the doctor, with an air of contemptuous disgust. "Is it your Florentine fashion to put the masters of the science of medicine on a level with men who do carpentry on broken limbs, and sew up wounds like tailors, and carve away excrescences as a butcher trims meat? Via! A manual art, such as any artificer might learn, and which has been practised by simple barbers like yourself—on a level with the noble science of Hippocrates, Galen, and Avicenna, which penetrates into the occult influences of the stars and plants and gems!—a science locked up from the vulgar!"

"No, in truth, maestro," said Nello, using his lather very deliberately, as if he wanted to prolong the operation to the utmost, "I never thought of placing them on a level: I know your science comes next to the miracles of Holy Church for mystery. But there, you see, is the pity of it"—here Nello fell into a tone of regretful sympathy —"your high science is sealed from the profane and the

vulgar, and so you become an object of envy and slander. I grieve to say it, but there are low fellows in this city— mere sgherri, who go about in nightcaps and long beards, and make it their business to sprinkle gall in every man's broth who is prospering. Let me tell you—for you are a stranger—this is a city where every man had need carry a large nail ready to fasten on the wheel of Fortune when his side happens to be uppermost. Already there are stories—mere fables doubtless—beginning to be buzzed about concerning you, that make me wish I could hear of your being well on your way to Arezzo. I would not have a man of your metal stoned, for though San Stefano was stoned, he was not great in medicine like San Cosmo and San Damiano. . . ."

"What stories? what fables?" stammered Maestro Tacco. "What do you mean?"

"Lasso! I fear me you are come into the trap for your cheese, Maestro. The fact is, there is a company of evil youths who go prowling about the houses of our citizens carrying sharp tools in their pockets;—no sort of door, or window, or shutter, but they will pierce it. They are possessed with a diabolical patience to watch the doings of people who fancy themselves private. It must be they who have done it—it must be they who have spread the stories about you and your medicines. Have you by chance detected any small aperture in your door, or window-shutter? No? W^ell, I advise you to look; for it is now commonly talked of that you have been seen in your dwelling at the Canto di Paglia, making your secret specifics by night: pounding dried toads in a mortar, compounding a salve out of mashed worms, and making your pills from the dried livers of rats which you mix with

15*

saliva emitted during the utterance of a blasphemous incantation—which indeed these witnesses profess to repeat."

"It is a pack of lies!" exclaimed the doctor, struggling to get utterance, and then desisting in alarm at the approaching razor.

"It is not to me, or any of this respectable company, that you need to say that, doctor. We are not the heads to plant such carrots as those in. But what of that? What are a handful of reasonable men against a crowd with stones in their hands? There are those among us who think Cecco d'Ascoli was an innocent sage—and we all know how he was burnt alive for being wiser than his fellows. Ah, doctor, it is not by living at Padua that you can learn to know Florentines. My belief is, they would stone the Holy Father himself, if they could find a good excuse for it; and they are persuaded that you are a necromancer, who is trying to raise the pestilence by selling secret medicines—and I am told your specifics have in truth an evil smell."

"It is false!" burst out the doctor, as Nello moved away his razor. "It is false! I will show the pills and the powders to these honourable signori—and the salve—it has an excellent odour—an odour of—of salve." He started up with the lather on his chin, and the cloth round his neck, to search in his saddle-bag for the belied medicines, and Nello in an instant adroitly shifted the shaving chair till it was in the close vicinity of the horse's head, while Sandro, who had now returned, at a sign from his master placed himself near the bridle.

"Behold, Messeri!" said the doctor, bringing a small box of medicines and opening it before them. "Let any signer apply this box to his nostrils and he will find an. honest odour of medicaments—not indeed of pounded

•gems, or rare vegetables from the East, or stones found in the bodies of birds; for I practise on the diseases of the vulgar, for whom heaven has provided cheaper and less powerful remedies according to their degree; and there are even remedies known to our science which are entirely free of cost—as the new iussis may be counteracted in the poor, who can pay for no specifics, by a resolute holding of the breath. And here is a paste which is even of savoury odour, and is infallible against melancholia, being ■concocted under the conjunction of Jupiter and Venus; and I have seen it allay spasms."

"Stay, Maestro," said Nello, while the doctor had his lathered face turned towards the group near the door, eagerly holding out his box, and lifting out one specific after another; "here comes a crying contadina with her baby. Doubtless she is in search of you; it is perhaps an opportunity for you to show this honourable company a proof of your skill. Here, buona donna! here is the famous doctor. Why, what is the matter with the sweet bimbo?"

This question was addressed to a sturdy-looking, broad-shouldered contadina, with her head-drapery folded about her face so that little was to be seen but a bronzed nose and a pair of dark eyes and eyebrows. She carried her child packed up in the stiff mummy-shaped case in which Italian babies have been from time immemorial introduced into society, turning its face a little towards her bosom, and making those sorrowful grimaces which women are in the habit of using as a sort of pulleys to draw down reluctant tears.

"Oh, for the love of the Holy Madonna!" said the woman, in a wailing voice; "will you look at my poor bimbo? I know I can't pay you for it, but I took it into

the Nunziata last night, and it's turned a worse colour than before; it's the convulsions. But when I was holding it before the Santissima Nunziata, I remembered they said there was a new doctor come who cured everything; and so I thought it might be the will of the Holy Madonna that I should bring it to you."

"Sit down. Maestro, sit down," said Nello. "Here is an opportunity for you; here are honourable witnesses who will declare before the Magnificent Eight that they have seen you practising honestly and relieving a poor woman's child. And then if your life is in danger, the Magnificent Eight will put you in prison a little while just to ensure your safety, and after that, their sbirri will conduct you out of Florence by night, as they did the zealous Frate Minore who preached against the Jews. What! our people are given to stone-throwing; but we have magistrates."

The doctor, unable to refuse, seated himself in the shaving chair, trembling, half with fear and half with rage, and by this time quite unconscious of the lather which Nello had laid on with such profuseness. He deposited his medicine-case on his knees, took out his precious spectacles (wondrous Florentine device!) from his wallet, lodged them carefully above his flat nose and high ears, and lifting up his brows, turned towards the applicant.

"O Santiddio! look at him," said the woman, with a more pitious wail than ever, as she held out the small mummy, which had its head completely concealed by dingy drapery wound round the head of the portable cradle, but seemed to be struggling and crying in a demoniacal fashion under this imprisonment. "The fit is on him!

Ohime! I know what colour he is; it's the evil eye oh!"

The doctor, anxiously holding his knees together to support his box, bent his spectacles towards the baby, and said cautiously, "It may be a new disease; unwind these rags, Monna!"

The contadina, with sudden energy, snatched off the encircling linen, when out struggled scratching, grinning, and screaming—what the doctor in his fright fully believed to be a demon, but what Tito recognised as Vaiano's monkey, made more formidable by an artificial blackness, such as might have come from a hasty rubbing up the chimney.

Up started the unfortunate doctor, letting his medicine box fall, and away jumped the no less terrified and indignant monkey, finding the first resting-place for his claws on the horse's mane, which he used as a sort of rope-ladder till he had fairly found his equilibrium, when he continued to clutch it as a bridle. The horse wanted no spur under such a rider, and, the already loosened bridle offering no resistance, darted off across the piazza, with the monkey, clutching, grinning and blinking on his neck.

"Il cavallo! Il Diavolo!" was now shouted on all sides by the idle rascals who gathered from all quarters of the piazza, and was echoed in tones of alarm by the stall-keepers, whose vested interests seemed in some danger; while the doctor, out of his wits with confused terror at the Devil, the possible stoning, and the escape of his horse, took to his heels with spectacles on nose, lathered face, and the shaving-cloth about his neck, crying—"Stop him! stop him! for a powder—a florin—stop him for a florin!" while the lads, outstripping him, clapped their hands and shouted encouragement to the runaway.

The cerretano, who had not bargained for the flight of his monkey along with the horse, had caught up his petticoats with much celerity, and showed a pair of particoloured hose above his contadina's shoes, far in advance of the doctor. And away went the grotesque race up the Corso degli Adimari — the horse with the singular jockey, the contadina with the remarkable hose, and the doctor in lather and spectacles, with furred mantle out-flying.

It was a scene such as Florentines loved, from the potent and reverend signer going to council in his lucco, down to the grinning youngster, who felt himself master of all situations when his bag was filled with smooth stones from the convenient dry bed of the torrent. The greyheaded Domenico Cennini laughed no less heartily than the younger men, and Nello was triumphantly secure of the general admiration.

"Aha!" he exclaimed, snapping his fingers when the first burst of laughter was subsiding. "I have cleared my piazza of that unsavoury flytrap, mi pare. Maestro Tacco will no more come here again to sit for patients than he will take to licking marble for his dinner."

"You are going towards the Piazza della Signoria, Messer Domenico," said Macchiavelli. "I will go with you, and we shall perhaps see who has deserved the palio among these racers. Come, Melema, will you go too?"

It had been precisely Tito's intention to accompany Cennini, but before he had gone many steps, he was called back by Nello, who saw Maso approaching.

Maso's message was from Romola. She wished Tito to go to the Via de' Bardi as soon as possible. She would see him under the loggia, at the top of the house, as she wished to speak to him alone.

CHAPTER XVII. UNDER THE LOGGIA.

The loggia at the top of Bardo's house rose above the buildings on each side of it, and formed a gallery-round quadrangular walls. On the side towards the street the roof was supported by columns; but on the remaining sides, by a wall pierced with arched openings, so that at the back, looking over a crowd of irregular, poorly-built dwellings towards the hill of Bogoli, Romola could at all times have a walk sheltered from observation. Near one of those arched openings, close to the door by which he had entered the loggia, Tito awaited her, with a sickening sense of the sunlight that slanted before him and mingled itself with the ruin of his hopes. He had never for a moment relied on Romola's passion for him as likely to be too strong for the repulsion created by the discovery of his secret; he had not the presumptuous vanity which might have hindered him from feeling that her love had the same root with her belief in him. But as he imagined her coming towards him in her radiant majesty, made so loveably mortal by her soft hazel eyes, he fell into wishing that she had been something lower, if it were only that she might let him clasp her and kiss her before they parted. He had had no real caress from ;her—nothing but now and then a long glance, a kiss, a pressure of the hand; and he had so often longed that they should be alone together. They were going to be alone now; but he saw her standing inexorably aloof from him. His heart gave a great throb as he saw the door move: Romola was there. It was all like a flash of

ROMOLA.

lightning: he felt, rather than saw, the glory about her head, the tearful appealing eyes; he felt, rather than heard, the cry of love with which she said, "Tito!"

And in the same moment she was in his arms, and sobbing with her face against his.

How poor Romola had yearned through the watches of the night to see that bright face! The new image of death; the strange bewildering doubt infused into her by the story of a life removed from her understanding and sympathy; the haunting vision, which she seemed not only to hear uttered by the low gasping voice, but to live through, as if it had been her own dream, had made her more conscious than ever that it was Tito who had first brought the warm stream of hope and gladness into her life, and who had first turned away the keen edge of pain in the remembrance of her brother. She would tell Tito everything; there was no one else to whom she could tell it. She had been restraining herself in the presence of her father all the morning; but now, that long pent-up sob mitjht come forth. Proud and self-controlled to all the world beside, Romola was as simple and unreserved as a child in her love for Tito. She had been quite contented with the days when they had only looked at each other; but now, when she felt the need of clinging to him, there was no thought that hindered her.

"My Romola! my goddess!" Tito murmured with passionate fondness, as he clasped her gently, and kissed the thick golden ripples on her neck. He was in paradise: disgrace, shame, parting—there was no fear of them any longer. This happiness was too strong to be marred by the sense that Romola was deceived in him; nay, he could only rejoice in her delusion; for, after all, concealment had been wisdom. The only thing he could regret was his

needless dread; if, indeed, the dread had not been worth suffering for the sake of this sudden rapture.

The sob had satisfied itself, and Romola raised her head. Neither of them spoke; they stood looking at each other's faces with that sweet wonder which belongs to young love—she with her long white hands on the dark-brown curls, and he with his dark fingers bathed in the streaming gold. Each was so beautiful to the other; each was experiencing that undisturbed mutual consciousness for the first time. The cold pressure of a new sadness on Romola's heart made her linger the more in that silent soothing sense of nearness and love; and Tito could not even seek to press his lips to hers, because that would be change.

"Tito," she said, at last, "it has been altogether painful. But I must tell you everything. Your strength will help me to resist the impressions that will not be shaken off by reason."

"I know, Romola—I know he is dead," said Tito; and the long lustrous eyes told nothing of the many wishes that would have brought about that death long ago if there had been such potency in mere wishes. Romola only read her own pure thoughts in their dark depths, as we read letters in happy dreams.

"So changed, Tito! It pierced me to think that it was Dino. And so strangely hard: not a word to my father; nothing but a vision that he wanted to tell me. And yet it was so piteous—the struggling breath, and the eyes that seemed to look towards the crucifix, and yet not to see it. I shall never forget it; it seems as if it would come between me and everything I shall look at."

Romola's heart swelled again, so that she was forced 4o break off. But the need she felt to disburden her mind to Tito urged her to repress the rising anguish. When she began to speak again, her thoughts had travellecj a Httle.

"It was strange, Tito. The vision was about our marriage, and yet he knew nothing of you."

"What was it, my Romola? Sit down and tell me," said Tito, leading her to the bench that stood near. A fear had come across him lest the vision should somehow or other relate to Baldassarre; and this sudden change of feeling prompted him to seek a change of position.

Romola told him all that had passed, from her entrance into San Marco, hardly leaving out one of her brother's words, which had burnt themselves into her memory as they were spoken. But when she was at the end of the vision, she paused; the rest came too vividly before her to be uttered, and she sat looking at the distance, almost unconscious for the moment that Tito was near her. His mmd was at ease now; that vague vision had passed over him like white mist, and left no mark. But he was silent, expecting her to speak again.

"I took it," she went on, as if Tito had been reading her thoughts, "I took the crucifix; it is down below in my bedroom."

"And now, my Romola," said Tito, entreatingly, "you will banish these ghastly thoughts. The vision was'an ordinary monkish vision, bred of fasting and fanatical ideas. It surely has no weight with you."

"No, Tito; no. But poor Dino, he believed it was a divine message. It is strange," she went on meditatively, "this life of men possessed with fervid beliefs that seem like madness to their fellow beings. Dino was not a vulgar fanatic; and that Fra Girolamo, his very voice i seems to have penetrated me with a sense that there is some truth in what moves them—some truth of which I know nothing."

"It was only because your feehngs were highly wrought, my Romola. Your brother's state of mind was no more than a form of that theosophy which has been the common disease of excitable dreamy minds in all ages; the same ideas that your father's old antagonist, Marsilio Ficino, pores over in the New Platonists; only your brother's passionate nature drove him to act out what other men write and talk about. And for Fra Girolamo, he is simply a narrow-minded monk, with a gift for preaching and infusing terror into the multitude. Any words or any voice would have shaken you at that moment. When your mind has had a little repose, you will judge of such things as you have always done before."

"Not about poor Dino," said Romola. "I was angry with him; my heart seemed to close against him while he was speaking; but since then I have thought less of what was in my own mind and more of what was in his. Oh, Tito! it was very piteous to see his young life coming to an end in that way. That yearning look at the crucifix when he was gasping for breath—I can never forget it. Last night I looked at the crucifix a long while, and tried to see that it would help him, until at last it seemed to me by the lamplight as if the suffering face shed pity."

"My Romola, promise me to resist such thoughts; they are fit for sickly nuns, not for my golden-tressed Aurora, who looks made to scatter all such twilight fantasies. Try not to think of them now; we shall not long be alone together."

The last words were uttered in a tone of tender beseeching, and he turned her face towards him with a gentle touch of his right hand.

Romola had had her eyes fixed absently on the arched opening, but she had not seen the distant hill; she had all the while been in the chapter-house, looking at the pale images of sorrow and death.

Tito's touch and beseeching voice recalled her; and now in the warm sunlight she saw that rich dark beauty which seemed to gather round it all images of joy—purple vines festooned between the elms, the strong corn perfecting itself under the vibrating heat, bright-winged creatures hurrying and resting among the flowers, round limbs beating the earth in gladness with cymbals held aloft, light melodies chanted to the thrilling rhythm of strings—all objects and all sounds that tell of Nature revelling in her force. Strange, bewildering transition from those pale images of sorrow and death to this bright youthfulness, as of a sun-god who knew nothing of night! What thought could reconcile that worn anguish in her brother's face— that straining after something invisible—with this satisfied strength and beauty, and make it intelligible that they belonged to the same world? Or was there never any re-concihng of them, but only a blind worship of clashing deities, first in mad joy and then in wailing? Romola for the first time felt this questioning need like a sudden uneasy dizziness and want of something to grasp; it was an experience hardly longer than a sigh, for the eager theorising of ages is compressed, as in a seed, in the momentary want of a single mind. But there was no answer to meet the need, and it vanished before the returning rush of young sympathy with the glad, loving beauty that beamed upon her in new radiance, like the dawn after we have looked away from it to the grey west.

"Your mind lingers apart from our love, my Romola,"

Tito said, with a soft reproachful murmur. "It seems a forgotten thing to you."

She looked at the beseeching eyes in silence, till the sadness all melted out of her own.

"My joy!" she said, in her full clear voice.

"Do you really care for me enough, then, to banish those chill fancies, or shall you always be suspecting me as the Great Tempter?" said Tito, with his bright smile.

"How should I not care for you more than for everything else? Everything I had felt before in all my life— about my father, and about my loneliness—was a preparation to love you. You would laugh at me, Tito, if you knew what sort of man I used to think I should marry—some scholar with deep lines in his face, like Alamanno Rinuccini, and with rather grey hair, who would agree with my father in taking the side of the Aristotelians, and be willing to live with him. I used to think about the love I read of in the poets, but I never dreamed that anything like that could happen to me here in Florence in our old library. And then you came, Tito, and were so much to my father, and I began to believe that life could be happy for me too."

"My goddess! is there any woman like you?" said Tito, with a mixture of fondness and wondering admiration at the blended majesty and simplicity in her.

"But, dearest," he went on, rather timidly, "if you minded more about our marriage, you would persuade your father and Messer Bernardo not to think of any more delays. But you seem not to mind about it."

"Yes, Tito, I will, I do mind. But I am sure my godfather will urge more delay now, because of Dino's death. He has never agreed with my father about disowning Dino, and you know he has always said that we

ROMOLA.

ought to wait until you have been at least a year in Florence. Do not think hardly of my godfather. I know he is prejudiced and narrow, but yet he is very noble. He has often said that it is folly in my father to want to keep his library apart, that it may bear his name; yet he would try to get my father's wish carried out. That seems to me very great and noble—that power of respecting a feeling which he does not share or understand."

"I have no rancour against Messer Bernardo for thinking you too precious for me, my Romola," said Tito: and that was true. "But your father, then, knows of his son's death?"

"Yes, I told him—I could not help it—I told him where I had been, and that I had seen Dino die; but nothing else; and he has commanded me not to speak of it again. But he has been very silent this morning, and has had those restless movements which always go to my heart; they look as if he were trying to get outside the prison of his blindness. Let us go to him now. I had persuaded him to try to sleep, because he slept little in the night. Your voice will soothe him, Tito; it always does."

"And not one kiss? I have not had one," said Tito, in his gentle reproachful tone, which gave him an air of dependence very charming in a creature with those rare gifts that seem to excuse presumption.

The sweet pink blush spread itself with the quickness of lisfht over Romola's face and neck as she bent towards him. It seemed impossible that their kisses could ever become common things.

"Let us walk once round the loggia," said Romola, "before we go down."

"There is something grim and grave to me always

about Florence," said Tito, as they paused in the front of the house, where they could see over the opposite roofs to the other side of the river, "and even in its merriment there is something shriU and hard—biting rather than gay. I wish we hved in Southern Italy, where thought is broken not by weariness, but by delicious languors such as never seem to come over the 'ingenia acerrima Florentina.' I should like to see you under that southern sun, lying among the flowers, subdued into mere enjoyment, while I bent over you and touched the lute and sang to you some little unconscious strain that seemed all one with the light and the warmth. You have never known that happiness of the nymphs, my Romola."

"No, Tito; but 1 have dreamed of it often since you came. I am very thirsty for a deep draught of joy—for a life all bright like you. But we will not think of it now, Tito; it seems to me as if there would always be pale sad faces among the flowers, and eyes that look in vain. Let us go."

CHAPTER XVIII.
THE PORTRAIT.

When Tito left the Via de' Bardi that day in exultant satisfaction at finding himself thoroughly free from the threatened peril, his thoughts, no longer claimed by the immediate presence of Romola and her father, recurred to those futile hours of dread in which he was conscious of having not only felt but acted as he would not have done if he had had a truer foresight. He would not have parted with his ring; for Romola, and others to whom it was a familiar object, would be a little struck with the apparent

ROMOLA.

sordidness of parting with a gem he had professedly cherished, unless he feigned as a reason the desire to make some special gift with the purchase-money; and Tito had at that moment a nauseating weariness of simulation. He was well out of the possible consequences that might have fallen on him from that initial deception, and it was no longer a load on his mind; kind fortune had brought him immunity, and he thought it was only fair that she should. Who was hurt by it? Any results to Baldassarre were too problematical to be taken into account. But he wanted now to be free from any hidden shackles that would gall him, though ever so little, under his ties to Romola. He was not aware that that very delight in immunity which prompted resolutions not to entangle himself again, was deadening the sensibilities which alone could save him from entanglement.

But, after all, the sale of the ring was a slight matter. Was it also a slight matter that little Tessa was under a delusion which would doubtless fill her small head with expectations doomed to disappointment? Should he try to see the little thing alone again and undeceive her at once, or should he leave the disclosure to time and chance? Happy dreams are pleasant, and they easily come to an end with daylight and the stir of life. The sweet, pouting, innocent, round thing! It was impossible not to think of her. Tito thought he should like some time to take her a present that would please her, and just learn if her stepfather treated her more cruelly now her mother was dead. Or, should he at once undeceive Tessa, and then tell Romola about her, so that they might find some happier lot for the poor thing? No: that unfortunate little incident of the cerretano and the marriage, and his allowing Tessa to part from him in delusion, must never be

known to Romola, and since no enlightenment could expel it from Tessa's mind, there would ahvays be a risk of betrayal; besides, even httle Tessa might have some gall in her when she found herself disappointed in her love— yes, she must be a little in love with him, and that might make it well that he should not see her again. Yet it was a trifling adventure such as a country girl would perhaps ponder on till some ruddy contadino made acceptable love to her, when she would break her resolution of secrecy and get at the truth that she was free. Dunqiie — good-by, Tessa! kindest wishes! Tito had made up his mind that the silly little affair of the cerretano should have no further consequences for himself; and people are apt to think that resolutions made on their own behalf will be firm. As for the fifty-five florins, the purchase-money of the ring, Tito had made up his mind what to do with some of them; he would carry out a pretty ingenious thought which would make him more at ease in accounting for the absence of his ring to Romola, and would also serve him as a means of guarding her mind from the recurrence of those monkish fancies which were especially repugnant to him; and with this thought in his mind, he went to the Via Gualfonda to find Piero di Cosimo, the artist who at that time was pre-eminent in the fantastic mythological design which Tito's purpose required.

Entering the court on which Piero's dwelling opened, Tito found the heavy iron knocker on the door thickly bound round with wool and ingeniously fastened with cords. Remembering the painter's practice of stuffing his ears against obtrusive noises, Tito was not much surprised at this mode of defence against visitors' thunder, and betook himself first to tapping modestly with his knuckles, and then to a more importunate attempt to shake the

door. In vain! Tito was moving away, blaming himself for wasting his time on this visit, instead of waiting till he saw the painter again at Nello's, when a little girl entered the court with a basket of eggs on her arm, went up to the door, and standing on tiptoe, pushed up a small iron plate that ran in grooves, and putting her mouth to the aperture thus disclosed, called out in a piping voice, "Messer Piero!"

In a few moments Tito heard the sound of bolts, the door opened, and Piero presented himself in a red nightcap and a loose brown serge tunic, with sleeves rolled up to the shoulder. He darted a look of surprise at Tito, but without further notice of him stretched out his hand to take the basket from the child, re-entered the house, and presently returning with the empty basket, said, "How much to pay?"

"Two grossoni, Messer Piero; they are all ready boiled, my mother says."

Piero took the coin out of the leathern scarsella at his belt, and the little maiden trotted away, not without a few upward glances of awed admiration at the surprising young signer.

Piero's glance was much less complimentary as he said,

"What do you want at my door, Messer Greco? I saw you this morning at Nello's; if you had asked me then, I could have told you that I see no man in this house without knowing his business and agreeing with him beforehand."

"Pardon, Messer Piero," said Tito, with his imperturbable good-humour; "I acted without sufficient reflection. I remembered nothing but your admirable skill in inventing pretty caprices, when a sudden desire for something of that sort prompted me to come to you."

The painter's manners were too notoriously odd to all the world for this reception to be held a special affront; but even if Tito had suspected any offensive intention, the impulse to resentment would have been less strong in him than the desire to conquer good-will.

Piero made a grimace which was habitual with him when he was spoken to with flattering suavity. He grinned, stretched out the corners of his mouth, and pressed down his brows, so as to defy any divination of his feelings under that kind of stroking.

"And what may that need be?" he said, after a moment's pause. In his heart he was tempted by the hinted opportunity of applying his invention.

"I want a very delicate miniature device taken from certain fables of the poets, which you will know how to combine for me. It must be painted on a wooden case —I will show you the size—in the form of a triptych. The inside may be simple gilding: it is on the outside I want the device. It is a favourite subject with you Florentines—the triumph of Bacchus and Ariadne; but I want it treated in a new way. A story in Ovid will give you the necessary hints. The young Bacchus must be seated in a ship, his head bound with clusters of grapes, and a spear entwined with vine-leaves in his hand: dark-berried ivy must wind about the masts and sails, the oars must be thyrsi, and flowers must wreathe themselves about the poop; leopards and tigers must be crouching before him, and dolphins must be sporting round. But I want to have the fair-haired Ariadne with him, made immortal with her golden crown—that is not in Ovid's story, but no matter, you will conceive it all—and above there must be young Loves, such as you know how to paint, shooting with roses at the points of their arrows—"

"Say no more!" said Piero. "I have Ovid in the vulgar tongue. Find me the passage. I love not to be choked with other men's thoughts. You may come in."

Piero led the way through the first room, where a basket of eggs was deposited on the open hearth, near a heap of broken egg-shells and a bank of ashes. In strange keeping with that sordid litter, there was a low bedstead of carved ebony, covered carelessly with a piece of rich oriental carpet, that looked as if it had served to cover the steps to a Madonna's throne; and a carved cassone, or large chest, with painted devices on its sides and lid. There was hardly any other furniture in the large room, except casts, wooden steps, easels and rough boxes, all festooned with cobwebs.

The next room was still larger, but it was also much more crowded. Apparently Piero was keeping the Festa, for the double door underneath the window which admitted the painter's light from above, was thrown open, and showed a garden, or rather thicket, in which fig-trees and vines grew in tangled trailing wildness among nettles and hemlocks, and a tall cypress lifted its dark head from a stifling mass of yellowish mulberry-leaves. It seemed as if that dank luxuriance had begun to penetrate even within the walls of the wide and lofty room; for in one corner, amidst a confused heap of carved marble fragments and rusty armour, tufts of long grass and dark feathery fennel had made their way, and a large stone vase, tilted on one side, seemed to be pouring out the ivy that streamed around. All about the walls hung pen and oil sketches of fantastic sea-monsters; dances of satyrs and menads; Saint Margaret's resurrection out of the devouring dragon; Madonnas with the supernal light upon them; studies of plants and grotesque heads; and on irregular rough shelves

a few books were scattered among great drooping bunches of corn, bullocks' horns, pieces of dried honeycomb, stones with patches of rare-coloured lichen, skulls and bones, peacocks' feathers, and large birds' wings. Rising from amongst the dirty litter of the floor were lay figures: one in the frock of a Vallombrosan monk, strangely surmounted by a helmet with barred visor, another smothered with brocade and skins hastily tossed over it. Amongst this heterogeneous still life, several speckled and white pigeons were perched or strutting, too tame to fly at the entrance of men; three corpulent toads were crawling in an intimate friendly way near the door-stone; and a white rabbit, apparently the model for that which was frightening Cupid in the picture of Mars and Venus placed on the central easel, was twitching its nose with much content on a box full of bran.

"And now, Messer Greco," said Piero, signing to Tito to sit down on a low stool near the door, and then standing over him with folded arms, "don't be trying to see everything at once, like Messer Domeneddio, but let me know how large you would have this same triptych."

Tito indicated the required dimensions, and Piero marked them on a piece of paper.

"And now for the book," said Piero, reaching down a manuscript volume.

"There's nothing about the Ariadne there," said Tito, giving him the passage; "but you will remember I want the crowned Ariadne by the side of the young Bacchus: she must have golden hair."

"Ha!" said Piero, abruptly, pursing up his lips again. "And you want them to be likenesses, eh?" he added, looking down into Tito's face.

Tito laughed and blushed. "I know you are great at

portraits, Messer Piero; but I could not ask Ariadne to sit for you, because the painting is a secret."

"There it is! I want her to sit to me. Giovanni Vespucci wants me to paint him a picture of Œdipus and Antigone at Colonos, as he has expounded it to me: I have a fancy for the subject, and I want Bardo and his daughter to sit for it. Now, you ask them; and then I'll put the likeness into Ariadne."

"Agreed, if I can prevail with them. And your price for the Bacchus and Ariadne?"

"Bale! If you get them to let me paint them, that will pay me. I'd rather not have your money: you may pay for the case."

"And when shall I sit for you?" said Tito, "for if we have one likeness, we must have two."

"I don't want your likeness—I've got it already," said Piero, "only I've made you look frightened. I must take the fright out of it for Bacchus."

As he was speaking, Piero laid down the book and went to look among some paintings, propped with their faces against the wall. Pie returned with an oil-sketch in his hand.

"I call this as good a bit of portrait as I ever did," he said, looking at it as he advanced. "Yours is a face that expresses fear well, because it's naturally a bright one. I noticed it the first time I saw you. The rest of the picture is hardly sketched; but I've painted yoit in thoroughly."

Piero turned the sketch, and held it towards Tito's eyes. He saw himself with his right hand uplifted, holding a wine-cup, in the attitude of triumphant joy, but with his face turned away from the cup with an expression of such intense fear in the dilated eyes and pallid lips, that

he felt a cold stream through his veins, as if he were being thrown into sympathy with his imaged self"

"You are beginning to look like it already," said Piero, with a short laugh, moving the picture away again. "He's seeing a ghost—that fine young man. I shall finish it some day, when I've settled what sort of ghost is the most terrible—whether it should look solid, like a dead man come to life, or half transparent, like a mist."

Tito, rather ashamed of himself for a sudden sensitiveness, strangely opposed to his usual easy self-command, said carelessly—

"That is a subject after your own heart, Messer Piero —a revel interrupted by a ghost.

You seem to love the blending of the terrible with the gay. I suppose that is the reason your shelves are so well furnished with death's-heads, while you are painting those roguish Loves who are running away with the armour of Mars. I begin to think you are a Cynic philosopher in the pleasant disguise of a cunning painter."

"Not I, Messer Greco; a philosopher is the last sort of animal I would choose to resemble. I find it enough to live, without spinning lies to account for life. Fowls cackle, asses bray, women chatter, and philosophers spin false reasons—that's the effect the sight of the world brings out of them. Well, I am an animal that paints instead of cackling, or braying, or spinning lies. And now, I think, our business is done; you'll keep to your side of the bargain about the .CEdipus and Antigone?"

"I will do my best," said Tito—on this strong hint, immediately moving towards the door.
"And you'll let me know at Nello's. No need to come here again."
ROMOLA.
"I understand," said Tito, laughingly, lifting his hand in sign of friendly parting.

CHAPTER XIX.

THE OLD man's HOPE.

Messer Bernardo del Nero was as inexorable as Romola had expected in his advice that the marriage should be deferred till Easter, and in this matter Bardo was entirely under the ascendancy of his sagacious and practical friend. Nevertheless, Bernardo himself, though he was as far as ever from any susceptibility to the personal fascination in Tito which was felt by others, could not altogether resist that argument of success which is always powerful with men of the world. Tito was making his way rapidly in high quarters. He was especially growing in favour with the young Cardinal Giovanni de' Medici, who had even spoken of Tito's forming part of his learned retinue on an approaching journey to Rome; and the bright young Greek, who had a tongue that was always ready without ever being quarrelsome, was more and more wished for at gay suppers in the Via Larga, and at Florentine games in which he had no pretension to excel, and could admire the incomparable skill of Piero de' Medici in the most graceful manner in the world. By an unfailing sequence, Tito's reputation as an agreeable companion in "magnificent" society made his learning and talent appear more lustrous: and he was really accomplished enough to prevent an exaggerated estimate from being hazardous to him. Messer Bernardo had old prejudices and attachments which now began to argue down the newer and feebler prejudice against the young Greek

stranger who was rather too supple. To the old Florentine it was impossible to despise the recommendation of standing well with the best Florentine families, and since Tito began to be thoroughly received into that circle whose views were the unquestioned standard of social value, it seemed irrational not to admit that there was no longer any check to satisfaction in the prospect of such a son-in-law for Bardo, and such a husband for Romola. It was undeniable that Tito's coming had been the dawn of a new life for both father and daughter, and the first promise had even been surpassed. The blind old scholar— whose proud truthfulness would never enter into that commerce of feigned and preposterous admiration which, varied by a corresponding measurelessness in vituperation, made the woof of all learned intercourse—had fallen into neglect even among his fellow-citizens, and when he was alluded to at all, it had long been usual to say that, though his blindness and the loss of his son were pitiable misfortunes, he was tiresome in contending for the value of his own labours; and that his discontent was a little inconsistent in a man who had been openly regardless of religious rites, and in days past had refused offers made to him from various quarters, if he would only take orders, without which it was not easy for patrons to provide for every scholar. But since Tito's coming, there was no longer the same monotony in the thought that Bardo's name suggested; the old man, it was understood, had left off his plaints, and the fair daughter was no longer to be shut up in dowerless pride, waiting for a parentado. The winning manners and growing favour of the handsome Greek who was expected to enter into the double relation of son and husband helped to make the new interest a thoroughly friendly one, and it was no longer a rare occurrence when a visitor enlivened the quiet library. Elderly men came from that indefinite prompting to renew former intercourse which arises when an old acquaintance begins to be newly talked about; and young men whom Tito had asked leave to bring once, found it easy to go again when they overtook him on his way to the Via de' Bardi, and, resting their hands on his shoulder, fell into easy chat with him. For it Avas pleasant to look at Romola's beauty; to see her, like old Firenzuola's type of womanly majesty, "sitting with a certain grandeur, speaking with gravity, smiling with modesty, and casting around, as it were, an odour of queenliness;"* and she seemed to unfold like a strong white lily under this genial breath of admiration and homage; it was all one to her with her new bright life in Tito's love.

Tito had even been the means of strengthening the hope in Bardo's mind that he might before his death receive the longed-for security concerning his library: that it should not be merged in another collection; that it should not be transferred to a body of monks, and be called by the name of a monastery; but that it should remain for ever the Bardi Library, for the use of Florentines. For the old habit of trusting in the Medici could not die out while their influence was still the strongest lever in the State; and Tito, once possessing the ear of the Cardinal Giovanni de' Medici, might do more even than Messer Bernardo towards winning the desired interest, for he could demonstrate to a learned audience the

* " Quando una donna h grande, ben formata, porta ben sua persona, siede con una certa grandezza, parla con gravita, ride con mo-destia, e finalmente getta quasi un odor di Regina; allora noi diciamo quella donna pare una maesta, ella ha una maesta."

Firenzuola: Delia Bdlezza delle Donne.

peculiar value of Bardi's collection. Tito himself talked sanguinely of such a result, willing to cheer the old man, and conscious that Romola repaid those gentle words to her father with a sort of adoration that no direct tribute to herself could have won from her.

This question of the library was the subject of more than one discussion with Bernardo del Nero when Christmas was turned and the prospect of the marriage was becoming near—but always out of Bardo's hearing. For Bardo nursed a vague belief, which they dared not disturb, that his property, apart from the library, was adequate to meet all demands. He would not even, except under a momentary pressure of angry despondency, admit to himself that the will by which he had disinherited Dino would leave Romola the heir of nothing but debts; or that he needed anything from patronage beyond the security that a separate locality should be assigned to his library, in return for a deed of gift by which he made it over to the Florentine Republic.

"My opinion is," said Bernardo to Romola, in a consultation they had under the loggia, "that since you are to be married, and Messer Tito will have a competent income, we should begin to wind up the affairs, and ascertain exactly the sum that would be necessary to save the library from being touched, instead of letting the debts accumulate any longer. Your father needs nothing but his shred of mutton and his macaroni every day, and I think Messer Tito may engage to supply that for the years that remain; he can let it be in place of the morgen-cap."

"Tito has always known that my life is bound up with my father's," said Romola; "and he is better to my father than I am: he delights in making him happy."

"Ah, he's not made of the same clay as other men, is he?" said Bernardo, smih'ng. "Thy father has thought of shutting woman's folly out of thee by cramming thee with Greek and Latin; but thou hast been as ready to believe in the first pair of bright eyes and the first soft words that have come within reach of thee, as if thou couldst say nothing by heart but Paternosters, like other Christian men's daughters."

"Now, godfather," said Romola, shaking her head playfully, "as if it were only bright eyes and soft words that made me love Tito! You know better. You know I love my father and you because you are both good; and I love Tito, too, because he is so good. I see it, I feel it, in everything he says and does. And he is handsome, too: why should I not love him the better for that? It seems to me beauty is part of the finished language by which goodness speaks. You know yoti must have been a very handsome youth, godfather"—she looked up with one of her happy, loving smiles at the stately old man— "you were about as tall as Tito, and you had very fine eyes; only you looked a little sterner and prouder, and "

"And Romola likes to have all the pride to herself?" said Bernardo, not inaccessible to this pretty coaxing. "However, it is well that in one way Tito's demands are more modest than those of any Florentine husband of fitting rank that we should have been likely to find for you; he wants no dowry."

So it was settled in that way between Messer Bernardo del Nero, Romola, and Tito. Bardo assented with a wave of the hand when Bernardo told him that he thought it would be well now to begin to sell property and clear off debts; being accustomed to think of debts and property

as a sort of tliick wood that his imagination never even penetrated, still less got beyond. And Tito set about winning Messer Bernardo's respect by inquiring, with his ready faculty, into Florentine money-matters, the secrets of the Alonti or public funds, the values of real property, and the profits of banking.

"You will soon forget that Tito is not a Florentine, godfather," said Romola. "See how he is learning everything about Florence."

"It seems to me he is one of the demoni, who are of no particular country, child," said Bernardo, smiling. "His mind is a little too nimble to be weighted with all the stuff we men carry about in our hearts."

Romola smiled too, in happy confidence.

CHAPTER XX.

THE DAY OF IIIE BETROTHAL.

It was the last week of the Carnival, and the streets of Florence were at their fullest and noisiest: there were the masqued processions, chanting songs, indispensable now they had once been introduced by Lorenzo; there was the favourite rigoletto, or round dance, footed "in piazza" under the blue frosty sky; there were practical jokes of all sorts, from throwing comfits to throwing stones— especially stones. For the boys and striplings, always a strong element in Florentine crowds, became at the height of Carnival-time as loud and unmanageable as tree-crickets, and it was their immemorial privilege to bar the way with poles to all passengers, until a tribute had been paid towards furnishing these lovers of strong sensations with suppers and bonfires: to conclude with the standing

entertainment of stone-throwing, which was not entirely monotonous, since the consequent maiming was various, and it was not ahvays a single person who was killed. So that the pleasures of the Carnival were of a chequered kind, and if a painter were called upon to represent them truly, he would have to make a picture in which there would be so much grossness and barbarity that it must be turned with its face to the wall, except when it was taken down for the grave historical purpose of justifying a reforming zeal which, in ignorance of the facts, might be unfairly condemned for its narrowness. Still there was much of that more innocent picturesque merriment which is never wanting among a people with quick animal spirits and sensitive organs: there was not the heavy sottishness which belongs to the thicker northern blood, nor the stealthy fierceness which in the more southern regions of the peninsula makes the brawl lead to the dagger-thrust. It was the high morning, but the merry spirits of the Carnival were still inclined to lounge and recapitulate the last night's jests, when Tito Melema was walking at a brisk pace on the way to the Via de' Bardi. Young Bernardo Dovizi, who now looks at us out of Raphael's portrait as the keen-eyed Cardinal da Bibbiena, was with him; and, as they went, they held animated talk about some subject that had evidently no relation to the sights and sounds through which they were pushing their way along the Por' Santa Maria. Nevertheless, as they discussed, smiled, and gesticulated, they both, from time to time, cast quick glances around them, and at the turning towards the Lung' Arno, leading to the Ponte Rubaconte, Tito had become aware, in one of these rapid surveys, that there was someone not far off him by whom he very much desired not to be recognised at that moment. His

  time and thoughts were thoroughly preoccupied, for he was looking forward to a unique occasion in his life: he was preparing for his betrothal, which was to take place on the evening of this very day. The ceremony had been resolved upon rather suddenly; for although preparations towards the marriage had been going forward for some time—chiefly in the application of Tito's florins to the fitting-up of rooms in Bardo's dwelling, which, the library excepted, had always been scantily furnished—it had been intended to defer both the betrothal and the marriage until after Easter, when Tito's year of probation, insisted on by Bernardo del Nero, would have been complete. But when an express proposition had come, that Tito should follow the Cardinal Giovanni to Rome to help Bernardo Dovizi with his superior knowledge of Greek in arranging a library, and there was no possibility of declining what lay so plainly on the road to advancement, he had become urgent in his entreaties that the betrothal might take place before his departure: there would be the less delay before the marriage on his return, and it would be less painful to part if he and Romola were outwardly as well as inwardly pledged to each other—if he had a claim which defied Messer Bernardo or anyone else to nullify it. For the betrothal, at which rings were exchanged and mutual contracts were signed, made more than half the legality of marriage, which was completed on a separate occasion by the nuptial benediction. Romola's feeling had met Tito's in this wish, and the consent of the elders had been won.

  And now Tito was hastening, amidst arrangements for his departure the next day, to snatch a morning visit to Romola, to say and hear any last words that were needful to be said before their meeting for the betrothal in the evening. It was not a time when any recognition could be pleasant that was at all likely to detain him; still less a recognition by Tessa. And it was unmistakably Tessa whom he had caught sight of moving along, with a timid and forlorn look, towards that very turn of the Lung' Arno which he was just rounding. As he continued his talk with the young Dovizi, he had an uncomfortable undercurrent of consciousness which told him that Tessa had seen him and would certainly follow him: there was no escaping her along this direct road by the Arno, and over the Ponte Rubaconte. But she would not dare to speak to him or approach him while he was not alone, and he would continue to keep Dovizi with him till they reached Bardo's door. He quickened his pace, and took up new threads of talk; but all the while the sense that Tessa was behind him, though he had no physical evidence of the fact, grew stronger and stronger; it was very irritating— perhaps all the more so because a certain tenderness and pity for the poor little thing made the determination to escape without any visible notice of her, a not altogether agreeable resource. Yet Tito persevered and carried his companion to the door, cleverly managing his "addio" without turning his face in a direction where it was possible for him to see an importunate pair of blue eyes; and as he went up the stone steps, he tried to get rid of unpleasant thoughts by saying to himself that after all Tessa might not have seen him, or, if she had, might not have followed him.

  But—perhaps because that possibility could not be relied on strongly—when the visit was over, he came out of the doorway with a quick step and an air of unconsciousness as to anything

that might be on his right hand or his left. Our eyes are so constructed, however, that
they take in a wide angle without asking any leave of our will; and Tito knew that there was a little figure in a white hood standing near the doorway—knew it quite well, before he felt a hand laid on his arm. It was a real grasp, and not a light, timid touch; for poor Tessa, seeing his rapid step, had started forward with a desperate effort. But when he stopped and turned towards her, her face wore a frightened look, as if she dreaded the effect of her boldness.

"Tessa!" said Tito, with more sharpness in his voice than she had ever heard in it before. "Why are you here? You must not follow me—you must not stand about doorplaces waiting for me."

Her blue eyes widened with tears, and she said nothing. Tito was afraid of something worse than ridicule, if he were seen in the Via de' Bardi with a girlish con-tadina looking pathetically at him. It was a street of high silent-looking dwellings, not of traffic; but Bernardo del Nero, or someone almost as dangerous, might come up at any moment. Even if it had not been the day of his betrothal, the incident would have been awkward and annoying. Yet it would be brutal—it was impossible— to drive Tessa away with harsh words. That accursed folly of his with the cerreiario —that it should have lain buried in a quiet way for months, and now start up before him as this unseasonable crop of vexation! He could not speak harshly, but he spoke hurriedly.

"Tessa, I cannot—must not talk to you here. I will go on to the bridge and wait for you there. Follow me slowly."

He turned and walked fast to the Ponte Rubaconte, and there leaned against the wall of one of the quaint little houses that rise at even distances on the bridge, looking towards the way by which Tessa would come. It would have softened a much harder heart than Tito's to see the little thing advancing with her round face much paled and saddened, since he had parted from it at the door of the "Nunziata." Happily it was the least frequented of the bridges, and there were scarcely any passengers on it at this moment. He lost no time in speaking as soon as she came near him.

"Now, Tessa, I have very little time. You must not cry. Why did you follow me this morning? You must not do so again."

"I thought," said Tessa, speaking in a whisper, and struggling against a sob that would rise immediately at this new voice of Tito's—"I thought you wouldn't be so long before you came to take care of me again. And the patrigno beats me, and I can't bear it any longer. And always when I come for a holiday I walk about to find you, and I can't. Oh, please don't send me away from you again! It has been so long, and I cry so now, because you never come to me. I can't help it, for the days are so long, and I don't mind about the goats and kids, or anything—and I can't "

The sobs came fast now, and the great tears. Tito felt that he could not do otherwise than comfort her. Send her away—yes; that he must do, at once. But it was all the more impossible to tell her anything that would leave her in a state of hopeless grief He saw new trouble in the background, but the difficulty of the moment was too pressing for him to weigh distant consequences.

"Tessa, my little one," he said, in his old caressing tones, "you must not cry. Bear with the cross patrigno a little longer. I will come back to you. But I'm going now to Rome—a long, long way off. I shall come back
in a few weeks, and then I promise you to come and see you. Promise me to be good and wait for me."

It was tlie well-remembered voice again, and the mere sound was half enough to soothe Tessa. She looked up at him with trusting eyes, that still glittered with tears, sobbing all the while, in spite of her utmost efforts to obey him. Again he said, in a gentle voice:

"Promise me, my Tessa."

"Yes," she whispered. "But you won't be long?"

"No, not long. But I must go now. And remember what I told you, Tessa. Nobody must know that you ever see me, else you will lose me for ever. And now, when I have left you, go straight home, and never follow me again. Wait till I come to you. Good-by, my little Tessa: I will come."

There was no help for it; he must turn and leave her without looking behind him to see how she bore it, for he had no time to spare. When he did look round he was in the Via de' Benci, where there was no seeing what was happening on the bridge; but Tessa was too trusting and obedient not to do just what he had told her.

Yes, the difficulty was at an end for that day; yet this return of Tessa to him, at a moment when it was impossible for him to put an end to all difficulty with her by undeceiving her, was an unpleasant incident to carry in his memory. But Tito's mind was just now thoroughly penetrated with a hopeful first love, associated with all happy prospects flattering to his ambition; and that future necessity of grieving Tessa could be scarcely more to him than the far-off cry of some little suffering animal buried in the thicket, to a merry cavalcade in the sunny plain. When, for the second time that day, Tito was hastening across the Ponte Rubaconte, the thought of Tessa caused

no perceptible diminution of his happiness. He was well muffled in his mantle, less, perhaps, to protect him from the cold than from the additional notice that would have been drawn upon him by his dainty apparel. He leaped up the stone steps by two at a time, and said hurriedly to Maso, who met him,

"Where is the damigella?"

"In the library; she is quite ready, and Monna Brigida and Messer Bernardo are already there with Ser Braccio, but none of the rest of the company."

"Ask her to give me a few minutes alone; I will await her in the salotto."

Tito entered a room which had been fitted up in the utmost contrast with the half-pallid, half-sombre tints of the library. The walls were brightly frescoed with "caprices" of nymphs and loves sporting under the blue among flowers and birds. The only furniture besides the red leather seats and the central table were two tall white vases, and a young faun playing the flute, modelled by a promising youth named Michelangelo Buonarotti. It was a room that gave a sense of being in the sunny open air.

Tito kept his mantle round him, and looked towards the door. It was not long before Romola entered, all white and gold, more than ever like a tall lily. Her white silk garment was bound by a golden girdle, which fell with large tassels; and above that was the rippling gold of her hair, surmounted by the white mist of her long veil, which was fastened on her brow by a band of pearls, the gift of Bernardo del Nero, and was now parted off her face so that it all floated backward.

"Regina mia!" said Tito, as he took her hand and kissed it, still keeping his mantle round him. He could not help going backward to look at her again, while she

Stood in calm delight, with that exquisite self-consciousness which rises under the gaze of admiring love.

"Romola, will you show me the next room now?" said Tito, checking himself with the remembrance that the time might be short. "You said I should see it when you had arranged everything."

Without speaking, she led the way into a long narrow room, painted brightly like the other, but only with birds and flowers. The furniture in it was all old; there were old faded objects for feminine use or ornament, arranged in an open cabinet between the two narrow windows;

above the cabinet was the portrait of Romola's mother; and below this, on the top of the cabinet, stood the crucifix which Romola had brought from San Marco.

"I have brought something under my mantle," said Tito, smiling; and throwing off the large loose garment, he showed the little tabernacle which had been painted by Piero di Cosimo. The painter had carried out Tito's intention charmingly, and so far had atoned for his long delay. "Do you know what this is for, my Romola?" added Tito, taking her by the hand, and leading her towards the cabinet. "It is a little shrine, which is to hide away from you for ever that remembrancer of sadness. You have done with sadness now; and we will bury all images of it—bury them in a tomb of joy. See!"

A slight quiver passed across Romola's face as Tito took hold of the crucifix. But she had no wish to prevent his purpose; on the contrary, she herself wished to subdue certain importunate memories and questionings which still flitted like unexplained shadows across her happier thought.

He opened the triptych and placed the crucifix within the central space; then closing it again, taking out the key, and setting the little tabernacle in the spot where the crucifix had stood, said,

"Now, Romola, look and see if you are satisfied with the portraits old Piero has made of us. Is it not a dainty device? and the credit of choosing it is mine."

"Ah, it is you—it is perfect!" said Romola, looking with moist joyful eyes at the miniature Bacchus with his purple clusters. "And I am Ariadne, and you are crowning me! Yes, it is true, Tito; you have crowned my poor life."

They held each other's hands while she spoke, and both looked at their imaged selves. But the reality was far more beautiful; she all lily-white and golden, and he with his dark glowing beauty above the purple red-bordered tunic.

"And it was our good strange Piero who painted it?" said Romola. "Did you put it into his head to paint me as Antigone, that he might have my likeness for this?"

"No, it was he who made my getting leave for him to paint you and your father, a condition of his doing this for me."

"Ah, I see now what it was you gave up your precious ring for, I perceived you had some cunning plan to give me pleasure."

Tito did not blench. Romola's little illusions about himself had long ceased to cause him anything but satisfaction. He only smiled and said,

"I might have spared my ring: Piero will accept no money from me; he thinks himself paid by painting you. And now, while I am away, you will look every day at those pretty symbols of our life together—the ship on the calm sea, and the ivy that never withers, and those Loves that have left off wounding us and shower soft petals that

e like our kisses; and the leopards and tigers, they are e troubles of your life that are all quelled now; and the range sea-monsters, with their merry eyes—let us see— ey are the dull passages in the heavy books, which have igun to be amusing since we have sat by each other."

"Tito mio!" said Romola, in a half-laughing voice of ve; "but you will give me the key?" she added, holding It her hand for it.

"Not at all!" said Tito, with playful decision, opening s scarsella and dropping in the little key. "I shall drown ni the Arno."

"But if I ever wanted to look at the crucifix again?"

"Ah! for that very reason it is hidden—hidden by .ese images of youth and joy."

He pressed a light kiss on her brow, and she said no ore, ready to submit, like all strong souls, when she felt) valid reason for resistance.

And then they joined the waiting company, which ade a dignified little procession as it passed along the Dnte Rubaconte towards Santa Croce. Slowly it passed, r Bardo, unaccustomed for years to leave his own house, alked with a more timid step than usual; and that slow ice suited well with the gouty dignity of Messer Bartolom-eo Scala, who graced the occasion by his presence, along ith his daughter Alessandra. It was customary to have ;ry long troops of kindred and friends at the sposalizio, betrothal, and it had even been found necessary in ne past to limit the number by law to no more than ?ir hundred two hundred on each side; for since the lests were all feasted after this initial ceremony, as well ; after the nozze, or marriage, the very first stage of latrimony had become a ruinous expense, as that scholarly enedict, Leonardo Bruno, complained in his own case.

But Bardo, who in his poverty had kept himself proudly free from any appearance of claiming the advantages attached to a powerful family name, would have no invitations given on the strength of mere friendship; and the modest procession of twenty that followed the sposi were, with three or four exceptions, friends of Bardo's and Tito's, selected on personal grounds.

Bernardo del Nero walked as a'vanguard before Bardo, who was led on the right by Tito, while Romola held her father's other hand. Bardo had himself been married at Santa Croce, and had insisted on Romola's being betrothed and married there, rather than in the little church of Santa Lucia, close by their house, because he had a complete mental vision of the grand church where he hoped that a burial might be granted him among the Florentines who had deserved well. Happily the way was short and direct, and lay aloof from the loudest riot of the Carnival, if only they could return before any dances or shows began in the great piazza of Santa Croce. The west was red as they passed the bridge, and shed a mellow light on the pretty procession, which had a touch of solemnity in the presence of the blind father. But when the ceremony was over, and Tito and Romola came out on to the broad steps of the church, with the golden links of destiny on their fingers, the evening had deepened into struggling starlight, and the servants had their torches lit.

As they came out a strange dreary chant, as of a Miserere, met their ears, and they saw that at the extreme end of the piazza there seemed to be a stream of people impelled by something approaching from the Borgo de' Greci.

"It is one of their masqued processions, I suppose,"

said Tito, who was now alone with Romola, while Bernardo took charge of Bardo.

And as he spoke there came slowly into view, at a height far above the heads of the on-lookers, a huge and ghastly image of Winged Time with his scythe and hourglass, surrounded by his winged children, the Hours. He was mounted on a high car completely covered with black, and the bullocks that drew the car were also covered with black, their horns alone standing out white above the gloom; so that in the sombre shadow of the houses it seemed to those at a distance as if Time and his children were apparitions floating through the air. And behind them came what looked like a troop of the sheeted dead gliding above blackness. And as they glided slowly, they chanted in a wailing strain,

A cold horror seized on Romola, for at the first moment it seemed as if her brother's vision, which could never be effaced from her mind, was being half fulfilled. She clung to Tito, who, divining what was in her thoughts, said—

"What dismal fooling sometimes pleases your Florentines ! Doubtless this is an invention of Piero di Cosimo, who loves such grim merriment."

"Tito, I wish it had not happened. It will deepen the images of that vision which I would fain be rid of."

"Nay, Romola, you will look only at the images of our happiness now. I have locked all sadness away from you."

"But it is still there—it is only hidden," said Romola, in a low tone, hardly conscious that she spoke.

"See, they are all gone now!" said Tito. "You will forget this ghastly mummery when we are in the light, and can see each other's eyes. My Ariadne must never look backward now—only forward to Easter, when she will triumph with her Care-dispeller."

BOOK II.

CHAPTER I.

FLORENCE EXPECTS A GUEST,

It was the seventeenth of November, 1494: more than eighteen months since Tito and Romola had been finally united in the joyous Easter time, and had had a rainbow-tinted shower of comfits thrown over them, after the ancient Greek fashion, in token that the heavens would shower sweets on them through all their double life.

Since that Easter time a great change had come over the prospects of Florence; and as in the tree that bears a myriad of blossoms, each single bud with its fruit is dependent on the primary circulation of the sap, so the fortunes of Tito and Romola were dependent on certain grand political and social conditions which made an epoch in the history of Italy,

In this very November, little more than a week ago, the spirit of the old centuries seemed to have re-entered the breasts of Florentines. The great bell in the Palace tower had rung out the hammer-sound of alarm, and the people had mustered with their rusty arms, their tools and impromptu cudgels, to drive out the Medici. The gate of San Gallo had been fairly shut on the arrogant, exasperat-

?ng Piero, galloping away towards Bologna with his hired horsemen frightened behind him, and on his keener young brother, the cardinal, escaping in the disguise of a Franciscan monk; and a price had been set on their heads. After that, there had been some sacking of houses, according to old precedent; the ignominious images, painted on the public buildings, of the men who had conspired against the Medici in days gone by, were effaced; the exiled enemies of the Medici were invited home. The half-fledged tyrants were fairly out of their splendid nest in the Via Larga, and the Republic had recovered the use of its will again.

But now, a week later, the great palace in the Via Larga had been prepared for the reception of another tenant; and if drapery roofing the streets with unwonted colour, if banners and hangings pouring out from the windows, if carpets and tapestry stretched over all steps and pavement on which exceptional feet might tread, were an unquestionable proof of joy, Florence was very joyful in the expectation of its new guest. The stream of colour flowed from the Palace in the Via Larga round by the Cathedral, then by the great Piazza della Signoria, and across the Ponte Vecchio to the Porta San Frediano—the gate that looks towards Pisa. There, near the gate, a platform and canopy had been erected for the Signoria; and Messer Luca Corsini, doctor of law, felt his heart palpitating a little with the sense that he had a Latin oration to read; and every chief elder in Florence had to make himself ready, with smooth chin and well-lined silk lucco, to walk in procession; and the well-born youths were looking at their rich new tunics after the French mode which was to impress the stranger as having a peculiar grace when worn by Florentines; and a large body of the

clergy, from the archbishop in his effulgence to the train of monks, black, white, and grey, were consulting betimes in the morning how they should marshal themselves, with their burden of relics and sacred banners and consecrated jewels, that their movements might be adjusted to the expected arrival of the illustrious visitor, at three o'clock in the afternoon.

An unexampled visitor! For.he had come through the passes of the Alps with such an army as Italy had not seen before: with thousands of terrible Swiss, well used to fight for love and hatred as well as for hire; with a host of gallant cavaliers proud of a name; with an unprecedented infantry, in which every man in a hundred carried an arquebus; nay, with cannon of bronze shooting not stones but iron balls, drawn not by bullocks but by horses, and capable of firing a second time before a city could mend the breach made by the first ball. Some compared the new comer to Charlemagne, reputed rebuilder of Florence, welcome conqueror of degenerate kings, regulator and benefactor of the Church; some preferred the comparison to Cyrus, liberator of the chosen people, restorer of the Temple. For he had come across the Alps with the most glorious projects: he was to march through Italy amidst the jubilees of a grateful and admiring people; he was to satisfy all conflicting complaints at Rome; he was to take possession, by virtue of hereditary right and a little fighting, of the kingdom of Naples; and from that convenient starting-point he was to set out on the conquest of the Turks, who were partly to be cut to pieces and partly converted to the faith of Christ. It was a scheme that seemed to befit the Most Christian King, head of a nation which, thanks to the devices of a subtle Louis the Eleventh, who had died in much fright as to his personal

prospects ten years before, had become the strongest of Christian monarchies; and this antitype of Cyrus and Charlemagne was no other than the son of that subtle Louis—the young Charles the Eighth of France.

Surely, on a general statement, hardly anything could seem more grandiose, or fitter to revive in the breasts of men the memory of great dispensations by which new strata had been laid in the history of mankind. And there was a very widely-spread conviction that the advent of the French King and his army into Italy was one of those events at which marble statues might well be believed to perspire, phantasmal fiery warriors to fight in the air, and quadrupeds to bring forth monstrous births— that it did not belong to the usual order of Providence, but was in a peculiar sense the work of God. It was a conviction that rested less on the necessarily momentous character of a powerful foreign invasion than on certain moral emotions to which the aspect of the times gave the form of presentiments: emotions which had found a very remarkalDle utterance in the voice of a single man.

That man was Fra Girolamo Savonarola, Prior of the Dominican convent of San Marco in Florence. On a September morning, when men's ears were ringing with the news that the French army had entered Italy, he had preahed in the Cathedral of Florence from the text, "Behold I, even I, do bring a flood of waters upon the earth." He believed it was by supreme guidance that he had reached just so far in his exposition of Genesis the previous Lent; and he believed the "flood of waters" — emblem at once of avenging wrath and purifying mercy— to be the divinely indicated symbol of the French army. His audience, some of whom were held to be among the choicest spirits of the age — the most cultivated men in

the most cultivated of Italian cities—believed it too, and listened with shuddering awe. For this man had a power rarely paralleled, of impressing his beliefs on others, and of swaying very various minds. And as long as four years ago he had proclaimed from the chief pulpit of Florence that a scourge was about to descend on Italy, and that by this scourge the Church was to be purified. Savonarola appeared to believe, and his hearers more or less waveringly believed, that he had a mission like that of the Hebrew prophets, and that the Florentines amongst whom his message was delivered were in some sense a second chosen people. The idea of prophetic gifts was not a remote one in that age: seers of visions, circumstantial heralds of things to be, were far from uncommon either outside or inside the cloister; but this very fact made Savonarola stand out the more conspicuously as a grand exception. While in others the gift of prophecy was very much like a farthing candle illuminating small corners of human destiny with prophetic gossip, in Savonarola it was like a mighty beacon shining far out for the warning and guidance of men. And to some of the soberest minds the supernatural character of his insight into the future gathered a strong attestation from the peculiar conditions of the age.

At the close of 1492, the year in which Lorenzo de' Medici died and Tito Melema came as a wanderer to Florence, Italy was enjoying a peace and prosperity unthreatened by any near and definite danger. There was no fear of famine, for the seasons had been plenteous in corn, and wine, and oil; new palaces had been rising in all fair cities, new villas on pleasant slopes and summits; and the men who had more than their share of these good things were in no fear of the larger number

who had less. For the citizens' armour was getting msty, and populations seemed to have become tame, licking the hands of masters who paid for a ready-made army when they wanted it, as they paid for goods of Smyrna. Even the fear of the Turk had ceased to be active, and the Pope found it more immediately profitable to accept bribes from him for a little prospective poisoning than to form plans either for conquering or for converting him.

Altogether, this world, with its partitioned empire and its roomy universal Church, seemed to be a handsome establishment for the few who were lucky or wise enough to reap the advantages of human folly: a world in which lust and obscenity, lying and treachery, oppression and murder, were pleasant, useful, and, when properly managed, not dangerous. And as a sort of fringe or adornment to the substantial delights of tyranny, avarice, and lasciviousness, there was the patronage of polite learning and the fine arts, so that flattery could always be had in the choicest Latin to be commanded at that time, and sublime artists were at hand to paint the holy and the unclean with impartial skill. The Church, it was said, had never been so disgraced in its head, had never shown so few signs of renovating, vital belief in its lower members; nevertheless it was much more prosperous than in some past days. The heavens were fair and smiUng above; and below there were no signs of earthquake.

Yet at that time, as we have seen, there was a rr.an in Florence who for two years and more had been preaching that a scourge was at hand; that the world was certainly not framed for the lasting convenience of hypocrites, libertines, and oppressors. From the midst of those smiling heavens he had seen a sword hanging—the sword of God's justice which was speedily to descend with puri-

Romola. I

fying punishment on the Church and the world. In brilliant Ferrara, seventeen years before, the contradiction between men's lives and their professed beliefs had pressed upon him with a force that had been enough to destroy his appetite for the world, and at the age of twenty-three had driven him into the cloister. He believed that God had committed to the Church the sacred lamp of truth for the guidance and salvation of men, and he saw that the Church, in its corruption, had become as a sepulchre to hide the lamp. As the years went on scandals increased and multiplied, and hypocrisy seemed to have given place to impudence. Had the world, then, ceased to have a righteous Ruler? Was the Church finally forsaken? No, assuredly: in the Sacred Book there was a record of the past in which might be seen as in a glass what would be in the days to come, and the book showed that when the wickedness of the chosen people, type of the Christian Church, had become crying, the judgments of God had descended on them. Nay, reason itself declared that vengeance was imminent, for what else would suffice to turn men from their obstinacy in evil? And unless the Church were reclaimed, how could the promises be fulfilled, that the heathens should be converted and the whole world become subject to the one true law? He had seen his belief reflected in visions—a mode of seeing which had been frequent with him from his youth up.

But the real force of demonstration for Girolamo Savonarola lay in his own burning indignation at the sight of wrong; in his fervent belief in an Unseen Justice that would put an end to the wrong, and in an Unseen Purity to which lying and uncleanness were an abomination. To his ardent, power-loving soul, believing in great ends, and

longing to achieve those ends by the exertion of its own strong will, the faith in a supreme and righteous Ruler became one with the faith in a speedy divine interposition that would punish and reclaim.

Meanwhile, under that splendid masquerade of dignities sacred and secular which seemed to make the life of lucky Churchmen and princely families so luxurious and amusing, there were certain conditions at work which slowly tended to disturb the general festivity. Ludovico Sforza—copious in gallantry, splendid patron of an incomparable Lionardo da Vinci—holding the ducal crown of Milan in his grasp, and wanting to put it on his own head rather than let it rest on that of a feeble nephew who would take very little to poison him, was much afraid of the Spanish-born old King Ferdinand and the Crown Prince Alfonso of Naples, who, not liking cruelty and treachery which were useless to themselves, objected to the poisoning of a near relative for the advantage of a Lombard usurper; the royalties of Naples again were afraid of their suzerain, Pope Alexander Borgia; all three were anxiously watching Florence, lest with its midway territory it should determine the game by underhand backing; and all four, with every small state in Italy, were afraid of Venice—Venice the cautious, the stable, and the strong, that wanted to stretch its arms not only along both sides of the Adriatic but across to the ports of the western coast.

Lorenzo de' Medici, it was thought, did much to prevent the fatal outbreak of such jealousies, keeping up the old Florentine alliance with Naples and the Pope, and yet persuading Milan that the alliance was for the general advantage. But young Piero de' Medici's rash vanity had quickly nullified the effect of his father's wary policy, and Ludovico Sforza, roused to suspicion of a league against him, thought of a move which would checkmate his adversaries: he determined to invite the French king to march into Italy and, as heir of the house of Anjou, to take possession of Naples. Ambassadors—"orators," as they were called in those haranguing times went and came; a recusant cardinal, determined not to acknowledge a Pope elected by bribery, and his own particular enemy, went and came also, and seconded the invitation with hot rhetoric; and the young king seemed to lend a willing ear. So that in 1493 the rumour spread and became louder and louder that Charles the Eighth of France was about to cross the Alps with a mighty army; and the Italian populations, accustomed, since Italy had ceased to be the heart of the Roman empire, to look for an arbitrator from afar, began vaguely to regard his coming as a means of avenging their wrongs and redressing their grievances.

And in that rumour Savonarola had heard the assurance that his prophecy was being verified. What was it that filled the ear of the prophets of old but the distant tread of foreign armies, coming to do the work of justice? He no longer looked vaguely to the horizon for the coming storm: he pointed to the rising cloud. The French army was that new deluge which was to purify the earth from iniquity; the French king, Charles VIII., was the instrument elected by God, as Cyrus had been of old, and all men who desired good rather than evil were to rejoice in his coming. For the scourge would fall destructively on the impenitent alone. Let any city of Italy, let Florence above all—Florence beloved of God, since to its ear the warning voice had been specially sent —repent and turn from its ways, like Nineveh of old, and the storm-cloud would roll over it and leave only refreshing rain-drops.

Fra Girolamo's word was powerful; yet now that the new Cyrus had already been three months in Italy, and was not far from the gates of Florence, his presence was expected there with mixed feelings, in which fear and distrust certainly predominated. At present it was not understood that he had redressed any grievances; and the Florentines clearly had nothing to thank him for. He held their strong frontier fortresses, which Piero de' Medici had given up to him without securing any honourable terms in return; he had done nothing to quell the alarming revolt of Pisa, which had been encouraged by his presence to throw off the Florentine yoke; and "orators," even with a prophet at their head, could win no assurance from him, except that he would settle everything when he was once within the walls of Florence. Still, there was the satisfaction of knowing that the exasperating Piero de' Medici had been fairly pelted out for the ignominious surrender of the fortresses, and in that act of energy the spirit of the Republic had recovered some of its old fire.

The preparations for the equivocal guest were not entirely those of a city resigned to submission. Behind the bright drapery and banners symbolical of joy, there were preparations of another sort made with common accord by government and people. Well hidden within walls there were hired soldiers of the Republic, hastily called in from the surrounding districts; there were old arms newly furbished, and sharp tools and heavy cudgels laid carefully at hand, to be snatched up on short notice; there were excellent boards and stakes to form barricades upon occasion, and a good supply of stones to make a surprising hail from the upper windows. Above all, there were people very strongly in the humour for fighting any personage who might be supposed to have designs of hectoring over them, having lately tasted that new pleasure with much relish. This humour was not diminished by the sight of occasional parties of Frenchmen, coming beforehand to choose their quarters, with a hawk, perhaps, on their left wrist, and, metaphorically speaking, a piece of chalk in their right hand to mark Italian doors withal; especially as credible historians imply that many sons of France were at that time characterised by something approaching to a swagger, which must have whetted the Florentine appetite for a little stone-throwing.

And this was the temper of Florence on the morning of the seventeenth of November, 1494.

CHAPTER II. THE PRISONERS.

The sky was grey, but that made little difference in the Piazza del Duomo, which was covered with its holy-day sky of blue drapery, and its constellations of yellow lilies and coats of arms. The sheaves of banners were unfurled at the angles of the Baptistery, but there was no carpet yet on the steps of the Duomo, for the marble was being trodden by numerous feet that were not at all exceptional. It was the hour of the Advent sermons, and the very same reasons which had flushed the streets with holiday colour were reasons why the preaching in the Duomo could least of all be dispensed with.

But not all the feet in the Piazza were hastening towards the steps. People of high aud low degree were moving to and fro with the brisk pace of men who had errands before them; groups of talkers were thickly scattered, some willing to be late for the sermon, others content not to hear it at all.

The expression on the faces of these apparent loungers was not that of men who are enjoying the pleasant laziness of an opening holiday. Some were in close and eager discussion; others were listening with keen interest to a single spokesman, and yet from time to time turned round with a scanning glance at any new passer-by. At the corner, looking towards the Via de'

Cerretani—just where the artificial rainbow light of the Piazza ceased, and the grey morning fell on the sombre stone houses— there was a remarkable cluster of the working people, most of them bearing on their dress or persons the signs of their daily labour, and almost all of them carrying some weapon, or some tool which might serve as a weapon upon occasion. Standing in the grey light of the street, with bare brawny arms and soiled garments, they made all the more striking the transition from the brightness of the Piazza. They were listening to the thin notary, Ser Cioni, who had just paused on his way to the Duomo. His biting words could get only a contemptuous reception two years and a half before in the Mercato, but now he spoke with the more complacent humour of a man whose party is uppermost, and who is conscious of some influence with the people.

"Never talk to me," he was saying, in his incisive voice, "never talk to me of bloodthirsty Swiss or fierce French infantry: they might as well be in the narrow passes of the mountains as in our streets; and peasants have destroyed the finest armies of our condottieri in time past, when they had once got them between steep precipices. I tell you, Florentines need be afraid of no army in their own streets."

"That's true, Ser Cioni," said a man whose arms and hands were discoloured by crimson dye, which looked like bloodstains, and who had a small hatchet stuck in his belt; "and those French cavaliers, who came in squaring themselves in their smart doublets the other day, saw a sample of the dinner we could serve up for them. I was carrying my cloth in Ognissanti, when I saw my fine Messeri going by, looking round as if they thought the houses of the Vespucci and the Agli a poor pick of lodgings for them, and eyeing us Florentines, like top-knotted cocks as they are, as if they pitied us because we didn't know how to strut. 'Yes, my fine GalH,' says I, 'stick out your stomachs, I've got a meat-axe in my belt that will go inside you all the easier;' when presently the old cow lowed,* and I knew something had happened—no matter what. So I threw my cloth in at the first doorway, and took hold of my meat-axe and ran after my fine cavaliers towards the Vigna Nuova. And, 'What is it, Guccio?' said I, when he came up with me. 'I think it's the Medici coming back,' said Guccio. Bembe! I expected so! And up we reared a barricade, and the Francesi looked behind and saw themselves in a trap; and up comes a good swarm of our Ciompi,** and one of them with a big scythe he had in his hand mowed off one of the fine cavalier's feathers:—it's true! And the lasses peppered a few stones down to frighten them. However, Piero de' Medici wasn't come after all; and it was a

* "Za vacca mtigUa" was the phrase for the sounding of tlie great bell in the tower of the Palazzo Veccliio.

** The poorer artisans connected with the wool trade—wool-beaters, carders, washers, &c.

pity; for we'd have left him neither legs nor wings to go away with again,"

"Well spoken, Oddo," said a young butcher, with his knife at his belt, "and it's my belief Piero will be a good while before he wants to come back, for he looked as frightened as a hunted chicken, when we hustled and pelted him in the piazza. He's a coward, else he might have made a better stand when he'd got his horsemen. But we'll swallow no Medici any more, whatever else the French king wants to make us swallow."

"But I like not those French cannon they talk of," said Goro, none the less fat for two years' additional grievances. "San Giovanni defend us! If Messer Dome-neddio means so well by us as your Frate says he does, Ser Cioni, why shouldn't he have sent the French another way to Naples?"

"Ay, Goro," said the dyer; "that's a question worth putting. Thou art not such a pumpkin-head as I took thee for. Why, they might have gone to Naples by Bologna, eh, Ser Cioni? or if they'd gone to Arezzo—we wouldn't have minded their going to Arezzo."

"Fools! It will be for the good and glory of Florence," Ser Cioni began. But he was interrupted by the exclamation, "Look there!" which burst from several voices at once, while the faces were all turned to a party who were advancing along the Via de' Cerretani.

"It's Lorenzo Tornabuoni, and one of the French noblemen who are in his house," said Ser Cioni, in some contempt at this interruption. "He pretends to look well satisfied—that deep Tornabuoni—but he's a Medicean in his heart: mind that."

The advancing party was rather a brilliant one, for there was not only the distinguished presence of Lorenzo

Tornabuoni, and the splendid costume of the Frenchman with his elaborately displayed white linen and gorgeous embroidery; there were two other Florentines of high birth in handsome dresses donned for the coming procession, and on the left hand of the Frenchman was a figure that was not to be eclipsed by any amount of intention or brocade—a figure we have often seen before. He wore nothing but black, for he was in mourning; but the black was presently to be covered by a red mantle, for he too was to walk in procession as Latin Secretary to the Ten. Tito Melema had become conspicuously serviceable in the intercourse with the French guests, from his familiarity with Southern Italy, and his readiness in the French tongue, which he had spoken in his early youth; and he had paid more than one visit to the French camp at Signa. The lustre of good fortune was upon him; he was smiling, listening, and explaining, with his usual graceful unpretentious ease, and only a very keen eye bent on studying him could have marked a certain amount of change in him which was not to be accounted for by the lapse of eighteen months. It was that change which comes from the final departure of moral youthfulness— from the distinct self-conscious adoption of a part in life. The lines of the face were as soft as ever, the eyes as pellucid; but something was gone—something as indefinable as the changes in the morning twilight.

The Frenchman was gathering instructions concerning ceremonial before riding back to Signa, and now he was going to have a final survey of the Piazza del Duomo, where the royal procession was to pause for religious purposes. The distinguished party attracted the notice of all eyes as it entered the piazza, but the gaze was not entirely cordial and admiring; there were remarks not altogether

allusive and mysterious to the Frenchman's hoof-shaped shoes—delicate flattery of royal superfluity in toes; and there was no care that certain snarlings at "Mediceans" should be strictly inaudible. But Lorenzo Tornabuoni possessed that power of dissembling annoyance which is demanded in a man who courts popularity, and to Tito's natural disposition to overcome ill-will by good-humour, there was added the unimpassioned feeling of the alien towards names and details that move the deepest passions of the native.

Arrived where they could get a good oblique view of the Duomo, the party paused. The festoons and devices that had been placed over the central doorway excited some demur, and Tornabuoni beckoned to Piero di Cosimo, who, as was usual with him at this hour, was lounging in front of Nello's shop. There was soon an animated discussion, and it became highly amusing from the Frenchman's astonishment at Piero's odd pungency of statement, which Tito translated literally. Even snarling on-lookers became curious, and their faces began to wear the half-smiling, half-humiliated expression of people who are not within hearing of the joke which is producing infectious laughter. It was a delightful moment for Tito, for he was the only one of the party who could have made so amusing an interpreter, and without any disposition to triumphant self-gratulation he revelled in the sense that he was an object of liking—he basked in approving glances. The rainbow light fell about the laughing group, and the grave church-goers had all disappeared within the walls. It seemed as if the piazza had been decorated for a real Florentine holiday.

Meanwhile in the grey light of the unadorned streets there were on-comers who made no show of linen and brocade, and whose humour was far from merry. Here, too, the French dress and hoofed shoes were conspicuous, but they were being pressed upon by a larger and larger number of non-admiring Florentines. In the van of the crowd were three men in scanty clothing; each had his hands bound together by a cord, and a rope was fastened round his neck and body, in such a way that he who held the extremity of the rope might easily check any rebellious movement by the threat of throttling. The men who held the ropes were French soldiers, and by broken Italian phrases and strokes from the knotted end of the rope, they from time to time stimulated their prisoners to beg. Two of them were obedient, and to every Florentine they had encountered had held out their bound hands and said in piteous tones,

"For the love of God and the Holy Madonna, give us something towards our ransom! We are Tuscans: we were made prisoners in Lunigiana."

But the third man remained obstinately silent under all the strokes from the knotted cord. He was very different in aspect from his two fellow-prisoners. They were young and hardy, and, in the scant clothing which the avarice of their captors had left them, looked like vulgar, sturdy mendicants. But he had passed the boundary of old age, and could hardly be less than four or five and sixty. His beard, which had grown long in neglect, and the hair which fell thick and straight round his baldness, were nearly white. His thick-set figure was still firm and upright, though emaciated, and seemed to express energy in spite of age—an expression that was partly carried out in the dark eyes and strong dark eyebrows, which had a strangely isolated intensity of colour in the midst of his yellow, bloodless, deep-wrinkled face with its lank grey

hairs. And yet there was something fitful in the eyes which contradicted the occasional flash of energy: after looking round with quick fierceness at windows and faces, they fell again with a lost and wandering look. But his lips were motionless, and he held his hands resolutely down. He would not beg.

This sight had been witnessed by the Florentines with growing exasperation. Many standing at their doors or passing quietly along had at once given money—some in half-automatic response to an appeal in the name of God, others in that unquestioning awe of the French soldiery which had been created by the reports of their cruel warfare, and on which the French themselves counted as a guarantee of immunity in their acts of insolence. But as the group had proceeded farther into the heart of the city, that compliance had gradually disappeared, and the soldiers found themselves escorted by a gathering troop of men and boys, who kept up a chorus of exclamations sufficiently intelligible to foreign ears without any interpreter. The soldiers themselves began to dislike their position, for, with a strong inclination to use their weapons, they were checked by the necessity for keeping a secure hold on their prisoners, and they were now hurrying along in the hope of finding shelter in a hostelry.

"French dogs!" "Bullock-feet!" "Snatch their pikes from them!" "Cut the cords and make them run for their prisoners. They'll run as fast as geese—don't you see they're web-footed?" These were the cries which the soldiers vaguely understood to be jeers, and probably threats. But everyone seemed disposed to give invitations of this spirited kind rather than to act upon them.

"Santiddio! here's a sight!" said the dyer, as soon as he had divined the meaning of the advancing tumult,

"and the fools do nothing but hoot. Come along!" he added, snatching his axe from his belt, and running to join the crowd, followed by the butcher and all the rest of his companions except Goro, who hastily retreated up a narrow passage.

The sight of the dyer, running forward with blood-red arms and axe uplifted, and with his cluster of rough companions behind him, had a stimulating effect on the crowd. Not that he did anything else than pass beyond the soldiers and thrust himself well among his fellow-citizens, flourishing his axe; but he served as a stirring symbol of street-fighting, like the waving of a well-known gonfalon. And the first sign that fire was ready to burst out was something as rapid as a little leaping tongue of flame: it was an act of the conjuror's impish lad Lollo, who was dancing and jeering in front of the ingenuous boys that made the majority of the crowd. Lollo had no great compassion for the prisoners, but being conscious of an excellent knife which was his unfailing companion, it had seemed to him from the first that to jump forward, cut a rope, and leap back again before the soldier who held it could use his weapon, would be an amusing and dexterous piece of mischief And now, when the people began to hoot and jostle more vigorously, Lollo felt that his moment was come—he was close to the eldest prisoner: in an instant he had cut the cord.

"Run, old one!" he piped in the prisoner's ear, as soon as the cord was in two; and himself set the example of running as if he were helped along with wings, like a scared fowl.

The prisoner's sensations were not too slow for him to seize the opportunity: the idea of escape had been continually present with him, and he had gathered fresh hope

from the temper of the crowd. He ran at once; but his speed would hardly have sufficed for him if the Florentines had not instantaneously rushed between him and his captor. He ran on into the piazza, but he quickly heard the tramp of feet behind him, for the other two prisoners had been released, and the soldiers were struggling and fighting their way after them, in such tardigrade fashion as their hoof-shaped shoes would allow—impeded, but not very resolutely attacked, by the people. One of the two younger prisoners turned up the Borgo di San Lorenzo, and thus made a partial diversion of the hubbub; but the main struggle was still towards the piazza, where all eyes were turned on it with alarmed curiosity. The cause could not be precisely guessed, for the French dress was screened by the impeding crowd.

"An escape of prisoners," said Lorenzo Tornabuom", as he and his party turned round just against the steps of the Duomo, and saw a prisoner rushing by them. "The people are not content with having emptied the Bargello the other day. If there is no other authority in sight they must fall on the sbirri and secure freedom to thieves. Ah! there is a French soldier: that is more serious."

The soldier he saw was struggling along on the north side of the piazza, but the object of his pursuit had taken the other direction. That object was the eldest prisoner, who had wheeled round the Baptistery and was running towards the Duomo, determined to take refuge in that sanctuary rather than trust to his speed. But in mounting the steps, his foot received a shock; he was precipitated towards the group of signori, whose backs were turned to him, and was only able to recover his balance as he clutched one of them by the arm.

It was Tito Melema who felt that clutch. He turned

his head, and saw the face of his adoptive father, Bal-dassarre Calvo, close to his own.

The two men looked at each other, silent as death: Baldassarre, with dark fierceness and a tightening grip of the soiled worn hands on the velvet-clad arm; Tito, with cheeks and lips all bloodless, fascinated by terror. It seemed a long while to them—it was but a moment.

The first sound Tito heard was the short laugh of Piero di Cosimo, who stood close by him and was the only person that could see his face.

"Ha, ha! I know what a ghost should be now."

"This is another escaped prisoner," said Lorenzo Tornabuoni. "Who is he, I wonder?"

"Some 7nadnian, surely," said Tito.

He hardly knew how the words had come to his lips: there are moments when our passions speak and decide for us, and we seem to stand by and wonder. They carry in them an inspiration of crime, that in one instant does the work of long premeditation.

The two men had not taken their eyes off each other, and it seemed to Tito, when he had spoken, that some magical poison had darted from Baldassarre's eyes, and that he felt it nishing through his veins. But the next instant the grasp on his arm had relaxed, and Baldassarre had disappeared within the church.

CHAPTER III.

AFTER-THOUGHTS.

"You are easily frightened, though," said Piero, with another scornful laugh. "My portrait is not as good as

the original. But the old fellow had a tiger look: I must go into the Duomo and see him again."

"It is not pleasant to be laid hold of by a madman, if madman he be," said Lorenzo Tornabuoni, in polite excuse of Tito, "but perhaps he is only a ruffian. We shall hear. I think we must see if we have authority enough to stop this disturbance between our people and your countrymen," he added, addressing the Frenchman.

They advanced towards the crowd with their swords drawn, all the quiet spectators making an escort for them. Tito went too: it was necessary that he should know what others knew about Baldassarre, and the first palsy of terror was being succeeded by the rapid devices to which mortal danger will stimulate the timid.

The rabble of men and boys, more inclined to hoot at the soldier and torment him than to receive or inflict any serious wounds, gave way at the approach of signori with drawn swords, and the French soldier was interrogated. He and his companions had simply brought their prisoners into the city that they might beg money for their ransom: two of the prisoners were Tuscan soldiers taken in Lunigiana; the other, an elderly man, was with a party of Genoese, with whom the French foragers had come to blows near Fivizzano. He might be mad, but he was harmless. The soldier knew no more, being unable to understand a word the old man said. Tito heard so far, but he was deaf to everything else till he was specially addressed. It was Tornabuoni who spoke.

"Will you go back with us, Melema? Or, since Messere is going off to Signa now, will you wisely follow the fashion of the times and go to hear the Frate, who will be like the torrent at its height this morning? It's what we must all do, you know, if we are to save our Medicean skins. should go if I had the leisure."

Tito's face had recovered its colour now, and he could make an effort to speak with gaiety.

"Of course I am among the admirers of the inspired orator," he said, smilingly; "but, unfortunately, I shall be occupied with the Segretario till the time of the procession."

"■ am going into the Duomo to look at that savage old man again," said Piero.

"Then have the charity to show him to one of the hospitals for travellers, Piero mio," said Tornabuoni. "The monks may find out whether he wants putting into a cage."

The party separated, and Tito took his way to the Palazzo Vecchio, where he was to find Bartolommeo Scala. It was not a long walk, but, for Tito, it was stretched out like the minutes of our morning dreams: the short spaces of street and piazza held memories, and previsions, and torturing fears, that might have made the history of months. He felt as if a serpent had begun to coil round his limbs. Baldassarre living, and in Florence, was a living revenge, which would no more rest than a winding serpent would rest until it had crushed its prey. It was not in the nature of that man to let an injury pass unavenged; his love and hatred were of that passionate fervour which subjugates all the rest of the being, and makes a man sacrifice himself to his passion as if it were a deity to be worshipped with self-destruction. Baldassarre had relaxed his hold, and had disappeared. Tito knew well how to interpret that: it meant that the vengeance was to be studied that it might be sure. If he had not uttered those decisive words—"He is a madman"—if he could have summoned up the state of mind, the courage, necessary for avowing his recognition of Baldassarre, would not the risk have been less? He might have declared himself to have had what he believed to be positive evidence of Baldassarre's death; and the only persons who could ever have had positive knowledge to contradict him, were Fra Luca, who was dead, and the crew of the companion galley, who had brought him the news of the encounter with the pirates. The chances were infinite against Baldassarre's having met again with any one of that crew, and Tito thought with bitterness that a timely, well-devised falsehood might have saved him from any fatal consequences. But to have told that falsehood would have re(|uired perfect self-command in the moment of a convulsive shock: he seemed to have spoken without any preconception—the words had leaped forth like a sudden birth that has been begotten and nourished in the darkness.

Tito was experiencing that inexorable law of human souls, that we prepare ourselves for sudden deeds by the reiterated choice of good or evil that gradually determines character.

There was but one chance for him now: the chance of Baldassarre's failure in finding his revenge. And— 'J'ito grasped at a thought more actively cruel than any he had ever encouraged before: might not his own unpre-uicditated words have some truth in them?—enough truth, at least, to bear him out in his denial of any declaration Baldassarre might make about him? The old man looked strange and wild; with his eager heart and brain, suffering Avas likely enough to have produced madness. If it were so, the vengeance that strove to inflict disgrace might be baffled.

But there was another form of vengeance not to be baffled by ingenious lying. Baldassarre belonged to a race to whom the thrust of the dagger seems almost as natural an impulse as the outleap of the tiger's talons. Tito shrank with shuddering dread from disgrace; but he had also that physical dread which is inseparable from a soft pleasure-loving nature, and which prevents a maa from meeting wounds and death as a welcome relief from disgrace. His thoughts flew at once to some hidden defensive armour that might save him from a vengeance which no subtlety could parry.

He wondered at the power of the passionate fear that possessed him. It was as if he had been smitten with a blighting disease that had suddenly turned the joyous sense of young life into pain.

There was still one resource open to Tito. He might have turned back, sought Baldassarre again, confessed everything to him—to Romola—to all the world. But he never thought of that. The repentance which cuts off all moorings to evil, demands something more than selfish fear. He had no sense that there was strength and safety in truth; the only strength he trusted to lay in his ingenuity and his dissimulation. Now that the first shock, which had called up the traitorous signs of fear, was well past, he hoped to be prepared for all emergencies by cool deceit—and defensive armour.

It was a characteristic fact in Tito's experience at this crisis, that no direct measures for ridding himself of Baldassarre ever occurred to him. All other possibilities passed through his mind, even to his own flight from Florence; but he never thought of any scheme for removing his enemy. His dread generated no active malignity, and he would still have been glad not to give pain to any mortal. He had simply chosen to make life easy to himself to carry his human lot, if possible, in such a way that it should pinch him nowhere; and the choice had, at various times, landed him in unexpected positions. The question now was, not whether he should divide the common pressure of destiny with his suffering fellow-men; it was whether all the resources of lying would save him from being crushed by the consequences ot that habitual choice.

CHAPTER IV.
INSIDE THE DUOMO.

When Baldassarre, with his hands bound together, and the rope round his neck and body, pushed his way behind the curtain, and saw the interior of the Duomo before him, he gave a start of astonishment, and stood still against the doorway. He had expected to see a vast nave empty of everything but lifeless emblems—side altars with candles unlit, dim pictures, pale and rigid statues— with perhaps a few worshippers in the distant choir following a monotonous chant. That was the ordinary aspect of churches to a man who never went into them with any religious purpose.

And he saw, instead, a vast multitude of warm, living faces, upturned in breathless silence towards the pulpit, at the angle between the nave and the choir. The multitude was of all ranks, from magistrates and dames of gentle nurture to coarsely clad artisans and country people. In the pulpit was a Dominican monk, with strong features and dark hair, preaching with the crucifix in his hand.

For the first few minutes Baldassarre noted nothing of his preaching. Silent as his entrance had been, some

eyes near the doorway had been turned on him with surprise and suspicion. The rope indicated plainly enough that he was an escaped prisoner, but in that case the church was a sanctuary which he had a right to claim; his advanced years and look of wild misery were fitted to excite pity rather than alarm; and as he stood motionless, with eyes that soon wandered absently from the wide scene before him to the pavement at his feet, those who had observed his entrance presently ceased to regard him, and became absorbed again in the stronger interest of listening to the sermon.

Among the eyes that had been turned towards him were Romola's: she had entered late through one of the side doors, and was so placed that she had a full view of the main entrance. She had looked long and attentively at Baldassarre, for grey hairs made a peculiar appeal to her, and the stamp of some unwonted suffering in the face, confirmed by the cord round the neck, stirred in her those sensibilities towards the sorrows of age, which her whole life had tended to develop. She fancied that his eyes had met hers in their first wandering gaze; but Baldassarre had not, in reality, noted her; he had only had a startled consciousness of the general scene, and the consciousness was a mere flash that made no perceptible break in the fierce tumult of emotion which the encounter with Tito had created. Images from the past kept urging themselves upon him like delirious visions strangely blended with thirst and anguish. No distinct thought for the future could shape itself in the midst of that fiery passion: the nearest approach to such thought was the bitter sense of enfeebled powers, and a vague determination to universal distrust and suspicion. Suddenly he felt himself vibrating to loud tones, which seemed

like the thundering echo of his own passion. A voice that penetrated his very marrow with its accent of triumphant certitude was saying—"The day of vengeance is at hand!"

Baldassarre quivered and looked up. He was too distant to see more than the general aspect of the preacher standing, with his right arm outstretched, lifting up the crucifix; but he panted for the threatening voice again as if it had been a promise of bliss. There was a pause before the preacher spoke again. He gradually lowered his arm. He deposited the crucifix on the edge of the pulpit, and crossed his arms over his breast, looking round at the multitude as if he would meet the glance of every individual face.

"All ye in Florence are my witnesses, for I spoke not in a corner. Ye are my witnesses, that four years ago, when there were yet no signs of war and tribulation, I preached the coming of the scourge. I lifted up my voice as a trumpet to the prelates and princes and people of Italy and said, The cup of your iniquity is full. Behold, the thunder of the Lord is gathering, and it shall fall and break the cup, and your iniquity, which seems to you as pleasant wine, shall be poured out upon you, and shall be as molten lead. And you, O priests, who say. Ha, ha! there is no Presence in the sanctuary—the Shechinah is nought—the Mercy-seat is bare: we may sin behind the veil, and who shall punish us? To you, I said, the presence of God shall be revealed in his temple as a consuming fire, and your sacred garments shall become a winding-sheet of flame, and for sweet music there shall be shrieks and hissing, and for soft couches there shall be thorns, and for the breath of wantons shall come the pestilence. Trust not in your gold and silver, trust not

in your high fortresses; for, though the walls were of iron, and the fortresses of adamant, the Most High shall put terror into your hearts and weakness into your councils, so that you shall be confounded and flee like women. He shall break in pieces mighty men without number, and put others in their stead. For God will no longer endure the pollution of his sanctuary; he will thoroughly purge his Church.

"And forasmuch as it is written that God will do nothing but he revealeth it to his servants the prophets, he has chosen me, his unworthy servant, and made his purpose present to my soul in the living word of the Scriptures, and in the deeds of his Providence; and by the ministry of angels he has revealed it to me in visions. And his word possesses me so that I am but as the branch of the forest when the wind of heaven penetrates it, and it is not in me to keep silence, even though I may be a derision to the scorner. And for four years I have preached in obedience to the Divine will: in the face of scoffing I have preached three things, which the Lord has delivered to me: that in these times God will regenerate his Church, and that before the regeneration must come the scourge over all Italy, and that these things will come quickly.

"But hypocrites who cloak their hatred of the truth Avith a show of love have said to me, 'Come now, Frate, leave your prophesyings: it is enough to teach virtue.' To these I answer: Yes, you say in your hearts, God lives afar off, and his word is as a parchment written by dead men, and he deals not as in the days of old, rebuking the nations, and punishing the oppressors, and smiting the unholy priests as he smote the sons of Eli. But I cry again in your ears: God is near and not afar off; His

judgments change not. He is the God of armies; the strong men who go up to battle are his ministers, even as the storm, and fire, and pestilence. He drives them by the breath of His angels, and they come upon the chosen land which has forsaken the covenant. And thou, O Italy, art the chosen land; has not God placed his sanctuary within thee, and thou hast polluted it? Behold! the ministers of his wrath are upon thee—they are at thy very doors."

Savonarola's voice had been rising in impassioned force up to this point, when he became suddenly silent, let his hands fall, and clasped them quietly before him. His silence, instead of being the signal for small movements amongst his audience, seemed to be as strong a spell to them as his voice. Through the vast area of the cathedral men and women sat with faces upturned, like breathing statues, till the voice was heard again in clear low tones.

"Yet there is a pause—even as in the days when Jerusalem was destroyed there was a pause that the children of God might flee from it. There is a stillness before the storm: lo, there is blackness above, but not a leaf quakes: the winds are stayed, that the voice of God's warning may be heard. Hear it now, O Florence, chosen city in the chosen land! Repent and forsake evil: do justice: love mercy: put away all uncleanness from among you, that the spirit of truth and holiness may fill your souls and breathe through all your streets and habitations, and then the pestilence shall not enter, and the sword shall pass over you and leave you unhurt.

"For the sword is hanging from the sky; it is quivering; it is about to fall! The sword of God upon the earth, swift and sudden! Did I not tell you, years ago, that I had beheld the vision and heard the voice? And behold, it is fulfilled! Is there not a king with his army at your gates? Does not the earth shake with the tread of horses and the wheels of swift cannon? Is there not a fierce multitude that can lay bare the land as with a sharp razor? I tell you the French king with his army is the minister of God: God shall guide him as the hand guides a sharp sickle, and the joints of the wicked shall melt before him, and they shall be mown down as stubble: he that fleeth of them shall not flee away, and he that escapeth of them shall not be delivered. And the tyrants who make to themselves a throne out of the vices of the multitude, and the unbelieving priests who traffic in the souls of men and fill the very sanctuary with fornication, shall be hurled from their soft couches into burning hell; and the pagans and they who sinned under the old covenant shall stand aloof and say: 'Lo! these men have brought the stench of a new wickedness into the everlast-ing fire.'

"But thou, O Florence, take the offered mercy. See! the Cross is held out to you: come and be healed. Which among the nations of Italy has had a token like unto yours? The tyrant is driven out from among you: the men who held a bribe in their left hand and a rod in their right are gone forth, and no blood has been spilled. And now put away every other abomination from among you, and you shall be strong in the strength of the living God. Wash yourselves from the black pitch of your vices, which have made you even as the heathens: put away the envy and hatred that have made your city as a nest of wolves. And there shall no harm happen to you: and the passage of armies shall be to you as the flight of birds, and rebellious Pisa shall be given to you again, and famine and pestilence shall be far from your gates, and you shall be as a beacon among the nations. But, mark! while you suffer the accursed thing to lie in the camp you shall be afflicted and tormented, even though a remnant among you may be saved."

These admonitions and promises had been spoken in an incisive tone of authority; but in the next sentence the preacher's voice melted into a strain of entreaty.

"Listen, O people, over whom my heart yearns, as the heart of a mother over the children she has travailed for! God is my witness that but for your sakes I would willingly live as a turtle in the depths of the forest, singing low to my Beloved, who is mine and I am his. For you I toil, for you I languish, for you my nights are spent in watching, and my soul melteth away for very heaviness. O Lord, thou knowest I am willing—I am ready. Take me, stretch me on thy cross: let the wicked who delight in blood, and rob the poor, and defile the temple of their bodies, and harden themselves against thy mercy—let them wag their heads and shoot out the lip at me: let the thorns press upon my brow, and let my sweat be anguish—I desire to be made like Thee in thy great love. But let me see of the fruit of my travail—let this people be savcu! Let me see them clothed in purity: let me hear their voices rise in concord as the voices of the angels: let them see no wisdom but in thy eternal law, no beauty but in holiness. Then they shall lead the v/ay before the nations, and the people from the four winds shall follow them, and be gathered into the fold of the blessed. For it is thy will, O God, that the earth shall be converted unto thy law: it is thy will that wickedness shall cease and love shall reign. Come, O blessed promise! and behold, I am willing—lay me on the altar: let my blood flow and the fire consume me; but let my witness be remembered among men, that iniquity shall not prosper for ever."

During the last appeal, Savonarola had stretched out his arms and lifted up his eyes to heaven; his strong voice had alternately trembled with emotion and risen again in renewed energy; but the passion with which he offered himself as a victim became at last too strong to allow of further speech, and he ended in a sob. Every changing tone, vibrating through the audience, shook them into answering emotion. There were plenty among them who had very moderate faith in the Prate's prophetic mission, and who in their cooler moments loved him little; nevertheless, they too were carried along by the great wave of feeling which gathered its force from sympathies that lay deeper than all theory. A loud responding sob rose at once from the wide multitude, while Savonarola had fallen on his knees and buried his face in his mantle. He felt in that moment the rapture and glory of martyrdom without its agony.

In that great sob of the multitude Baldassarre's had mingled. Among all the human beings present, there was perhaps not one whose frame vibrated more strongly than his to the tones and words of the preacher; but it had vibrated like a harp of which all the strings had been wrenched away except one. That threat of a fiery inexorable vengeance—of a future into which the hated sinner might be pursued and held by the avenger in an eternal grapple, had come to him like the promise of an unquenchable fountain to unquenchable thirst. The doctrines of the sages, the old contempt for priestly superstitions, had fallen away from his soul like a forgotten language: if he could have remembered them, what answer

could they have given to his great need Hke the answer given by this voice of energetic conviction? The thunder of denunciation fell on his passion-wrought nerves with all the force of self-evidence: his thought never went beyond it into questions—he was possessed by it as the war-horse is possessed by the clash of sounds. No word that was not a threat touched his consciousness; he had no fibre to be thrilled by it. But the fierce exultant delight to which he was moved by the idea of perpetual vengeance found at once a climax and a relieving outburst in the preacher's words of self-sacrifice. To Baldassarre those words only brought the vague triumphant sense that he too was devoting himself—signing with his own blood the deed by which he gave himself over to an unending fire, that would seem but coolness to his burning hatred.

"I rescued him—I cherished him—if I might clutch his heart-strings for ever! Come, O blessed promise! Let my blood flow; let the fire consume me!"

The one chord vibrated to its utmost. Baldassarre clutched his own palms, driving his long nails into them, and burst into a sob with the rest.

CHAPTER V.

OUTSIDE THE DUOMO.

While Baldassarre was possessed by the voice of Savonarola, he had not noticed that another man had entered through the doorway behind him, and stood not far off, observing him. It was Piero di Cosimo, who took no heed of the preaching, having come solely to look at the escaped prisoner. During the pause, in which the preacher and his audience had given themselves up to

ROMOLA.

inarticulate emotion, the new comer advanced and touched Baldassarre on the arm. He looked round with the tears still slowly rolling down his face, but with a vigorous sigh, as if he had done with that outburst. The painter spoke to him in a low tone:—

"Shall I cut your cords for you? I have heard how you were made prisoner,"

Baldassarre did not reply immediately; he glanced suspiciously at the officious stranger. At last he said, "If you will."

"Better come outside," said Piero.

Baldassarre again looked at him suspiciously; and Piero, partly guessing his thought, smiled, took out a knife, and cut the cords. He began to think that the idea of the prisoner's madness was not improbable, there was something so peculiar in the expression of his face. "Well," he thought, "if he does any mischief, he'll soon get tied up again. The poor devil shall have a chance, at least."

" Yon are afraid of me," he said again, in an undertone; "you don't want to tell me anything about yourself"

Baldassarre was folding his arms in enjoyment of that long-absent muscular sensation. He answered Piero with a less suspicious look and a tone which had some quiet decision in it.

"No, I have nothing to tell."

"As you please," said Piero, "but perhaps you want shelter, and may not know how hospitable we Florentines are to visitors with torn doublets and empty stomachs. There's an hospital for poor travellers outside all our gates, and, if you liked, I could put you in the way to one. There's no danger from your French soldier. He has been sent off."

Baldassarre nodded, and turned in silent acceptance of the offer, and he and Piero left the church together.

"You wouldn't like to sit to me for your portrait, should you?" said Piero, as they went along the Via dell' Orinolo, on the way to the gate of Santa Croce. "I am a painter: I would give you money to get your portrait."

The suspicion returned into Baldassarre's glance, as he looked at Piero, and said decidedly, "No."

"Ah!" said the painter, curtly. "Well, go straight on, and you'll find the Porta Santa Croce, and outside it there's an hospital for travellers. So you'll not accept any service from me?"

"I give you thanks for what you have done already. I need no more."

"It is well," said Piero, with a shrug, and they turned away from each other.

"A mysterious old tiger!" thought the artist, "well worth painting. Ugly—with deep lines—looking as if the plough and the harrow had gone over his heart, A fine contrast to my bland and smiling Messer Greco — my Bacco trionfante, who has married the fair Antigone in contradiction to all history and fitness. Aha! his scholar's blood curdled uncomfortably at the old fellow's clutch."

When Piero re-entered the Piazza del Duomo the multitude who had been listening to Fra Girolamo were pouring out from all the doors, and the haste they made to go on their several ways was a proof how important they held the preaching which had detained them from the other occupations of the day. The artist leaned against an angle of the Baptistery and watched the departing crowd, delighting in the variety of the garb and of the keen characteristic faces—faces such as IMasaccio

had painted more than fifty years before: such asDomenico Ghirlandajo had not yet quite left off painting.

This morning was a pecuHar occasion, and the Frate's audience, ahvays muhifarious, had represented even more completely than usual the various classes and political parties of Florence. There were men of high birth, accustomed to public charges at home and abroad, who had become newly conspicuous not only as enemies of the Medici and friends of popular government, but as thorough Piagnoni, espousing to the utmost the doctrines and practical teaching of the Frate, and frequenting San Marco as the seat of another Samuel; some of them men of authoritative and handsome presence, like Francesco Valori, and perhaps also of a hot and arrogant temper, very much gratified by an immediate divine authority for bringing about freedom in their own way; others, like Soderini, with less of the ardent Piagnone, and more of the wise politician. There were men, also of family, like Piero Capponi—simply brave undoctrinal lovers of a sober republican liberty, who preferred fighting to arguing, and had no particular reasons for thinking any ideas false that kept out the Medici and made room for public spirit. At their elbows were doctors of law whose studies of Ac-cursius and his brethren had not so entirely consumed their ardour as to prevent them from becoming enthusiastic Piagnoni: Messer Luca Corsini himself, for example, who on a memorable occasion yet to come was to raise his learned arms in street stone-throwing for the cause of religion, freedom and the Frate. And among these dignities who carried their black lucco or furred mantle with an air of habitual authority, there was an abundant sprinkling of men with more contemplative and sensitive faces; scholars inheriting such high names as Strozzi and .Acciajoli, who were already minded to take the cowl and join the community of San Marco; artists, wrought to a new and higher ambition by the teaching of Savonarola, like that young painter who had lately surpassed himself in his fresco of the Divine Child on the wall of the Frate's bare cell—unconscious yet that he would one day himself wear the tonsure and the cowl, and be called Fra Bartolommeo. There was the mystic poet Girolamo Benevieni hastening, perhaps, to carry tidings of the beloved Frate's speedy coming to his friend Pico della Miran-dola, who was never to see the light of another morning. There were well-born women attired with such scrupulous plainness that their more refined grace was the chief distinction between them and their less aristocratic sisters. There was a predominant proportion of the genuine popo-lani or middle class, belonging both to the Major and Minor Arts, conscious of purses threatened by war-taxes. And more striking and various, perhaps, than all the other classes of the Frate's disciples, there was the long stream of poorer tradesmen and artisans, whose faith and hope in his Divine message varied from the rude undiscriminat-ing trust in him as the friend of the poor and the enemy of the luxurious oppressive rich, to that eager tasting of all the subtleties of biblical interpretation which takes a peculiarly strong hold on the sedentary artisan, illuminating the long dim spaces beyond the board where he stitches, with a pale flame that seems to him the light of Divine science.

But among these various disciples of the Frate were scattered many who were not in the least his disciples. Some were Mediceans who had already, from motives of fear and policy, begun to show the presiding spirit of the popular party a feigned deference. Others were sincere advocates of a free government, but regarded Savonarola simply as an ambitious monk—half sagacious, half fanatical —who had made himself a powerful instrument with the people, and must be accepted as an important social fact. There were even some of his bitter enemies: members of the old aristocratic anti-Medicean party—determined to try and get the reins once more tight in the hands of certain chief families; or else licentious young men, who detested him as the kill-joy of Florence. For the sermons in the Duomo had already become political incidents, attracting the ears of curiosity and malice, as well as of faith. The men of ideas, like young Niccolo Macchiavelli, went to observe and write reports to friends away in country villas; the men of appetites, like Dolfo Spini, bent on hunting down the Frate as a public nuisance who made game scarce, went to feed their hatred and lie in wait for grounds of accusation.

Perhaps, while no preacher ever had a more massive influence than Savonarola, no preacher ever had more heterogeneous materials to work upon. And one secret of the massive influence lay in the highly mixed character of his preaching. Baldassarre, wrought into an ecstasy of self-martyring revenge, was only an extreme case among the partial and narrow sympathies of that audience. In Savonarola's preaching there were strains that appealed to the very finest susceptibilities of men's natures, and there were elements that gratified low egoism, tickled gossiping curiosity, and fascinated timorous superstition. His need of personal predominance, his labyrinthine allegorical interpretations of the Scriptures, his enigmatic visions, and his false certitude about the Divine intentions, never ceased, in his own large soul, to be ennobled by that fervid piety, that passionate sense of the infinite, that active sympathy, that clear-sighted demand for the subjection of selfish interests to the general good, which he had in common with the greatest of mankind. But for the mass of his audience all the pregnancy of his preaching lay in his strong assertion of supernatural claims, in his denunciatory visions, in the false certitude which gave his sermons the interest of a political bulletin; and having once held that audience in his mastery, it was necessary to his nature— it was necessary for their welfare—that he should keep the mastery. The effect was inevitable. No man ever struggled to retain power over a mixed multitude without suffering vitiation: his standard must be their lower needs, and not his own best insight.

The mysteries of human character have seldom been presented in a way more fitted to check the judgments of facile knowingness than in Girolamo Savonarola; but we can give him a reverence that needs no shutting of the eyes to fact, if we regard his life as a drama in which there were great inward modifications accompanying the outward changes. And up to this period, when his more direct actioh on political affairs had only just begun, it is probable that his imperious need of ascendancy had burned undiscernibly in the strong flame of his zeal for God and man.

It was the fashion of old, when an ox was led out for sacrifice to Jupiter, to chalk the dark spots, and give the offering a false show of unblemished whiteness. Let us fling away the chalk, and boldly say,—the victim is spotted, but it is not therefore in vain that his mighty heart is laid on the altar of men's highest hopes.

CHAPTER VI.
THE GARMENT OF FEAR.

At six o'clock that evening most people in Florence were glad the entrance of the new Charlemagne was fairly over. Doubtless when the roll of drums, the blast of trumpets, and the tramp of horses along the Pisan road began to mingle with the pealing of the excited bells, it was a grand moment for those who were stationed on turreted roofs, and could see the long-winding terrible pomp on the background of the green hills and valley. There was no sunshine to light up the splendour of banners, and spears, and plumes, and silken surcoats, but there was no thick cloud of dust to hide it, and as the picked troops advanced into close view they could be seen all the more distinctly for the absence of dancing glitter. Tall and tough Scotch archers, Swiss halberdiers fierce and ponderous, nimble Gascons ready to wheel and climb, cavalry in which each man looked like a knight-errant with his indomitable spear and charger—it was satisfactory to be assured that they would injure nobody but the enemies of God! With that confidence at heart it was a less dubious pleasure to look at the array of strength and splendour in nobles and knights, and youthful pages of choice lineage—at the bossed and jewelled sword-hilts, at the satin scarfs embroidered with strange symbolical devices of pious or gallant meaning, at the gold chains and jewelled aigrettes, at the gorgeous horse-trappings and brocaded mantles, and at the transcendent canopy carried by select youths above the head of the Most Christian King. To sum up with an old diarist,

wliose siDelling and diction halted a little behind the wonders of this royal visit,— "fit gran tnagriificenza."

But for the Signoria, who had been waiting on their platform against the gates, and had to march out at the right moment, with their orator in front of them, to meet the mighty guest, the grandeur of the scene had been somewhat screened by unpleasant sensations. If Messer Luca Corsini could have had a brief Latin welcome depending from his mouth in legible characters, it would have been less confusing when the rain came on, and created an impatience in men and horses that broke off the delivery of his well-studied periods, and reduced the representatives of the scholarly city to offer a make-shift welcome in impromptu French. But that sudden confusion had created a great opportunity for Tito. As one of the secretaries he was among the officials who were stationed behind the Signoria, and with whom these highest dignities were promiscuously thrown when pressed upon by the horses.

"Somebody step forward and say a few words m. French," said Soderini. But no one of high importance chose to risk a second failure. "You, Francesco Gaddi —you can speak." But Gaddi, distrusting his own promptness, hung back, and pushing Tito, said, "You, Melema."

Tito stepped forward in an instant, and, with the air of profound deference that came as naturally to him as walking, said the few needful words in the name of the Signoria; then gave way gracefully, and let the king pass on. His presence of mind, which had failed him in the terrible crisis of the morning, had been a ready instrument this time. It was an excellent livery-servant that never forsook him when danger was not visible. But when he

ROMOLA.

was complimented on his opportune service, he laughed it off as a thing of no moment, and to those who had not witnessed it, let Gaddi have the credit of the improvised welcome. No wonder Tito was popular: the touchstone by which men try us is most often their own vanity.

Other things besides the oratorical welcome had turned out rather worse than had been expected. If everything had happened according to ingenious preconceptions, the Florentine procession of clergy and laity would not have found their way choked up and been obliged to take a make-shift course through the back streets, so as to meet the king at the Cathedral only. Also, if the young monarch under the canopy, seated on his charger with his lance upon his thigh, had looked more like a Charlemagne and less like a hastily modelled grotesque, the imagination of his admirers would have been much assisted. It might have been wished that the scourge of Italian wickedness and "Champion of the honour of women" had had a less miserable leg, and only the normal sum of toes; that his mouth had been of a less reptilian width of slit, his nose and head of a less exorbitant outline. But the thin leg rested on cloth of gold and pearls, and the face was only an interruption of a few square inches in the midst of black velvet and gold, and the blaze of rubies, and the brilliant tints of the embroidered and bepearled canopy,— "fii gran fnagni/icenza."

And the people had cried Francia, Francia! with an enthusiasm proportioned to the splendour of the canopy which they had torn to pieces as their spoil, according to immemorial custom; royal lips had duly kissed the altar: and after all mischances the royal person and retinue were lodged in the Palace of the Via Larga, the rest of the nobles and gentry were dispersed among the great

houses of Florence, and the terrible soldiery were encamped in the Prato and other open quarters. The business of the day was ended.

But the streets still presented a surprising aspect, such as Florentines had not seen before under the November stars. Instead of a gloom unbroken except by a lamp burning feebly here and there before a saintly image at the street corners, or by a stream of redder light from an open doorway, there were lamps suspended at the windows of all houses, so that men could walk along no less securely and commodiously than by day,— "fii gran magnifice7iza."

Along those illuminated streets Tito Melema was walking at about eight o'clock in the evening, on his way homeward. He had been exerting himself throughout the day under the pressure of hidden anxieties, and had at last made his escape unnoticed from the midst of after-supper gaiety. Once at leisure thoroughly to face and consider his circumstances, he hoped that he could so adjust himself to them and to all probabilities as to get rid of his childish fear. If he had only not been wanting in the presence of mind necessary to recognise Baldassarre under that surprise!—it would have been happier for him on all accounts; for he still winced under the sense that he was deliberately inflicting suffering on his father: he would very much have preferred that

Baldassarre should be prosperous and happy. But he had left himself no second path now: there could be no conflict any longer: the only thing he had to do was to take care of himself

While these thoughts were in his mind he was advancing from the Piazza di Santa Croce along the Via dei Benci, and as he neared the angle turning into the Borgo Santa Croce his ear was struck by a music which was not that of evening revelry, but of vigorous labour the music of the anvil. Tito gave a slight start and quickened his pace, for the sounds had suggested a welcome thought. He knew that they came from the workshop of Niccolo Caparra, famous resort of all Florentines who cared for curious and beautiful iron-work.

"What makes the giant at work so late?" thought Tito. "But so much the better for me. I can do that little bit of business to-night instead of to-morrow morning."

Preoccupied as he was, he could not help pausing a moment in admiration as he came in front of the workshop. The wide doorway, standing at the truncated angle of a great block or "isle" of houses, was surmounted by a loggia roofed with fluted tiles, and supported by stone columns with roughly carved capitals. Against the red light framed in by the outline of the fluted tiles and columns stood in black relief the grand figure of Niccolo, with his huge arms in rhythmic rise and fall, first hiding and then disclosing the profile of his firm mouth and powerful brow. Two slighter ebony figures, one at the anvil, the other at the bellows, served to set off his superior massiveness.

Tito darkened the doorway with a very different outline, standing in silence, since it was useless to speak until Niccolo should deign to pause and notice him. That was not until the smith had beaten the head of an axe to the due sharpness of edge and dismissed it from his anvil. But in the meantime Tito had satisfied himself by a glance round the shop that the object of which he was in search had not disappeared.

Niccolo gave an unceremonious but good-humoured nod as he turned from the anvil and rested his hammer on his hip.

"What is it, Messer Tito? Business?"

"Assuredly, Niccolo; else I should not have ventured to interrupt you when you are working out of hours, since I take that as a sign that your work is pressing."

"I've been at the same work all day—making axes and spear-heads. And every fool that has passed my shop has put his pumpkin-head in to say, 'Niccolo, wilt thou not come and see the King of France and his soldiers?' and I've answered, 'No: I don't want to see their faces—I want to see their backs.'"

"Are you making arms for the citizens, then, Niccolo, that they may have something better than rusty scythes and spits in case of an uproar?"

"We shall see. Arms are good, and Florence is likely to want them. The Frate tells us we shall get Pisa again, and I hold with the Frate; but I should be glad to know how the promise is to be fulfilled, if we don't get plenty of good weapons forged? The Frate sees a long way before him; that I believe. But he doesn't see birds caught with winking at them, as some of our people try to make out. He sees sense, and not nonsense. But you're a bit of a Medicean, Messer Tito Melema. Ebbene! so I've been myself in my time, before the cask began to run sour. What's your business?"

"Simply to know the price of that fine coat of mail I saw hanging up here the other day. I want to buy it for a certain personage who needs a protection of that sort under his doublet."

"Let him come and buy it himself, then," said Niccolo, bluntly. "I'm rather nice about what I sell, and whom I sell to. I like to know who's my customer."

"I know your scruples, Niccolo. But that is only defensive armour: it can hurt nobody."

"True: but it may make the man who wears it feel himself all the safer if he should want to hurt somebody. No, no: it's not my own work; but it's fine work of Maso of Brescia; I should be loth for it to cover the heart of a scoundrel, I must know who is to wear it."

"Well, then, to be plain with you, Niccolo mio, I want it myself," said Tito, knowing it was useless to try persuasion. "The fact is, I am likely to have a journey to take—and you know what journeying is in these times. You don't suspect me of treason against the Republic?"

"No, I know no harm of you," said Niccolo, in his blunt way again. "But have you the money to pay for the coat? For you've passed my shop often enough to know my sign: you've seen the burning account-books. I trust nobody. The price is twenty florins, and that's because it's second-hand. You're not likely to have so much, money with you. Let it be till to-morrow."

"I happen to have the money," said Tito, who had been winning at play the day before, and had not emptied his purse. "I'll carry the armour home with me."

Niccolo reached down the finely wrought coat, which fell together into little more than two handfuls.

"There, then," he said, when the florins had been told down on his palm. "Take the coat. It's made to cheat sword, or poniard, or arrow. But, for my part, I would never put such a thing on. It's like carrying fear about with one."

Niccolo's words had an unpleasant intensity of meaning for Tito. But he smiled and said,—

"Ah, Niccolo, we scholars are all cowards. Handling the pen doesn't thicken the arm as your hammer-wielding does. Addio!"

He folded the armour under his mantle, and hastened across the Ponte Rubaconte.

CHAPTER VII.

THE YOUNG WIFE,

While Tito was hastening across the bridge with the new-bought armour under his mantle, Romola was pacing up and down the old library, thinking of him and longing for his return.

It was but a few fair faces that had not looked forth from windows that day to see the entrance of the French king and his nobles. One of the few was Romola's. She had been present at no festivities since her father had died—died quite suddenly in his chair, three months before.

"Is not Tito coming to write?" he had said, when the bell had long ago sounded the usual hour in the evening. He had not asked before, from dread of a negative; but Romola had seen by his listening face and restless movements that nothing else was in his mind.

"No, father, he had to go to a supper at the cardinal's: you know he is wanted so much by everyone," she answered, in a tone of gentle excuse.

"Ah! then perhaps he will bring some positive word about the library; the cardinal promised last week," said Bardo, apparently pacified by this hope.

He was silent a little while; then, suddenly flushing, he said,—

"I must go on without him, Romola. Get the pen. He has brought me no new text to comment on; but I must say what I want to say about the New Platonists. I shall die and nothing will have been done. Make haste, my Romola."

"I am ready, father," she said, the next minute, holding the pen in her hand.

But there was silence. Romola took no note of this for a little while, accustomed to pauses in dictation; and when at last she looked round inquiringly, there was no change of attitude.

"I am quite ready, father!"

Still Bardo was silent, and his silence was never again broken.

Romola looked back on that hour with some indignation against herself, because even with the first outburst of her sorrow there had mingled the irrepressible thought, "Perhaps my life with Tito will be more perfect now."

For the dream of a triple life with an undivided sum of happiness had not been quite fulfilled. The rainbow-tinted shower of sweets, to have been perfectly typical, should have had some invisible seeds of bitterness mingled with them; the crowned Ariadne, under the snowing roses, had felt more and more the presence of unexpected thorns. It was not Tito's fault, Romola had continually assured herself He was still all gentleness to her, and to her father also. But it was in the nature of things—she saw it clearly now—it was in the nature of things that no one but herself could go on month after month, and year after year, fulfilling patiently all her father's monotonous exacting demands. Even she, whose sympathy with her father had made all the passion and religion of her young years, had not always been patient, had been inwardly very rebellious. It was true that before their marriage, and even for some time after, Tito had seemed more unwearying than herself; but then, of course, the effort had the

ease of novelty. We assume a load with confident readiness, and up to a certain point the growing irksomeness of pressure is tolerable; but at last the desire for relief can no longer be resisted. Roniola said to herself that she had been very foolish and ignorant in her girlish time: she was wiser now, and would make no unfair demands on the man to whom she had given her best woman's love and worship. The breath of sadness that still cleaved to her lot while she saw her father month after month sink from elation into new disappointment as Tito gave him less and less of his time, and made bland excuses for not continuing his own share of the joint work—that sadness was no fault of Tito's, she said, but rather of their inevitable destiny. If he stayed less and less with her, why, that was because they could hardly ever be alone. His caresses were no less tender: if she pleaded timidly on any one evening that he should stay with her father instead of going to another engagement which was not peremptory, he excused himself with such charming gaiety, he seemed to linger about her with such fond playfulness before he could quit her, that she could only feel a little heartache in the midst of her love, and then go to her father, and try to soften his vexation and disappointment, while inwardly her imagination was busy trying to see how Tito could be as good as she had thought he was, and yet find it impossible to sacrifice those pleasures of society which were necessarily more vivid to a bright creature like him than to the common run of men. She herself would have liked more gaiety, more admiration: it was true, she gave it up willingly for her father's sake—she would have given up much more than that for the sake even of a slight wish on Tito's part. It was clear that their natures differed widely; but

perhaps it was no more than the inherent difference between man and woman, that made her affections more absorbing. If there were any other difference she tried to persuade herself that the inferiority was on her side. Tito was really kinder than she was, better tempered, less proud and resentful; he had no angry retorts, he met all complaints with perfect sweetness; he only escaped as quietly as he could from things that were unpleasant.

It belongs to every large nature, when it is not under the immediate power of some strong unquestioning emotion, to suspect itself, and doubt the truth of its own impressions, conscious of possibilities beyond its own horizon. And Romola was urged to doubt herself the more by the necessity of interpreting her disappointment in her life with Tito, so as to satisfy at once her love and her pride. Disappointment? Yes, there was no other milder word that would tell the truth. Perhaps all women had to suffer the disappointment of ignorant hopes, if she only knew their experience. Still, there had been something peculiar in her lot: her relation to her father had claimed unusual sacrifices from her husband. Tito had once thought that his love would make those sacrifices easy; his love had not been great enough for that. She was not justified in resenting a self-delusion. No! resentment must not rise: all endurance seemed easy to Romola rather than a state of mind in which she would admit to herself that Tito acted unworthily. If she had felt a new heartache in the solitary hours with her father through the last months of his life, it had been by no inexcusable fault of her husband's; and now—it was a hope that would make its presence felt even in the first moments when her father's place was empty—there was no longer any importunate claim to divide her from Tito; their young lives would flow in one cuirenl, and their true marriage would begin.

But the sense of something hke guilt towards her father in a hope that grew out of his death, gave all the more force to the anxiety with which she dwelt on the means of fulfilling his supreme wish. That piety towards his memory was all the atonement she could make now for a thought that seemed akin to joy at his loss. The laborious simple life, pure from vulgar corrupting ambitions, embittered by the frustration of the dearest hopes, imprisoned at last in total darkness—a long seed-time without a harvest—was at an end now, and all that remained of it besides the tablet in Santa Croce and the unfinished commentary on Tito's text, v/as the collection of manuscripts and antiquities, the fruit of half a century's toil and frugality. The fulfilment of her father's life-long ambition about this library was a sacramental obligation for Romola.

The precious relic was safe from creditors, for when the deficit towards their payment had been ascertained, Bernardo del Nero, though he was far from being among the wealthiest Florentines, had advanced the necessary sum of about a thousand florins——a large sum in those days—accepting a lien on the collection as a security.

"The State will repay me," he had said to Romola, making light of the service, which had really cost him some inconvenience. "If the cardinal finds a building, as he seems to say he will, our Signoria may consent to do the rest. I have no children, I can afford the risk."

But within the last ten days all hopes in the Medici had come to an end: and the famous Medicean collections in the Via Larga were themselves in danger of dispersion.

French agents had ah-eady begun to see that such very fine antique gems as Lorenzo had collected belonged by right to the first nation in Europe; and the Florentine State, which had got possession of the Medicean library, was likely to be glad of a customer for it. With a war to recover Pisa hanging over it, and with the certainty of having to pay large subsidies to the French king, the State was likely to prefer money to manuscripts.

To Romola these grave political changes had gathered their chief interest from their bearing on the fulfilment of her father's wish. She had been brought up in learned seclusion from the interests of actual life, and had been accustomed to think of heroic deeds and great principles as something antithetic to the vulgar present, of the Pnyx and the Forum as something more worthy of attention than the councils of living Florentine men. And now the expulsion of the Medici meant little more for her than the extinction of her best hope about her father's library. The times, she knew, were unpleasant for friends of the Medici, like her godfather and Tito: superstitious shopkeepers and the stupid rabble, were full of suspicions; but her new keen interest in public events, in the outbreak of war, in the issue of the French king's visit, in the changes that were likely to happen in the State, was kindled solely by the sense of love and duty to her father's memory. All Romola's ardour had been concentrated in her affections. Her share in her father's learned pursuits had been for her little more than a toil which was borne for his sake; and Tito's airy brilliant faculty had no attraction for her that was not merged in the deeper sympathies that belong to young love and trust. Romola had had contact with no mind that could stir the larger possibilities of her nature; they lay folded and crushed like embryonic wings, making no element in her consciousness beyond an occasional vague uneasiness.

But this new personal interest of hers in public affairs had made her care at last to understand precisely what influence Fra Girolamo's preaching was likely to have on the turn of events. Changes in the form of the State were talked of, and all she could learn from Tito, whose secretaryship and serviceable talents carried him into the heart of public business, made her only the more eager to fill out her lonely day by going to hear for herself what it was that was just now leading all Florence by the ears. This morning, for the first time, she had been to hear one of the Advent sermons in the Duomo, When Tito had left her, she had formed a sudden resolution, and after visiting the spot where her father was buried in Santa Croce, had walked on to the Duomo. The memory of that last scene with Dino was still vivid within her whenever she recalled it, but it had receded behind the experience and anxieties of her married life. The new sensibiHties and questions which it had half awakened in her were quieted again by that subjection to her husband's mind which is felt by every wife who loves her husband with passionate devotedness and full reliance. She remembered the effect of Fra Girolamo's voice and presence on her as a ground for expecting that his sermon might move her in spite of his being a narrow-minded monk. But the sermon did no more than slightly deepen her previous impression, that this fanatical preacher of tribulations was after all a man towards whom it might be possible for her to feel personal regard and reverence. The denunciations and exhortations simply arrested her attention. She felt no terror, no pangs of conscience: it was the roll of distant

thunder, that seemed grand, but could not shake her. But when she heard Savonarola invoke martyrdom, she sobbed with the rest: she felt herself penetrated with a new sensation—a strange sympathy with something apart from all the definable interests of her life. It was not altogether unlike the thrill which had accompanied certain rare heroic touches in history and poetry; but the resemblance was as that between the memory of music, and the sense of being possessed by actual vibrating harmonies.

But that transient emotion, strong as it was, seemed to lie quite outside the inner chamber and sanctuary of her life. She was not thinking of Fra Girolamo now; she was listening anxiously for the step of her husband. During these three months of their double solitude she had thought of each day as an epoch in which their union might begin to be more perfect. She was conscious of being sometimes a little too sad or too urgent about what concerned her father's memory—a little too critical or coldly silent when Tito narrated the things that were said and done in the world he frequented—a little too hasty in suggesting that by living quite simply as her father had done, they might become rich enough to pay Bernardo del Nero, and reduce the difficulties about the library. It was not possible that Tito could feel so strongly on this last point as she did, and it was asking a great deal from him to give up luxuries for which he really laboured. The next time Tito came home she would be careful to suppress all those promptings that seemed to isolate her from him. Romola was labouring, as every loving woman must, to subdue her nature to her husband's. The great need of her heart compelled her to strangle, with desperate resolution, every rising impulse of suspicion, pride, and resentment; she felt equal to any self-infliction that would

save her from ceasing to love. That would have been like the hideous nightmare in which the Avorld had seemed to break away all round her, and leave her feet overhanging the darkness. Romola had never distinctly imagined such a future for herself; she was only beginning to feel the presence of effort in that clinging trust which had once been mere repose.

She waited and listened long, for Tito had not come straight home after leaving Niccolo Caparra, and it was more than two hours after the time when he was crossing the Ponte Rubaconte that Romola heard the great door of the court turning on its hinges, and hastened to the head of the stone steps. There was a lamp hanging over the stairs, and they could see each other distinctly as he ascended. The eighteen months had produced a more definable change in

Romola's face than in Tito's: the expression was more subdued, less cold, and more beseeching, and, as the pink flush overspread her face now, in her joy that the long waiting was at an end, she was much lovelier than on the day when Tito had first seen her. On that day, any on-looker would have said that Romola's nature was made to command, and Tito's to bend; yet now Romola's mouth was quivering a little, and there was some timidity in her glance.

He made an effort to smile, as she said,

"My Tito, you are tired, it has been a fatiguing day: is it not true?"

Maso was there, and no more was said until they had crossed the antechamber and closed the door of the library behind them. The wood was burning brightly on the great dogs; that was one welcome for Tito, late as he was, and Romola's gentle voice was another.

He just turned and kissed her, when she took off his

mantle, then went towards a high-backed chair placed for him near the fire, threw himself into it, and flung away his cap, saying, not peevishly, but in a fatigued tone of remonstrance, as he gave a slight shudder,

"Romola, I wish you would give up sitting in this library. Surely our own rooms are pleasanter in this chill weather."

Romola felt hurt. She had never seen Tito so indifferent in his manner; he was usually full of lively solicitous attention. And she had thought so much of his return to her after the long day's absence! He must be very weary.

"I wonder you have forgotten, Tito," she answered, looking at him, anxiously, as if she wanted to read an excuse for him in the signs of bodily fatigue. "You know I am making the catalogue on the new plan that my father wished for; you have not time to help me, so I must work at it closely."

Tito, instead of meeting Romola's glance, closed his eyes and rubbed his hands over face and hair. He felt he was behaving unlike himself, but he would make amends to-morrow. The terrible resurrection of secret fears, which, if Romola had known them, would have alienated her from him for ever, caused him to feel an alienation already begun between them—caused him to feel a certain repulsion towards a woman from whose mind he was in danger. The feeling had taken hold of him unawares, and he was vexed with himself for behaving in this new cold way to her. He could not suddenly command any affectionate looks or words; he could only exert himself to say what might sei"ve as an excuse.

"I am not well, Romola; you must not be surprised if I am peevish."

"Ah, you have had so much to tire you to-day," said Romola, kneehng down close to him, and laying her arm on his chest while she put his hair back caressingly.

Suddenly she drew her arm away with a start, and a gaze of alarmed inquiry.

"What have you got under your tunic, Tito? Something as hard as iron."

"It ts iron—it is chain armour," he said at once. He was prepared for the surprise and the question, and he spoke quietly, as of something that he was not hurried to explain.

"There was some unexpected danger to-day, then?" said Romola, in a twie of conjecture. "You had it lent to you for the procession?"

"No; it is my own. I shall be obliged to wear it constantly, for some time."

"What is it that threatens you, my Tito?" said Romola, looking terrified, and clinging to him again.

"Everyone is threatened in these times, who is not a rabid enemy of the Medici. Don't look distressed, my Romola—this armour will make me safe against covert attacks."

Tito put his hand on her neck and smiled. This little dialogue about the armour had broken through the new crust, and made a channel for the sweet habit of kindness.

"But my godfather, then," said Romola; "is not he, too, in danger? And he takes no precautions—ought he not? since he must surely be in more danger than you, who have so little influence compared with him."

"It is just because I am less important that I am in more danger," said Tito, readily. "I am suspected constantly of being an envoy. And men like Messer Bernardo are protected by their position and their extensive family connections, which spread among all parties, while I am a Greek that nobody would avenge."

"But, Tito, is it a fear of some particular person, or only a vague sense of danger, that has made you think of wearing this?" Romola was unable to repel the idea of a degrading fear in Tito, which mingled itself with her anxiety.

"I have had special threats," said Tito, "but I must beg you to be silent on the subject, my Romola. I shall consider that you have broken my confidence, if you mention it to your godfather."

"Assuredly I will not mention it," said Romola, blushing, "if you wish it to be a secret. But, dearest Tito," she added, after a moment's pause, in a tone of loving anxiety, "it will make you very wretched."

"What will make me wretched?" he said, with a scarcely perceptible movement across his face, as from some darting sensation.

"This fear.—this heavy armour. I can't help shuddering as I feel it under my arm. I could fancy it a story of enchantment — that some malignant fiend had changed your sensitive human skin into a hard shell. It seems so unlike my bright, light-hearted Tito!"

"Then you would rather have your husband exposed to danger, when he leaves you?" said Tito, smiling. "If you don't mind my being poniarded or shot, why need I mind? I will give up the armour—shall I?"

"No, Tito, no. I am fanciful. Do not heed what I have said. But such crimes are surely not common in Florence? I have always heard my father and godfather say so. Have they become frequent lately?"

"It is not unlikely they will become frequent, with the bitter hatreds that are being bred continually."

Romola was silent a few moments. She shrank from insisting further on the subject of the armour. She tried to shake it off.

"Tell me what has happened to-day," she said, in a dieerful tone. "Has all gone off well?"

"Excellently well. First of all, the rain came and put an end to Luca Corsini's oration, which nobody wanted to hear, and a ready-tongued personage—some say it was Gaddi, some say it was Melema, but really it was done so quickly no one knows who it was—had the honour of giving the Christianissimo the briefest possible welcome in bad French."

"Tito, it was you, I know," said Romola, smiling brightly, and kissing him. "How is it you never care about claiming anything? And after that?"

"Oh! after that, there was a show of armour and jewels, and trappings, such as you saw at the last Florentine giostra, only a great deal more of them. There was strutting, and prancing, and confusion, and scrambling, and the people shouted, and the Christianissimo smiled from ear to ear. And after that there was a great deal of flattery, and eating, and play. I was at Tornabuoni's. I will tell you about it to-morrow."

"Yes, dearest, never mind now. But is there any more hope that things will end peaceably for Florence, that the Republic will not get into fresh troubles?"

Tito gave a shrug. "Florence will have no peace but what it pays well for; that is clear."

Romola's face saddened, but she checked herself, and said, cheerfully, "You would not guess where I went today, Tito. I went to the Duomo, to hear Fra Girolamo."

Tito looked startled: he had immediately thought of Baldassarre's entrance into the Duomo: but Romola gave his look another meaning.

"You are surprised, are you not? It was a sudden thought. I want to know all about the public affairs now, and I determined to hear for myself what the Frate promised the people about this French invasion."

"Well, and what did you think of the prophet?"

"He certainly has a very mysterious power, that man. A great deal of his sermon was what I expected; but once I was strangely moved—I sobbed with the rest."

"Take care, Romola," said Tito, playfully, feeling relieved that she had said nothing about Baldassarre; "you have a touch of fanaticism in you. I shall have you seeing visions, like your brother."

"No; it was the same with everyone else. He carried them all with him; unless it were that gross Dolfa Spini, whom I saw there making grimaces. There was even a wretched-looking man, with a rope round his neck —an escaped prisoner, I should think, who had run in for shelter—a very wild-eyed old man: I saw him with great tears rolling down his cheeks, as he looked and listened quite eagerly."

There was a slight pause before Tito spoke.

"I saw the man," he said, "the prisoner. I was outside the Duomo with Lorenzo Tornabuoni when he ran in. He had escaped from a French soldier. Did you see him when you came out?"

"No, he went out with our good old Piero di Cosimo. I saw Piero come in and cut off his rope, and take him out of the church. But you want rest, Tito? You feel ill?"

"Yes," said Tito, rising. The horrible sense that he

must live in continual dread of what Baldassarre had said or done pressed upon him like a cold weight.

CHAPTER Vni.

THE PAINTED RECORD.

Four days later, Romola was on her way to the house of Piero di Cosimo, in the Via Gualfonda. Some of the streets through which she had to pass were lined with Frenchmen who were gazing at Florence, and with Florentines who were gazing at the French, and the gaze was not on either side entirely friendly and admiring. The first nation in Europe, of necessity finding itself, when out of its own country, in the presence of general inferiority, naturally assumed an air of conscious preeminence; and the Florentines, who had taken such pains to play the host amiably, were getting into the Avorst humour with their too superior guests.

For after the first smiling compliments and festivities were over—after wondrous Mysteries with unrivalled machinery of floating clouds and angels had been presented in churches—after the royal guest had honoured Florentine dames with much of his Most Christian ogUng at balls and suppers, and business had begun to be talked of—it appeared that the new Charlemagne regarded Florence as a conquered city, inasmuch as he had entered it with his lance in rest, talked of leaving his viceroy behind him, and had thoughts of bringing back the Medici. Singular logic this appeared to be on the part of an elect instrument of God! since the policy of Piero de' Medici, disowned by the people, had been the only offence of Florence against the majesty of France, And Florence was deter-

^^O ROMOLA.

mined not to submit. The determination was being expressed very strongly in consultations of citizens inside the Old Palace, and it was beginning to show itself on the broad flags of the streets and piazze wherever there was an opportunity of flouting an insolent Frenchman. Under these circumstances the streets were not altogether a pleasant promenade for well-born women; but Romola, shrouded in her black veil and mantle, and with old Maso by her side, felt secure enough from impertinent observation.

And she was impatient to visit Piero di Cosimo. A copy of her father's portrait as Œdipus, which he had long ago undertaken to make for her, was not yet finished; and Piero was so uncertain in his work—sometimes, when the demand was not peremptory, laying aside a picture for months; sometimes thrusting it into a corner or coffer, where it was likely to be utterly forgotten—that she felt it necessary to watch over his progress. She was a favourite with the painter, and he was inclined to fulfil any wish of hers, but no general inclination could be trusted as a safeguard against his sudden whims. He had told her the week before that the picture would perhaps be finished by this time; and Romola was nervously anxious to have in her possession a copy of the only portrait existing of her father in the days of his blindness, lest his image should grow dim in her mind. The sense of defect in her devotedness to him made her cling with all the force of compunction as well as affection to the duties of memory. Love does not aim simply at the conscious good of the beloved object: it is not satisfied without perfect loyalty of heart; it aims at its own completeness.

Romola, by special favour, was allowed to intrude upon the painter without previous notice. She lifted the

iron slide and called Piero in a flute-like tone, as the little maiden with the eggs had done in Tito's presence. Piero was quick in answering, but when he opened the door he accounted for his quickness in a manner that was not complimentary.

"Ah, Madonna Romola, is it you? I thought my eggs were come; I wanted them."

"I have brought you something better than hard eggs, Piero. Maso has got a little basket full of cakes and confetti for you," said Romola, smiling, as she put back her veil. She took the basket from Maso, and, stepping into the house, said,—

"I know you like these things when you can have them without trouble. Confess you do."

"Yes, when they come to me as easily as the light does," said Piero, folding his arms and looking down at the sweetmeats as Romola uncovered them and glanced at him archly. "And they are come along with the light now," he added, lifting his eyes to her face and hair with a painter's admiration, as her hood, dragged by the weight of her veil, fell backward.

"But I know what the sweetmeats are for," he went on; "they are to stop my mouth while you scold me. Well, go on into the next room, and you will see I've done something to the picture since you saw it, though it's not finished yet. But I didn't promise, you know: I take care not to promise:

'Chi promette e non mantiene L'anima sua non va mai bene.'"

The door opening on the wild garden was closed now, and the painter was at work. Not at Romola's picture, however. That was standing on the floor, propped against

the wall, and Piero stooped to lift it, that he might carry it into the proper light. But in lifting away this picture, he had disclosed another—the oil-sketch of Tito, to which he had made an important addition within the last few days. It was so much smaller than the other picture that it stood far within it, and Piero, apt to forget where he had placed anything, was not aware of what he had revealed as, peering at some detail in the painting which he held in his hands, he went to place it on an easel. But Romola exclaimed, flushing with astonishment,

"That is Tito!"

Piero looked round, and gave a silent shrug. He was vexed at his own forgetfulness.

She was still looking at the sketch in astonishment; but presently she turned towards the painter, and said with puzzled alarm,

"What a strange picture! When did you paint it? What does it mean?"

"A mere fancy of mine," said Piero, lifting off his skull-cap, scratching his head, and making the usual grimace by which he avoided the betrayal of any feeling. "I wanted a handsome young face for it, and your husband's was just the thing."

He went forward, stooped down to the picture, and lifting it away with its back to Romola, pretended to be giving it a passing examination, before putting it aside as a thing not good enough to show.

But Romola, who had the fact of the armour in her mind, and was penetrated by this strange coincidence of things which associated Tito with the idea of fear, went to his elbow and said,—

"Don't put it away; let me look again. That man with the rope round his zieck—I saw him—I saw you come to

him in the Duomo. What was it that made you put him into a picture with Tito?"

Piero saw no better resource than to tell part of the truth.

"It was a mere accident. The man was running away—running up the steps, and caught hold of your husband: I suppose he had stumbled. I happened to be there, and saw it, and I thought the savage-looking old fellow was a good subject. But it's worth nothing—it's only a freakish daub of mine," Piero ended, contemptuously, moving the sketch away with an air of decision, and putting it on a high shelf. "Come and look at the Œdipus."

He had shown a little too much anxiety in putting the sketch out of her sight, and had produced the very impression he had sought to prevent—that there was really something unpleasant, something disadvantageous to Tito, in the circumstances out of which the picture arose. But this impression silenced her: her pride and delicacy shrank from questioning further, where questions might seem to imply that she could entertain even a slight suspicion against her husband. She merely said, in as quiet a tone as she could.

"He was a strange piteous-looking man, that prisoner. Do you know anything more of him?"

"No more: I showed him the way to the hospital, that's all. See now, the face of Œdipus is pretty nearly finished; tell me what you think of it."

Romola now gave her whole attention to her father's portrait, standing in long silence before it.

"Ah!" she said at last, "you have done what I wanted. You have given it more of the listening look. My good

Piero"—she turned towards him with bright moist eyes—' "I am very grateful to you."

"Now, that's what I can't bear in you women," said Piero, turning impatiently, and kicking aside the objects that littered the floor—"you are always pouring out feelings where there's no call for them. Why should you be grateful to me for a picture you pay me for, especially when I make you wait for it? And if I paint a picture, I suppose it's for my own pleasure and credit to paint it well, eh? Are you to thank a man for not being a rogue or a noodle? It's enough if he himself thanks Messer Domeneddio, who has made him neither the one nor the other. But women think walls are held together with honey."

"You crusty Piero! I forgot how snappish you are. Here, put this nice sweetmeat in your mouth," said Romola, smiling through her tears, and taking something very crisp and sweet from the little basket.

Piero accepted it very much as that proverbial bear that dreams of pears might accept an exceedingly mellow "swan-egg" — really liking the gift, but accustomed to have his pleasures and pains concealed under a shaggy coat.

"It's good. Madonna Antigone," said Piero, putting his fingers in the basket for another. He had eaten nothing but hard eggs for a fortnight. Romola stood opposite him, feeling her new anxiety suspended for a little while by the sight of this naive enjoyment.

"Good-by, Piero," she said, presently, setting down the basket. "I promise not to thank you if you finish the portrait soon and well. I will tell you, you were bound to do it for your own credit."

"Good," said Piero, curtly, helping her with much deftness to fold her mantle and veil round her.

"I'm glad she asked no more questions about that sketch," he thought, when he had closed the door behind her. "I ^ould be sorry for her to guess that I thought her fine husband a good model for a coward. But I made light of it; she'll not think of it again."

Piero was too sanguine, as open-hearted men are apt to be when they attempt a little clever simulation. The thought of the picture pressed more and more on Romola as she walked homeward. She could not help putting together the two facts of the chain armour and the encounter mentioned by Piero between her husband and the prisoner, which had happened on the morning of the day when the armour was adopted. That look of terror which the painter had given Tito, had he seen it? What could it all mean?

"It means nothing," she tried to assure herself. "It was a mere coincidence. Shall I ask Tito about it?" Her mind said at last, "No: I will not question him about anything he did not tell me spontaneously. It is an offence against the trust I owe him." Her heart said, "I dare not ask him."

There was a terrible flaw in the trust: she was afraid of any hasty movement, as men are who hold something precious and want to believe that it is not broken.

CHAPTER IX.

A MOMENT OF TRIUMPH.

"The old fellow has vanished; went on towards Arezzo the next morning; not liking the smell of the French, I suppose, after being their prisoner. I went to the hospital to inquire after himj I wanted to know if those broth-

making monks had found out whether he was in his right mind or not. However, they said he showed no signs of madness—only took no notice of questions, and seemed to be planting a vine twenty miles off. He was a mysterious old tiger. I should have liked to know something more about him."

It was in Nello's shop that Piero di Cosimo was speaking, on the twenty-fourth of November, just a week after the entrance of the French. There was a party of six or seven assembled at the rather unusual hour of three in the afternoon; for it was a day on which all Florence was excited by the prospect of some decisive political event. Every lounging-place was full, and every shopkeeper who had no wife or deputy to leave in charge stood at his door with his thumbs in his belt; while the streets were constantly sprinkled with artisans pausing or passing lazily like floating splinters, ready to rush forward impetuously if any object attracted them.

Nello had been thrumming the lute as he half sat on the board against the shop window, and kept an outlook towards the piazza.

"Ah," he said, laying down the lute, with emphasis, "I would not for a gold florin have missed that sight of the French soldiers waddling in their broad shoes after their runaway prisoners! That comes of leaving my shop to shave magnificent chins. It is always so: if ever I quit this navel of the earth something takes the opportunity of happening in my piazza."

"Yes, you ought to have been there," said Piero, in his biting way, "just to see your favourite Greek look as frightened as if Satanasso had laid hold of him. I like to see your ready smiling Messeri caught in a sudden wind and obliged to show their lining in spite of themselves.

What colour do you think a man's liver is, who looks like a bleached deer as soon as a chance stranger lays hold of him suddenly?"

"Piero, keep that vinegar of thine as sauce to thine own eggs! What is it against my bel erudito that he looked startled when he felt a pair of claws upon him and saw an unchained madman at his elbow? Your scholar is not like those beastly Swiss and Germans, whose heads are fit for nothing but battering-rams, and who have such large appetites that they think nothing of taking a cannon-ball before breakfast. We Florentines count some other qualities in a man besides that vulgar stuff called bravery, which is to be got by hiring dunderheads at so much per dozen. I tell you, as soon as men found out they had more brains than oxen they set the oxen to draw for them, and when we Florentines found out that we had more brains than other men we set them to fight for us."

"Treason, Nello!" a voice called out from the inner sanctum; "that is not the doctrine of the State. Florence is grinding its weapons; and the last well-authenticated vision announced by the Frate was Mars standing on the Palazzo Vecchio with his arm on the shoulder of San Giovanni Battista, who was offering him a piece of honeycomb."

"It is well, Francesco," said Nello, "Florence has a few thicker skulls that may do to bombard Pisa with; there will still be the finer spirits left at home to do the thinking and the shaving. And, as for our Piero here, if he makes such a point of valour, let him carry his biggest brush for a weapon and his palette for a shield, and challenge the widest-mouthed Swiss he can see in the -Prato to a single combat."

"Va, Nello," growled Piero, "thy tongue runs on as usual, like a mill when the Aino's full—whether there's grist or not."

"Excellent grist, I tell thee. For it would be as reasonable to expect a grizzled painter like thee to be fond of getting a javelin inside thee as to expect a man whose wits have been sharpened on the classics to like having his handsome face clawed by a wild beast."

"There you go, supposing you'll get people to put their legs into a sack because you call it a pair of hosen," said Hero. "Who said anything about a wild beast, or about an unarmed man rushing on battle? Fighting is a trade, and it's not my trade. I should be a fool to run after danger, but I could face it if it came to me."

"How is it you're so afraid of the thunder then, my Piero?" said Nello, determined to chase down the accuser. "You ought to be able to understand why one man is shaken by a thing that seems a trifle to others—you who hide yourself with the rats as soon as a storm comes on."

"That is because I have a particular sensibility to loud sounds; it has nothing to do with my courage or my conscience."

"Well, and Tito Melema may have a peculiar sensibility to being laid hold of unexpectedly by prisoners who have run away from French soldiers. Men are born with antipathies; I myself can't abide the smell of mint. Tito was born with an antipathy to old prisoners who stumble and clutch. Ecco!"

There was a general laugh at Nello's defence, and it was clear that Piero's disinclination towards Tito was not shared by the company. The painter, with his undecipherable grimace, took the tow from his scarsella and stuffed his ears in indignant contempt, while Nello went on triumphantly,—

"No, my Piero, I can't afford to have my bel erudito decried; and Florence can't afford it either, with her scholars moulting off her at the early age of forty. Our Phoenix Pico just gone straight to Paradise, as the Frate has informed us; and the incomparable Poliziano, not two months since, gone to—well, well, let us hope he is not gone to the eminent scholars in the Malebolge."

"By the way," said Francesco Cei, "have you heard that Camilla Rucellai has outdone the Frate in her prophecies? She prophesied two years ago that Pico would die in the time of lilies. He has died in November. 'Not at all the time of lilies,' said the scorners. 'Go to!' says Camilla; 'it is the lilies of France I meant, and it seems to me they are close enough under your nostrils.' I say, 'Euge, Camilla!' If the Frate can prove that anyone of his visions has been as well fulfilled, Pll declare myself a Piagnone to-morrow."

"You are something too flippant about the Frate, Francesco," said Pietro Cennini, the scholarly. "We are all indebted to him in these weeks for preaching peace and quietness, and the laying aside of party quarrels. They are men of small discernment who would be glad to see the people slipping the Frate's leash just now. And if the Most Christian King is obstinate about the treaty to-day, and will not sign what is fair and honourable to Florence, Fra Girolamo is the man we must trust in to bring him to reason."

"You speak truth, Messer Pietro," said Nello; "the Frate is one of the firmest nails Florence has to hang on—at least, that is the opinion of the most respectable chins I have the honour of shaving. But young Messer Niccolo was saying here the other morning—and doubtless

Francesco means the same thing—there is as wonderful a power of stretching in the meaning of visions as in Dido's bull's hide. It seems to me a dream may mean whatever comes after it. As our Franco Sacchetti says, a woman dreams overnight of a serpent biting her, breaks a drinking-cup the next day, and cries out, 'Look you, I thought something would happen—it's plain now what the serpent meant.'"

"But the Prate's visions are not of that sort," said Cronaca. "He not only says what will happen—that the Church will be scourged and renovated, and the heathens converted—he says it shall happen quickly. He is no slippery pretender who provides loopholes for himself,— he is—"

"What is this? what is this?" exclaimed Nello, jumping off the board, and putting his head out at the door. "Here are people streaming into the piazza, and shouting. Something must have happened in the Via Larga. Aha!" he burst forth with delighted astonishment, stepping out, laughing, and waving his cap.

All the rest of the company hastened to the door. News from the Via Larga was just what they had been waiting for. But if the news had come into the piazza, they were not a little surprised at the form of its advent. Carried above the shoulders of the people, on a bench apparently snatched up in the street, sat Tito Melema, in smiling amusement at the compulsion he was under. His cap had slipped off his head, and hung by the becchetto which was wound loosely round his neck; and as he saw the group at Nello's door he lifted up his fingers in beckoning recognition. The next minute he had leaped from the bench on to a cart filled with bales, that stood in the broad space between the Baptistery and the steps of the Duomo, while the people swarmed round him with

the noisy eagerness of poultry expecting to be fed. But there was silence when he began to speak in his clear mellow voice—

"Citizens of Florence! I have no warrant to tell the news except your will. But the news is good, and will harm no man in the telling. The Most Christian King is signing a treaty that is honourable to Florence. But you owe it to one of your citizens, who spoke a word worthy of the ancient Romans—you owe it to Piero Capponi!"

Immediately there was a roar of voices.

"Capponi! Capponi! What said our Piero?" "Ah! he wouldn't stand being sent from Herod to Pilate!" "We knew Piero!" "Orsu! Tell us, what did he say?"

When the roar of insistance had subsided a little, Tito began again—

"The Most Christian King demanded a little too much —was obstinate—said at last, 'I shall order my trumpets to sound.' Then, Florentine citizens! your Piero Capponi, speaking with the voice of a free city, said, 'If you sound your trumpets, we will ring our bells!' He snatched the copy of the dishonouring conditions from the hands of the secretary, tore it in pieces, and turned to leave the royal presence."

Again there were loud shouts—and again impatient demands for more.

"Then, Florentines, the high majesty of France felt, perhaps for the first time, all the majesty of a free city. And the Most Christian King himself hastened from his place to call Piero Capponi back. The great spirit of your Florentine city did its work by a great word, without need of the great actions that lay ready behind it. And the King has consented to sign the treaty, which preserves the honour, as well as the safety, of Florence. The banner

of France will float over every Florentine galley in sign of amity and common privilege, but above that banner will be written the word 'Liberty!'

"That is all the news I have to tell; is it not enough?— "" since it is for the glory of every one of you, citizens of Florence, that you have a fellow-citizen who knows how to speak your will."

As the shouts rose again, Tito looked round with inward amusement at the various crowd, each of whom was elated with the notion that Piero Capponi had somehow represented him—that he was the mind of which Capponi was the mouthpiece. He enjoyed the humour of the incident, which had suddenly transformed him, an alien and a friend of the Medici, into an orator who tickled the ears of the people blatant for some unknown good which they called liberty. He felt quite glad that he had been laid hold of and hurried along by the crowd as he was coming out of the palace in the Via Larga with a commission to the Signoria. It was very easy, very pleasant, this exercise of speaking to the general satisfaction: a man who knew how to persuade need never be in danger from any party; he could convince each that he was feigning with all the others. The gestures and faces of weavers and dyers were certainly amusing when looked at from above in this way.

Tito was beginning to get easier in his armour, and at this moment was quite unconscious of it. He stood with one hand holding his recovered cap, and with the other at his belt, the light of a complacent smile in his long lustrous eyes, as he made a parting reverence to his audience, before springing down from the bales—when suddenly his glance met that of a man who had not at all the amusing aspect of the exulting weavers, dyers, and.

wool-carders. The face of this man was clean shaven, his hair close-clipped, and he wore a decent felt hat. A single glance would hardly have sufficed to assure anyone but Tito that this was the face of the escaped prisoner who had laid hold of him on the steps. But to Tito it came not simply as the face of the escaped prisoner, but as a face with which he had been familiar long years before.

It seemed all compressed into a second—the sight of Baldassarre looking at him, the sensation shooting through him like a fiery arrow, and the act of leaping from the cart. He would have leaped down in the same instant, whether he had seen Baldassarre or not, for he was in a hurry to be gone to the Palazzo Vecchio: this time he had not betrayed himself by look or movement, and he said inwardly that he should not be taken by surprise again; he should be prepared to see this face rise up continually like the intermittent blotch that comes in diseased vision. But this reappearance of Baldassarre so much more in his own likeness tightened the pressure of dread: the idea of his madness lost its likelihood now he was shaven and clad like a decent though poor citizen. Certainly, there was a great change in his face; but how could it be otherwise? And yet, if he were perfectly sane—in possession of all his powers and all his learning—why was he lingering in this way before making known his identity? It must be for the sake of making his scheme of vengeance more complete. But he did linger: that at least gave an opportunity lor flight. And Tito began to think that flight was his only resource.

But while he, with his back turned on the Piazza del Duomo, had lost the recollection of the new part he had been playing, and was no longer thinking of the many things which a ready brain and tongue made easy, but

of a few things which destiny had somehow made very difficult, the enthusiasm which he had fed contemptuously was creating a scene in that piazza in grand contrast with the inward drama of self-centred fear which he had carried away from it.

The crowd, on Tito's disappearance, had begun to turn their faces towards the outlets of the piazza in the direction of the Via Larga, when the sight of mazzieri, or mace-bearers, entering from the Via de' Martelli, announced the approach of dignitaries. They must be the syndics, or commissioners charged with the effecting of the treaty; the treaty must be already signed, and they had come away from the royal presence. Piero Capponi was coming—the brave heart that had known how to speak for Florence. The effect on the crowd was remarkable; they parted with softening, dropping voices, subsiding into silence,—and the silence became so perfect that the tread of the syndics on the broad pavement, and the rustle of their black silk garments, could be heard, like rain in the night. There were four of them; but it was not the two learned doctors of law, Messer Guidantonio Vespucci and Messer Domenico Bonsi, that the crowd waited for; it was not Francesco Valori, popular as he had become in these late days. The moment belonged to another man, of firm presence, as little inclined to humour the people as to humour any other unreasonable claimants—loving order, like one who by force of fortune had been made a merchant, and by force of nature had become a soldier. It was not till he was seen at the entrance of the piazza that the silence was broken, and then one loud shout of "Capponi, Capponi! Well done, Capponi!" rang through the piazza.

The simple, resolute man looked round him with grave joy. His fellow-citizens gave him a great funeral two years later, when he had died in fight: there were torches carried by all the magistracy, and torches again, and trains of banners. But it is not known that he felt any joy in the oration that was delivered in his praise, as the banners waved over his bier. Let us be glad that he got some thanks and praise while he lived.

CHAPTER X. THE avenger's SECRET.

It was the first time that Baldassarre had been in the Piazza del Duomo since his escape. He had a strong desire to hear the remarkable monk preach again, but he had shrunk from reappearing in the same spot where he had been seen half naked, with neglected hair, with a rope round his neck—in the same spot where he had been called a madman. The feeling, in its freshness, was too strong to be overcome by any trust he had in the change he had made in his appearance; for when the words "some madman, surely," had fallen from Tito's lips, it was not their baseness and cruelty only that had made their viper sting—it was Baldassarre's instantaneous bitter consciousness that he might be unable to prove the words false. Along with the passionate desire for vengeance which possessed him had arisen the keen sense that his power of achieving the vengeance was doubtful. It was as if Tito had been helped by some diabolical prompter, who had whispered Baldassarre's saddest secret in the traitor's ear. He was not mad; for he carried within him that piteous stamp of sanity, the clear consciousness of shattered faculties; he measured his own feebleness. With the first movements of vindictive rage awoke a vague caution, like that of a wild beast that is fierce but feeble —or like that of an insect whose little fragment of earth has given way, and made it pause in a palsy of distrust. It was this distrust, this determination to take no step which might betray anything concerning himself, that had made Baldassarre reject Piero di Cosimo's friendly advances.

He had been equally cautious at the hospital, only telling, in answer to the questions of the brethren there, that he had been made a prisoner by the French on his way from Genoa. But his age, and the indications in his speech and manner that he was of a different class from the ordinary mendicants and poor travellers who were entertained in the hospital, had induced the monks to offer him extra charity: a coarse woollen tunic to protect him from the cold, a pair of peasant's shoes, and a few danari, smallest of Florentine coins, to help him on his way. He had gone on the road to Arezzo early in the morning; but he had paused at the first little town, and had used a couple of his danari to get himself shaved, and to have his circle of hair clipped short, in his former fashion. The barber there had a little hand-mirror of bright steel: it was a long while, it was years, since Baldassarre had looked at himself, and now, as his eyes fell on that hand-mirror, a new thought shot through his mind. "Was he so changed that Tito really did not know him?" The thought was such a sudden arrest of impetuous currents, that it was a painful shock to him: his hand shook like a leaf as he put away the barber's arm and asked for the mirror. He wished to see himself before he was shaved. The barber, noticing his tre-mulousness, held the mirror for him.

No, he was not so changed as that. He himself had known the wrinkles as they had been three years ago; they were only deeper now: there was the same rough, clumsy skin, making little superficial bosses on the brow, like so many cipher marks; the skin was only yellower, only looked more like a lifeless rind. That shaggy white beard—it was no disguise to eyes that had looked closely at him for sixteen years—to eyes that ought to have searched for him with the expectation of finding him changed, as men search for the beloved among the bodies cast up by the waters. There was something different in his glance, but it was a difference that should only have made the recognition of him the more startling; for is not a known voice all the more thrilling when it is heard as a cry? But the doubt was folly: he had felt that Tito knew him. He put out his hand and pushed the mirror away. The strong currents were rushing on again, and the energies of hatred and vengeance were active once more.

He went back on the way towards Florence again, but he did not wish to enter the city till dusk; so he turned aside from the highroad, and sat down by a little pool shadowed on one side by alder-bushes still sprinkled with yellow leaves. It was a calm November day, and he no sooner saw the pool than he thought its still surface might be a mirror for him. He wanted to contemplate himself slowly, as he had not dared to do in the presence of the barber. He sat down on the edge of the pool, and bent forward to look earnestly at the image of himself.

Was there something wandering and imbecile in his face something like what he felt in his mind?

Not now; not when he was examining himself with a look of eager inquiry: on the contrary, there was an intense purpose in his eyes. But at other times? Yes, it must be so: in the long hours when he had the vague aching of an unremembered past within him when he seemed to sit in dark loneliness, visited by whispers which died out mockingly as he strained his ear after them, and by forms that seemed to approach him and float away as he thrust out his hand to grasp them in those hours, doubtless, there must be continual frustration and amazement in his glance. And, more horrible still, when the thick cloud parted for a moment, and, as he sprang forward with hope, rolled together again, and left him helpless as before; doubtless then, there was a blank confusion in his face, as of a man suddenly smitten with blindness.

Could he prove anything? Could he even begin to allege anything, with the confidence that the links of thought would not break away? Would any believe that he had ever had a mind filled with rare knowledge, busy with close thoughts, ready with various speech? It had all slipped away from him—that laboriously gathered store. Was it utterly and for ever gone from him, like the waters from an urn lost in the wide ocean? Or, was it still within him, imprisoned by some obstruction that might one day break asunder?

It might be so; he tried to keep his grasp on that hope. For, since the day when he had first walked feebly from his couch of straw, and had felt a new darkness within him under the sunlight, his mind had undergone changes, partly gradual and persistent, partly sudden and fleeting. As he had recovered his strength of body, he had recovered his self-command and the energy of his will; he had recovered the memory of all that part of his

life which was closely inwrought with his emotions; and he had felt more and more constantly and painfully the uneasy sense of lost knowledge. But more than that—• once or twice, when he had been strongly excited, he had seemed momentarily to be in entire possession of his past self, as old men doze for an instant and get back the consciousness of their youth: he seemed again to see Greek pages and understand them, again to feel his mind moving unbenumbed among familiar ideas. It had been but a flash, and the darkness closing in again seemed the more horrible; but might not the same thing happen again for longer periods? If it would only come and stay long enough for him to achieve a revenge—devise an exquisite suffering, such as a mere right arm could never inflict!

He raised himself from his stooping attitude, and, folding his arms, attempted to concentrate all his mental force on the plan he must immediately pursue. He had to wait for knowledge and opportunity, and while he waited he must have the means of living without beggary. What he dreaded of all things now was, that anyone should think him a foolish, helpless old man. No one must know that half his memory was gone: the lost strength might come again; and if it were only for a little while that might be enough.

He knew how to begin to get the information he wanted about Tito. He had repeated the words "Bratti Ferravecchi" so constantly after they had been uttered to him, that they never slipped from him for long together. A man at Genoa, on whose finger he had seen Tito's ring, had told him that he bought that ring at Florence, of a young Greek, well dressed, and with a handsome dark face, in the shop of a rigattiere called Bratti

Ferravecchi, in the street also called Ferravecchi, This discovery had caused a violent agitation in Baldassarre. Until then he had clung with all the tenacity of his fervid nature to his faith in Tito, and had not for a moment believed himself to be wilfully forsaken. At first he had said, "My bit of parchment has never reached him; that is why I am still toiling at Antioch. But he is searching; he knows where I was lost; he will trace me out, and find me at last." Then, when he was taken to Corinth, he induced his owners, by the assurance that he should be sought out and ransomed, to provide securely against the failure of any inquiries that might be made about him at Antioch; and at Corinth he thought joyfully, "Here, at last, he must find me. Here he is sure to touch, whichever way he goes." But before another year had passed, the illness had come from which he had risen with body and mind so shattered that he was worse than worthless to his owners except for the sake of the ransom that did not come. Then, as he sat helpless in the morning sunlight, he began to think, "Tito has been drowned, or they have made him a prisoner too. I shall see him no more. He set out after me, but misfortune overtook him. I shall see his face no more." Sitting in his new feebleness and despair, supporting his head between his hands, with blank eyes and lips that moved uncertainly, he looked so much like a hopelessly imbecile old man, that his owners were contented to be rid of him, and allowed a Genoese merchant, who had compassion on him as an Italian, to take him on board his galley. In a voyage of many months in the Archipelago and along the sea-board of Asia Minor, Baldassarre had recovered his bodily strength, but on landing at Genoa he had so weary a sense of his desolateness that he almost wished he had died of that

illness at Corinth. There was just one possibility that hindered the wish from being decided: it was that Tito might not be dead, but living in a state of imprisonment or destitution; and if he lived, there was still a hope for Baldassarre—faint, perhaps, and likely to be long deferred, but still a hope, that he might find his child, his cherished son again; might yet again clasp hands and meet face to face with the one being who remembered him as he had been before his mind was broken.

In this state of feeling he had chanced to meet the stranger who wore Tito's onyx ring, and though Baldassarre would have been unable to describe the ring beforehand, the sight of it stirred the dormant fibres, and he recognised it. That Tito nearly a year after his father had been parted from him, should have been living in apparent prosperity at Florence, selling the gem which he ought not to have sold till the last extremity, was a fact that Baldassarre shrank from trying to account for; he was glad to be stunned and bewildered by it, rather than to have any distinct thought; he tried to feel nothing but joy that he should behold Tito again. Perhaps Tito had thought that his father was dead; somehow the mystery would be explained. "But at least I shall meet eyes that will remember me; I am not alone in the world."

And now again Baldassarre said, "I am not alone in the world; I shall never be alone, for my revenge is with me."

It was as the instrument of that revenge, as something merely external and subservient to his true life, that he bent down again to examine himself with hard curiosity— not, he thought, because he had any care for a withered, forsaken old man, whom nobody loved, whose soul was like a deserted home, where the ashes were cold upon thq

hearth, and the walls were bare of all but the marks of what had been. It is in the nature of all human passion, the lowest as well as the highest, that there is a point at which it ceases to be properly egoistic, and is like a fire kindled within our being to which everything else in us is mere fuel.

He looked at the pale black-browed image in the water till he identified it with that self from which his revenge seemed to be a thing apart; and he felt as if the image too heard the silent language of his thought.

"I was a loving fool—I worshipped a woman once, and believed she could care for me; and then I took a helpless child and fostered him; and I watched him as he grew, to see if he would care for me only a little—care for me over and above the good he got from me. I would have torn open my breast to warm him with my life-blood if I could only have seen him care a little for the pain of my wound. I have laboured, I have strained to crush out of this hard life one drop of unselfish love. Fool! men love their own delights; there is no delight to be had in me. And yet I watched till I believed I saw what I watched for. When he was a child he lifted soft eyes towards me, and held my hand willingly: I thought, this boy will surely love me a little: because I give my life to him and strive that he shall know no sorrow, he will care a little when I am thirsty—the drop he lays on my parched lips will be a joy to him. . . . Curses on him! I wish I may see him lie with those red lips white and dry as ashes, and when he looks for pity I wish he may see my face rejoicing in his pain. It is all a lie—this world is a lie—there is no goodness but in hate. Fool! not one drop of love came with all your striving: life has not given you one drop. But there are deep draughts in this world

for hatred and revenge. I have memory left for that, and there is strength in my arm—there is strength in my will —and if I can do nothing but kill him—"

But Baldassarre's mind rejected the thought of that brief punishment. His whole soul had been thrilled into immediate unreasoning belief in that eternity of vengeance where he, an undying hate, might clutch for ever an undying traitor, and hear that fair smiling hardness cry and moan with anguish. But the primary need and hope was to see a slow revenge under the same sky and on the same earth where he himself had been forsaken and had fainted with despair. And as soon as he tried to concentrate his mind on the means of attaining his end, the sense of his weakness pressed upon him like a frosty ache. This despised body, which was to be the instrument of a sublime vengeance, must be nourished and decently clad. If he had to wait he must labour, and his labour must be of a humble sort, for he had no skill. He wondered whether the sight of written characters would so stimulate his faculties that he might venture to try and find work as a copyist: that might win him some credence for his past scholarship. But no! he dared trust neither hand nor brain. He must be content to do the work that was most like that of a beast of burden: in this mercantile city many porters must be wanted, and he could at least carry weights. Thanks to the justice that struggled in this confused world in behalf of vengeance, his limbs had got back some of their old sturdiness. He was stripped of all else that men would give coin for.

But the new urgency of this habitual thought brought a new suggestion. There was something hanging by a cord round his bare neck; something apparently so paltry that the piety of Turks and Frenchmen had spared it a tiny parchment bag blackened with age. It had hung round his neck as a precious charm when he was a boy, and he had kept it carefully on his breast, not believing that it contained anything but a tiny scroll of parchment rolled up hard. He might long ago have thrown it away as a relic of his dead mother's superstition; but he had thought of it as a relic of her love, and had kept it. It was part of the piety associated with such hrevi, that they should never be opened, and at any previous moment in his life Baldassarre would have said that no sort of thirst would prevail upon him to open this little bag for the chance of finding that it contained, not parchment, but an engraved amulet which would be worth money. But now a thirst had come like that which makes men open their own veins to satisfy it, and the thought of the possible amulet no sooner crossed Baldassarre's mind than with nervous fingers he snatched the breve from his neck. It all rushed through his mind the long years he had worn it, the far-off sunny balcony at Naples looking towards the blue waters, where he had leaned against his mother's knee; but it made no moment of hesitation: all piety now was transmuted into a just revenge. He bit and tore till the doubles of parchment were laid open, and then it was a sight that made him pant—there was an amulet. It was very small, but it was as blue as those far-off waters; it was an engraved sapphire, which must be worth some gold ducats. Baldassarre no sooner saw those possible ducats than he saw some of them exchanged for a poniard. He did not want to use the poniard yet, but he longed to possess it. If he could grasp its handle and feel its edge, that blank in his mind—that past which fell away continually—would not make him feel so cruelly helpless: the sharp steel that despised talents and eluded

strength would be at his side, as the unfailing friend of ieeble justice. There was a sparkling triumph under Bal-dassarre's black eyebrows as he replaced the little sapphire inside the bits of parchment and wound the string tightly round them.

It was nearly dusk now, and he rose to walk back towards Florence. With his danari to buy him some bread, he felt rich: he could lie out in tlae open air, as he found plenty more doing in all corners of Florence. And in the next few days he had sold his sapphire, had added to his clothing, had bought a bright dagger, and had still a pair of gold florins left. But he meant to hoard that treasure carefully: his lodging was an outhouse with a heap of straw in it, in a thinly inhabited part of Oltrarno, and he thought of looking about for work as a porter.

He had bought his dagger at Bratti's. Paying his meditated visit there one evening at dusk, he had found that singular rag-merchant just returned from one of his rounds, emptying out his basketful of broken glass and old iron amongst his handsome show of heterogeneous second-hand goods. As Baldassarre entered the shop, and looked towards the smart pieces of apparel, the musical instruments, and weapons, that were displayed in the broadest light of the window, his eye at once singled out a dagger that hung up high against a red scarf. By buying that dagger he could not only satisfy a strong desire, he could open his original errand in a more indirect manner than by speaking of the onyx ring. In the course of bargaining for the weapon he let drop, with cautious carelessness, that he came from Genoa, and had been directed to Bratti's shop by an acquaintance in that city who had bought a very valuable ring there. Had the respectable trader any more such rings?

Whereupon Bratti had much to say as to the unUkeli-hood of such nngs being within reach of many people, with much vaunting of his own rare connections, due to his known wisdom and honesty. It might be true that he was a pedlar—he chose to be a pedlar; though he was rich enough to kick his heels in his shop all day. But those who thought they had said all there was to be said about Bratti, when they had called him a pedlar, were a good deal further off the truth than the other side of Pisa. How was it that he could put that ring in a stranger's way? It was, because he had a very particular knowledge of a handsome young sign or, who did not look quite so fine a feathered bird when Bratti first set eyes on him as he did at the present time. And by a question or two Baldassarre extracted, without any trouble, such a rough and rambling account of Tito's life as the pedlar could give, since the time when he had found him sleeping under the Loggia de' Cerchi. It never occurred to Bratti that the decent man (who was rather deaf, apparently, asking him to say many things twice over) had any curiosity about Tito; the curiosity was doubtless about himself, as a truly remarkable pedlar.

And Baldassarre left Bratti's shop, not only with the dagger at his side, but with a general knowledge of Tito's conduct and position—of his early sale of the jewels, his immediate quiet settlement of himself at Florence, his marriage, and his great prosperity.

"What story had he told about his previous life— about his father?"

That was a question to which it would be difficult for Baldassarre to discover the answer. Meanwhile, he wanted to learn all he could about Florence. But he found, to his acute distress, that of the new details he learned he

could only retain a few, and those only by continual repetition; and he began to be afraid of listening to any new discourse, lest it should obliterate what he was already striving to remember.

The day he was discerned by Tito in the Piazza del Duomo, he had the fresh anguish of this consciousness in his mind, and Tito's ready speech fell upon him like the mockery of a glib, defying demon.

As he went home to his heap of straw, and passed by the booksellers' shops in the Via del Garbo, he paused to look at the volumes spread open. Could he by long gazing at one of those books lay hold of the slippery threads of memory? Could he, by striving, get a firm grasp somewhere, and lift himself above these waters that flowed over him?"

He was tempted, and bought the cheapest Greek book he could see. He carried it home and sat on his heap of straw, looking at the characters by the light of the small window; but no inward light arose on them. Soon the evening darkness came; but it made little difference to Baldassarre. His strained eyes seemed still to see the white pages with the unintelligible black marks upon them.

CHAPTER XL

FRUIT IS SEED.

"My Romola," said Tito, the second morning after he had made his speech in the Piazza del Duomo, "I am to receive grand visitors to-day; the Milanese Count is coming again, and the Seneschal de Beaucaire, the great favourite of the Cristianissimo, I know you don't care to go through smiling ceremonies with these rustling magnates, whom we are not likely to see again; and as they will want to look at the antiquities and the library, perhaps you had better give up your work to-day, and go to see your cousin Brigida."

Romola discerned a wish in this intimation, and immediately assented. But presently, coming back in her hood and mantle, she said, "Oh, what a long breath Florence will take when the gates are flung open, and the last Frenchman is walking out of them! Even you are getting tired, with all your patience, my Tito; confess it. Ah, your head is hot."

He was leaning over his desk, writing, and she had laid her hand on his head, meaning to give a parting caress. The attitude had been a frequent one, and Tito was accustomed, when he felt her hand there, to raise his head, throw himself a little backward, and look up at her. But he felt now as unable to raise his head as if her hand had been a leaden cowl. He spoke instead, in a light tone, as his pen still ran along.

"The French are as ready to go from Florence as the wasps to leave a ripe pear when they have just fastened on it."

Romola, keenly sensitive to the absence of the usual response, took away her hand and said, "I am going, Tito."

"Farewell, my sweet one. I must wait at home. Take Maso with you."

Still Tito did not look up, and Romola went out without saying any more. Very slight things make epochs in married life, and this morning for the first time she admitted to herself not only that Tito had changed, but that he had changed towards her. Did the reason lie in herself? She might perhaps have thought so, if there had not been the facts of the armour and the picture to suggest some external event which was an entire mystery to her.

But Tito no sooner believed that Romola was out of the house than he laid down his pen and looked up, in delightful security from seeing anything else than parchment and broken marble. He was rather disgusted with himself that he had not been able to look up at Romola and behave to her just as usual. He would have chosen, if he could, to be even more than usually kind; but he could not, on a sudden, master an involuntary shrinking from her, which, by a subtle relation, depended on those very characteristics in him that made him desire not to fail in his marks of affection. He was about to take a step which he knew would arouse her deep indignation: he would have to encounter much that was unpleasant before he could win her forgiveness. And Tito could never find it easy to face displeasure and anger; his nature was one of those most remote from defiance or impudence, and all his inclinations leaned towards preserving Romola's tenderness. He was not tormented by sentimental scruples

which, as he had demonstrated to himself by a very rapid course of argument, had no relation to solid utility; but his freedom from scruples did not release him from the dread of what was disagreeable. Unscrupulousness gets rid of much, but not of toothache, or wounded vanity, or the sense of loneliness, against which, as the world at present stands, there is no security but a thoroughly healthy jaw, and a just, loving soul. And Tito was feeling intensely at this moment that no devices could save him from pain in the impending collision with Romola; no persuasive blandness could cushion him against the shock towards which he was being driven like a timid animal urged to a desperate leap by the terror of the tooth and the claw that are close behind it.

The secret feeling he had previously had that the tenacious adherence to Bardo's wishes about the library had become under existing difficulties a piece of sentimental folly, which deprived himself and Romola of substantial advantages, might perhaps never have wrought itself into action but for the events of the past week, which had brought at once the pressure of a new motive and the outlet of a rare opportunity. Nay, it was not till his dread had been aggravated by the sight of Baldassarre looking more like his sane self, not until he had begun to feel that he might be compelled to flee from Florence, that he had brought himself to resolve on using his legal right to sell the library before the great opportunity offered by French and Milanese bidders slipped through his fingers. For if he had to leave Florence he did not want to leave it as a destitute wanderer. He had been used to an agreeable existence, and he wished to carry with him all the means at hand for retaining the same agreeable conditions. He wished among other things to cany Romola

with him, and not, if possible, to carry any infamy. Success had given him a growing appetite for all the pleasures that depend on an advantageous social position, and at no moment could it look like temptation to him, but only like a hideous alternative, to decamp under dishonour, even with a bag of diamonds, and incur the life of an adventurer. It was not possible for him to make himself independent even of those Florentines who only greeted him with regard; still less was it possible for him to make himself independent of Romola. She was the wife of his first love—he loved her still; she belonged to that furniture of life which he shrank from parting with. He winced under her judgment, he felt uncertain how far the revulsion of her feeling towards him might go; and all that sense of power over a wife which makes a husband risk betrayals that a lover never ventures on, would not suffice to counteract Tito's uneasiness. This was the leaden weight which had been too strong for his will, and kept him from raising his head to meet her eyes. Their pure light brought too near him the prospect of a coming struggle. But it was not to be helped: if they had to leave Florence, they, must have money; indeed, Tito could not arrange life at all to his mind without a considerable sum of money. And that problem of arranging life to his mind had been the source of all his misdoing. He would have been equal to any sacrifice that was not unpleasant. The rustling magnates came and went, the bargains had been concluded, and Romola returned home; but nothing grave was said that night. Tito was only gay and chatty, pouring forth to her, as he had not done before, stories and descriptions of what he had witnessed during the French visit. Romola thought she discerned an effort in his liveliness, and attributing it to the consciousness in

him that she had been wounded in the morning, accepted the effort as an act of penitence, inwardly aching a httle at that sign of growing distance between them—that there* was an offence about which neither of them dared to speak.

The next day Tito remained away from home until late at night. It was a marked day to Romola, for Piero di Cosimo, stimulated to greater industry on her behalf by the fear that he might have been the cause of pain to her in the past week, had sent home her father's portrait. She had propped it against the back of his old chair, and had been looking at it for some time, when the door opened behind her, and Bernardo del Nero came in.

"It is you, godfather! How I wish you had come sooner: it is getting a little dusk," said Romola, going towards him.

'T have just looked in to tell you the good news, for I know Tito is not come yet," said Bernardo. "The French king moves off to-morrow; not before it is high time. There has been another tussle between our people and his soldiers this morning. But there's a chance now of the city getting into order once more and trade going on."

"That is joyful," said Romola. "But it is sudden, is it not? Tito seemed to think yesterday that there was little prospect of the king's going soon."

"He has been well barked at, that's the reason," said Bernardo, smiling. "His own generals opened their throats pretty well, and at last our Signoria sent the mastiff of the city, Fra Girolamo. The Cristianissimo was frightened at that thunder, and has given the order to move, I'm afraid there'll be small agreement among us when he's gone, but, at anyrate, all parties are agreed in

being glad not to have Florence stifled with soldiery any longer, and the Frate has barked this time to some purpose. Ah, what is this?" he added, as Romola, clasping him by the arm, led him in front of the picture. "Let us see."

He began to unwind his long scarf while she placed a seat for him.

"Don't you want your spectacles, godfather?" said Romola, in anxiety that he should see just what she saw.

"No, child, no," said Bernardo, uncovering his grey head, as he seated himself with firm erectness. "For seeing at this distance, my old eyes are perhaps better than your young ones. Old men's eyes are like old men's memories; they are strongest for things a long way off."

"It is better than having no portrait," said Romola, apologetically, after Bernardo had been silent a little while. "It is less like him now than the image I have in my mind, but then that might fade with the years." She rested her arm on the old man's shoulder as she spoke, drawn towards him strongly by their common interest in the dead.

"I don't know," said Bernardo. "I almost think I see Bardo as he was when he was young, better than that picture shows him to me as he was when he was old. Your father had a great deal of fire in his eyes when he was young. It was what I could never understand, that he, with his fiery spirit, which seemed much more impatient than mine, could hang over the books and live with shadows all his life. However, he had put his heart into that."

Bernardo gave a slight shrug as he spoke the last words, but Romola discerned in his voice a feeling that accorded with her own.

"And he was disappointed to the last," she said, involuntarily. But immediately fearing lest her words should be taken to imply an accusation against Tito, she went on almost hurriedly, "If we could only see his longest, dearest wish fulfilled just to his mind!"

"Well, so we may," said Bernardo, kindly, rising and putting on his cap. "The times are cloudy now, but fish are caught by waiting. Who knows? When the wheel has turned often enough, I may be Gonfaloniere yet before I die; and no creditor can touch these things." He looked round as he spoke. Then, turning to her, and patting her cheek, said, "And you need not be afraid of my dying; my ghost will claim nothing. I've taken care of that in my will."

Romola seized the hand that was against her cheek, and put it to her lips in silence.

"Haven't you been scolding your husband for keeping away from home so much lately? I see him everywhere but here," said Bernardo, willing to change the subject.

She felt the flush spread over her neck and face as she said, "He has been very much wanted; you know he speaks so well. I am glad to know that his value is understood."

"You are contented then. Madonna Orgogliosa?" said Bernardo, smiling, as he moved to the door.

"Assuredly."

Poor Romola! There was one thing that would have made the pang of disappointment in her husband harder to bear: it was, that anyone should know he gave her cause for disappointment. This might be a woman's weakness, but it is closely allied to a woman's nobleness. She who willingly lifts up the veil of her married life has profaned it from a sanctuary into a vulgar place.

;66 ROMOLA.

CHAPTER XII. A REVELATION.

The next day Romola, like every other Florentine, was excited about the departure of the French. Besides her other reasons for gladness, she had a dim hope, which she was conscious was half superstitious, that those new anxieties about Tito, having come with the burdensome guests, might perhaps vanish with them. The French had been in Florence hardly eleven days, but in that space she had felt more acute unhappiness than she had known in her life before. Tito had adopted the hateful armour on the day of their arrival, and though she could frame no distinct notion why their departure should remove the cause of his fear—though, when she thought of that cause, the image of the prisoner grasping him, as she had seen it in Piero's sketch, urged itself before her and excluded every other—still, when the French were gone, she would be rid of something that was strongly associated with her pain.

Wrapped in her mantle she waited under the loggia at the top of the house, and watched for the glimpses of the troops and the royal retinue passing the bridges on their way to the Porta San Piero, that looks towards Siena and Rome. She even returned to her station when the gates had been closed, that she might feel herself vibrating with the great peal of the bells. It was dusk then, and when at last she descended into the library, she lit her lamp, with the resolution that she would overcome the agitation that had made her idle all day, and sit down to work at her copying of the catalogue, Tito had left home early in the morning, and she did not expect him yet. Before he came she intended to leave the library, and sit in the pretty saloon, with the dancing nymphs and the birds. She had done so every evening since he had objected to the library as chill and gloomy.

To her great surprise, she had not been at work long before Tito entered. Her first thought was, how cheerless he would feel the wide darkness of this great room, with one little oil-lamp burning at the farther end, and the fire nearly out. She almost ran towards him.

"Tito, dearest, I did not know you would come so soon," she said, nervously, putting up her white arms to unwind his becchetto.

"I am not welcome then?" he said, with one of his brightest smiles, clasping her, but playfully holding his head back from her.

"Tito!" She uttered the word in a tone of pretty, loving reproach, and then he kissed her fondly, stroked her hair, as his manner was, and seemed not to mind about taking off his mantle yet. Romola quivered with delight. All the emotions of the day had been preparing in her a keener sensitiveness to the return of this habitual manner. "It will come back," she was saying to herself, "the old happiness will perhaps come back. He is like himself again."

Tito was taking great pains to be like himself; his heart was palpitating with anxiety.

"If I had expected you so soon," said Romola, as she at last helped him to take off his wrappings, "I would have had a little festival prepared to this joyful ringing of

the bells. I did not mean to be here in the library when you came home."

"Never mind, sweet," he said, carelessly. "Do not think about the fire. Come—come and sit down."

There was a low stool against Tito's chair, and that was Romola's habitual seat when they were talking together. She rested her arm on his knee, as she used to do on her father's, and looked up at him while he spoke. He had never yet noticed the presence of the portrait, and she had not mentioned it—thinking of it all the more.

"I have been enjoying the clang of the bells for the first time, Tito," she began. "I like being shaken and . deafened by them: I fancied I was something like a Bacchante possessed by a divine rage. Are not the people looking very joyful to-night?"

"Joyful after a sour and pious fashion," said Tito, with a shrug. "But, in truth, those who are left behind in Florence have little cause to be joyful; it seems to me, the most reasonable ground of gladness would be to have got out of Florence."

Tito had sounded the desired key-note without any trouble, or appearance of premeditation. He spoke with no emphasis, but he looked grave enough to make Romola ask rather anxiously,

"Why, Tito? Are there fresh troubles?"

"No need of fresh ones, my Romola. There are three strong parties in the city, all ready to fly at each other's throats. And if the Frate's party is strong enough to frighten the other two into silence, as seems most likely, life will be as pleasant and amusing as a funeral. They have the plan of a Great Council simmering already; and if they get it, the man who sings sacred Lauds the loudest

will be the most eligible for office. And besides that, the city will be so drained by the payment of tliis great subsidy to the French king, and by the war to get back Pisa, that the prospect would be dismal enough without the rule of fanatics. On the whole, Florence will be a delightful place for those worthies who entertain themselves in the evening by going into crypts and lashing themselves; but for everything else, the exiles have the best of it. For my own part, I have been thinking seriously that we should be wise to quit Florence, my Romola."

She started. "Tito, how could we leave Florence? Surely you do not think I could leave it—at least, not yet —not for a long while." She had turned cold and trembling, and did not find it quite easy to speak. Tito must know the reasons she had in her mind.

"That is all a fabric of your own imagination, my sweet one. Your secluded life has made you lay such false stress on a few things. You know I used to tell you, before we were married, that I wished we were somewhere else than in Florence. If you had seen more places and more people, you would know what I mean when I say that there is something in the Florentines that reminds me of their cutting spring winds. I like people who take life less eagerly; and it would be good for my Romola, too, to see a new life. I should like to dip her a little in the soft waters of forgetfulness."

He leaned forward and kissed her brow, and laid his hand on her fair hair again; but she felt his caress no more than if he had kissed a mask. She was too much agitated by the sense of the distance between their minds to be conscious that his lips touched her.

"Tito, it is not because I suppose Florence is the pleasantest place in the world that I desire not to quit it.

Romola.

It is because I—because we have to see my father's wish fulfilled. My godfather is old; he is seventy-one; we could not leave it to him."

"It is precisely those superstitions which hang about your mind like bedimming clouds, my Romola, that make one great reason why I could wish we were two hundred leagues from Florence. I am obliged to take care of you in opposition to your own will: if those dear eyes, that look so tender, see falsely, I must see for them, and save my wife from wasting her life in disappointing herself by impracticable dreams."

Romola sat silent and motionless: she could not blind herself to the direction in which Tito's words pointed: he wanted to persuade her that they might get the library deposited in some monastery, or take some other ready means to rid themselves of a task, and of a tie to Florence; and she was determined never to submit her mind to his judgment on this question of duty to her father; she was inwardly prepared to encounter any sort of pain in resistance. But the determination was kept latent in these first moments by the heart-crushing sense that now at last she and Tito must be confessedly divided in their wishes. He was glad of her silence, for, much as he had feared the strength of her feeling, it was impossible for him, shut up in the narrowness that hedges in all merely clever, unimpassioned men, not to over-estimate the persuasiveness of his own arguments. His conduct did not look ugly to himself, and his imagination did not suffice to show him exactly how it would look to Romola. He went on in the same gentle, remonstrating tone.

"You know, dearest—your own clear judgment always showed you—that the notion of isolating a collection of books and antiquities, and attaching a single name to them

for ever, was one that had no valid, substantial good for its object: and yet more, one that was liable to be defeated in a thousand ways. See what has become of the Medici collections! And, for my part, I consider it even blameworthy to entertain those petty views of appropriation: why should anyone be reasonably glad that Florence should possess the benefits of learned research and taste more than any other city? I understand your feeling about the wishes of the dead; but wisdom puts a limit to these sentiments, else lives might be continually wasted in that sort of futile devotion—like praising deaf gods for ever. You gave your life to your father while he lived; why should you demand more of yourself?"

"Because it was a trust," said Romola, in a low but distinct voice. "He trusted me, he trusted you, Tito. I did not expect you to feel anything else about it—to feel as I do—but I did expect you to feel that."

"Yes, dearest, of course I should feel it on a point where your father's real welfare or happiness was concerned; but there is no question of that now. If we believed in purgatory, I should be as anxious as you to have masses said; and if I believed it could now pain your father to see his library preserved and used in a rather different way from what he had set his mind on, I should share the strictness of your views. But a little philosophy should teach us to rid ourselves of those air-woven fetters that mortals hang round themselves, spending their lives in misery under the mere imagination of weight. Your mind, which seizes ideas so readily, my Romola, is able to discriminate between substantial good and these brain-wrought fantasies. Ask yourself, dearest, what possible good can these books and antiquities do stowed together under your father's name in Florence, more than they would do if they were divided or carried elsewhere? Nay, is not the very dispersion of such things in hands that know how to value them one means of extending their usefulness? This rivalry of Italian cities is very petty and illiberal. The loss of Constantinople was the gain of the whole civilised world."

Romola was still too thoroughly under the painful pressure of the new revelation Tito was making of himself, for her resistance to find any strong vent. As that fluent talk fell on her ears there was a rising contempt within her, which only made her more conscious of her bruised, despairing love, her love for the Tito she had married and believed in. Her nature, possessed with the energies of strong emotion, recoiled from this hopelessly shallow readiness which professed to appropriate the widest sympathies and had no pulse for the nearest. She still spoke like one who was restrained from showing all she felt. She had only drawn away her arm from his knee and sat with her hands clasped before her, cold and motionless as locked waters.

"You talk of substantial good, Tito! Are faithfulness, and love, and sweet grateful memories, no good? Is it no good that we should keep our silent promises on which others build because they believe in our love and truth? Is it no good that a just life should be justly honoured? Or, is it good that we should harden our hearts against all the wants and hopes of those who have depended on us? What good can belong to men who have such souls? To talk cleverly, perhaps, and find soft couches for themselves, and live and die with their base selves as their best companions."

Her voice had gradually risen till there was a ring of scorn in the last words; she made a slight pause, but he saw there were other words quivering on her lips, and he chose to let them come.

"I know of no good for cities or the world if they are to be made up of such beings. But I am not thinking of other Italian cities and the whole civilised world—I am thinking of my father, and of my love and sorrow for him, and of his just claims on us. I would give up anything else, Tito,—I would leave Florence,—what else did I live for but for him and you? But I will not give up that duty. What have I to do with your arguments? It was a yearning of ii's heart, and therefore it is a yearning of mine."

Her voice, from having been tremulous, had become full and firm. She felt that she had been urged on to say all that it was needful for her to say. She thought, poor thing, there was nothing harder to come than this struggle against Tito's suggestions as against the meaner part of herself.

He had begun to see clearly that he could not persuade her into assent: he must take another course, and show her that the time for resistance was past. That, at least, would put an end to further struggle; and if the disclosure were not made by himself to-night, to-morrow it must be made in another way. That necessity nerved his courage; and his experience of her affectionateness and unexpected submissiveness, ever since their marriage until now, encouraged him to hope that, at last, she would accommodate herself to what had been his will.

"I am sorry to hear you speak in that spirit of blind persistence, my Romola," he said, quietly, "because it obliges me to give you pain. But I partly foresaw your opposition, and as a prompt decision was necessary, I avoided that obstacle, and decided without consulting you.

The very care of a husband for his wife's interest compels him to that sej^arate action sometimes—even when he has such a wife as you, my Romola."

She turned her eyes on him in breathless inquiry.

"I mean," he said, answering her look, "that I have arranged for the transfer, both of the books and antiquities, where they will find the highest use and value. The books have been bought for the Duke of Milan, the marbles and bronzes and the rest are going to France; and both will be protected by the stability of a great Power, instead of remaining in a city which is exposed to ruin."

Before he had finished speaking, Romola had started from her seat, and stood up looking down at him, with tightened hands falling before her, and, for the first time in her life, with a flash of fierceness in her scorn and anger.

"You have sold them?" she asked, as if she distrusted her ears.

"I have," said Tito, quailing a little. The scene Avas unpleasant—the descending scorn already scorched him.

"You are a treacherous man!" she said, with something grating in her voice, as she looked down at him.

She was silent for a minute, and he sat still, feeling that ingenuity was powerless just now. Suddenly she turned away, and said, in an agitated tone, "It may be hindered—I am going to my godfather."

In an instant Tito started up, went to the door, locked it, and took out the key. It was time for all the masculine predominance that was latent in him to show itself. But he was not angry; he only felt that the moment was eminently unpleasant, and that when this scene was at an end he should be glad to keep away from Romola for a little while. But it was absolutely necessary first that she should be reduced to passiveness.

"Try to calm yourself a little, Romola," he said, leaning in the easiest attitude possible against a pedestal under the bust of a grim old Roman. Not that he was inwardly easy: his heart palpitated a little with a moral dread, against which no chain-armour could be found. He had locked in his wife's anger and scorn, but he had been obHged to lock himself in with it; and his blood did not rise with contest—his olive cheek was perceptibly paled.

Romola had paused and turned her eyes on him as she saw him take his stand and lodge the key in his scarsella. Her eyes were flashing, and her whole frame seemed to be possessed by impetuous force that wanted to leap out in some deed. AH the crushing pain of disappointment in her husband, which had made the strongest part of her consciousness a few minutes before, was annihilated by the vehemence of her indignation. She could not care in this moment that the man she was despising as he leaned there in his loathsome beauty—she could not care that he was her husband; she could only feel that she despised him. The pride and fierceness of the old Bardi blood had been thoroughly awaked in her for the first time.

"Try at least to understand the fact," said Tito, "and do not seek to take futile steps which may be fatal. It is of no use for you to go to your godfather. Messer Bernardo cannot reverse what I have done. Only sit down. You would hardly wish, if you were quite yourself, to make known to any third person what passes between us in private."

Tito knew that he had touched the right fibre. But she did not sit down; she was too unconscious of her body voluntarily to change her attitude.

"Why can it not be reversed?" she said, after a pause. "Nothing is moved yet."

"Simply because the sale has been concluded by written agreement; the purchasers have left Florence, and I hold the bonds for the purchase-money."

"If my father had suspected you of being a faithless man," said Romola, in a tone of bitter scorn, which insisted on darting out before she could say anything else, "he would have placed the library safely out of your power. But death overtook him too soon, and when you were sure his ear was deaf, and his hand stiff, you robbed him." She paused an instant, and then said, with gathered passion, "Have you robbed somebody else, who is 7iot dead? Is that the reason you wear armour?"

Romola had been driven to utter the words as men are driven to use the lash of the horsewhip. At first, Tito felt horribly cowed; it seemed to him that the disgrace he had been dreading would be worse than he had imagined it. But soon there was a reaction: such power of dislike and resistance as there was within him was beginning to rise against a wife whose voice seemed like the herald of a retributive fate. Her, at least, his quick mind told him that he might master.

"It is useless," he said, coolly, "to answer the words of madness, Romola. Your peculiar feeling about your father has made you mad at this moment. Any rational person looking at the case from a due distance will see that I have taken the wisest course. Apart from the influence of your exaggerated feelings on him, I am convinced that Messer Bernardo would be of that opinion."

"He would not!" said Romola. "He lives in the hope of seeing my father's wish exactly fulfilled. We spoke of it together only yesterday. He will help me

yet. Who are these men to whom you have sold my father's property ? "

"There is no reason why you should not be told, except that it signifies little. The Count di San Severino and the Seneschal de Beaucaire are now on their way with the king to Siena."

"They may be overtaken and persuaded to give up their purchase," said Romola, eagerly, her anger beginning to be surmounted by anxious thought.

"No, they may not," said Tito, with cool decision.

"Why?"

"Because I do not choose that they should."

"But if you were paid the money?—we will pay you the money," said Romola.

No words could have disclosed more fully her sense of alienation from Tito; but they were spoken with less of bitterness than of anxious pleading. And he felt stronger, for he saw that the first impulse of fury was past.

"No, my Romola. Understand that such thoughts as these are impracticable. You would not, in a reasonable moment, ask your godfather to bury three thousand florins in addition to what he has already paid on the library. I think your pride and delicacy would shrink from that."

She began to tremble and turn cold again with discouragement, and sank down on the carved chest near which she was standing. He went on in a clear voice, under which she shuddered, as if it had been a narrow cold stream coursing over a hot cheek.

"Moreover, it is not my will that Messer Bernardo should advance the money, even if the project were not an utterly wild one. And I beg you to consider, before you take any step or utter any word on the subject, what will be the consequences of your placing yourself in opposition

to me, and trying to exhibit your husband in the odious h'ght which your own distempered feehngs cast over him. What object will you serve by injuring me with Messer Bernardo? The event is irrevocable, the library is sold, and you are my wife."

Every word was spoken for the sake of a calculated effect, for his intellect was urged into the utmost activity by the danger of the crisis. He knew that Romola's mind would take in rapidly enough all the wide meaning of his speech. He waited and watched her in silence.

She had turned her eyes from him, and was looking on the ground, and in that way she sat for several minutes. When she spoke, her voice was quite altered,—it was quiet and cold.

"I have one thing to ask."

"Ask anything that I can do without injuring us both, Romola."

"That you will give me that portion of the money which belongs to my godfather, and let me pay him."

"I must have some assurance from you, first, of the attitude you intend to take towards me."

"Do you believe in assurances, Tito?" she said, with a tinge of returning bitterness.

"From you, I do."

"I will do you no harm. I shall disclose nothing. I will say nothing to pain him or you. You say truly, the event is irrevocable."

"Then I will do what you desire to-morrow morning."

"To-night, if possible," said Romola, "that we may not speak of it again."

"It is possible," he said, moving towards the lamp, while she sat still, looking away from him with absent eyes.

Presently he came and bent down over her, to put a piece of paper in her hand. "You will receive something in return, you are aware, my Roraola?" he said, gently, not minding so much what had passed, now he was secure; and feeling able to try and propitiate her.

"Yes," she said, taking the paper, without looking at him, "I understand."

"And you will forgive me, my Romola, when you have had time to reflect." He just touched her brow with his h'ps, but she took no notice, and seemed really unconscious of the act.

She was aware that he unlocked the door and went out. She moved her head and listened. The great door of the court opened and shut again. She started up as if some sudden freedom had come, and going to her father's chair where his picture was propped, fell on her knees before it, and burst into sobs.

CHAPTER XIII.
BALDASSARRE MAKES AN ACQUAINTANCE.

When Baldassarre was wandering about Florence in search of a spare outhouse where he might have the cheapest of sheltered beds, his steps had been attracted towards that sole portion of ground within the walls of the city which is not perfectly level, and where the spectator, lifted above the roofs of the houses, can see beyond the city to the protecting hills and far-stretching valley, otherwise shut out from his view except along the welcome opening made by the course of the Arno. Part of that ground has been already seen by us as the hill of Bogoli, at that time a great stone quarry; but the side towards which Baldassarre directed his steps was the one that sloped down behind the Via de' Bardi, and was most commonly called the hill of San Giorgio. Bratti had told him that Tito's dwelling was in the Via de' Bardi; and, after surveying that street, he turned up the slope of the hill which he had observed as he was crossing the bridge. If he could find a sheltering outhouse on that hill, he would be glad: he had now for some years been accustomed to live with a broad sky about him: and, moreover, the narrow passes of the streets, with their strip of sky above, and the unknown labyrinth around them, seemed to intensify his sense of loneliness and feeble memory.

The hill was sparsely inhabited, and covered chiefly by gardens; but in one spot was a piece of rough ground jagged with great stones, which had never been cultivated since a landsUp had ruined some houses there towards the end of the thirteenth century. Just above the edge of this broken ground stood a queer httle square building, looking like a truncated tower roofed in with fluted tiles, and close by was a small outhouse, apparently built up against a piece of ruined stone wall. Under a large half-dead mulberry-tree that was now sending its last fluttering leaves in at the open doorways, a shrivelled, hardy old woman was untying a goat with two kids, and Baldas-sarre could see that part of the outbuilding was occupied by live stock; but the door of the other part was open, and it was empty of everything but some tools and straw. It was just the sort of place he wanted. He spoke to the old woman; but it was not till he got close to her and shouted in her ear, that he succeeded in making her understand his want of a lodging, and his readiness to pay for it. At first he could get no answer beyond shakes of the head and the words, "No—no lodging," uttered in the muffled tone of the deaf But, by dint of persistence, he made clear to her that he was a poor stranger from a long way over seas, and could not afford to go to hostelries; that he only wanted to lie on the straw in the outhouse, and would pay her a quattrino or two a week for that shelter. She still looked at him dubiously, shaking her head and talking low to herself; but presently, as if a new thought occurred to her, she fetched a hatchet from, the house, and, showing him a chump that lay half covered with litter in a corner, asked him if he would chop that up for her: if he would, he might lie in the outhouse for one night. He agreed, and Monna Lisa stood with her arms akimbo to watch him, with a smile of gratified cunning, saying low to herself.

"It's lain there ever since my old man died. What then? I might as well have put a stone on the fire. He chops very well, though he does speak with a foreign tongue, and looks odd. I couldn't have got it done cheaper. And if he only wants a bit of straw to lie on, I might make him do an errand or two up and down the hill. Who need know? And sin that's hidden's half forgiven. He's a stranger: he'll take no notice of her. And I'll tell her to keep her tongue still."

The antecedent to these feminine pronouns had a pair of blue eyes, which at that moment were applied to a large round hole in the shutter of the upper window. The shutter was closed, not for any penal reasons, but because only the opposite window had the luxury of glass in it: the weather was not warm, and a round hole four inches in diameter served all the purposes of observation. The hole was unfortunately a little too high, and obliged the small observer to stand on a low stool of a rickety character; but Tessa would have stood a long while in a much more inconvenient position for the sake of seeing a little variety in her life. She had been drawn to the opening at the first loud tones of the strange voice speaking to Monna Lisa; and darting gently across her room every now and then to peep at something, she continued to stand there until the wood had been chopped, and she saw Baldassarre enter the outhouse, as the dusk was gathering, and seat himself on the straw.

A great temptation had laid hold of Tessa's mind; she would go and take that old man part of her supper, and talk to him a little. He was not deaf like Monna Lisa, * "Peccato celato c mezzo perdonato."

and besides she could say a great many things to him that it was no use to shout at Monna Lisa who knew them aheady. And he was a stranger—strangers came from a long way off and went away again, and Uved nowhere in particular. It was naughty, she knew, for obedience made the largest part in Tessa's idea of duty; but it would be something to confess to the padre next Pasqua, and there was nothing else to confess except going to sleep sometimes over her beads, and being a little cross with Monna Lisa because she was so deaf; for she had as much idleness as she liked now, and was never frightened into telling white lies. She turned away from her shutter with rather an excited expression in her childish face, which was as pretty and pouting as ever. Her garb was still that of a simple contadina, but of a contadina prepared for a festa: her gown of dark green serge, with its red girdle, was very clean and neat, she had the string of red glass beads round her neck, and her brown hair, rough from curliness, was duly knotted up and fastened with the silver pin. She had but one new ornament, and she was very proud of it, for it was a fine gold ring.

She sat on the low stool, nursing her knees, for a minute or two, with her little soul poised in fluttering excitement on the edge of this pleasant transgression. It was quite irresistible; she had been commanded to make no acquaintances, and warned that if she did, all her new happy lot would vanish away, and be like a hidden treasure that turned to lead as soon as it was brought to the daylight; and she had been so obedient that when she had to go to church she had kept her face shaded by her hood and had pursed up her lips quite tightly. It was true her obedience had been a little helped by her own dread lest the alarnring stepfather Nofri should turn

up even in this quarter, so far from the Por' del Prato, and beat her at least, if he did not drag her back to work for him. But this old man was not an acquaintance; he was a poor stranger going to sleep in the outhouse, and he probably knew nothing of stepfather Nofri; and, besides, if she took him some supper, he would like her, and not want to tell anything about her. Monna Lisa would say she must not go and talk to him, therefore Monna Lisa must not be consulted. It did not signify what she found out after it had been done.

Supper was being prepared, she knew—a mountain of macaroni, flavoured with cheese, fragrant enough to tame any stranger. So she tripped downstairs with a mind full of deep designs, and first asking with an innocent look what that noise of talking had been, without waiting for an answer, knit her brow with a peremptory air, something like a kitten trying to be formidable, and sent the old woman upstairs; she chose to eat her supper down below. In three minutes Tessa with her lantern in one hand and a wooden bowl of macaroni in the other, was kicking gently at the door of the outhouse, and Baldassarre, roused from sad reverie, doubted in the first moment whether he was awake as he opened the door and saw this surprising little handmaid, with delight in her wide eyes, breaking in > on his dismal loneliness.

"I've brought you some supper," she said, lifting her mouth towards his ear and shouting, as if he had been deaf like Monna Lisa. "Sit down and eat it, while I stay with you."

Surprise and distrust surmounted every other feeling in Baldassarre, but, though he had no smile or word of gratitude ready, there could not be any impulse to push away this visitant, and he sank down passively on his

Straw again, while Tessa placed herself close to him, put the wooden bowl on his lap, and set down the lantern ui front of them, crossing her hands before her, and nodding at the bowl with a significant smile, as much as to say, "Yes, you may really eat it." For, in the excitement of carrying out her deed, she had forgotten her previous thought that the stranger would not be deaf, and had fallen into her habitual alternative of dumb show and shouting.

The invitation was not a disagreeable one, for he had been gnawing a remnant of dried bread, which had left plenty of appetite for anything warm and relishing. Tessa watched the disappearance of two or three mouthfuls without speaking, for she had thought his eyes rather fierce at first; but now she ventured to put her mouth to his ear again and cry—

"I like my supper, don't you?"

It was not a smile, but rather the milder look of a dog touched by kindness but unable to smile, that Baldassarre turned on this round blue-eyed thing that was caring about him.

"Yes," he said; "but I can hear well—I'm not deaf"

"It is true; I forgot," said Tessa, lifting her hands and clasping them. "But Monna Lisa is deaf, and I live with her. She's a kind old woman, and I'm not frightened at her. And we live very well: we have plenty of nice things. I can have nuts if I like. And I'm not obliged to work now. I used to have to work, and I didn't like it; but I liked feeding the mules, and I should like to see poor Giannetta, the little mule, again. We've only got a goat and two kids, and I used to talk to the goat a good deal, because there was nobody else but Monna Lisa. But now I've got something else — can you guess what it is?"

She drew her head back, and looked with a challenging smile at Baldassarre, as if she had proposed a difficult riddle to him."

"No," said he, putting aside his bowl, and looking at her dreamily. It seemed as if this young prattling thing were some memory come back out of his own youth.

"You like me to talk to you, don't you?" said Tessa, "but you must not tell anybody. Shall I fetch you a bit of cold sausage?"

He shook his head, but he looked so mild now that Tessa felt quite at her ease.

"Well, then, I've got a little baby. Such a pretty bambinetto, with little fingers and nails! Not old yet; it was born at the Nativita, Monna Lisa says. I was married one Nativita, a long, long while ago, and nobody knew. O Santa Madonna! I didn't mean to tell you that!"

Tessa set up her shoulders and bit her lip, looking at Baldassarre as if this betrayal of secrets must have an exciting effect on him too. But he seemed not to care much; and perhaps that was in the nature of strangers.

"Yes," she said, carrying on her thought aloud, "you are a stranger; you don't live anywhere or know anybody, do you?"

"No," said Baldassarre, also thinking aloud, rather than consciously answering, "I only know one man."

"His name is not Nofri, is it?" said Tessa, anxiously.

"No," said Baldassarre, noticing her look of fear. "Is that your husband's name?"

That mistaken supposition was very amusing to Tessa. She laughed and clapped her hands as she said,—

"No, indeed! But I must not tell you anything about my husband. You would never think what he is—not at all like Nofri!"

She laughed again at the delightful incongruity between the name of Nofri—which was not separable from the idea of the cross-grained stepfather—and the idea of her husband.

"But I don't see him very often," she went on, more gravely. "And sometimes I pray to the Holy Madonna to send him oftener, and once she did. But I must go back to my bimbo now. I'll bring it to show you to-morrow. You would like to see it. Sometimes it cries and makes a face, but only when it's hungry, Monna Lisa says. You wouldn't think it, but Monna Lisa had babies once, and they are all dead old men. My husband says she will never die now, because she's so well dried. I'm glad of that, for I'm fond of her. You would like to stay here to-morrow, shouldn't you?"

"I should like to have this place to come and rest in, that's all," said Baldassarre. "I would pay for it, and harm nobody."

"No, indeed; I think you are not a bad old man. But you look sorry about something. Tell me, is there anything you shall cry about when I leave you by yourself? I used to cry once."

"No, child; I think I shall cry no more."

"That's right; and I'll bring you some breakfast, and show you the bimbo. Good-night."

Tessa took up her bowl and lantern, and closed the door behind her. The pretty loving apparition had been no more to Baldassarre than a faint rainbow on the blackness to the man who is wrestling in deep waters. He hardly thought of her again till his dreamy waking passed into the more vivid images of disturbed sleep.

But Tessa thought much of him. She had no sooner entered the house than she told Monna Lisa what she had done, and insisted that the stranger should be allowed to come and rest in the outhouse when he liked. The old woman, who had had her notions of making him a useful tenant, made a great show of reluctance, shook her head, and urged that Messer Naldo would be angry if she let any one come about the house. Tessa did not believe that. Naldo had said nothing against strangers who lived nowhere; and this old man knew nobody except one person, who was not Nofri.

"Well," conceded Monna Lisa, at last, "if I let him stay for awhile and carry things up the hill for me, thou must keep thy counsel and tell nobody."

"No," said Tessa, "I'll only tell the bimbo."

"And then," Monna Lisa went on, in her thick undertone, "God may love us well enough not to let Messer Naldo find out anything about it. For he never comes here but at dark; and as he was here two days ago, it's likely he'll never come at all till the old man's gone away again."

"Oh, me! Monna," said Tessa, clasping her hands, "I wish Naldo had not to go such a long, long way sometimes before he comes back again."

"Ah, child, the world's big, they say. There are places behind the mountains, and if people go night and day, night and day, they get to Rome, and see the Holy Father."

Tessa looked submissive in the presence of this mystery, and began to rock her baby, and sing syllables

of vague loving meaning, in tones that imitated a triple chime.

The next morning she was unusually industrious in the prospect of more dialogue and of the pleasure she should give the poor old stranger by showing him her baby. But before she could get ready to take Baldassarre his breakfast, she found that Monna Lisa had been employing him as a drawer of water. She deferred her paternosters, and hurried down to insist that Baldassarre should sit on his straw, so that she might come and sit by him again while he ate his breakfast. That attitude made the new companionship all the more delightful to Tessa, for she had been used to sitting on straw in old days along with her goats and mules.

"I will not let Monna Lisa give you too much work to do," she said, bringing him some steaming broth and soft bread. "I don't like much work, and I dare say you don't. I like sitting in the sunshine and feeding things. Monna Lisa says work is good, but she does it all herself, so I don't mind. She's not a cross old woman; you needn't be afraid of her being cross. And now, you eat that, and I'll go and fetch my baby and show it you."

Presently she came back with the small mummy-case in her arms. The mummy looked very lively, having unusually large dark eyes, though no more than the usual indication of a future nose.

"This is my baby," said Tessa, seating herself close to Baldassarre. "You didn't think it was so pretty, did you? It is like the little Gesu, and I should think the Santa Madonna would be kinder to me now, is it not true? But I have not much to ask for, because I have everything now — only that I should see my husband oftener. You may hold the bambino a little if you like,

but I think you must not kiss him, because you might hurt him."

She spoke this prohibition in a tone of soothing excuse, and Baldassarre could not refuse to hold the sr.all package. "Poor thing! poor thing!" he said, in a deep voice which had something strangely threatening in its apparent pity. It did not seem to him as if this guileless loving little woman could reconcile him to the world at all, but rather that she was with him against the world, that she was a creature who would need to be avenged.

"Oh, don't you be sorry for me," she said; "for though I don't see him often, he is more beautiful and good than anybody else in the world. I say prayers to him when he's away. You couldn't think what he is!"

She looked at Baldassarre with a wide glance of mysterious meaning, taking the baby from him again, and almost wishing he would question her as if he wanted very much to know more.

"Yes, I could," said Baldassarre, rather bitterly.

"No, I'm sure you never could," said Tessa, earnestly. "You thought he might be Nofri," she added, with a triumphant air of conclusiveness. "But never mind; you couldn't know. What is your name?"

He rubbed his hand over his knitted brow, then looked at her blankly and said, "Ah, child, what is it?"

It was not that he did not often remember his name well enough; and if he had had presence of mind now to remember it, he would have chosen not to tell it. But a sudden question appealing to his memory, had a paralysing effect, and in that moment he was conscious of nothing but helplessness.

Ignorant as Tessa was, the pity stirred in her by his blank look taught her to say,

"Never mind: you are a stranger, it is no matter about your having a name. Good-by now, because I want my breakfast. You will come here and rest when you like; Monna Lisa says you may. And don't you be unhappy, for we'll be good to you."

"Poor thing!" said Baldassarre again.

END OF VOL. I.

Printed in Great Britain
by Amazon